a deadly choice

"There is the cup," the witch reminded Caith quietly, at last, when the pain had made him near mindless, and the fear of dying had traded places with a fear that he would live far too long. "Do not reject me. Take it. It is healing. Your suffering is all your own doing."

"It is not!" Caith cried. He had learned not to suffer lies in patience, and not to be put upon. "Three times and four times no, and to *hell* with you, madam."

"Have it as you will," she declared; she abruptly took her weight from the bedside. A wave of giddiness came over him as his life went flooding out. He was dying . . .

FAERY IN
SHADOW

C. J. Cherryh

A Del Rey® Book
BALLANTINE BOOKS • NEW YORK

A Del Rey® Book
Published by Ballantine Books

Library of Congress Catalog Card Number: 94–94145

ISBN 0-345-37279-4

Manufactured in the United States of America

First Edition: September 1994

10 9 8 7 6 5 4 3 2 1

FAERY IN
SHADOW

CHAPTER
ONE

THE WATER FLOWED first from a spring in Teile, clear as glass, and out of the loch in broad Gleann Teile it emerged rich, peat-dark, its brown-stained bubbles swirling over tumbled basalt. Guagach was the name of this stream, and it plunged through sun-touched bracken and over rock as it began its chute into Gleann Fiain, a noisy fall into a barren chasm, whence it issued whispering and babbling madness. It was born bright and clear and clean on the mountains, it became one thing in the peat of Gleann Teile, and it became something else again in that pool, down among the dark-leaved trees of Gleann Fiain. A single shaft of sunlight pierced the branches and spread itself through the spray in a rainbow that made the woods and rocks seem the blacker about that boiling cauldron.

That was Teile's farewell to Guagach, and beyond that deep pool, Guagach went so stained and darksome that its very voice became subdued. It flowed sluggish and deep, among black reeds, along cheerless banks of black rock in an autumn forest, beneath thickets which maintained only slick rags of foliage.

The fish that came by ill luck out of sunny Teile and fell down into that pool, the fish that ventured farther through the dark water and swam close to the overhang of a certain haunted bank, found a current foul with a

1

reek of terror and of evil, and cold with upwellings out
of hidden depth. That fish fled with all its silver might,
lone mote of Teile's sunlight racing through the dark of
Fiain; but darkness followed it, and overtook it, and it
was gone.

A swirl of water marked the surface, a little glint of
sunlight striking the darkness that Guagach had become,
a slight roiling of the waters which might indeed have
been a cold upwelling out of some hidden fissure; or it
might have been some great dark swimmer turning near
the surface—but that thing would have been great indeed,
and so dark it cast nothing back that the day gave it.

A trio of bubbles danced in the whirlpool it left. A
brown leaf fell in the treachery of a breeze, as if the evil
in the water had caused the limbs above the stream to
move and to rattle.

If that was the cause, it was a very vile thing which
lived beneath that willow, and travelers would be well-
advised to take some other course than that stony,
breakneck path which led down the fell. Such travelers
would have been wiser still to seek at once back to the
braes of Gleann Teile and their sunlight.

But Caith mac Sliabhin and his companion walked
beside the darksome water under that autumn dearth of
leaf, and Caith never lifted his head until a breeze
sported ashore and touched him with its cold.

Then he wrapped his grey storm-cloak about him, realizing how dark the path had become since they had
left the pool behind; while his companion cast a look
toward the dark water and that spinning leaf, and
walked down to lean over the brink, hands on kilted
thighs.

Caith paid him no heed. A great many things distracted Dubhain, half of them nonsensical—a butterfly,
the flutter of a leaf, the rising of a bubble in a brook.

"Waugh, here's something foul!" said Dubhain. He
bent and, gathering up a pebble, skipped it across the

water, making a neat stitch of ripples across the darkness, and one white-frothed splash where it disappeared among the reeds.

Caith looked askance at him and walked on along the stream-bank, a tired young man in a worn grey cloak and a dark red hunting plaid, with shoes the worse for miles and weather. In all that bleak shadow he was the only light, his red hair catching the occasional sun and reminding this glen what bright color was. But his countenance was grim, settled young into the habit of dour thought. He carried a sword beneath that cloak, keeping it as close as he kept secrets, never letting it to daylight: it was a cursed blade. And for other protection he had on a cord about his neck an elf-shot, a stone which running water had pierced. If he looked through this stone, so the man who had given it to him had claimed, he might discern truth from illusion. But he seldom cared to look, and, long after he had taken the gift, it had occurred to him that the man who had given him the stone had never told him which was truth, whether it was the world through which men walked, believing, or the world he could see through the river-pierced stone.

It seemed pointless now to wonder, and perhaps self-tormenting. His dreams were haunted, and there was nothing of his possessions that was not fey and dreadful, even that stone. It was his hope yet to do good in the world, but no chance had ever come to him that had not brought disaster.

As for the youth Dubhain, who overtook him, skipping heedlessly through the dark and moribund thicket—Dubhain was all the name he owned, and he was perhaps sixteen, the wily, light-fingered sixteen the roads might make of a wicked boy.

Or perhaps it was only his slight stature that made Dubhain seem young at all. His hair was as dark as a thought of sin, his sloe eyes twinkled beneath a wayward forelock and danced with mischief in a face as dusky as the shadow in this woods. He might have been some sprite of merry malice, some prankish pan. His face was more apt to grin than to smile, and if he frowned, why, it was thundercloud and a clashing of black brows; but far more often it was the grin, a flash of white, square teeth, and soon a skip and a hop of quick bare feet. Dubhain had never liked shoes. He laughed and, barefoot, danced over the leaves as if the noisome wind gave him pleasure. His ragged shirt and his dark hunting-tartan skirled with his turns as he skipped atop one rock and another and another, until he squatted above the trail Caith mac Sliabhin walked.

He pitched a stone then to strike Caith's back.

Caith whirled. His hand lit on his sword hilt and his eyes burned. "Damn you!" he cried, footsore from the descent and unhappy with the place they had come to. "I weary of you!"

"Oh-ho," said Dubhain. "Do you now, mac Sliabhin?"

And Dubhain flung up a ragged arm and whirled his way down the rocks like a wisp of wind, like an evil thought sped on its mischief. He landed on two bare feet amongst the leaves, hands on thighs. "But perhaps ye'd play tag, man?"

"Damn you," Caith said again, despairing. "Damn your roads and your mischief and your skipping about! This place is fouler and fouler!"

"Does it not suit you? I had thought it would."

Caith waved a furious arm, without the sword. "Be gone from me! Leave me in peace!"

"Oh-ho, oh-ho!" Dubhain whirled again and skipped up onto the rocks, skipped and spun and landed on two feet, tottering precariously. "That's the way, man! That's the way!" He pointed toward the dark of the forest ahead. "Go, ye need me not, is that the way of it? Ye wish't me harm? Go to, go to, hae joy of the road or find your own! I'll not stay ye, not I, not Dubhain!" A further skip carried him up and up to the very crest of the rocks, a flash of bare legs and ragged dark kilt. "Wish me harm, do ye? Wish for me again and wish three times, man, and cry me sweet mercy, before I come and go where ye wish me most!"

"A plague on your wishes!" Caith cried in despair, for now he suspected Dubhain had led him this long weary trek for one of his damnable pranks. "Faithless wretch!"

"My merry friend, my sweet companion, my darling murderer—*go to!*"

It was only Dubhain's voice that lingered, echoing down the glen. Dubhain was gone, spun off the rock as if the darkling air had swallowed him. Caith scrambled for that vantage in a fit of temper, barked his shin on the rock as his foot slipped on wet stone, and slid halfway down again.

Fey laughter sounded at his side, and then behind him, echoing among the rocks. Another stone sped and hit him full in the chest as he turned to see. This was no pebble. He winced and caught for balance, seeing the wisp of white shirt flit through the brush and fly away.

"Dubhain!"

"That's once!" the voice taunted him. "Wish and call my name again, but nae sae easily d' ye gain my help again, my merry murderer, my sweet, my darling oath-breaker! Wish me with all your heart and tainted soul!"

"Traitor!"

"Once in dread, d' ye call me; once in pain; once in bitter anguish, that ye maun do, t' that ye maun descend, my Caith, before ye hae the Calling of me again!"

The wisp of white lost itself in the shadow of the woods, as uncatchable as the taunt ringing after him. Caith slumped against the rocks with his hand to his chest, looked down and saw a stain of blood on his shirt where the rock had struck him, over the heart.

Such were all Dubhain's blows, heart's-blood and numbing in their pain. But Dubhain was his only companion, and companionship of any sort had become so precious to him that with Dubhain's going, a black despair came pouring over his soul. It was pride and weariness of body that had made him dismiss Dubhain, the misery of a man half-mad with his own damnation and the darkness of the roads he was doomed to travel in the world.

"Dubhain," he whispered to the lonely winds, and *"Dubhain, damn you, come back!"* he shouted in his rage. He slid down from the rocks, landed on two feet on the mold and the fallen leaves; and in desperation he cast himself heavily to both knees and held wide his hands. "Dubhain, I beg you, see?"

But nothing answered him, not even the mocking laughter he cursed and courted.

The path came and went in the woods, wove to the stream-side and left it and returned, random and reasonless. The wind rattled the black, ragged branches as the sun sneaked shame-faced behind the hills and lost its last light in grey clouds.

The spatter of rain and the peal of thunder that heralded the storm was injury upon insult. Caith looked to that quarter of the sky, with nothing to see above him but bare branches and dark clouds scudding above them, low and heavy with rain. He cursed his luck and asked himself why he did not abandon this ill-chosen direction and go back to Teile. But so little grace he had with the powers of the Sidhe, he feared he might lose Dubhain forever if he failed to make amends. So he kept going as he had been going, telling himself again and again it was no more than one of Dubhain's cursed jokes, and that sooner or later Dubhain would come back to enjoy it.

Then a wind bitter as the heart of winter roared down the deep glen, tearing the last of the autumn leaves from the branches and ruffling the dark waters, and with a gasp and an indignant curse, Caith wrapped his grey cloak about himself and held on to it, shaken by the blast.

This was too much. The miles he had walked in his exile lay heavier and heavier on him, and his wounding was as much in his dreams as in the flesh, and as much in his trust as in his body. Good sense told him to seek shelter in the rocks and pull leaves up against his cloak, against the rain he knew would come, except that Dubhain had left him, and he dared not lie down in such a place and risk falling asleep.

If he did so, his dreams, he had all faith in them, would be surpassing fair. That was his torment. The dark spilling down with the clouds was his enemy, the sleep which urged at him was his nightly bane, his erstwhile companion was his appointed tormentor, and, as he loved and loathed Dubhain with all the confusion of his damned soul, he called to him and kept going, desperate in the cold and the coming dark. "Dubhain!" he shouted into the storm; and, *Dubhain*, said the rain on the leaves beneath his feet. *Dubhain*, the leaves overhead whispered; *Dubhain*, the vile waters bubbled—but the darkening air did not give him up again.

Dubhain was Sidhe, one of the dark kind, a power who served other powers; but Dubhain was, in the interludes of his appointed punishment, his truest and only friend, and he knew of an increasing certainty that Dubhain had spoken to him from his Sightedness, and that the three callings of him must be, Dubhain had said it, each in misery more acute than the last. That was Dubhain's geas: to See a thing and then recklessly to bring it on them both—never to their good.

For having the Sight, Dubhain had told him once, *having the Sight, man, is no' a great blessing. Such merry, merry sights I See, and what may I do, hey, but make sport on 't?*

That is the worth of it all, a jest, a jape, a merriment. So laugh, man, ye laugh not oft enough . . .

Thunder cracked. The rain came blasting down,

stinging his face. Having prepared no shelter, Caith
knew well enough the choice a man caught out had before him: walk or freeze to death in the autumn night—
but he knew as surely that he had no power, even
willfully, to sit down to rest in despite of the Sidhe. The
bright lords would not abide it—they were not done
with their plans, and his humbling this evening had not
sufficed: Dubhain had not even returned to mock him.
Therefore the parting was something not to Dubhain's
pleasure, therefore it was some Power's working, and
therefore Dubhain had goaded him and left him—in
Dubhain's own most twisted humor, making him deserve what a more mindful fate had forced upon him.
And well away Dubhain would stay, until the issue of
it: Dubhain was frequently many things, even loyal, but
Dubhain had no taste for suffering with him.

*Once in dread, once in pain, once in bitter an-
guish . . .*

Plague take the Sidhe! he thought, and immediately a
harder spate of rain spattered through the leaves, pat-
tered noisily onto the forest mold and pocked Guagach's black water. He shook his head, wrapped his
cloak about himself and kept walking, in patience such
as he could summon—put his hand on an overgrown
stone to steady himself in stepping over a deadfall, and
saw stone eyes and a domed head.

He drew back his hand. It was that startling, the old
image. Most were gone. But one found them, the banished gods, the lords of hell—the lord of the wheel, this
one was, the wheel mostly weathered away, the god
staring into the vines and the dark, powerless, now, as
the stone gods the farmers built into walls, for the welfare of their crops and cattle. Or dug out of older walls,
to patch a gap in the sheep-fences. He brushed by it, offering it nothing, equally destitute, and more concerned
with the powers of the heavens than of hell tonight, that
bid fair to soak him to the skin and force him to some
shivering cover before the dawn, wherever he could

find it. But the encounter troubled him, in the way things could that touched the Sight he had, nothing to warn a man of anything reasonable, only a feeling of unease in the moment, a sign of lurking power, it might be, or of ruin and overthrow in the night.

Damn the wretch that deserted him, all for a merry prank, and left him to slog ankle deep through tributary streams, all active with the downpour, to fight his way through bracken clumps, and guess where the water's edge was. He was wet through and through, the lightnings made him anxious for more reason than old gods, and he was in no good humor for Dubhain's jokes, not his vanishings, nor his excuses, nor his light-minded good humor.

But on a gust came another scent besides the smell of peat-water and stone—a faint, rain-washed waft of smoke, carried from somewhere hereabouts.

He paused and turned his face to that wind, troubled by the sudden evidence of human presence and suspecting that the makers of that fire were either a danger to him or in mortal danger from him, if only by the fact that he had arrived in this glen.

The autumn boughs about him were all a-toss on the wind, the light that penetrated this deep rift between the hills was fast-fading into starless night, and the wind that carried that scent of smoke gusted out of the west and down off the braes of Gleann Fiain. He blinked rain from his eyes, turned his back sullenly to the wind and the scent it carried, and held his cloak close against the numbing cold, deliberately setting himself to walk again in the direction he had been going, refusing the temptation of a fire and shelter, and hoping to avoid the inhabitants of this place entirely, if somehow the Sidhe had no need of his troubling them.

But he could not put Dubhain's warning out of his mind, now.

Dread from the woods or dread from the heights, might it be? He had been wet many a time and cold many a night, and long as the morning might be in coming, he was strong enough, he was well-used to the road and the weather, and far too canny to make the mistakes that killed a man. Granted, he would go hungry, this night: they had eaten the last of the meal yesterday, and he had lost the flask in the falls—but hunger was no great novel thing, and thirst he could hardly complain of: water in liberal abundance was pouring down his neck and soaking his shoes, with no hope of better until the sun rose tomorrow—but the streamside course was what he chose, picking his way along the water's edge as the black waters muttered and chuckled in cynic laughter beneath the splash of the rain. Guagach grew swollen as the new-born brooks came spilling down from the heights to their corrupting, while the sun slipped away behind the rain-drowned walls of the glen, forcing a man to watch his step and mind the slick rocks.

In that uncertain light, as he waded a stream that fed Guagach's black strength, he saw, just beyond the reeds, a powerful swirling and dimpling of Guagach's rain-pocked surface, as if some powerful stroke had troubled it. The bottom near him sighed up bubbles which burst in the rain, yielding up an unexpected fetid air and an intimation of chill nether depths.

He did not like that. He liked it less when he saw the black surface wrinkle with another unexpected current where a rock sheltered it from the driving rain—a curious thing to see, here in the near dark, and the loneliness of this glen, a great fish, perhaps, or an underwater spring.

The branches above him rattled, wind-tossed, an ill-omened, cold sound, as if the very trees shivered. With a twitch of his shoulders, he put himself briskly on his way, careful on the tumble of rocks that made the banks here, that turned too readily and clattered underfoot. He made the crossing of another rill, holding to the branches of an old willow that overhung the place. With that hasty passage over the unsteady stones, he reached the bank of Guagach again, where other willows, bare-branched with oncoming winter, came between him and the dark water. He felt somehow safer then, knee-deep in dead, rain-wet bracken and walking on solid ground, though the shadows were thicker. That brink to him seemed unaccountably perilous and he was glad to leave it.

Then behind him two stones clattered, as if a foot had disturbed them. He spun about to see, hand on the hilt of his sword, looking through a veil of willow-branches.

He waited. Nothing stirred further. He walked on with an ear to his backtrail, the bracken whispering against his legs and cracking underfoot. The wind went roaring through the woods, and the water of the hills babbled and laughed beneath the gale.

Then he heard a sharp, fierce clatter of stones at his back.

He spun around again, but the willows and the night obscured the source of the sound that had been at once so plain and abruptly ended.

He did not like that. He did not like that at all. He had the feeling he had in a throng of people, when he heard a move at his back and faced a sudden innocence. He had all too often been the victim of that game. But this was no village bully he shared the woods with. This had no sound of a human prank. It might be Dubhain—but he had no confidence it was anything so friendly.

Another rattle, then a rolling clatter that did not stop, a sound as if the very stones of the river-bottom rose up in frenzied pursuit of him. A scent of rot rode the wind that blasted at his back, and hearing that rattling come closer, he cast a glance over his shoulder as he walked, trying, as one might with the dark Sidhe, to pass as respectfully and rapidly as he could out of its territory. That glance spied movement in the blowing willow-strands, the clattering redoubled, and then horror rose up in him, making him doubt whether it was wiser to walk, rather than to run.

He compromised and walked a little faster, seeking not to disrespect it, but not to give it his attention again either, at which such things might grow dangerously bolder. He tried to make no sound louder than the natural wind, but that was no use: it came clattering and rattling with louder force, and as much as he feared to run and acknowledge a Sidhe presence, only a fool could pretend he was alone in this woods—a woods, he began to be sure, old and utterly merciless itself, giving him no help at all and promising him no safety. Branches tore at his cloak and raked his face and his knees. He snatched the coarse, rain-soaked cloth close about him and set his other hand on his sword to keep it from banging about his side. He dared not draw it against the creature that moved behind him—iron having no power over the oldest things and over the darkest, the very things a man would most wish to keep away from him, so that a man risked more with a weapon than without it. Worse, it was gaining slightly, as best he could judge, and a Sidhe thing, once a man began to run, would run too, until human strength gave out—which his would quickly, hungry and weary as he was. The cold had already numbed his feet beyond sensibility and the lightning that lit the forest turned it to a creature of a thousand reaching arms and claws all shaking in the wind.

He averted his face from the rake of a branch, forged ahead with his arms and found his path ahead hindered by branches he had no time to go around. He tore desperately through thorny brush, his heart hammering in the clatter of that nameless thing that pursued. His breath rasped, but nothing so loud as that breathing at his back, whose rattle was the rattle of ill-joined bones or the clack and clatter of stones in the spate.

Thunder boomed out and panic jolted him: he abandoned the cautionary hold on his sword-hilt and his resolve to walk quietly through this threat: he leapt to the top of a deadfall and over, plunged uphill along what might still be a trail, or only a deception of the forest, thinking now that his only safety might lie uphill, away from the water this thing haunted. The elf-shot stone leapt and thumped at his neck and face as he bolted across an open space with the rattling closer and closer behind him. He dived through a thicket to the peril of his eyes, fending branches with his hands and tearing his shoulders and his legs and his cloak through the snags.

Run and run again, along a leaf-slick slope which ran white with a rain-fed rill: he leaped over that clean water, which might barrier some things, but he no longer believed that running water would give this haunt any pause.

In his desperation, then, he recalled the smoke he had smelled on the wind, and drove upslope and back again as his last resort, while his heart beat to bursting and he heard the rattle of bones close behind him, between the peals of thunder.

He crested a rise, tore through brush he had not seen in the dark and found himself snagged in a deeper thornbrake, gripped by a fear so smothering his throat could find no breath for Dubhain's name—panicked as a child in the dark, he tore a way through the thorns by main strength, raking his arms and his legs and his face. His cloak snagged fast: he turned desperately to free himself, pulling with both his hands as the clattering came up the slope at him. He caught a glimpse of a shadow that lurched with every rattling, a glistening shape that broke the brush under it and kept coming, immune to the thorns.

Terror gripped him. He ripped the cloth free and ran, dodging and ducking beneath low limbs on the slope, overleaping deadfalls and rocks and slogging through boggy ground, up and up the steep, forced to hands and knees at last on the rain-slick leaves and the mire, while the rattling thing came up behind him, the clack and clatter of bones and horror all misgathered. Something struck heavily at his heel, raked his leg and thudded against the earth with a wet and slippery suck of mud and flesh.

"Dubhain!" The name broke free at that hurting touch, the cry cracked his throat, was sob and gasp for wind in two desperate heaves that caught a stitch in his side. In the strength of sheer terror he scrambled ahead of the creature, stumbled through a sudden thinning of the trees and in among clumps of whin on a steep, unwooded hillside.

"Dubhain!" He pressed a hand to the stitch in his side, running uphill with everything he had left—fell once and a second time to his knees on wet grass and in blind horror scrambled up again and kept running, weaving among the scattered clumps of gorse.

A lightning-stroke lit the way between two bushes: lit a white-shirted shape so suddenly in his path that he skidded and sprawled on his aching side, one glance to the white-shirted villain who loomed above him and another, full of horror, to the slope below and its humped shapes of lightning-lit gorse. He scrambled up again, caught Dubhain's arm and dragged him along in uphill flight, on the very dregs of the breath he had in him.

"Och, now!" Dubhain cried, plucking away his hand. "Let be, let be, man! Whence this dreadsome haste?"

The slope was sparse grass above, gorse and shattered stone below; and when, Dubhain balking, Caith cast a second look back—nothing at all showed in pursuit of them.

"Hoosht, hey," said Dubhain, all awash in the driving rain, his dark hair streaming in the lightning-flicker, as he leaned on his knees and drew a quick breath. His square-toothed grin was quite merry when he had it. "And will that be your first calling? —D' ye beg me? Is it 'Damn you, Dubhain?' or is it, 'Fair, kind Dubhain, my friend Dubhain, my sweet Dubhain—' "

"A plague on your humor!" Caith coughed. His side

was a knotted misery and his wounded ankle a burning one; his flesh shrank under the pealing thunder-strokes and the cold battering of the rain, and he grasped Dubhain's warm arm and held to him for fear of Dubhain's vanishing a second time, as the smell of smoke came strongly to him on the wind.

So he had run to the very place he had tried to avoid going. His teeth began to chatter. He was chilled to the soul, fearful of what manner of folk might have their claim on that fire and that shelter.

But meanwhile his left leg was aching from the ankle to the knee. He limped a tentative step uphill, and a burning pain shot up the inner leg, as if poison were moving in it. He flailed out wildly for balance, and at once Dubhain caught his arm and flung that arm across his shoulders, bearing him up the slope as if his weight were nothing to him.

He failed to struggle. He had no wish to be abandoned on this barren slope, and he had a keen terror that Dubhain might well leave him here, Dubhain being mad and fey and bound by geas. But he had no great desire to go where Dubhain was taking him, either.

"Foolish man," Dubhain chided him the while, "poor, foolish man, fighting against shadows and powers, now ye maun speak me fair."

"Brave Dubhain, my fine Dubhain,—" His breath rasped through a raw throat. He was held in Dubhain's warmth and Dubhain's unlikely strength, supported through the driving rain and thunderous dark with a force he could neither resist nor trust.

Perhaps Dubhain had come to help him—he had been in dread, and in pain, and perhaps the wounding was the anguish Dubhain's fey saying foretold.

"Again," Caith gasped, reeling and staggering in that warm, inexorable embrace, "Dubhain, I beg you, I ask you. Is that enough to make amends, a second and a third time—oft as ye like, Dubhain, I ask."

"Nay." Dubhain's arm tightened about his waist, and

Dubhain's hand on his wrist hauled him up despite his faltering steps. "Nay, sweet Caith, I can nae hear ye yet, I can nae listen t' ye, the thunder drowns your voice, though I do love ye well, my Caith, and bear ye safe—hoosht, now, ye see, ye see, here's rest for ye!"

Caith blinked the rain from his eyes and saw the crest of the hill taking on a man-made shape, the low ridge of a cottage roof. The place showed no light: its shutters were tight and let nothing escape. But its smoke came to him, smelling of wood-fire rather than the peat more common in Teile; and, most madly, most heart-breakingly wonderful . . . smelling of bread recently baked.

They passed a pen beside a shed. Goats stared at them in slit-eyed curiosity, in the lightning strokes. A ewe bleated, rain-soaked and frightened by the thunder. Caith stared back, helplessly carried past the rough railings, affrighted at where Dubhain was taking him, seeing in the goats and the sheep a figure of the trapped and the damned in this cursed night, of himself and Dubhain penned here together with something more fell than he could reckon of hunting him through the storm. He could beg Dubhain to loose all the animals into the dark. But that was no kindness to a sheep. It was what it was.

And it was not kindness close at his side, which bore him limping and stumbling along in the storm—it was not kindness that Dubhain served tonight or any night.

"The shed," Caith protested as Dubhain took him toward the cottage door. "We can lodge there, Dubhain. We have no need to trouble these folk at all—"

The house with its lightless shutters might be as dreadful on its own terms as that woods down in the deep glen; but there was that smell of baking, that argued for some gentler presence—and he feared they might be some innocent folk, a family, children, even, all chances he feared with the fear of the damned. He tried at the very last to push free and to stand on his

own feet, but the wounded leg gave way beneath him
and the ankle turned as Dubhain haled him up to the
door, at which Dubhain rapped cheerfully.

"Help, hey!" Dubhain sang out. "Travelers in need of
shelter—och, help for me master, have mercy, ho!"

"Give o'er!" Caith gasped, and shoved away and
leaned instead against the stone wall, for Dubhain's humors appalled and frightened him. He caught at
Dubhain's white-shirted arm, warm despite the chill of
the rain on them both, and got only Dubhain's broad
grin and a toss of Dubhain's head as a peephole in the
door shot open. Dubhain instantly stood a-tiptoe, pre-
senting himself to be seen, instantly suffering in pitiful,
rain-drenched shivers.

"Me master," Dubhain cried, as the golden light from
within fell on his face and shoulders. "Oh, mercy,
there's something hunting in the woods! Mercy, let us
in!" He seized up Caith in his arms, dragging him all
unwilling into that light. "We're perishing of the cold
out here! Hae ye mercy, let us in!"

An eye stared out that peephole and scanned the dark
behind them. In no case to walk even as far as the shed,
Caith hung within Dubhain's arms, teeth chattering,
hoping in the honest part of his heart for that spyhole to
be thrown fast shut and Dubhain's cleverness for once
thwarted. Dubhain was a familiar damnation to him,
one he knew how to suffer and endure tonight, only so
long as Dubhain did not abandon him to that rattling
thing by the riverside, only so that horror was not this
moment snuffling and sucking and rattling its way up
the slope like all the bones risen from some hallowless
and dreadful bog.

In that latter thought he cast a look past Dubhain's
shoulder, onto a slope lightning-lit and overgrown with
whin, full of shapes any one of which might be that
creature.

The bar thumped within the house and the door
swung open, dazzling his eyes with firelight and mak-

ing of the tenant only a hazed shadow as Dubhain
dragged him inside perforce, into warmth and light.

Then in that tidy small house, as the householder shut
the door and the bar dropped down with a sound like
doom, the shivering and the dread came on him in earnest, the pain in his leg grown all-encompassing. Caith
caught his balance on one foot, then gripped Dubhain's
shirt for fear of fainting in the warm air, as Dubhain
turned him to regard their host.

Caith saw three things: a door warded with iron and
with knotted rowan-sprigs, a charm against faery (but
not against faery *bidden* enter); a youth, fair as the
Sidhe himself, all golden in the firelight; and a sword in
that youth's hand the blade of which gleamed with
lamplight and the point of which threatened his unde-
fended heart. By the shimmering of the blade, the hand
holding the hilt was trembling, which could give the
helpless object of that fear no comfort.

Dubhain, to be sure, stood holding him to the fore
like a shield, for the Sidhe had no love of iron at all.

CHAPTER

TWO

"THERE IS THE fire," the young man said, although the sword never dropped its line toward Caith's heart. "Sit there, if you wish."

"Your mercy," Caith breathed, in what voice he had left him. He struggled lamely to turn in that direction, and solicitously Dubhain bore him toward the hearth, past a table on which was set a supper: a half a loaf of bread, a bit of white cheese, a pitcher with a chipped rim ... things better than gold to Caith's eyes; he hoped for the offer of a supper and shelter even while he was hurting too much to think of courtesies or escapes.

But the setting of two plates caught his attention. Two earthen brown cups, and two plates with crumbs on them—so it was in no anticipation of visitors that table had been laid. More, a rough-spun curtain screened the end of the room.

"Me master thanks you," Dubhain said to the youth, facing him about, "thanks you from the bottom of his heart."

"Have mercy," Caith said through his teeth, ill-liking Dubhain's false and dangerous courtesy, while he felt the iron strength of Dubhain's fingers bruise his arm to the bone.

"Och, me master," Dubhain said against his ear, set-

ting him down on the warm fieldstone hearth, and began to unfasten his cloak pin. Caith struck at Dubhain's
hand to prevent him. Resist more than that, he dared
not, dared not provoke doubt or alarm the youth more
than he was alarmed already. In bringing him under this
roof, Dubhain had gained a hostage for his good behavior, a hostage who stood looking doubtfully on them
both, sword in hand. "The cold hae tried him so,"
Dubhain said to the youth.

"A plague on your pity," Caith rasped, hugging his
sodden limbs into a knot about his sword, his teeth
chattering with a racket like the boggy thing below.
The pain in his leg had shot to his groin, now, burning
and aching at the same time. His stocking was ripped,
and the wound that showed through the raveling was
muddy and already purpling with corruption. That
sight made him shiver more than from the cold, seeing death inexorably climbing his leg to his vitals.

"Badbh and Macha," he moaned, although no gods
had help for him against this. He felt desolate of every
hope. He had never a doubt that evil was his lot, both
the doing and the suffering of it, but he had never foreseen himself a cripple, or dying convulsed from some
foul creature's poison, with no reason for it ever offered
him.

"Ah," said Dubhain, and stripped down his stocking and laid hands on the wound. Warmth and pain
were both in that touch, a pang so delicious and so
acute that Caith let the sword fall and threw back both
hands to brace himself against the hearthstones. Back
went his head and the breath hissed between his teeth
as Dubhain's hand moved and sent heat and cold at
once bone-deep. He could not see for that instant,
could not get his breath; some shout seemed to hang
in the numbed, blind air, and it might well have been
his.

"He hae set his foot amiss," Dubhain was saying,
then, to the youth who hovered, firelit, behind Dubhain's

shoulder. "A wrenching of the joint, I think. —There, me master, there, lean yourself against the stone. 'T will pass, 't will pass, ye'll take nae harm of your foolishness."

Dubhain lifted his hands from his ankle. There was no wound. The flesh was unscarred. Caith stared at it with a helpless loathing of the power that went singing through his veins like strong drink—at once corrupting judgment and wit, telling him he had no need of leaning against anything, or of rest tonight or any night. It was too much force. It was not a human thing, yet his body must contain it, quivering; and the blood buzzed in his ears, making him ache to get up and walk and be rid of it; but the breath would not come fast enough, even so, and he was near to fainting. More, he realized the threat still hung over him: the drawn sword in the youth's hands had never gone to sheath—in dazed calculation of which, he took the belt of his own sword, and, still struggling for his breaths, giddily passed it over his head and shoved the sheathed blade aside on the hearth-stones, out of convenient reach.

"Peace," he said. "The gods' peace, man, I am no bandit, and my lad is no thief."

"There is bread," said the youth, "and milk and butter." Saying which, he walked away toward the door and, with a wary and misgiving glance at them, took up the sheath of the sword and put it away with a hiss of metal. "I have little to spare, but be welcome to it."

So the young freeholder invited them reluctantly to his supper, and at the very moment, from behind the curtain at the back of the room, there peered a young woman's face—as fair-haired as the youth, she was, and gloriously beautiful.

"Aha," Dubhain said with immediate and lascivious interest, and the youth was all dismay.

"Firinne," he chided her.

"What harm?" she asked gently, this Firinne, and

Caith felt he had heard no sound in all his wandering so
entrancing as that soft voice. She came out from behind
her curtain into the lamplight, and he found nothing else
in all the world to look at.

It was, perhaps, the spell the house cast, in its quaint
homeliness, the work of her hands, he was now sure—
the sum of all those things a man under his terms of
exile could never enjoy. Perhaps it was only the unex-
pectedness of her, so quiet and gracious and so giving
of her hospitality—but in that one unguarded moment
he would have given up the last shred of his soul if she
would look at him kindly and never realize the danger
that had taken shelter under her roof—

Not, to be sure, that his thoughts of her were altogether pure, even in the instant of seeing her; but he set
any desire of her as far off as he could put it, and at
once, for all their safety. He was willing to adore her for
no other thing than that she was fair and gracious and
brave enough to welcome strangers in her house—
precisely that bravery which most folk lacked toward
things of the Sidhe, and especially toward strangers unexpected on their doorsteps. It seemed that true gentleness of heart in her, to which Dubhain's care of him
could never attain.

At least that was what he wished to see: he gazed at
her from the depths of his bartered soul, while she set
about the housewifely business of setting him and
Dubhain a generous plate of food and pouring them a
cup of milk apiece from the chipped pitcher on her
table—to a houseless wanderer's eyes there was beauty
in every simple thing Firinne did, a grace he had seen
before in a girl no more than a child.

"She is my wife," the youth said sternly, unneedfully
sternly, and Caith glanced at the youth to find him
standing near the door and beside his sword. The warning fell harshly on Firinne's gracious welcome; and in a
second breath Caith did not at all believe it was the

truth. The young householders were as alike as brother and sister could possibly be.

But, sitting spent and rain-soaked on a stranger's hearth and expecting supper on his charity, he dared not call the young man a liar to his face.

"Aye," he said meekly. " 'T is your house, man, and we your most grateful guests. We give good peace to this roof, tonight and hereafter."

The young man seemed in better sorts then, and to make firm the point, Caith reached left-handed for his sword and sword-belt, which lay, at a stretch, still within his reach. With his fingertips he pushed it aside on the hearth-stones, moving the sheathed point of the sword as far as he could push it, at which gesture the young householder looked at last mollified.

"Caith is my name," he said, and if his red Dun Mhor tartan or the luck that was on his house was at all known here, the youth gave no sign of knowing either: nor did he himself recognize the brown and gold plaid the householder wore. "Mac Gaelan," Caith added, which was the name he used when he wished to avoid awkwardness in chance meetings, and it was the name he wished to the bottom of his heart were his—the one which, if it were indeed his, would make him less blood-guilty than he was and his soul less damned. He rested against the fire-warmed stones at Dubhain's side, awaiting courteous response, and watched the young man take the food the young woman had prepared, to offer it to them himself.

"My name," the youth said, when they had received their supper from his hands, "is Ceannann mac Ceannann. My wife's is Firinne."

"My lad here," Caith said wryly, "is Dubhain. A fatherless orphan." He took a sip from the cup of milk, and Dubhain drank his with a slant-eyed glance aside at him, full of wicked mirth—for it was obligation a Sidhe gave and accepted with that small sup of milk, obligation and a binding to favor. He knew what was settled on them, and Dubhain surely knew, but most likely their hosts did not.

And when they had both drunk and eaten, Caith was content merely to rest his back against the stones of the fireplace while his rain-soaked clothing dried on his body. He would have been grateful to sit all night in that condition, fed and warmed inside, but the young host brought them blankets, and Firinne absented herself behind the curtain, to sleep, one supposed.

"Take off your wet clothes," Ceannann said, "and wrap in these. There's wood to keep the fire high tonight."

Caith hesitated. He was reluctant as always to show his back in view of strangers, because of the scars that marked it; but, more practically speaking, the clothes he wore were all the property he owned in the world; and being, as they were, all his protection from strangers' curiosity, he had far rather let them dry on his body than sit naked in a strange house, with the thunder walking over the rooftree to remind him there was a haunted woods downslope and that this was a stranger house than most.

Besides, the youth had asked no questions of him, had asked not even those few questions which any proper host had a right to ask a stranger under his roof. So one could conclude that one of them at least was not honest in the other's sight: that Ceannann, with some ill intent toward them, cared not at all who they were, or that Ceannann wished he had left the door shut to them. It was an uneasy silence that had settled in the house— but he was too weary to tell clever lies to the boy, not with Dubhain's chancy humor at his elbow.

Far better to keep silence, he thought. His belly held the young couple's food, his chilled flesh was warmed by their fire, at which he seemed to have at least grudging welcome, and there was the gentleness of Firinne's presence behind the curtain to reassure him. He undid the laces of his shirt, while beside him Dubhain shrugged out of his clothes without a blush of shame and wrapped himself in the offered blanket—warmth which was no necessity to Dubhain, this willful power which had abandoned him in the woods and then dragged him to this doubtful refuge; but, oh, aye, Dubhain was willing enough for any sensation the mortal world could offer him, especially the pleasurable ones.

"Och," Dubhain said, grinning, as Caith reached after the blanket Ceannann offered him. " 'T is a fine, gentle man, a courteous host, for such an out-of-the-way place. D'ye not thank our host, my master?"

"From the heart," Caith said fervently, since Dubhain obliged him to say something; and because he was anxious to persuade the youth of their gratitude and their harmlessness. There were hurts fouler than the scratch the thing in the dark had laid on him. There was host-murder, for one.

Make me not slay them, Caith wished, heart-deep, of whatever powers drove Dubhain tonight. He suddenly felt their own presence as Sidhe-touched and unstable. *Leave them in peace, they've dealt well with us, they've sheltered us, they've fed us, can ye ask more?*

He knew the power that drove him—he believed it was the same as drove Dubhain, and, knowing how fickle and touchy the bright Sidhe were, and how treacherous it might be to have them put any wish, good or ill, on this house, he was twice anxious to settle down in quiet. So he wrapped himself in the blanket, leaned forward without a word to the youth, disposed his clothing beside Dubhain's, and sank back again, snuggled against the fire-warmed stones. He was sore and aching from his exertions, for all Dubhain's ministrations; and now that the shivers were all out of him, now that the youth had given up pointing swords at him, and now that he had the young couple's leftover supper in his stomach, he felt himself slipping with unaccountable rapidity toward sleep he dared not risk.

He watched, slit-eyed, the boy move his chair over by the door, where, evidently, he meant to sit watch over them. The youth sat down, arms folded—he watched them a long, long while like that, as if he believed they might perform some miraculous transformation like the Sidhe in the fables; but Caith leaned his head back against the stones, feigning sleep, eyes mostly shut, now.

The young man had, at the same time, set himself by the sheathed sword he had rested beside the door, Caith did not miss that—while Firinne remained modestly behind her curtain, tucked in for the night, he supposed.

Beside him, Dubhain stretched like a cat and began a soft snoring—the Sidhe could indeed sleep, if it pleased them, and his own pleasure pleased Dubhain, at any time, the wretch; but no Sidhe had to snore, for what Caith knew, and what he knew was considerable. Dubhain was being mortal for the night, noisily, as it were, laying the business on thick as butter. Caith yearned to shake him until he rattled, wishing him to stop his jokes, if only under this roof, but, oh, Dubhain would never take that quietly, no, Dubhain would wake the house and the nearest neighbors with his contrition, so Caith bore with it, and tried not to listen to it, or to think how much he longed for sleep.

The youth never moved, and there was no sound from behind the curtain, while the storm spattered the shutters and a leak from the thatch started plunking rhythmically into a bucket set, no longer oddly, between the table and the wall ... a tame little leak, a steady one; then another leak started, which spatted onto the warm stones of the hearth, where the cant of the stones channeled it into the fire ... not a bad roof, it was, and no bugs in the house: the young couple were good, careful householders—it was honest industry that had made of this lonely place what it was, and Firinne's bread-making had not a smidge of grit in it. That was care. Good cheese. Thank the goats, as well. He began to dismiss his unease in the house. Folk who set out their bucket when it rained were not slovens, and most bandits were not careful housekeepers ... no bandits that he had met, at least, and he had grown up among rough men, in his fostering.

So peace to the house, Caith wished them, and tried to have a kindly feeling toward the young man trying so hard to keep himself awake, and to be both hospitable and fearsome at once. The lad had not had his practice at sitting watch, that was soon clear, and had not his uneasy conscience, more to the mark, to keep him awake. The lad's head began to nod, sank and jerked up by several turns, over a long while.

Then, determined lad, he quietly gathered up the sword from beside him, wrapped his arms about it for a prop and stayed awake half of another hour, before he nodded off.

Caith rested his eyes, that much he dared, Dubhain being beside him; but sleep tonight he still dared not venture, not at all sure he could keep from nightmares after the fright he had had in the woods, and not wishing to alarm the house with his terrors and his outcries in his sleep—for pride's sake, if nothing else. Something he felt about the young man set his back up, and made him rivalrous, he did not even know why, but he would not make a fool of himself with Ceannann to witness it, nor trust himself to Ceannann's watch.

So he lay listening to one storm pass, and heard its sister move in a little time later, not unusual for the mountain heights, where one cloud and another could sail along behind a ridge and surprise a traveler who thought the weather fine and safe. He heard the thunder walk above the roof and listened to the wind shriek around the eaves—heard the thumping of something against the house, one of the hanging stones that would hold down the thatch, he decided, swinging against the stone wall. Meanwhile the water plunked on into the bucket and onto the hearth, and that little stream ran red and gold to its meeting with the fire, that ruffled and thumped in the wind down the chimney. Another ill-tempered spatter of rain struck the door and the shutters, but the sister-storm walked away, too, across the deep glen and away, muttering.

He stirred to feed the fire from time to time—the lad by the door was oblivious by now—and Dubhain had given up snoring, truly asleep, it might be. The fire and the night was finally all his own, and he settled back with a sigh.

A man should be easy in such a house. He decided even he could be, for a little while before the dawn, and let himself slip further than he had thought he would dare, just to the very edge of slumber. The young householder had stirred once, and tucked his sword closer, perhaps trying a while more to keep awake, but he posed no threat, and by small moments, and especially on the edge of morning, Caith let himself slip over the edge of sleep.

Immediately he was sorry, because in his dream he found himself in a woods. A sidh existed here, as it stood in Fiach, beyond Teile. Each of the two was a mound within the woods, each supported two uprights and a slanted stone to rest above it. They were passages to each other, and they were the same. When he looked at the sidh before him, he did not know what land he was in, whether looking in or looking out. That was how it confused a man. He was alarmed, for it was very seldom his dreams brought him to this sight, the heart of either woods. Always it betokened some meeting. He wished to return, now, to the cottage fireside, but when he tried to do that in his dream, faery was all about him, a mazy woods the secrets to which he did not know, and out of which, against the Sidhe's will, he could never escape, nor prevent what waited for him to witness.

A pond and a stream existed just the other side of the woods, in the midst of a broad meadow, and he drifted toward that meadow as if every path now bent itself to bring him here ... as perhaps it must. He came to the bank of what seemed an ordinary stream, but when he stood on the brink and looked down, the surface of that stream was starry vastness and a giddy fall to forever awaiting any failing of balance on the dew-wet grass. It might be death to fall into it. It might be a passage more fearful than the sidh offered him. A mortal willing to stand on the very edge of this stream and wish with all his heart would see anything in the mortal realm or in faery that he desired.

A face took shape for him, an old man, Cinnfhail, it was, king in Dun Gorm, far away, and a red-haired young man, Raghallach, his son ... and he had not willfully thought of them, but his heart must have traveled that way, thinking on the peaceful cottage, and he was both afraid and glad: he had never looked to see Raghallach again, face-to-face, it was at him he most longed to look, and yet he feared this dream was ominous ... for he could not glance away from Cinnfhail, or maintain the sense of where he was.

"Listen," Cinnfhail the king said in his dream. "Listen to me, mac Gaelan." While around them the darkness gathered and the rumble of thunder rolled, until he was standing with Cinnfhail in a stairway, with shadows all about them. He knew where this was. He knew what the king would say, foolish old man, telling him things he had no wish to hear.

"I'll leave now," he said to Cinnfhail, and tried, but Cinnfhail's face was still in front of him, while the rain dripped off the eaves, and lightning lit the stableyard, every detail sharp-edged and terrible. It was no longer Raghallach with them, it was the king's shieldman, grim as his master.

"Where are you going, mac Gaelan?" the old king asked. "Do you know?"

He knew. He tried not to think of it, but the old king said, " 'T is Dun Mhor, is it?" And when he tried to leave, the king caught his arm. "Mac Gaelan, listen, king Gaelan is dead, do you hear? Sliabhin is king now in Dun Mhor—the queen has hanged herself . . . whatever passes in Dun Mhor these days, it is not a hall I would ever guest in."

He grew angry . . . rage and lifelong hurt overwhelmed all his judgment, though it was no news, none of it. His father dead before he could ever meet him, his mother hanged for shame of Sliabhin's bed . . . that news had brought him this far from Dun na nGall, from the sea, to a house that should have helped him, and this . . . *this* furtive, shameful meeting.

"You were my father's friend. So the price of your friendship is a meal and a horse. That's well. A man should know his friends."

"Mind your tongue," the shieldman muttered.

"He has cause," the king said. "Mac Gaelan—" He stayed Caith with a hand against his shoulder. "Go back to Dun na nGall. For the gods' sake go home."

"Dun Mhor is my home. My *brother* is still in their hands. I will tell you something, lord of Dun Gorm; I had something of Sliabhin's kind of fostering from *my* foster father. I know what a whip feels like, my lord; and *no*, I'll not leave my brother to Sliabhin. And for my father's and my mother's murder—where on the gods' own earth should I go, tell me that, until I have killed that man?"

"A kinslayer has no rest in the world. Whatever his cause."

"Sliabhin's no kin of mine! I'll not *own* him mine. He murdered my father—his own brother! He raped my mother, with my father's corpse not cold in the hall! —Let me tell you, Cinnfhail king, if any man could have come and set matters right, it *might* have been my father's friend, but I see how things sit here at Dun Gorm, and you leave me no choice. No. I'll kill Sliabhin myself, with no qualm!"

There was terror in the old king's eyes. "Stay," Cinnfhail said, stopping him a second time, this time with the biting grip of a hand still powerful. "I cannot let you go. —Mac Gaelan! Stop and listen to me! . . . You'll have the horse, and whatever else you need. Go back to Dun na nGall, or go ahead to Gleann Fiach and rue it—rue it all your life. I don't think you know . . . you don't want to know more than I said in hall. *Listen to me*, for the gods' sake, lad, listen. *You don't know who you are!*"

The cold went to Caith's bones. *Bastard*, his foster father had hurled at him often enough. So maybe that was the reason Gaelan had sent him to be fostered out, at birth. "Old man," he said, "it was no grand place my father sent me. Maybe he had little choice in his relatives. Sure enough he had little in his brother. And bastard, am I, then? Whose bastard? Yours?"

"Sliabhin's."

He lashed out with his bare right hand, but the shieldman brought his arm in the way and held him fast. The breath stifled in him, not alone from the strangling hold on his neck. "Liar," he said. "Gods, you whoreson liar!"

"Stay!" the king said to his man. "Let him go."

"Lord," the shieldman protested.

"Let him go, I say." And to Caith, "Lad, Sliabhin had his way with Gaelan's wife, long before. Gaelan knew it. They gave out the babe was stillborn—but they carried him secretly to Dun na nGall. Do you understand me? To do her mercy, likeliest it was some other hand that let Sliabhin's men into Dun Mhor. And if it's true she hanged herself, surely she repented—but do you yet understand me? The younger boy, Brian—may be Sliabhin's son. At least by

what they whisper, the younger son is safe in
Sliabhin's hands if anyone is."

It all fitted then, all the pieces of his life. He set them
all in order, his hand on his sword, in this dream that
played itself out, relentless, unwelcome.

"I will give you the best help that I can. Only go
back to Dun na nGall. You are Sliabhin's true son. The
Sidhe have set a curse on him, on all his line. Leave
justice to them. Nothing can mend what is."

"You forget. I have a brother in Dun Mhor."

"A brother you've never seen. Sliabhin's son."

"Why, then, my true brother still, would he not be?"

"Don't be a fool! Sliabhin's son and in Sliabhin's
keeping. You can do the lad nothing but harm."

"I can get him out of there."

"For the gods' sake, lad—"

"You promised me a horse."

A horse, a horse, a horse, echoed through his dream.
And the dark and the storm took away the place, and
the king. He sent it away—he refused to remember the
ride, the hell-bent ride away from there. He gained
command of his dream again, and sent away the visions
in the gulf of stars, and stood safe on the bank, unwilling to see more.

But, oh, he had no dearth of foolish wishes. He
stood there, at risk of that unthinkable fall, and as in
all his other dreams of this place, he wished for that
vision that hurt him most—a pleasant glen far to the
north, a young boy growing, and a young man becoming, and a girl, Raghallach's sister, the king's daughter, he might easily have loved. It threatened him not
for what it was, which was everything it should be. It
threatened him because he was forevermore a creature of the Sidhe, and this was the hold they had on
him: that they could damn him to destroy this place
by his very longing for it. The boy who had been his
brother, Raghallach, who might have been his friend,
the girl who might someday have been his wife—with

the Sight the Sidhe had lent him, he had Seen what he would bring on them if he had his own way—and when he so much as dreamed, as now, of possessing that place regardless of the danger, the leaves of faery turned black when he touched them, the grass smoked under his feet, the golden fruit turned to worms and corruption under his fingers.

He waked without passing back through the sidh, and knew that tears were running on his face. He wiped his arm across his eyes, felt the rough blanket of a stranger's generosity wrapped about him, and opened his eyes on a place which for the moment, he could not recall—as he could not recall, most alarmingly, what might be that shadow suddenly looming against the fire.

Deirdre? he asked himself.

But it was only Firinne, bending and offering him a cup of milk, her pale hair a halo against the firelight. He held his blanket about him and took the cup. Outside, a lark was singing in precious foolishness. And his heart beat in a longing as deadly for the peace of this place as it was for the one in his dreams.

She had only been fourteen, the girl back in Teile, when he had first and last laid eyes on her; he had never spoken to her at all—nor ever would, now, nor have her see his face again.

"Thank you," he whispered. Waking was their secret, between them. Beside him Dubhain either slept or wandered free in that way trustful Sidhe might; Ceannann drowsed in his chair with his sword still in his arms, his fair head fallen against it.

"Would you more?" Firinne asked, when he had drunk half the cup, and he was for some reason not sure she meant the milk.

Prudently he shook his head, only looking at her—an exile could do that much, surely, and a good wife could forgive a stranger his moment's foolishness. He lacked all experience with good and peaceful houses. But she was staring at him, too, gazing into his eyes longer than any giving of a cup warranted, and he wondered if he could altogether have mistaken her meaning. She had no shyness toward him, that was plain; he was not, he flattered himself, an unhandsome man. She smelled of spice and flowers, of grass and wood-smoke, she smelled of home and welcome—the girl in Teile would almost be of an age with this young woman, now, and he had not reckoned that in his dream. Almost of that age—would she not be, after five years? She would have grown to womanhood, dreamed of love, longed for children—

The fire crackled with a new-laid stick of wood and the heat was burning his shoulder, but he could not readily find the will to move, conscious as he was suddenly of his nakedness, and his position as a guest under this roof. For a moment he imagined himself staying in this place a day or so, and seeing how matters would go between them. Perhaps she was unhappy in this desolate place. Perhaps in a day or so he would find Firinne alone . . . and ask her what her thoughts were, whether her husband spoke for them both and by her choice—or enjoy what she was willing to give, if that was the story here, and if that was what the Sidhe had brought him here to do, and if that was why the dream of the sidh.

Ceannann stirred from sleep. The chair thumped level on the floor, the very crack of judgment, and Firinne flinched away.

So did he. "I'll dress," he said, setting the cup beside him on the stones. His heart was beating hard. He had already been fool enough for one day; adultery might lie easier on a man's conscience than murder, but it so easily led to murders, and if the Sidhe thought to lead another mac Sliabhin into that old story, by the Badbh, they could find themselves another goat. This one was for the open sky and the hills, before he deserved the fate the Sidhe had once

tried to give him. This one was for escaping this
house as quickly as his legs could carry him, if there
was still escape possible from what the Sidhe de-
signed ... for he feared, he feared with the strength
of premonition that he had indeed just grazed past
some darkness that touched on the Sidhe's business,
here, if it was not the business of that beast downslope. There were easy ways and hard ways to do
what the Sidhe required, either would serve their pur-
poses, and he could not be out of this young couple's
house quickly enough. He reached out a discreet arm
to retrieve his clothing, modest as any maiden, and,
having recaptured his shirt, he nudged Dubhain
sharply in the ribs, and passed him the half-drained
cup as Dubhain lifted his head. "Drink, rascal, and
thank this good wife."

This he said as Ceannann watched him from the corner.

"Thank ye," Dubhain said in all solemnity, sat up,
leaning on one hand, and drained the cup to the last.
Then he stood up with his blanket gathered about
him, returned the cup to Firinne and bowed with extrav-
agant courtesy. "Thank ye indeed, woman, and again,
and the third time."

The color came and went in Firinne's face at that fey
saying. She retreated in confusion toward the door, saying that she had to see to the livestock, and lifted the
bar as Caith hastily pulled on his shirt. He intended now
to dress and have them out the door while she was out
of the house and about the chores—and before Ceannann could ask him any close questions.

But Firinne stopped cold in that doorway. Her hands
rose up before her and fluttered down helplessly to her
sides. "Oh," she said, and "Oh," and: "Oh, Ceannann,
it's taken the fence, oh, the poor things, Lugh defend
us—"

She rushed out into the wet yard and Ceannann ran
after her, sword in hand. Caith gathered himself to his

feet in sickened surmise what the poor things might be, and what manner of creature might have taken a fence down last night.

"Damn," he said under his breath, and to Dubhain: "I warned you, I said we should sleep in the shed. Our luck has struck them, and they did not deserve it, Dubhain, they in no wise deserved this."

Dubhain hit him in the ribs. "Hae the sight of her addled your wits, man? Come, dress, that lad has a sword, will ye contest him mother-naked? They will be in no good mind toward us."

Caith belted his plaid about him in haste, not pausing for his shoes—caught up his sheathed sword on his way to the door to see what the damage might be, and whether there was help to give.

"Caith," Dubhain protested, and got before him in the doorway.

But there was no need of his hurrying and no help he could give the couple, who stood amid the overthrown rails of their sheep pen. Rain-hammered tufts of wool lay everywhere, hung in sodden clumps from the railings, made islands in the puddles that lay like lakes about, where something heavy had trod.

"I was awake!" Ceannann was protesting to Firinne. "I was awake the night long, it never could have come so quietly. They've burst the pen, that's all, they've but lost a bit of hide breaking the fences, they're gone over the hill—"

"No!" Firinne cried when he seemed determined to go that way looking for them; she caught his sleeve and held him with both her hands. "No, no, and no!"

"And how shall we live without them? What shall we do?" Ceannann pried her hands from his shirt and she took hold again. "Leave be, Firinne, they'll be lost and cold, I know them, I know where to hunt them!"

"In the belly of that beast," Caith said, walking out into the yard despite Dubhain's objections, and pointed with his sheathed sword toward the deep glen. Hope hurt when it was vain, and the boy was being the fool. There was all too much of wool about, with the railings scattered wider than any escaping goat could fling them. "The beast from the woods came in the dark and the thunder, lad, it came in the height of the storm, and all of us did sleep last night, never deceive yourself, I saw you."

"Fool," whispered Dubhain, and turned about to face him, close at his shoulder. But it was said.

"Liar!" Ceannann came striding toward them, his sword in his hand.

"No liar, boy. We all did sleep."

Ceannann had stopped. Anger suffused his face. "Are you hers? Has *she* sent you? Is it to swords now, and now that we have no hope and no livelihood, you come to murder us in our beds?"

"Boy." Caith held wide his hands, putting his still-sheathed sword clearly far from his drawing-hand, despite Dubhain's anxious pull at his sleeve. "I outran that thing last night, and no one sent me. I bring you no harm at my own wish, by the gods I swear it. You and your wife have done us nothing in the wide world but good, and I swear to you I know nothing at all of any woman who might have sent us—I know nothing of her, nor ever wish to know."

" 'Know nothing of her'! It could never pass our wards before! This is your fault!"

"Forgive me. I'll be on my way, in the absence of welcome, I and my lad." He held up his empty hand, trying to disengage. "I offer you no quarrel, for any reason."

"You're no chance travelers. What brought you here? What do you want of us?"

"Naught but the freedom to cross your yard, naught but to walk along the ridge there, and away from your land. Sheep-stealers we are not, lad, and if we were bent on mischief, we were inside to do it while you slept."

"Liar, I say!"

"Have done!" He turned to go in, saw a flash of metal in the tail of his eye and spun back, his sword up crosswise. Sheath clashed with naked blade, and he shoved Ceannann back angrily and hard. "Have done, I say! I'd spit you, boy, and that would be worse to this—wife—of yours than a dozen goats in that thing's belly. —Tell him, girl!"

"Please!" cried Firinne, trying to set herself between Ceannann and him. "Please! Take our food and go, go away, please—oh, Ceannann, don't, don't, it's mad, they had nothing to do with it at all, they said it was abroad last night, it was the thunder covered it—"

"It drew about it its ain silence," said Dubhain. "For cup of milk, for hearth and bread I return ye truth: it crept up after us, it cast a silence about itself so that it had no need of thunder, but closer than the pens it durst not come, because of the wards, the rowan and the iron." Dubhain swept a hand toward the door and window. "Me, ye welcomed. Had it rapped sae politely as we, would you have guested it sae fair as us and fed it milk and fine bread?"

Firinne made a warding-sign against the Eye, while Ceannann backed away, the sword sinking in his hand.

"Faery," said Ceannann. "They are Sidhe!"

"Only he," said Caith, putting Dubhain behind him. "—You need have no fear of him. You gave him a cup and he took it. Peace be on your house."

He turned his back to their aggrieved faces and, with the assurance Dubhain's eye was on them, went back inside to put on his stockings and his shoes and pull his shirt to rights, Dubhain holding them from the doorway the while.

And it did occur to him, while he was inside alone, to raid the stores the couple had hanging from the rafters and steal food at least for their next meal. Of clothing Dubhain owned no more than he stood in, kilt and shirt, feet all bare, never a crumb of provisions to his name, never a thought to a next meal—while he walked the world little richer, except the sword and his thorn-torn cloak.

Nor ever doomed to be richer, Caith thought, slinging the cloak about his shoulders, and taking a last look about the table and the cup sitting there—they had not a cup or a plate to their name, either, and the young freeholders had several. A cup would be very welcome, on cold mornings, and a pan to cook with, twice so. A meal for the evening would go very well, seeing they might take no time to hunt.

But he left it all, and walked out their door with Dubhain in close attendance from the door sill, Dubhain trying to plead something with him, but he was not listening. His eyes were on Ceannann and Firinne standing in their ruined sheepfold, the young couple looking at the ground around about, as if they hoped even yet they might find some track, some evidence of an escape.

They looked around, then, and, perhaps at the grimness they saw in his face, or at something they saw in Dubhain's, Ceannann put his arm about Firinne and drew her behind him as if they might murder her in parting. The terror on two innocent faces and the desperate plight into which this attack had set them made him yearn to do something to prove himself better than they feared—such as staying and helping Ceannann search the hills for their flock, in the case one or two goats might have escaped, their kind being somewhat nimbler and far cannier than a sheep.

But their faces invited no such offer of help—Ceannann's was hostile and suspicious, irrecoverable words had passed between them, already, and given Firinne's perhaps simple-hearted approach to him and the Sidhe-touched doom he had already felt in the house, he was all too anxious to be away.

"Let us go," he said to Dubhain. "Let us bring no more harm on these folk."

"Nay, thou forgettest, thou hast no longer my summoning." Dubhain skipped a step across a puddle, light and barefoot to the bitter morning chill. Dubhain looked back at him, then, a wicked grin on his dusky face. "Ask them, man. Ask them whence they come and why they lodge in this lonely place. Does curiosity fail thee?"

"I ask them nothing," he muttered, and waved his sword at Dubhain to send him ahead of him down the hill and away. "We've done them harm enough! Of mercy, let them be!" An acute foreboding was on him now, an overwhelming anxiousness to be off their land, so vivid a foreboding that he felt a sweat start on his body, and he overtook Dubhain in the sloping yard and caught him by the arm. As well grasp the stone of the mountain—and Dubhain was so happy with the world this morning. "Of mercy," he hissed into Dubhain's ear. "D' ye hear me, Sidhe? Take it of me later. Take what you will. Bring nothing on their heads!"

"They hae brought it on themselves and will deserve more," Dubhain said, and, turning in his grip, tilted his head. Wild, dark eyes leered at him from beneath Dubhain's thick forelock, brown eyes which glowed with inward red like embers, and Dubhain grinned. "Is 't not ever the way of men?"

"Let be, let be!" He flung the cozening rascal a step farther downhill. Chill had settled over his skin, as if the storm had come back and obscured the wan morning sun. He stalked away down the hill alone, Dubhain lingering behind to spite him and frighten him, and where he went now he cared not at all, only that he distance himself from this cottage and from Ceannann's suspicions as quickly as his legs could carry him, before more and worse befell the two of them, or pushed him into some fatal confrontation with the boy: that was the pattern he saw shaping, his house had had enough of jealous rage, and he had shed blood enough over it.

"Hoosht! Hey!" Dubhain overtook him effortlessly, skipping along beside him on the rain-wet grass. "What a leave-taking! And you a king's son! Who ever taught you courtesy?"

"The same who taught me murder," he said shortly, and strode on downhill, toward the woods below, the quickest way off the hill. For a time he heard nothing at all, not even Dubhain's footsteps near him.

But there was no shaking Dubhain or his humor.

"The Sidhe decreed," Dubhain declared cheerfully, skipping up beside him, when he was well toward the trees and the dark depths of the glen, "the Sidhe foreknew what would happen here i' the night. *Draiocht* and *geas*, d' ye nae feel the weaving of webs and black witchery in this place? D' ye nae feel Necessity weighing every word and syllable?"

"A plague I say!" Caith tried to walk faster, blind in his going, and slid down a rain-slick patch of grass, almost under the trees.

Draiocht.

Sorceries. And by that, he knew that there was indeed no trail through this glen but one, and that his cursed temper was leading him down and down again beneath the trees and toward the black water. All his course into and through this valley was alike, no matter what his choosing. His path brought the shadow in the deep glen up the hill or brought him down to the shadow, it was all the same.

And it was another Shadow which skipped blithely by him.

"Things are greatly out of joint here," Dubhain said, mincing along a bank of dead fern. "Look ye, how the forest comes sae neatly up to the hill where that pretty pair have made their nest. And the burn here below winds a' through it, convenient for mischief."

"Let be, I say!"

"D' ye go a-hunting to-day, sweet Caith?"

"I do nothing! I brought them nothing, I take nothing away from this place, I do them no harm and I mean them none!"

"Necessity, necessity, necessity . . ."

"Be quiet!" Caith slouched on down the decline of the hill in a dour and bitter mind, discovered the black water in front of him, and found that, as the only open ground afforded him, he must walk beside that stream.

And why he did not then set his face back toward Teile and the sunlight he could not reason with himself, even while he walked doggedly in the other, hellbound direction. He wished with all his heart to go home now—but home was a deception: Teile held too much of temptation, in the presence of what he loved, and he could not bear it any longer, as he could not bear the deluded peace of that cottage another moment. A young man denying the truth before his eyes and hiding it with his temper, a girl become foolish and placating toward him, as if that would ever make him better than he was—it touched too many of his own wounds: the truth was something he had to keep constant and clear before him, and rage at his fate and shifting of blame was something he could never afford. There was danger all about that place, and that boy was a fool.

"Geas, my sweet prince. A curse is on this land as strong and as bluidy as your own. Ye feel it. Oh, aye, ye can See it in the water and in the clouds. Blood, blood, and blood."

"Damn your Seeing!" He thrust a branch from his path and climbed along the uneven bank, below a place where great boulders had erupted from the side of the mountain, rock grey and black and shattered in some ancient violence. Dead bracken brushed his legs with last night's rain, as cold as dead flesh. Fallen leaves

were black and rotten underfoot, a few rags still clinging to the trees, dripping with water.

"Rash, my Caith, rash," Dubhain chided him. "And
where are ye going now, sae angry, d' ye know?"

He had no more idea than before where he was going
now or even whether following the brook would lead
him the quickest way out of this accursed glen. Reason
told him, now that it was too late, that he should have
taken the climb from the cottage to the high hills and
over the heathery heights the sunlight loved, however
cold the nights in the mountains above. What drove him
to take this darksome path he feared was not reason,
and it was a minuscule part of his torment that he constantly knew better than he did. But he dared not go
back across the young couple's land, that was the solitary resolution he had formed, and he clung to it as the
only way of escape from the Sidhe's doings, no matter
what power had brought him here. He might only have
brushed against it. It might mean nothing to him. It was
not self-delusion: there was the chance, please the
Badbh, of walking out of this.

The bank went level a time, and dead, dry bracken
gave way to a margin of leaf-mold at the water's
edge. Then it was a less breathless walk for a space,
but gradually the outcrops of tumbled stone thrust
closer and closer to the stream, forcing them closer to
its brink, where, about the occasional black rocks that
had tumbled down into the water, Guagach murmured
with a dizzy sound, and became a white, stained rap-
ids.

That, Caith hoped, might mark the convenient range
of the creature that he suspected lived in it, although the
Badbh knew it could go on dry land if it liked. He
walked beside that white-frothing water, and Dubhain
skipped along the perilous rocks, sometimes peering
into the still side-pools of the stream and then running
to catch up.

"Why, man," Dubhain said, "ye are sae glum today.

Shall I amuse you? Shall I? —Hoosht, man, something is coming. My ears hear it. Are ye deaf? Or is it human folk at all that hear this thing?"

Dubhain's chatter often had more of mischief than of sense; this morning, it had become tormenting noise to him. Then the meaning came to him as well as the mischief, and he stopped still, knowing Dubhain both warned and mocked him of what was fated for him in this valley. He looked helplessly about him, scanning for ambushes, and gazed up the pillared darkness of the autumn stream course, where a great fall of rocks came near the stream and left only a narrow muddy bank.

Then his ears caught what Dubhain's faery sense had surely caught before him, the moving of many horses together, a warning treacherous and sourceless in this narrow, rocky place. Trees and rocks cast echoes this way and that, but, as best he could tell, it came from downstream and ahead of them. They were walking the only path that offered itself, and that left them exposed and vulnerable, after leaving abundant tracks along a bank where he was suddenly, reasonlessly certain that no intrusion was welcome.

And their tracks led straight to the cottage on their backtrail.

"O gods," he said, looking back.

"Come along, man, shall we play these riders a joke?"

"Damn you!"

He flung off Dubhain's hand. Dubhain's nostrils flared, his head came up and the red showed clear within his eyes. " 'T is the weird on this land that the Sidhe hae decreed," Dubhain said, gazing at him as if his flesh were no barrier to those red eyes at all. "And thou 'rt within it, thou, and I." The voice hissed and whispered like a spring within deep rocks. "O my sweet prince, that sword ye carry mends less than most of its kind. Will ye draw? And what will ye seek with it?

Blood? But whose, my sweet murderer?" Dubhain grasped his arm and drew him aside, while the noise of horses and riders came closer and clearer through the woods, a jangling and jingling of harness, a splashing of shallow water and hooves striking mud and stone just around the winding of the stream.

Dubhain dragged him perforce toward a den in the tumbled boulders. He resisted, and Dubhain's grip became stronger, became ice, became watery cold in which sense and resistance drowned: Caith staggered at the last and the bank and the forest reeled in a cold haze. He fell down into this dizziness and knew himself cradled in Dubhain's arms, down in that dark place among the rocks, as half a score of riders came by so near their concealment that a spatter of rotten leaves struck his arm and leg. He struggled to be free, and to take his own fate into his hands, but now his whole body grew numb.

"Sleep," Dubhain whispered against his ear, and stroked the hair aside from it. Dubhain hummed a tune and breathed that humming into his brain like the gentle thrum of bees in summer heat, the purring of a cat, the sighing of the wind in midsummer leaves. "Sleep, sweet Caith. What they will do is geas and neither you nor I can stay it. 'T is the trouble men are always having. Ye gae sae blind through the world."

The sound of the riders died away. Caith's wits reeled and spun and the sound filled his ears, become a whisper of a voice, the roaring of the sea.

"Blood," Dubhain whispered, "d' ye nae taste it, d' ye nae smell it, my prince?"

It washed between him and the sun, like a stinking flood, like a darkening curtain.

" 'T is geas," Dubhain said while the tumbling went on and on into dark, and the earth shook under hoofbeats. There was blood, and there was fire. Perhaps it was all in memory.

"All Necessity," the voice whispered. "And where

there is blood to be shed, thou 'rt most apt. The Sidhe weep for thee, my damned prince; and use thee, for they hae nae gentler weapon."

"Do not make me See this, Dubhain, no more, no more . . ."

"Nay, nay, I make thee blind, I make thee deaf, I unweave the pattern of thy sense, my Caith. I gie thee nae Sight to trouble thee, thou willt go blind to the doing of the deed. How tender thou art. And how passionate is thy mischief in the world." Dubhain gently traced the line of his cheek and smiled his merry, wicked smile. "Sleep and dream, sleep and dream, most dear and damned fool."

The humming filled his ears, and there was nothing beyond that but the dark.

Quiet came.

Came an acute pain of cramped sleeping, of limbs settled not where he would have disposed them, one leg unnaturally bent in the cold and the damp. Caith saw shadowed stone above his head, felt cold earth beneath him, and with a grimace stirred and levered himself from the icy crevice in the rocks where Dubhain had abandoned him.

Two things he knew immediately about the world. One was the smell of smoke on the wind, and the other was the sun standing at afternoon above the skeletal trees and the rocks. It had been morning. He was not even assured it was the same day. And when he had gained his feet, there was nothing he could do in this knowledge but to lean his elbows against the stone which had sheltered him. He smothered his anger and clenched his fists against his skull, to draw still breaths of reason and to try not to weep or to shout in his rage.

"Dubhain," he whispered then hollowly, lifting his face to the woods at large. "Dubhain, is it over now, will you come, or have you any more for me? Are they dead, those two? And was it by my hand? For the gods' sake, *let me remember*!"

The wind blew, stirring the black water, sending dead leaves down onto the surface, raising the stench of death and rot.

"Sweet Dubhain, fair Dubhain, Dubhain thou hell-spawn, what happened? What have I done? What am I to do? Where am I to go? Can ye not come and tell me at least that, Dubhain?"

Bubbles rose and burst, nothing more.

"D' you leave me now? D' you leave me to my own devices, Dubhain? I warn you, I warn you, wight, they are not always to the Sidhe's liking!"

The forest gave back not so much as an echo. The trampled earth proved the horsemen were no dream. And the reversed hoof-prints, filling with muddy water, proved that some of the riders at least had ridden back again.

"Dubhain!"

Let the riders hear him. Let them kill him. Let them try their luck against his charmed, cursed life. He walked, knowing (he had no knowledge how) that it was not at him those riders aimed. And if they should come for him, why, let Dubhain bestir himself to save him, let Dubhain soil his pretty hands—

It was back along the trail he walked, back all the way they had come, a track where horses had struggled to find footing; but their going had made a clear passage for him, especially where they had left the stream-side and climbed through the barren-limbed woods, up and up the hill.

He followed that unmistakable scar on the land. He had no fear himself of meeting the riders now—a fey rage was on him. They could not kill him: he could not, himself, be so fortunate, since where the Sidhe sent him, there was harm to be done. He had to know. He could not go blindly on into this valley, not knowing what he had done, or what the harm was—

The way darkened. It was the sidh again. It was the walk down a familiar, dreadful path, that he did not want to take, but he could only go ahead, knowing the place ahead, no cottage, but a fortress, and once he had thought of it, a gate and a door he did not want to enter, yet must.

Behind this door a man sat in a chair by the fire. The light was on his face, a face much like his own if bitter years had touched it. The man's hair and beard were his own burning red, faded with years; and the plaid was the red and black of Dun Mhor ... like the guards, around him, more and more of them appearing in the shadows of his dream. Essential details were changed. He could not, in his confusion, tell which.

"Who *are* you?" Sliabhin asked now as he had asked him that night, and the lie was as ready as it had been:

"A messenger, my lord of Dun Mhor. Hagan sends, from Dun na nGall, asking you send the other boy."

Sliabhin got to his feet, while his heart pounded. The cloak about him covered the red plaid that would kill him and the sword that would kill Sliabhin. There was no way out now. Not from the moment he had passed the door.

"So," Sliabhin said, and walked aside, a half step out of reach, among his men. *My father,* Caith thought, seeing that likeness to himself at every point, as the sweat gathered on his palms. "So Hagan wants the boy sent?" Sliabhin asked. "I find that passing strange."

"It's the elder son, lord, Caith. So Hagan said to me. Caith has heard rumors—" He let his voice trail off in intimidated silence, playing the messenger of ill news. "Lord, they have had to lock him away for fear he'll break for the south, or do himself some harm. He mourns for his brother. He's set some strange idea into his head that he has to see the boy or die. I'm to bring the lad, by your leave, lord."

A long time Sliabhin stood staring at him, this elder image of himself. "How does Caith fare?" Sliabhin asked, in a tone Caith had not expected could come from a mouth so hard and bitter. A soft question. Tender. As if it mattered. It was some evil dream—this man, his true father, asking the question he had longed all his days to hear a different father ask.

"Sorrowing for his mother, I hear." There was a knot in Caith's throat. He went on in this oblique argument. "If Caith could see the lad, lord, that he's well—it might bring him to a better mind. He knows whose son he is."

"Tell me,—messenger. What color Hagan's beard?"

"Bright red, lord. A scar grays it."

Sliabhin nodded slowly. "And how fares my neighbor?"

"Lord?"

"Cinnfhail." Sliabhin's brow darkened. His voice roughened. "You'll have passed through Gleann Gleatharan. *How fares Cinnfhail?*"

"Well enough, lord."

"If," said Sliabhin, "you had denied being with Cinnfhail I would have taken it very ill,—*Caith.*"

Caith snatched out his sword, throwing back his cloak. All about him men drew—and Sliabhin stopped everything with a move of his hand.

"I've waited for you." Sliabhin's voice was soft. "I was sure you would come someday, somehow."

Things were askew. Things had gone astray from the truth. He no longer knew the course of this dream, or where it would take him. "I came to kill you—for Gaelan's death. But I heard another tale, in Dun Gorm. And which is true,—*father*? Who sent me to that whoreson to foster? Was it Gaelan? Or yourself?"

"Who is your companion?" Sliabhin asked, turning his shoulder from the menace of his sword. "Some other of Gleatharan's fine young lads?"

"Oh, that." Caith kept the point and the distance between them, and took a lighter tone, an easier stance, realizing he had company in this dream. "Dubhain is his name. One of Hagan's whore's sons. I've gotten used to such comrades—I get on well with them, father, any sort of cutthroat. That's a skill they taught me well—your cousin Hagan and his crew. Why not? We breed such merry sorts,—*father*." He gained a step on Sliabhin, but sideways, as a man moved to block him. It all stopped again. "Pirates. Brigands. Are these my brothers? How many did you beget—and on *what*, when you tired of my mother?"

"Enough!" Sliabhin's face congested. He lifted a shaking hand, empty. "It was Gaelan—Gaelan tormented her. She and I loved, boy—*loved*—you'd not know that. Oh, yes, whelp, I saved your life. I rode—myself—and bestowed you in safety where and as I could, or Gaelan would have given you up for wolfbait. He gave out you were stillborn. He beat her—hear me? He *beat* your mother!"

More of truths and half truths shuttled back and forth in this tapestry of lies.

"Where's Brian? Where's my brother?"

"You'll not be taking your brother anywhere tonight, my lad."

"I want to see him."

"What's he to you?"

"A whim, father, like you."

"Put up the sword. *Put it up!*"

He doubted. He doubted, and the room went to and fro, and spun around again, into branches and dark. He saw the sidh ahead of him through the woods—the upright stones, the place within the shadow, but he lost it among the trees. He felt moist ground under his hands, grasped a branch to aid him on the slope, slow and deliberate as a dream. Horses' hoofprints scarred the mud. He had slept, he had dreamed, he followed a band of horsemen. There was no sidh, and it was Gleann Fiain, not Fiach . . .

The riders he tracked . . . he had no idea at all why he should count them as evil. Their riding through the woods, as sinister as it had seemed when Dubhain had drawn him off the trail ... might, he reasoned with himself, be on some mission of good. They might be hunters in pursuit of the bane in the glen: they might be honest men of some lord with a lawful right to ride this land. He might be utterly, fatally mistaken in following them, blinded by the Sidhe and by his cursed disposition to fear harm in everyone's actions. He was his father's son—it was no fault of the Sidhe that he saw weapons on the men and believed they were for using. . . .

Stone was about him, not branches. There was a wooden cage, and in that, a smallish, half-starved, dark-haired boy; this, *this*, the truth in the cellars of Dun Mhor. There were chains, and in those chains, Raghallach, next a reeking brazier ... burns on his body, bleeding wounds, and no sense within his eyes.

There was his father ... was Sliabhin, with his bandits about him, the lord of this hell in the vaults of Dun Mhor. "Sliabhin," Caith said ever so softly, seeing everything in ruins—his last and furtive hope of home and wholeness. He felt sick, forever fouled, from his origins to this hour. "Father mine, d' ye know I'd half believed ye until now? And, Brian? —Brian, is it you?"

Whether the caged boy heard at all he could not tell. Swords came out of sheaths all about the room ... his was in his right hand, though Sliabhin's own stayed within its sheath. An oilpot bubbled softly, and sent up its acrid, stinking reek. An ember snapped.

"I've killed your men upstairs," he said, baiting them all—such a deed as he intended now wanted anger, not blood as chilled as his ran at this sight. "I've killed every one I could reach and I've driven off the rest. There are no women here. No children. It's a fortress of bandits, father, this house of ours. And tell me again how my mother died. A suicide, was it? Was *that* for love of you?"

Sliabhin's face twisted. "Shut your mouth!"

"Why would ye not call me home long ago—to your loving care? Hagan—was nothing to what you've done here."

"Listen to me, Caith." Sliabhin took on a tone of reason. He moved closer, among the swords. "This whelp's no son of mine. Brian is hers and his—not mine. Gaelan taught him to hate me—his son . . ."

"Take your sword. I'll kill you one way or the other, I swear I will."

"The boy's not my son! You *are*!"

"Are you sure? Could we ever be *sure*?"

That touched the quick. Caith saw the hate, the terrible, terrible hatred. "Boy," said Sliabhin, on another step toward him, "I kept you up there—safe in Dun na nGall. Safe, all these years. Gaelan would have killed you!"

"The way you're killing my brother? —Brian. Brian, lad—" He moved closer to the cage, shifting ever so carefully. "I'm your brother Caith, Brian, d' ye hear me? I've come for you."

Perhaps the boy had passed beyond all capability of speech—or trust. Caith reached out his left hand through the bars, his eyes never leaving Sliabhin. And felt a hand grip his own, a small hand, all thin and weak and desperate.

And in that instant's distraction Sliabhin's men shifted like so many wolves in a pack.

"Face me!" Caith said, his sword aimed for Sliabhin. "Come on, man, draw."

A small shake of the head. "I'd not kill you."

"Why not? I'll wager you were never sure—never sure which of us was yours, or if either is. Isn't that what eats at you? Aye, you loved my mother. You wanted her more than you loved her—and *still* you'll never know."

Steel hissed its way to light: Sliabhin drew.

Caith disengaged his left hand with a gentle tug, his eyes all for Sliabhin now. Dark blurred around him, with his father closing on him, the men moving in from all sides. He seized the brazier one-handed, slung it the circuit of the room, hurling red coals and irons across the planks. The oilpot fell, and spread fire. He heard a man scream, lost his resolve not to look, then heard another, whirled, spitted the man that came at him—

"Patricide." Sliabhin held to him, clutching at his clothes, the plaid of Dun Mhor. "Patricide, twice as damned."

All about him, the shrieks of burning men. One ran at him, crazed with pain. All about him the alarm dinned—*help, fire, assault* . . .

Dark, then, and the rake of branches across his cheek. He was looking for the sidh. He looked for a way out . . . and followed the tracks of riders on the slope. Not to a fortress—to a cottage. To two innocents . . . no kin of his.

Perhaps, he thought, breathless on the long, wooded rise, perhaps he should turn aside, go back, forget the fate of the young couple on their hill. Perhaps that simple act would thwart the Sidhe that drove him, or bring Dubhain back to protest his change of mind; perhaps he should sit down where he was and refuse to budge until Dubhain did return to misguide and mislead him . . . but innocence was no match for such men, and, whether it was geas or his own damnation that led him, he was apt for the Sidhe's mischief, having a disposition that secrets were not for keeping (too many he had endured in his life) and that darknesses were for throwing light on (few the men that loved him for it). But, worst of all, now, now, in the labored beating of his heart, he had the hope that these visions meant something, the hope that Caith mac Sliabhin might yet accomplish something in the world to redeem himself—that, too, might be within the Sidhe's plans, his fondest, most foolish hope . . . a chance, a gift like other faery gifts, all unwarned.

He knew the Sidhe, that, having no fault, they needed have no mercy ... but he went places he knew were foolish, because he could never tell the difference between meddling they wanted and meddling they did not ... knowing they had to give an escape, they *had* to give him one chance.

So here he walked at the edge of a woods in which he had no right to trespass, in a stronger and stronger reek of smoke ... at the crest of the hill, now, seeking just that small vantage farther on the steep slope he prayed would show him he was all wrong in his assumptions, that it was only Firinne at soap-making, or some ordinary, homely reason for so much fire.

But, failing to see any such sight, and still following the horses' muddy prints in the grass, he ventured a little closer, knowing—*knowing*, damn the impulses that drove him first one way and then another, that his returning might bring down on the young pair the very harm he had come here to prevent. Ceannann might well and reasonably assume the worst of his return here. The riders might have come here with every right, and they might now, with every right of lordship, be hunting him, if the young couple had reported strangers pursuing undeclared business in the glen.

Still, he could see the smoke billowing from the hilltop, and the smoke that came to him did not have the smell of a tame fire. Bits of wool from the earlier destruction had flown even here, and clung on brush and grass stems. Every sign about him spoke of harm and hurt, from the beast, the fire, and the riders out of the glen, while the Sidhe left him without counsel in the matter.

His own curiosity was touched now, a desperate, foolish curiosity which he had generally learned to ignore, to Dubhain's sometime frustration and occasional delight ... for never yet had he escaped what the Sidhe desired of him, and it seemed he could not now—or had not—Macha, he could not account for the time, he did not know where he had been, or how long he had been unaware—he did not even know if his memories of his waking were true or some Sidhe deception.

He hesitated, a tormented, defiant impulse toward one direction and the other, so intense he shivered in his indecision; but last of all he slapped his leg in frustration and skirted the hill along the horses' track, bent on finding the answer here, constantly seeing the plume of smoke, white and abundant, rising above the hill, and, as he saw it farther around the track, above the stonework of the cottage itself. So much of the structure being stone, he still hoped that he might be altogether mistaken in his fears, and that he would find the cottage unharmed—in which event he swore to pass quietly and quickly from this place, if the Sidhe would only let him reach the woods again—constantly he laid out such patterns of escape for himself, ready, always, to bolt from the Sidhe's plans, knowing, always, that from something the Sidhe wished to go amiss, there would be no time to bolt and no ready escape if ever he gained the will.

But when he came within view of the house, he saw the thatch was burned: the smoke was going up from the mere shell of what had been a house, and furnishings, and all. The posts of the sheepfold stood with the railings scattered, and the shed was knocked flat. With all that before him, his heart sank to the pit of his stomach.

So much destruction, and for the taking of two harmless folk? he asked the Sidhe in silence. And he asked himself, disquieted, utterly: Badbh and Macha, . . . could I by any imagining have done this myself, and not know? And could the riders be hunting *me*?

He could not but come closer, to the very wall of the house, trying to see what had happened here; and the whisper of a footfall warned him as he went past the corner. He spun about in alarm, drew at the flash of a sword—but young Ceannann did not rush blindly to the attack, this time: he waited grimly on his guard, perhaps in fear of him, perhaps in doubt of his reasons or his guilt, he did not know.

"Where is Firinne?" he asked Ceannann, the only question he thought the boy might be willing to hear; and it did for a moment seem to take the breath out of the lad.

"Who *are* you?" Ceannann cried. "Who *are* you but her servant?"

"A second time, this 'her.' I know no 'her,' boy, unless you mean the thing that took the goats, and such as that is, I do doubt it sent the horsemen."

"Laugh as you like," Ceannann said, bringing the sword up, and Caith stepped back a pace out of fighting range and kept his sword out of line.

"I am not laughing, boy. I came back to help if I could. If we must be at blows, at least tell me the reason. Who were these men?"

The youth looked the more distracted, the more desperate, longing to believe him, perhaps, but fearing him—very wisely, since there was everything wrong about him. *Draiocht* and *geas*, Dubhain had said. It was here. It might be staying the lad's hand, as it had brought him back here—but it did not inspire the boy to trust him.

"Peace," Caith said. "You cannot kill me, not me, lad. And I know your thinking, that a quick end would be so much easier than going on from here, but will you have those men get away free? —Where is Firinne?"

The sword lifted, trembling with such violence the sun flashed from it like lightnings—then crashed point to the muddy, trampled earth. The lad was weeping when he turned away, and found no place to lean his head but the stone of the ravaged cottage wall.

"Ye know the fay," Caith said, "and ye know—ye

know, lad, that there was a Sidhe beneath your roof last night. But he wished you peace."

"Is this peace?" Ceannann cried, tears on his face, and swung the muddied sword an arc about him. "Is this peace, that's come on us?"

"Where is Firinne, man? Was she in the house? Did they take her away? What happened here?"

Ceannann drew a ragged breath. A helpless gesture, the boy made, with his empty left hand, and a second one before he found a voice to answer that. "They took her with them. —I was out searching. I hoped . . . I hoped maybe a goat or two . . . We quarreled, and I still had hope . . . Oh, gods, if I had listened to her and been home—"

"I smelled the burning," Caith said, and forbore to tell how he had seen the riders pass: the youth regarded them with suspicion enough already, and had not asked him regarding Dubhain's whereabouts, that was how scattered the lad's thoughts were—but small fault to him for that. "I tracked the horses. They came from along the brook, upward to the hill."

"I know whose they are. I know where they come from."

"Then whose are they? Creatures of this woman you speak of?"

The boy turned to look at him, with bleak and burning eyes. "Her men. Yes. And are you not one?"

"I came down from Teile. I know no one in Gleann Fiain, only the name of the place. But while we stand here talking, we might be on their track."

"I have nothing but what I stand in."

"Nor I," Caith said, made a motion of his hand toward the trail, slid his sword back into its sheath and started walking, hoping, by that, that the boy would listen, and follow, and he did: Ceannann overtook him, still with his sword unsheathed, and rubbing with the back of his hand at the tear-tracks on his face, which only spread the soot.

"Is your friend below?" Ceannann remembered to ask, finally, when they were halfway down the hill.

"Dubhain? He comes and he goes."

Ceannann gave him a second look, not seeming to trust that answer—small wonder, Caith thought: but what choice had the lad? They descended the rest of the hill in that uneasy silence, a long space of it, until they were all but within the woods again.

Then the boy cast him a misgiving glance, as if he were having second thoughts about this place, or him, or Dubhain's whereabouts and abilities.

"Where do you come from?" Ceannann asked him, at that last moment.

"From Teile. I told you. Mind your feet, lad." It was rough ground, and the boy misstepped, with his eyes set suspiciously on him, not the tree roots that laddered the ground. Ceannann scowled, but he went surely enough in the woods once he paid attention to his steps.

Not so graceless or unclever a boy, Caith thought, then, far from it: he was Firinne's very image. Ceannann had that true white skin that no sun could tan, on which the wind only brought a blush, give or take the smudges. His eyes were the clearest sea-green Caith had ever seen: granted, he had not met Firinne's gaze so closely except by firelight, but he was sure they would be that color, given all the other likenesses. Wife be damned: the hair, the lines, the face, everything said close kinship between the two. Brother and sister they had to be.

And the same line of thinking said that Firinne in soldiers' hands would not fare safely unless those men held a great dread of the woman who had sent them.

But that was not a thought to put forth aloud, not to the boy, and not now, when they could go no faster nor do more for the girl than they were already doing.

Dubhain, Caith wished silently, desperately, into the forest shade. *Dubhain, Dubhain, do you hear me?*

But of Dubhain there was still no wisp nor shadow. He felt keenly, the farther down the hill and the deeper into the forest they went, the despair rooted in the place. And Dubhain's absence began to weigh on him like a foreboding of harm. *Once in dread, once in pain ...*

It isn't enough, Caith thought with a sudden chill. He's vanished into thin air, damn him, while the riders were up there burning the cottage and kidnapping Firinne. It's only once he counts my calling, up there with the beast in the dark. Or this is one of his damnable jokes.

But whatever offense I gave ye, ye cursed wight, surely, surely I paid for it. Did I not? Is worse yet to come?

They reached the stream and the path again, where tracks of riders crossed each other in the mud, and he marked how Ceannann half-knelt to have a close look at the ground—seeing whether his footprints overlaid the horses' hoofprints. Canny lad, Caith thought, to be certain whether the trampled earth told the same story he had told him up by the house. He saw the glance Ceannann darted at a new print of his, by the others, that were filling with water. And he read what Ceannann might well read there, granted he thought about it.

"Whence did you follow them?" Ceannann asked. "How long ago?"

"From hiding. I heard them riding along the river. I saw no reason to bid any strangers the good of the day. But I saw the way they were tending and they had the look of trouble."

He knew already how short Ceannann's temper was: he wished he could mend matters in his answer, besides that there were hours missing in his account, which Ceannann was surely reckoning—such as how the riders had come and done their work and gone off another way, and still met their old trail, that his footprints overlay by considerable.

His, and only his, Dubhain's bare feet not having touched here.

"Dubhain and I had words," he said, trying to patch that matter at least, "and being the vain and silly ass he is,—" That for Dubhain, that for the woods at large if he had the Sidhe's attention, "—he cast a sleep on me and left me, when the riders came through."

Taunting Dubhain was another thing he realized as rash the moment he heard himself doing it: troubles enough had fallen on their heads, and Dubhain was not the only Sidhe who might be listening to a foolish man trying to mend and cobble the story he told—a tale which clearly Ceannann did not altogether find reasonable, since Ceannann had never yet sheathed his sword, so long as they had been walking in this haunted woods, and walked most often at his back.

And perhaps, Caith thought, Ceannann had his own cause to fear the Sidhe—they had deserved their fate, Dubhain had gibed this morning, to his indignation at the time Dubhain had said it; but it might be true in the balances of the Sidhe, which had nothing to do with mortal justice.

Or perhaps Ceannann's thoughts were set only, desperately, on Firinne. Ceannann had said not a thing further about Dubhain, nor had Ceannann quarreled with his account of what had happened, only set out at a breathless space along the track the riders had left, once they had left the place where all tracks crossed.

"Have a care," Caith advised him. "Silence is an ally, too."

"Take care for yourself," Ceannann retorted, hardly pausing. "It's no good if they reach her lands. No one can go there against her will."

"*Her* lands. *Her* will. —What," Caith asked, with the sun sinking fast behind the hills, now, and the trees around the narrow bank growing darker with the

shadow of the deep glen as they walked, "what happens
to be your quarrel with this woman? Who is she, that
she has such guards about her?"

He was recalling the faery-wards, the iron and the
rowan, he was recalling how Dubhain had had to be
asked in, and most of all he was asking himself now the
same question which Dubhain had bidden him wonder
in the morning, how they came to have their house up
the hill from such a dreadful brook as that, and biding
in such apparent contentment there.

"The lady of Dun Glas," Ceannann said shortly. "I
was her harper. I fell in love with her maid. We ran
away together."

Doubtless such things had happened in the wide
world. But as the truth, it made a fine ballad.

"You've fair readiness with a sword," Caith said. "Of
what harper did you learn that? And where is this Dun
Glas? Is it in Gleann Fiain?"

Ceannann glanced darkly back at him, only that, for
an answer.

"Are they all in that lady's hall," Caith asked, "so
fair-haired and green-eyed as you both? I thought at
first glance you were brother and sister. But I have been
mistaken before now."

Ceannann turned on him. "My *wife*, man! By the
Badbh, you're fond of other people's business!"

"Clearly I'm mis—"

Came a sound, the faintest of sounds, a single stone
rattling against another, which cast Caith's thoughts instantly back to the night and the dark and the rain. In
that way it had begun, signaling there was something
else abroad—or someone.

"—taken," he went on quietly, and, under his breath:
"—Something clattered."

"I heard." There was panic in Ceannann's eyes. But
the sound did not come again, which made Caith think
rather less of bogles starting up their evening's mischief
and rather more of a misplaced mortal foot.

"Does your beast—hunt by evening?"

"By night. Always by night."

They were standing in too much quiet in this deathly woods, with only the sluggish voice of the brook beside them, and whoever had misstepped was undoubtedly aware both of his mistake and their sudden silence.

"Well, well," Caith said aloud, and more loudly: "it's pranks he's playing, now. —Dubhain, you foolish fellow, where have you gotten to?"

"What are you doing?" Ceannann hissed, resisting his sudden hard grip on his arm. "Let me—"

"Get to cover. —Dubhain? —I *detest* his humors. Hide and seek like a very fool!" And under his breath, as Ceannann resisted him: "—Get ye down the bank, lad. Whoever dislodged that stone knows we heard. The trap will shut. There's treacherous ground here. —*Dubhain, you cursed wight, I weary of ye, do ye hear me?*"

He held Ceannann an instant longer, hoping the ambushers might delay their assault to account for an unexpected third man. "Sheath the sword," he said softly. "It flashes. Let's walk, only walk, quietly, lad, and set us something solid at our backs. If we have to run, we meet at the rocks up there."

Ceannann made a shaky disposal of the sword into its sheath and they walked, as calmly as two men could, while the presence in the woods waited . . . for something.

A movement caught Caith's eye: and in that instant Ceannann tore free of his light hold and bolted. Shadows parted from the brush and the rocks in pursuit, while Caith stepped behind a thick-boled oak, squatted down and stole a glance upslope to see how many others Ceannann's headlong flight might draw out.

A dozen at least, Macha pity the boy, who was clearly not going to reach the rocks. Caith took a quick breath, then committed himself to the unguarded straight course along Guagach's margin, below the outcrop, and then behind it.

"Dubhain," he muttered, ducking down into the scant cover he could find in the brush, right on the black water's brink. "Dubhain. D' ye hear?"

Fool, he cursed himself bitterly. *And what way else would our enemies lay an ambush, but ahead, the way we would follow . . . Macha, where were my wits?*

He watched the chase upslope, Ceannann miraculously dodging this way and that like a hare before the hounds. Ceannann, driven from two sides, made a desperate uphill jump over a deadfall and tried to go on climbing from that disadvantage.

At which Caith shook his head and wished not to watch. *Wrong choice, boy,* he thought, seeing how the pursuers came in from the flanks, while the boy had lost all his advantage of agility in that straight, panicked flight uphill.

There was no more to do for the boy. He eased into better cover while all their attention was on the youth, wrapped his grey, mud-stained cloak about him for cover in the autumn thicket, and called himself a coward for sitting here while the boy went foolishly into ambush.

But the boy was nothing to him, he told himself, the boy had distrusted him, gone at him with a drawn sword, while his was still in its sheath. The lad had acted the fool this morning, or he and Dubhain might have been there when the riders came. He had acted the fool just now, bolting like that, disregarding all advice—he deserved everything he got.

He heard Ceannann curse the bandits to their faces, and winced before he heard the thump that followed. He should have done something, he thought, in pity. But it was too late; and more, he thought, stealing a cautious look upslope, through the drab leaves and the dead bracken, they were carrying the boy off in one piece. The riders that had stolen Firinne evidently wished to take Ceannann alive—which was not at all a surety in his case, and he could do nothing for either of the young folk by rushing out of cover and impaling himself on their swords. Caution was the better course. Follow quietly and find out what he had to deal with.

Besides, when the Sidhe wished to tilt the balances, they could make sights and thoughts and recollections fall clean out of a man's head. It had happened to him this morning and now perhaps it was happening with the ambushers, or perhaps they were more interested in taking Ceannann away than in finding Ceannann's recent companion ... because only three or four of them came back along the stream and searched the area, beating the brush with their swords and bow-staves in what might suffice for another fool-catching, but not, thank the Badbh, for a man experienced in escapes and in hunting and being hunted: he stayed very still, as one searcher trod almost on his foot and bashed the bushes overhead, sending down a drift of dead leaves.

But after a little time of desultory searching the last few searchers followed the others away, downstream, where, the thought came to him, they might have Firinne as well.

But being not the lad's sort of fool, he stayed in his concealment until he was certain the riders were gone. Then he crept out carefully and set out on the riders' trail, wrapping the uncertain color of the cloak around him and watching very carefully the woods about him. It had been an effective ambush, and he did not at all put it past them to play the same trick twice, figuring that the man they had missed catching might follow them and fall headlong into—

At his back, amid the trees and the thickets, a horse snorted and moved.

His hand lit on his sword and he had the sword half from its sheath as the thinnest of grey shadows shifted among the dead leaves at his very shoulder, shifted like a trick of the eye's edge, and glimmered like the moon in daylight. He turned his head, and in that eldritch shining, turned the rest of him to face the tall figure which had stepped out of his nights and into his waking, if indeed he waked at all.

"Ah, well," he said. "Where one of you fails, why, look for the other." He drew his sword the rest of the way, cold and murder-cursed iron, which the Sidhe loathed, all the while remembering what pain could be. To curse Dubhain was one thing; but to strike at Nuallan . . . the bright Sidhe were in their way more terrible. The Fair Folk could strip his anger from him with a gesture and leave his soul naked in the world, that was what Nuallan might do to him—for a whim or for a lesson. He already felt the roots of his soul loosened in Nuallan's presence, as if a breath might whirl it away from him.

"Peace," said Nuallan. And if Ceannann and Firinne had reminded him of the bright Sidhe, the illusion vanished in the terror of Nuallan's beauty, in the gaze of eyes that pierced him to the soul and a fairness that was itself only a seeming the elf wore. Nuallan moved his hand as if he were sweeping some spiderweb from the path, and the sword in his hand gave downward gently, a weight grown slowly too heavy.

"Fear not me," Nuallan said. That hand brushed his face as well, and memory twisted in his soul like a knife, the recollection of all the hope he had ever had and lost. "Would you serve the Sidhe, man?"

In that moment he must wish it, in the way of a man forsworn of every loyalty, and still, at the call of his king, heart-loyal. Nuallan knew that; and the terrible compassion in the Sidhe's asking was as hurtful to mortal pride and mortal hopes as another bath in memory. "You are gentler," Nuallan said. "Your curses fall and perish, your heart is yea and nay, you are quicksilver. We are changeless and our blades are baneful to the soul, being not made for the flesh. —Would you serve the Sidhe?"

"You know that I have no choice." A calm settled on him at that second asking, like the numbness after a wound and before the pain begins. "Is it this Ceannann you want? And will you give me Dubhain back?"

"Do not curse Dubhain so. He loves you, man, for all his wickedness." Nuallan reached and gathered up the elfshot which hung at Caith's neck, fingering this act of rebellion ever so gently. "So do I love thee, despite thy treasons. Never look at him or me with this. The sight would blast you."

And letting fall the stone, Nuallan turned and walked away, where a horse waited, saddleless, pale as the moonrise. Dathuil was the horse's name. He had been Caith's once; that grace and that power was another thing he had lost, or only thought he had once owned.

And when Nuallan seized Dathuil's mane and leapt to his back, the horse leapt away into shadow and into faery.

"A plague on you!" Caith shouted after him, left in darkness, and clenched the elf-shot stone in his fist. *"A plague on you and all the Sidhe!"*

For now that Nuallan had named the thing he should never do, and told him the consequence, that seed was there to take root in his perverse heart and spread and grow with insidious swiftness. Thus Nuallan dealt with a rebel. He had never looked on Dubhain or Nuallan through the stone. He carried it against other seemings and traps, and he had never truly wished to look at them until now.

But now, knowing Dubhain's wicked nature and his gift for shape-shifting, and after Nuallan's challenge, he must walk beside Dubhain and lie beside him in the dark and not look at him as he really was?

There was no faith left him, no trust, no truth. It slid away with Nuallan, back into faery. The lightning only fell; it could not be blamed that flesh burned and human souls withered in the light of a beauty they could never have.

But the world shook and shivered again. He felt the closeness of earth about him, and was blind a moment, with the feeling of smothering.

Then breath came back. A small boy lay in the woods, sprawled unconscious at his feet, and, seeing it, Caith felt time slip about him and the anguish fresh as the moment. "Brian," he called—in dreams, sometimes things changed, there was always hope.

But Nuallan was also in this dream. Nuallan stepped into his path and a chill came over him, a realization that, again, essential things were different, but the words and the deeds were all set, all necessary . . . all in vain.

"Let him go," he cried . . . had cried, then. "Let my brother go! I never rescued him to give him to you!"

"But you didn't save him," Nuallan said. "Was that not the bargain, mac Sliabhin? Would you ask more, now? Would you change the bargain?"

Change the bargain, the words echoed through the dream, ominous, fraught with danger. He managed a laugh, despairing as it was, and brief, for the Sidhe glow brightened and he stood in a small clearing beside the water, where a sleeping band of riders sat on sleeping horses, heads bowed, bodies slumped, the rain on them like jewels, as if time had stopped here and all the world were wrapped in nightmares. Not the riders he had sought, no. These were long, long ago.

"They should not have come here," said a Sidhe voice, out of the darkness.

"No man should," said another.

"Now, now mac Sliabhin, what will you pay," asked Nuallan, "to free the boy from *us*?"

Caith turned a bleak look on him, blinking against raindrops. "Why, whatever I have, curse you. Take me. Let the rest go—all of them. I'm worth it. Am I not what ye've most longed to have—one of Sliabhin's blood in your hands? And I'm far more guilty than the boy."

"You've not asked what the curse is," said Nuallan.

"You'll tell me when it pleases you."

"Torment," said Nuallan, "to suffer torment all your days, mac Sliabhin. The boy, oh, aye, he can be free. We accept your offering: he's no matter to us. The curse is yours alone."

"Then let him go!"

"I shall do more than that," Nuallan said, and bent and gathered the boy up into his arms ever so gently, as if Brian had been no weight at all. Nuallan bore him to the sleeping riders, the faery light about him falling palely on their faces. It was Raghallach foremost among them; and Cinnfhail's shieldman; and others of Gleatharan—and Nuallan set Brian in Raghallach's arms on the saddlebow, sleeping child in the keeping of the sleeping rider, whose face was bruised and battered with wounds from Dun Mhor's cellars.

"What have you done?" Caith asked in horror. "Sidhe, what have you done?"

"Ah," said Nuallan, looking at him, with the answer he already knew. "But they will get on well, don't you think? —Raghallach will remember a thing he never did; but 't will seem to him he was a great hero. The boy will remember the brave warrior who bore him away and took him safe to Gleatharan. Oh, aye, they'll wake at dawn, and think themselves all heroes, and so men will say of them forever. Is that not generous of me?"

Caith let out a breath and clenched his fists. But it looked so apt, the tired, small boy, asleep in safety, the honest man who sheltered him. "You could make him forget the rest," he said, as he had said once before. . . .

"You've nothing left to trade."

"Of your mercy, if it exists."

The bargain stood. Exists, exists, exists, rang through the sidh, and the dreaming began to fade. He drew a deep breath, feeling at first entombed in the sidh—then all at once a chill gust. He came out, this time. He breathed deep night about him, saw darkness in which the stars shone bright above the skeleton trees of Gleann Fiain—for faery stole time from a man, as well; the moon *had* risen in the mortal world, and other things might have changed by minute changes in the dream.

"Dubhain," he whispered, and stood there bereft and afraid, until a step disturbed the ground behind him, and a presence breathed at his nape.

It might have been anything, in this fey, fell woods. Something vital might have changed.

"Dubhain?"

Something touched him. He spun about, the hair rising at his nape. It breathed again at his back.

"Dubhain, damn ye!"

And again. He spun to face it—hand on sword. It was indeed Dubhain, with his hair shading his dark eyes in the moonlight.

"I did nae hear ye, man, understand. Nuallan hae sent me."

"To do what?"

"Och, men burning and doing mischief." Dubhain scratched beneath his arm and shook his thick dark hair back with a flash of eye quickly obscured. He pointed then along the stream course where the men had taken Ceannann. "Witchery, man. It fills the wind of this vale like smoke and the bog-stench."

"Are they dead?"

"Is 't the lad or the lass ye inquire of?"

"Plague on you! What hurt did they do them?"

"Why, a scratch or two, a bit of sport, nothing lasting. But I hae followed them a time. Mayhap I disturbed that sport." Dubhain waved his hand again toward the black water and the far bank, where the woods grew thick and shadows were impenetrable. "A merry lot of bandits, and well on their way, now ye've betrayed the lad to them. I would hae thought ye'd do better, my prince. What, saved yourself and left your host to such knavery?"

"So Nuallan sent you."

"He hae nae love of sorcery, nay, not at all. The *draiocht* sets his teeth on edge. And, aye, he sends ye. Shall I carry ye, man?"

Caith whirled away from him, sought with his eyes an escape he knew was not there. The black trees stood about him like prison bars. Teile was far away. He would never walk that path back to it, now. The Sidhe would see to that. Fate would. Nightly his dreams tormented him, with what he could not touch without killing.

Necessity.

"Caith, sweet Caith, *brave* Caith, . . ."

He shut his eyes; and when he opened them he had clenched his hand on the elfshot stone, with no idea why. Then he wondered . . . his mind flew to it like ravens to corruption . . . what Dubhain truly was, without his fond illusions.

No, he told himself.

No. 'T is Nuallan's trap. Nuallan was angry about the stone, and he set me a temptation with it to teach me a lesson. I would be a greater fool than I have been, if I gave way to curiosity.

But his hand stayed locked about the stone, and in another corner of his mind he asked himself what good advice the Sidhe had ever given him, or to what good thing the Sidhe had ever led him.

Which led ineluctably to wondering, not for the first time, what the Sidhe had given to him for a companion, and to what he attached the trust a man had to bestow on some living creature or wither in his soul. For all he knew, Dubhain might be something as dreadful and damning as lived in this glen.

But he turned to look at Dubhain only with mortal eyes, at the dark hair and dusky boy's face. "Oh, aye,"

Caith said, all quietly. "What haste? Where shall we go?"

"Why," said Dubhain, "wherever pleases."

"How far?"

"Why, as far as pleases me, sweet Caith. There's mischief to do, thou 'rt apt for 't, and I maun bear thee."

"Hellspawn," he said in despair. "Than Nuallan, thou 'rt far the fairer."

"I?" Rare perplexity came to Dubhain's face. "Than the great Sidhe? Ye do mistake him, man."

"Or mistake you." Cold touched the nape of his neck. "Take me where I must go, Dubhain."

A moment the perplexity lingered. Then Dubhain threw the hair from his eyes and shook himself, loosening his clothes, undoing his belt. " 'T is a favor I do ye," Dubhain paused to say, frowning the while, and his eyes showed a faint glow, like slumbering ember. "Ye do know that."

"Silence is a great trial to you, is it?"

"Mind your impudence!" And having said, Dubhain drew a great breath, popped a smooth stone into his mouth, and greyed to shadow, and to utter dark, until his clothes fell all in a heap. A great black horse came down on all fours with a toss of his head, midnight forelock and mane swinging over an eye glowing red with hellfire. The pooka spurned the clothing underfoot, kicked up his heels with a spin perilously close to Caith's body, and danced a careful and wicked arc just out of reach.

"Play me no tricks." Caith bent and gathered up Dubhain's garments, rolled them up and bound them in the belt with Dubhain's little pouch of oddments, ignoring all the pooka's threats. With that in hand, he seized the mane that streamed and flowed over his hands like smoke, and from that moment Dubhain stood still, from that moment it was very easy to mount—Dubhain all but flowed under him as he swung himself up and landed astride.

Dubhain whirled then and plunged straight for the water, altogether as if he would try a pooka's dearest trick, and drown his rider forthwith.

But Dubhain breasted that dark stream, scattering droplets in the moonlight and making of Guagach's threat a moment of grace and beauty—Dubhain could *not* forbear to take a skip through the beast's own hunting ground on his way, and Caith's heart was in his throat until Dubhain came out on the farther bank, coursing up the leafy slope beyond with never a jolt in his stride. Dubhain shook the water from his mane, a second moonlit scatter of drops, as he struck out through the skeletal woods, taking deadfalls and skirting thickets as smoothly as a dream.

No man could fall off a pooka's back. And Dubhain delighted to run him under branches and over jumps—but all without a sound of hoofbeats now: it was the wind they were racing, and the dark, and a company of kidnappers of a sort that reeked of Sidhe doings.

The *draiocht* sets his teeth on edge, Dubhain had said of Nuallan.

Black sorcery. And a beast that had surely heard Dubhain's wanton challenge of it.

CHAPTER
THREE

DOWN A WOODED hill Dubhain went, and over a jump no mortal horse could have taken nor any rider keep his seat over bareback, except it was a pooka's mane a man clung to.

Never a pooka could lose a rider while the pooka wished to keep him—but Dubhain in this shape was far more fey and more wicked than Dubhain on two feet. Dubhain in this shape was a killer, and it must try his pooka soul to refrain from wickedness, with a river constantly near him to offer the temptation.

Even Dathuil could not have matched Dubhain stride for stride now. Water lay in front of them, Guagach in another winding, it might be: Dubhain splashed across it in a black ecstasy of mischief, scattered water beneath his hooves with a splash he need not have touched the world to make, and if something in its deep lair was growing more irate by the instant, why, thought Caith, it surely recognized in the pooka a cousin, another creature of the river-deep and the cold waters, power without moderation.

Scatheless still, Dubhain struck out through the thinning woods, past the last few trees—for by moonlight he was in his element, and challenging the beast to catch him, when nothing in faery could keep his pace in the mortal world. He drew the wind into his nostrils and

73

those nostrils glowed with the fire in his blood; but nothing so baneful as the fire in his eye, in which madness—Caith saw it roll at him—blazed full.

At that, Caith wound his free hand deep in the smoke of Dubhain's mane and held himself wary of any sudden break for the water, fearing now that any sense in which Dubhain knew him was altogether lost—that Dubhain would finally, in a moment he had feared might one day come, take his life.

The trees gave way to a broad water-meadow, where Guagach flowed into a broad loch.

And if Dubhain had run before, now he flew, his long, black body coursing above the grassy loch shore, moving to the hiss and whuff of his breaths, but with never a sound from his hooves since that splash through the brook.

"Dubhain!" Caith called into his back-laid ears; and the dark head lifted and turned. An eye full of balefire regarded him the space of half a dozen strides—if Dubhain saw anything but the night and a rider who might have borne any name, been any Man, any enemy. Fire from Dubhain's nostrils lit the steam of his breath, and he kicked out in mid-stride, only to scare his rider, and because the thought sailed through Dubhain's wicked mind. The wind became like ice. The dry grass passed beneath in a blur and there were other such kicks, jolts to make his rider think of falling . . . wilder and madder Dubhain was growing, and Caith knew not now whether they were even on the track Nuallan had wished them to take, or whether *draiocht* might have seized on Dubhain and turned him to its own dark purpose.

Again the ground changed, and became a road beneath Dubhain's hooves. Then slowly, lightly at first and then louder and louder, a thunder grew, which was Dubhain's hooves upon the mortal earth.

Then Dubhain ran not silken-smooth, but with the earthy violence of any horse at full pace, his hooves hit-ting rain-wet ground in the moonlight, the featureless meadow flying past on their left and the shimmering surface of the broad loch on the other, sparkling black beneath the stars.

A shadow showed on that road ahead, a little knot of something beneath the stars, growing closer and closer with every stride of Dubhain's legs.

"Who are they ahead of us?" Caith asked, for if they had come to what Dubhain was chasing, he reasoned that Dubhain's sense might—might, in some degree, return, now. "Dubhain, are they enemies, or no?"

There was no response at all but a tossing of Dubhain's head: the pace never slacked.

"Are they our enemies?" Caith cried desperately. "Dubhain, stop! Stop, and use your wits!"

Dubhain did the perverse opposite, a palpable increase in his pace until it seemed that mortal or immortal sinew must tear and bone shatter, so thunderously he ran. The wind caught Caith's cloak and his hair, and Dubhain's mane all but blinded him.

"Damn you!" Caith cried. He wished desperately to stop, now. He did not wish to be carried blindly into what he did not understand, or start a fight only because Dubhain plunged fecklessly into some strangers' midst. He saw the riders swept nearer and nearer, saw one turn in his saddle and saw the alarm spread among the others.

"Damn you!" he cried, while his free hand necessarily sought the hilt of the sword that hung at his side, and he had no hold at all on Dubhain. "Who are they? What cause do they serve? *Stop*, damn your scattered wits, Dubhain! Hold back a little!"

Dubhain but snorted and threw his head.

"Dubhain, will ye make me their murderer for no reason, thou damned fool? Slow, let me at least find out who they are!"

But for his own protection, Dubhain giving him no sign of understanding, he pulled the cursed blade from its sheath and held it at the side and not in the riders' sight—calmer now: now that he had that familiar weight in his hand, he was himself headed down the track of deadly, practiced estimations—where his first targets must be if it came to blows, to what quarter the first would break in flight, and what he should do if Dubhain perversely stopped in the midst of them.

He was ice cold, now that he believed Dubhain would force him to it, will he, nil he; and now that he had a weapon drawn. They were twenty or more, these riders, and in the narrowing distance and the starlight he made out a paleness about the head of one: Firinne, of a certainty, her hair astream in the wind—and near her, less bright, shone the pallor of Ceannann's hair.

When he saw that, he was for a single breath completely willing to ride in among them and deal death on the bandits that had abducted two innocents and burned their cottage. But then a reasonable doubt held him—because he had no clear knowledge what side the Sidhe had cast him on, whether rescue or revenge or any cruel trick of harm and guilt such as the bright Sidhe loved to play on mortals. If the men threatened to kill their prisoners, and he could not stop—if Dubhain had utterly lost his reason and was sweeping honest men to hell, there was nothing he could do to prevent it except let himself be killed . . . and that, that, he had not the courage to accept: he had tried that escape long since, and the Sidhe would not have him escape so easily as that, not their dearest, most useful weapon.

"Hold," he muttered, when they were coming up on the riders' backs, and them going at all their speed. "Dubhain, *damn* you . . ."

Then he saw the hindmost rider turn in the saddle, saw the arm outstretched straight at him and felt a blow to his shoulder as if he had ridden full tilt into a branch: that was what his shocked wits believed in the instant the blow spun him half from Dubhain's moving body. He snatched after Dubhain's mane with his left hand in blind confidence he would not fall, his right still holding the sword he did not wish to lose.

But, from the moment of that blow, the pooka-ride seemed slowed, and things began to happen in eerie stateliness—he found himself falling, which was impossible: no chance blow could take him from Dubhain's back—

Unless Dubhain willed—or unless it were a Power great enough to overwhelm a Sidhe.

He was thinking that, as his right leg slid helplessly over Dubhain's rump and his body hurtled through empty air.

He met the ground; he skidded over stones with a violence at once appalling and numbing, a battering tumble over reeds and water and unyielding rock until at last he found a stopping place, his back strained and his legs at a crazily twisted rest.

That was well enough, he thought, he was still whole, he had stopped moving—he lay there dazed, the wind knocked out of him, eyes open in contemplation of the dark and the shock.

The earth beneath him shook with the thump of hooves. *They will ride me down*, was his first thought; and hard upon it came the realization that, for all that the pain was comparatively dull now, he might well be dying, anyway, if he could not soon get a whole breath into his body.

He had been shot, he decided. He could not, through the general dull pain, tell where the arrow had gone. But he wanted a breath so badly his wits were hazing and no breath would come into his throat, for the life of him . . .

"Dubhain," he tried to say aloud; but without breath, he could not utter a word, could not even keep his wits from scattering.

Was this what you Saw, Dubhain? Draiocht to sever us one from the other? Draiocht greater than you could defeat? Badbh curse you, what a time to leave me.

Perhaps his legs were shattered. Perhaps everything was. He struggled with his arm to lift himself, and at the black verge of fainting, rolled onto his back and got a thin, small gasp into his throat.

Then the dark of his vision became a black of night again, and he saw a ring of horsemen towering above him, against the starry night.

The Badbh take you, he railed on Nuallan. Is this your plan? It lacks, it verily lacks in many points, lord Sidhe . . .

One rider urged his horse forward until it blotted out half his view of the sky, the stirrup all but over his head.

Perhaps, Caith thought, then, they would not even dismount, perhaps they would kill him and never give him a chance with the sword. He lay expecting the stroke, thinking, with some satisfaction, That for your plans, my prideful lord Nuallan. Now what will you do?

Then he wondered distractedly what had become of Firinne, or if she were with them now, and what side she took in the affair; but to look full circle about him would cost him pain, afford them sport, and perhaps cost things to Firinne he could not, in his confused condition, reckon of.

"Bring him," the rider above him said, with a sweeping gesture; and riders dismounted.

This was beyond his expectations. He closed the fingers of his right hand, expecting the hilt of his sword, but he could not feel it there. He moved his hand searching for it—and the flash of pain told him exactly where the arrow had hit.

Fool, he said to himself.

One of them set a foot on that wrist and trod down. In a progression of events suddenly grown too rapid for his wits to deal with, the men held him against the ground, and one laid hand on the shaft of the arrow, a touch that shot ice and fire through his bones and rendered him near senseless.

"Best not draw it," one said. "Only break the shaft."

Dubhain!

The arrow pressed sideways in the wound; pain shot to the roots of his teeth and the depths of his gut. A sharp crack, then, a jolt to the marrow of his bones. *"Dubhain!"* he thought he breathed, while the world went darker than it was. One of them laughed, and nothing of help came thundering in. A horse stamped and shifted, but it was a creature of flesh and blood, with the sound of bridle-rings.

They gathered him off his back, then, another grating of the broken stub in the wound; and held him on his knees while they ordered someone to get down from his horse. Then they hauled him up onto legs that would not altogether bear his weight and aimed him at that horse's side. They cuffed and struck him until half-fainting, he made shift to mount for himself.

They had to help him all the same, pushing from below; and when he had dragged himself into the saddle he sat swaying to the horse's sidesteps as someone else climbed awkwardly up behind him and leaned and righted the saddle.

This hurt him. He bore it with a rolling of his head and a haziness of mind that made him think he might faint and fall again, arrow and all.

Arms came gently about him. "I'll hold you," the man said, a thin and subdued voice; and when the horse began to move and the swaying carried him back against the body behind him, Caith gave himself up completely to it, reasoning with the shreds of memory and sense that yet survived, that he knew the voice, that it was Ceannann behind him and Ceannann's arms that held him—the fool who had brought him to this, and him now the second fool, for this boy's sake.

Is it enough, Dubhain? Once in dread, once in pain, once in bitter anguish—was this what you Saw, and did none of the rest matter?

But where are you, Dubhain? Can you hear me at all?

To be among enemies, while the arrow was moving in his flesh at every stride of the horse, an arrow which they had only to lay hands on to cause him unspeakable agony—this was not what he had bargained for with the Sidhe.

Dubhain!

Consciousness came and went in an endless haze. But it seemed to him at last that a black mass had crouched at the end of the cheerless loch, and that the steep mountains which walled the glen went on beyond that place and wound and wove patterns against the night.

Draiocht and *geas.*

Caith beheld the keep through half-lidded eyes, in what he began at last to perceive as more and less of pain, in the troughs of which he could live and think and breathe, on the waves of which he could only exist. The laboring of his heart and the hoofbeats of the double-burdened horse seemed to observe the same cycle. But where he was now in the world or what these men were, he began to forget. His world had shrunk to the mere rhythm of his breaths, and that outside was all too burdened by detail for a busy mind to deal with.

Draiocht and *geas.* Black sorcery and dire necessity.

He blinked again, or perhaps more than blinked—the mass of stone was much nearer, as if the horse beneath him had flown with a pooka's speed, bearing him to hell and river-depth—or was it the loch it had sought all along?

The hill and the keep ahead, beneath the stars and the mountain wall, had the shape of a beast, some old delver as flat and broad of body as a tortoise. Two guard towers at either end made its legs, the scope of outlying ringwalls made its mass. It might begin to move. It might rise up and walk. That would be a re-

markable thing. It might roam the land devouring fools
and destroying as it went . . . a stony thing, old and difficult to reason with. . . .

Another blink and the beast crouched very near indeed. Desolation was about it. A hall, Caith thought
critically of its master, should have pasturages; should
have cottages and fields and such homely things as hay-
ricks and fences and orchards about it. Here was nothing but the loch, locked amid the barren steep
mountains. What kind of management was this, and
what of the people in the glen? Were they all bandits,
and the young couple in the cottage hitherto unmo-
lested?

Draiocht.

Things changed rapidly now, and he tried to keep his
eyes open and his mind at reasoning, however scattered,
as they rode. He wandered in his wits a space, and then
to his relief that green place began to surround him,
ever so much fairer than a hellish dark courtyard with
all its clatter of horses and equipment, ever so much
more hopeful than the agony he faced there.

In the greenwood, Nuallan might listen to him.
Nuallan might have a reason for things, and an answer
for him, however difficult. He called Nuallan's name in
his dream, and he decided he would walk farther, perhaps find the starry mere again, and not come back to
the pain until he was resting.

Or farther than that. He had always believed it a risk
to his life, to go beyond the mere. He could not say
why he thought so, but it was to try, now. His life was
ebbing out of him, and far better to be here for ever
than there for the rest of the night.

Still, still, as he wandered, nothing seemed right: it
was only featureless meadow, at first, and he could not
find the mere or the woods. Then he did see the edge of
the woods, and went toward it, and under its shade,
thinking he must have arrived on the wrong side; but

the woods he wandered looked far wilder than the faery he had known.

But abruptly there was a silver gate in that woods, and beyond its shining bars he could see the faery he knew, the woods, the meadow, the stream that ran with stars.

He had never known there was a gate. He had never come at faery from this vantage before. He tried the gate and found it locked against him.

Worse, the sky was growing darker: the moon in faery was fast setting, and he was locked outside its bounds, in a dreadful woods the rules of which he did not know.

Someone was speaking, cursing someone or something. He felt a standing horse shift wearily under him, a jolt that brought the world back in all its grimness and pain. The rider behind him was still holding him in the saddle, the racket of chain rattling through the works of the iron gate sounded like doom, and after what he had seen in the realm of faery, he feared now he was outcast from all hope, that it was not even Ceannann who clasped him about the ribs, but some dire thing wellcontent, for now, to have this little joke on its prey.

The chain clanked taut. The second gate groaned open on its hinges, and a ratchet thumped, taking up chain for a door no attack would find easy. There were pavings, beyond the momentary eclipse of the arch, a starlit stone courtyard beyond the horse's ears, and the animal climbed the cobbled track with a jolt that threw him back against the man that held him and stole his senses for a moment. A wall loomed over them, they passed beneath the threat of the portcullis, and onto a steep, winding, walled ascent, where the pain now lodged in his shoulder found a new summit.

Then he felt that he was falling—being dragged off the horse by creatures he could not recognize: he tried to defend himself and jolted his wound, after which came another darkness, in which he was aware of sound, and movement, and the clatter of horses on the cobbles.

After that came the swearing of a groom, and other such ordinary sounds as attended a stable-yard. Hell, he decided, had its mundanity, its solidity, its harried, ill-tempered horse-grooms and bored men-at-arms. He could understand this place.

Some time passed. He had not been aware for a moment, then opened his eyes, lying on his back on cold stone, with a light in his face and with a woman leaning above him, so strange a sight he struggled to maintain it and to comprehend the vision, whether it was faery or hell or yet some third thing. Lantern light gleamed above her shoulders like a pair of small suns or the eyes of a misshapen beast. A shadow glistening with gilt embroidery, this woman leaned above him, and laid a finger on his brow.

"Draw the arrow," she said, at which he tried to protest that he had had enough of pain and wished simply to die, if die he could, without that further cruelty; but several men came and held him fast.

While they held him, the woman kept her finger in the center of his brow, and a touch of ice and balm went spreading outward from that spot between his brows. They moved his arm and it did not much hurt; they cut the shirt then and began to cut the arrow free, which he thought must have gone somewhere about the bone— once came a jolting strange feeling as something grated, but the woman was there, her hand was there, and the pain in his shoulder was only enough to advise him what they were doing. Most clearly he could feel the pull and the working of the arrow, and he looked desperately at the woman as his only source of comfort. But something changed behind her, and he looked—saw the god, the pillar with fixed eyes, the god in the vines and the sheep-fences, him of the wheel—he saw a rising of smoke in the courtyard, and a dance of shadows writhing across mortared stone.

Then living bodies moved between him and the shadows, and the pain became acute. He heard a thunder in the earth or in his ears.

Then the barb came out, and it seemed the very earth gave way beneath him, so vertiginous the relief, so immediate the panic he felt as the woman took her hand away and the pain hit him anew, one red wash across his senses, blurring lights and movements into giddy trails like comets across the night.

Her hand rested again on the wound, and after a little, the agony ebbed to something bearable. "There," she said gently; and warmth followed, not painful and not quite without pain either, but far, far more ease of body than he had had a moment ago.

"There." Her hand brushed his brow.

"Beware of her!" a woman's voice cried, and there followed the sharp sound of a blow, and a man's curse and other, harder blows.

Trouble surged about him—Ceannann's foolishness, he thought, recalling that Ceannann's foolishness had had no little to do with bringing him into his plight: he was angry with Ceannann, and had no sympathy left, while he drifted in that touch and that cessation of an otherwise excruciating pain.

But—Firinne? Had that been Firinne?

"Who is he?" the woman asked out of the darkness of his sky.

"A wanderer," said a voice.

Firinne? He strained to look that way, and did, into the eye-hurting light and impenetrable shadow between the lanterns. He caught a pale gleam just within the edge of the light, indeed, Firinne's loose hair, and Firinne's troubled face. For her, he did feel concern: he tried to lift his head and speak to her, but the sight hazed for him into another whirling comet and his head fell back against the unforgiving stone.

"A traveler," said Ceannann's voice. "He has nothing to do with us. Moragacht, let him go."

No one let him go, of course. He lost interest in the conversation and drifted. He tried to go back to that dream he had been having, however grim and dangerous: he had his wits better in order, now, and he might find a way through the silver gate.

But now he could not find the gate. All his sight was of a dead forest and a black stream, which poisoned the trees that grew above it.

CHAPTER

FOUR

SOMEONE MOVED TOWARD him, with a soft rustling of drapery. That stealthy sound wanted quick attention, and Caith waked among soft cushions, with a dazed, distant memory of hurt.

Daylight slanted dustily into a stone-walled room from a window partially shuttered, as a mass of gold and dusk and lavender whispered to his bedside, a richly clad woman who settled on the very edge of his mattress and offered him a jeweled cup.

Do I know this woman? he asked himself, bewildered, wondering how he had arrived in this room and this bed . . . as if he had fallen back into some foreign, strange existence that he ought somehow to remember.

She brought the cup toward his lips and he lifted his head to take the drink; his mouth was dry as dust and his throat was sore, another legacy of a night which seemed to have nothing to do with this place or this moment.

But as the cold rim touched his lips, he suffered a second, frightening doubt, recalling how a drink taken or a morsel of food eaten under a roof might bind a man in hospitality and obligation to a power forever. So, with weak and unhappy resolution, he sank back and refused her offering.

She drew back the cup with a little frown. Then he

did not understand why he had not known her—for the woman was none other than Firinne; and he remembered how, at daybreak in the cottage, Firinne had leaned close to him and also offered him a cup; and he remembered how he had felt immediately, strangely aroused, as he was now, with only a dim thought of present danger and far less concern for an hour from now.

"There is no harm," she said. Rose and rue laced richly through the warmth and the dusty dryness of the chamber. He heard the beating of his own heart, saw the press of her breasts against her gown, and was enveloped in the whisper of damask and the sweet smell of her as she leaned close to slip her arm beneath his neck.

But he had not grown up in blind trust of things as they seemed; and, as a man, he had had shaken what little he had thought he knew. He had mistaken her at first. Or now. He was not, now, in possession of his wits, and knew it, but he would not slide further down that slope of trust and abandon himself utterly to someone's demands. A second time he turned his face away and a second time the lady withdrew the cup. She let his head down, slipped her arm free, and a gentle hand brushed the hair from his brow. "There," she said, "am I your enemy? Was I ever your enemy? —I had thought not."

"What manner of place is this?" His own voice fell strange and muffled on his ears, or it was the light-headedness he felt. He reached and felt tentatively of his shoulder, where there was only a profound numbness, as if that entire quarter of his body had died to pain or sensation. On its evidence, he could not prove there had ever been an arrow, or a pooka-ride, or such overwhelming pain, and bright sun slanted through the window-slit, through the lazy drifting dust—so he had slept here some little while, however much of the night had remained when the men had hauled him into the courtyard.

But had there ever been such men, if there had been no arrow?

And Firinne, a prisoner in that dark journey, wore her long hair now in elegant braids and rich ribbons and jewels, and had on a damask robe with gilt embroidery that a queen might envy. How did he reconcile that?

And where was the pain and the threat and the force of this place, that he had experienced last night?

"A far place from your hill," he murmured, "from your goats and your sheep, goodwife."

"Hush, enough silliness. I have things to do and you must drink." She slipped her arm beneath him. A third time the cup came to his lips, chill and sweating and smelling of the wine inside. Her bosom was close to him. Her slender arm held him against that rich, perfumed warmth. "For me, sweet, drink. Be not so stubborn, love."

Stubborn, or prideful, once lost and knowing himself foolish: for these very faults the great Sidhe damned him, too. But he took nothing in faery or on earth on another's terms, not even so sweet and kind terms as these. A third time and at the last moment, he turned his face aside, so that some of the wine spilled and ran over his cheek and his jaw and trickled down to pool in the hollow of his throat.

Probably it had run down and stained the sheets, too. Most probably she was angry with him now. For a moment he held his eyes averted, wondering why he must be so contrary a fool to everyone he met, and thinking then that it was most remarkable strength in her slight arm, to hold his head so long against her heart. Perhaps it was the carrying of water and the spinning of wool that had made a crofter wife so steady and so strong of arm, but he was uneasy and looked back to know what did have him in its embrace.

From the tail of his eye, the woman was not Firinne. The woman holding him was dark of hair, burning of eye and hard of mouth. He felt a moment of acute

panic, wondering what had befallen him, wondering
how he could know what was the truth at all, and felt
the elfshot stone lying against his shoulder, where its
cord had disposed it.

But, he reasoned with himself, if she were truly any
dark power she would have taken that from him first.

If a dark Sidhe in fact had the power to take it.

"Drink," she said. "It would be the better for you."

"Three times no," he said hoarsely, remembering
more and more vividly the courtyard of the castle and
the lanterns and the hands that had both healed and
hurt. The woman was Firinne again, to the straight gaze
of his eye. She cradled his head steadily against her
bosom and waited for his compliance.

But three times was a magic number. It was a barrier
against faery he had drawn about him by those three re-
fusals. And perhaps his head was the clearer by it, because he considered a breath or two before challenging
her further, and wondered if perhaps there had never
been a Firinne at all. Firinne, if she were a wife to
Ceannann, had not behaved with any wifely loyalty, that
early morning in the cottage, and him a stranger, and
her husband asleep, and the house in uneasiness with
the recent storm.

Perhaps if there was a changeling involved, the sub-
stitution had happened long ago, and the changeling
might seem one thing to one man's eyes, and have a
completely different seeming to another man—perhaps,
he thought, *that* was the strange likeness of Firinne and
Ceannann. Perhaps there had never been a lady of Dun
Glas, or a harper, or any of the nonsense Ceannann had
told him, and it was all, all Ceannann and Firinne who
warred with magic and arrows in the dark.

But everything had been Ceannann's story, none of
Firinne's. And where had Ceannann gone and what had
become of him who—he thought—had held him with
some gentleness on the ride here, and defended Firinne
with some measure of courage?

He thought he remembered that for the truth. He was confused about what he did remember, but that made him less, rather than more, trustful. And perhaps at last the woman's arm did grow weary or her patience had worn thin: she slipped her arm from beneath him and withdrew the cup.

She was slighter than Firinne. When he expected to see something different, he could see the signs of age about her mouth from moment to moment, tiny fracturings which drew down in anger.

And knowing that she had meant to deceive him and perhaps to do him greater ill than her men had done, there was no reason in all the world why he could not reach out even one-handed and make her his prisoner, and thereafter get himself free of this castle and all its riddles.

But as he chanced to look full into the lady's eyes, he found himself incapable of violence against her, any more than he could have flung himself from Dubhain's back in full flight.

Yet that fall had indeed happened. And Dubhain was not here, when they could in no wise be parted.

She sat there on his bedside a long while, silent and unmoving long enough for her to become a shadow in his vision. He became, in the way of his fevered wits, more keenly aware of the sunlight beyond the shadow she was—aware of the light picking out a haze of dust motes and becoming a veil over boxes and shelves and cupboards, all of the same woods, appointments such as a comfortable bedroom might hold. Only the dust was in motion, only the dust proved to him that the whole world had not ceased movement, and only the sunlight proved to him that the world was going about its ordinary business outside this room, and beyond the lady's shadow.

Then, subtle and slow as the movement of the dust, he began to feel the stirrings of her magic. By such infinitesimal degrees the pain in his shoulder began again, so that it must have been growing for some few moments before it even drew his attention—pain most acute where the arrow had struck, as if the healing were slowly, inexorably unweaving itself.

All this while, the lady sat silent with the cup in her hand, with a meditative look on her face, and him knowing the comfort in that cup she offered, but not the price of it—except a man might guess, and fear what she was. She had no pity. She had no kindness. He understood that now. She was waiting for him to realize what was happening to him and then to take fright and beg the cup of her.

Of the great Sidhe, aye, of lord Nuallan, he might beg a favor, but, then—the great Sidhe might give it, if it pleased lord Nuallan so to give, and give like a lord, he would, because it pleased him to do good sometimes, for its own sake.

But the lady who waited so patiently and so demurely for a sign of terror in him, while the pain grew and grew, while his skin seemed to part and moisture to run down beneath his arm and soak the mattress—in her—in her, he told himself, there was no spark of generosity, and be *damned* to her.

"There is the cup," she reminded him quietly, at last, when the pain had made him near mindless, and the fear of dying had traded places with a fear that he would live far too long. She offered the cup a fourth time.

"Do not reject me. Take it. It is healing, it is surcease of all your pain, love. Your suffering is all your own doing."

"No, it is not!" He had learned of Dubhain and Nuallan to suffer no lies in patience, and not to be put upon. He knew the wiles of the Sidhe and, in his agony, this accusation and blame-shifting sounded so very, damnably, cursedly like them, offering help with the one hand and taking a man's soul with the other. "Three times and four times no, and to *hell* with you, madam."

"Have it as you will," she declared; and abruptly took her weight from the bedside, which slight shift of the mattress sent agony through him. A wave of giddiness came over him as his life went flooding out, soaking his shirt and the bedclothes. He was dying, and because she was lurking in the world, he did not grasp at all after life or beg her for anything: he bent his fading sense instead to find that green place again, that river, that shore, for it was his dearest hope (and one he had never confessed to Dubhain) that Nuallan might at his last breath receive him.

But it was only desolation he found, a grey waste, a barren shore, and a dead, chill loch. A black horse was running in that wilderness, red of eye, trailing a mane and tail like smoke as it turned toward him. "Dubhain!" he cried, holding out his arms in the faint and only hope that the Sidhe had sent Dubhain for him, and that the ride was not, after all, to hell, but to faery for good and for ever this time.

The pooka thundered down on him and reared up at the last instant, its hooves above his head; then it diminished in the blink of an eye. Dubhain stood there, naked, his eyes glowing with that same bright hellfire.

"Have you come to carry me?" Caith asked. And with no little trepidation: "And where must you take me, Dubhain?"

"Why, 't is yourself maun carry me," Dubhain said, so unexpectedly he knew it was a dream of meaning, or perhaps he had truly come to this bleak place on the rim of faery, and his body was growing cold in the lady's bed. *Me, me, me*, the hills gave back, with a peal like iron bells, so he could not forget it, even through the pain.

The cold wind roared and chill knifed at his wound; *me, me, me*, the hills still said, but Dubhain faded away.

Then the hills themselves did. Something wrenched at his very soul, while it clung tenaciously to his body, until he was spinning naked in the winds, above the retreating hills, and falling backward, and headfirst—his shoulders landed thump! against the mattress.

The lady took her hand from his shoulder, all besmirched with blood.

". . . There, now," she said, " 't will not bleed."

But the pain was no less. It settled at the seat of his joints and the roots of the teeth and the floor of the bowels and hurt with every beat of his heart.

"There remains," the lady said, with his blood still on her fingers, "the cup. —You will not die, man. Never expect that mercy. Drink, or I will pour it out now. Will you have the pain or will you have the cup?"

She leaned above him, a smell of perfume turned sharp with fever and with blood. She took the cup from the bedside and offered it to him again. It was difficult to frame a word at all, so acute and all-consuming was the pain.

Fool, and: *fool*, said a voice, his own sanity, perhaps, retreating deep inside him: *it hurts so, take it, take it while you can. Of what matter to you is another master or another mistress? Can two be worse than one? Take the cup, and let the lady and the bright Sidhe battle it out if they covet you so.*

"No," said the sullen voice that burst out of him, his damnable pride or the Sidhe's own answer, he had no least idea.

Then slowly, in his stricken gaze, she tipped the cup and poured out the liquid that promised ease of pain. It was red like blood, it made a thick stream, and it spattered her skirts where it fell.

"You will greatly regret it," she said. "You will pray me that I ask again, before I am done with you."

He turned his face from her and her threats, reeled back, dizzied, against the blood-soaked bedclothes, and sought only to breathe between the tides of hurt.

There was silence a moment. Then she dropped the cup ringing on the stone floor. The ringing became a booming, a thunder of a great cauldron overset on the stones, a cauldron that rumbled and rocked to rest. Its depths were darkness and within that darkness were the old Images, the hammer and the hanging noose, in a throng of staring statues, not Sidhe, but the blank-eyed gods of the grove and the torches . . .

Came the sharp grit of dust between sole and stone, and the rustle of heavy skirts passing his bed. He blinked at the dust-motes dancing their vital, timeless motion in mortal sunlight, and the smell of roses lingered as the steps gritted away, away, away above his head. He heard the door open, but not—

—not shut. That, through all the haze of misery, came clear to him.

He tilted his head back despite the pain, saw the cup and not the cauldron lying on the stones, saw not the lords of the dead, but cabinets, and the door left open wide, wide as the window that let in the healing sun.

He clenched his teeth and struggled to raise himself from the blood-soaked mattress. If he could once get on his feet, he thought, his head would be clearer. If he could once get his body to move, he could overcome the pain. Better the window, he decided. If he could get out it unseen, if he could get to the roofs and over the walls of this place—or, if nothing was in reach, it had to be the hall, there to find some weapon against the lady's magic, dark magic, stone magic. Against the caldron and the hammer there was Sidhe magic, that had not utterly deserted him, there was mortal iron, that he trusted more—Macha, if he could find him a sword, his own sword . . . or anyone's at all . . . and get him out of this place. . . .

The sweat broke out on his skin as he swung his feet off the bed, and felt his shoes there—foolish, that small delay might be, but he had no idea where he was going, or over what, through the window and over the roof slates, perhaps, thereafter, onto sharp, stony ground—no help to cripple himself. The cup stayed a cup and the wine made a puddle on the floor in front of him. The dust danced in the wind from the open door. Well enough. He drew on the ragged stockings, one-handed and sweating. He arranged his shoes and slipped his feet into them, everything in good order.

But when he straightened to stand up, his head spun, and he caught at the bedstead. He pulled himself up, fighting the weakness and the descent into dark—took a step, tried to fix his sight on the sunlight and the dust, but the whirling dance confused him, and his weakened knees at the second step forgot which way to bend. He went down with his arm on the edge of the bed, knocking a small table against the wall with a scrape and clatter like doom.

The hall outside rang with alarm and running footsteps. The hell with the door, then, he said to himself, and, bracing his other arm against the mattress, tried to turn for the window and get a knee under him, as armed men spilled into the room. In his ears the cauldron was booming again, and he looked around at the men, slack-jawed, in hopes of them doing for him what he could not manage at the moment, and lifting him to his feet.

There were four of them that he could see, armed in metal and leather, and their cloaks were grey. Bandits, he would have judged such a scowling lot of faces outside a lady's bower; but servants of her magic, they might be, servants of the cauldron, of the ringing hammer, the stone magic, the flint way ... Ye fools, he thought to say to them, to warn them he served other, younger powers; fools, he should tell them, the old gods have gone below, the Sidhe have their gates locked, the silver, unaccustomed gates ... but he owed them not even that much warning, not reckoning the bloodiness they served.

Pain shot through his arm with their laying hands on him, but he had measured that before it came, as he had marked the dagger that came within his reach as they drew him up. He had but to reach out for it and return it beneath its owner's jaw—but the man fell on him,

then, leaving it stuck fast in bone as the man's weight
carried him backward against the bed. Life's blood
flooded onto his hand and chest as he slid down, as if
there was not enough of his own about ... he slid off
the mattress edge and, with all the strength he had left,
twisted over and flung himself up to gain the door, balance deserting him.

He was already falling before one of them fell atop
him. He struck the stone floor with one man's weight
on his back, with others hauling at his arms. Thereafter
he could make only small, miserable movements of his
limbs, sick with pain, as they lifted him up by the sound
arm and the wounded one.

The cauldron boomed again, the stone walls and the
cupboards spun giddily about, the stone gods stared at
him, with cold, blank eyes. The pain came and went in
flashes that blinded him to the light as they half-carried
him for the hall—but he was aware of the doorway, and
tried to resist there, bracing his foot. They dragged him
past it. He saw a projection of stone halfway down the
hall, braced his foot and his knee and tried resistance
there, but he could not hold it.

Beyond that was dark and flashes of light, whirling
comets of torches and the eyes of staring gods, then the
banging of a doorway, a spiraling descent down stone
steps, in a dizzy confusion of sun from window-slits
and the echoing thunder and darkness between. Shouts
echoed from below and above as they went down and
down, amid the clatter of metal-guarded boots and the
rattle of scale and mail.

An open space gaped suddenly on the right, a blur of
dim light, in which, astonishingly vivid, a vaulted ceiling arching down to earth and water, closed off with
bars. Down a last flight of steps they haled him, to a
vast, muddy-floored space beneath that barrel vault.
Water lapped in pewter daylight beyond that grating and
half the width of the vault itself, where it made a
muddy bank.

Here they hurled him onto wet, dark earth, and one cursed him bitterly and kicked him twice in the groin before he could double to protect himself.

"Stop!" someone cried, and the next blow did not come. In bewilderment, in the booming of the cauldron and the trailing flare of grey sunlight, he turned his face from the wet earth, trying to determine whether this intervenor had help for him, or some other claim on him.

Firinne's pale face shone through black iron bars. And in her presence he did try: he hurled himself for his feet in his guards' distraction and snatched at a dagger in a man's belt. Blows rained on the back of his head and his shoulders, but he kept his hold on the hilt while the man wrestled with him to prevent his drawing it.

Then an arm slipped around his neck and hauled at him, that weight and another one bearing him down, the third man suddenly pulling and not pushing. He came down on that man, facing the grating again, in doubt of his sanity—for it was not Firinne imprisoned behind the bars, but Ceannann, and the booming and thunder drowned all sound in his ears.

Things after that went very slowly. He saw Ceannann flinch and avert his eyes from the beating the guards gave him, but he watched Ceannann, wondering why he was there. Eventually, weary of kicking him, they dragged him up to hit him, and he floated through the air sidelong, it taking a long time until he hit the muddy ground, which came all too hard and sudden, and jolted his wound beyond all enduring.

"Dubhain!" he murmured through the blood, thinking the guards gone, and rubbed at the film blurring his sight. "Nuallan, lord,—"

Once in dread, once in pain, once in bitter anguish.
"Dubhain!"

"Names are useful," a guard said, dragging him up halfway by the hair. He blinked at that film-darkened sight, dismayed at his own foolishness, and the guard, for his part, grinned at him before he flung him down like a soiled rag and kicked him in the wounded shoulder.

They could have killed him, then. He could no longer prevent any blow they chose to give him, and a few more blows did fall, desultory, none so devastating as that one, before they exhausted their energies or their imagination and went away up the stairs.

A door thundered shut. A bolt shot and echoed through the vault. Water lapped. Water dripped. The least sound echoed in this place. He wondered dazedly whether it would hurt worse to turn his cheek from the disgusting mud, and if that sogginess he felt under him was water or his own blood.

"Is he dead?" a high voice said clearly, and the scuff of a foot resounded on stone.

No, he thought. He could not possibly be so fortunate. The lady had promised him that.

"I see him breathing," a lower voice said. Ceannann's, he thought. "Better he were dead."

Perhaps the lady's men would come back for more amusement, or perhaps let him lie. If he lay long enough he supposed he might get breath enough to fight them again, but his wounds were all new and, by his experience, had a day or so to go before they hurt their worst.

At which time, if no better happened, he would still be here, for whatever disposition they chose to make of him.

Geas and *draiocht*, Dubhain had warned him. Necessity and sorceries had combined against him. Now he knew that Dubhain's abandoning him had been definitive, and that it was not Dubhain's sort of magic which lay about this place, not Nuallan's sort either. No arrow of a common soldier could have separated him from the pooka. No such men as these could have stopped Dubhain. Names slithered out of the dark, old names, flint names, stone names, the gods of the deep groves and the thunder—names they still danced to in the

woods, names the wheel-fires burned for on the hills, at
the falling of the leaves,. . . at the dying of the year, as
the sun wandered south from his staying-post . . .

Stay, they begged the sun, and rolled their wheels of
fire through the night, until they died in light-reflecting
meres.

Stay, they pleaded, and hung the straw-men, now,
that was all. It was Lugh men worshipped and not
Belenos. The bright Sidhe kept the balances, and the
geassi bound the magic in the world . . . could a witch
be so rash as that, to defy the Sidhe and wake the lords
of hell?

Or a man be so foolish as to betray the Names by
which the Sidhe could be conjured, and bound . . . even
Nuallan's, who deserved it? It was not mere bad luck:
the *draiocht* was at work about him, making the nets
tighter, constraining his choices, making advantage out
of inadvertency—he had not been to blame, not
wholly . . .

But that changed nothing. And he was alive now because it pleased them . . . if he had use left in him, now
that they had gained the Names . . .

The thoughts turned over and over, to the lap of the
loch water against the shore, to the echoing movements
of his fellow prisoners, if prisoners they were . . . on
such waves and such cycles of thought the pain came
and went, until they found a level that stayed constant,
until not knowing the danger he was in seemed worse
than knowing.

He lifted his cheek from the cold mud, blinking
through the haze that obscured his eyes, finding his
lower limbs twisted in some uncomfortable puzzle he
was too dazed to untangle. The cold of the ground had
ceased to be a comfort, it made his wound ache, and as
he tried to look about him, one foot fell limply past the
other and solved the tangle without his having to think
about it.

"Dubhain," he said faintly, in forlorn and dying hope.

His mouth was cut and swollen. He was all over blood and his movements discovered new pains, at sudden, irretrievable angles on his way to sitting up. He had said the Names. What could he do worse by saying them again?

And the Sidhe deserved it, who had led him to this pass. "Dubhain, damn you—"

For he still entertained the faintest hope that Dubhain would answer, now, finally, perversely having played his bloody trick—he clung to the hope that Dubhain *could* answer, if Dubhain could hear him, wherever he was.

But all he saw was Ceannann squatting at the bars of his cell, pale face and white hands ghostly above Ceannann's plain dark clothing.

"O man," Ceannann said, and grimaced and shook his head as though the gory sight of him were too unpleasant. "Man—"

Caith groaned and rolled over on his better arm to cast a look beyond to the loch and the fading daylight, hoping for intervention either bright or dark.

But there was only sweating, aged stone and water on that side; and in the tail of his eye, another such grating, behind which Firinne stood, the real Firinne, he might believe or disbelieve. There were two cells, on left and on right of him, it was not, after all, that they were changing shape—he resolved that much of the puzzle, and it wounded his pride that he had been beaten in Ceannann's sight, and in Firinne's; most of all, that he had lost every fight since he had come here, then foolishly blurted out one name that Ceannann and Firinne had not, evidently, told them, and one that they would not have known.

So rather than sit in their sight like a drunkard in the mud, he got one knee under him and made shift to get up. It tore his wound. Cold sweat broke out on him from head to foot, and he fell—tried to get his legs beneath him, and saw Firinne wince as if it had been her own pain.

"Damn," he said when he had breath. "Damn," —for it was curse after that, or weep. He hung his head down to catch his breath, then made the third try—set one foot beneath him, and one hand, the other swinging useless as if the arrow were still in it. Not an elegant sight.

He considered his next attempt, added another foot, staggered upright like a newborn calf and reeled to left and right. He felt himself falling, and instead, in a desperate, tilted series of steps, crashed against Firinne's cage and caught at the bars with the hand that would hold at all.

"My friend is cursed late," he declared, in a voice gone ragged. As humor it was exceeding poor; it was Dubhain's own kind of joke, which won nothing from Firinne but a pitying shake of her head and a despairing look.

"But late or not," he said, fearing that all this shouting after Dubhain sounded mad, "—he may well be planning our rescue. The lad is fond of schemes." Leaning his good shoulder against the bars to support himself, he found the chain that locked the grating and felt, one-handed, after the joining of it, making a gentle clanking of chain which woke echoes off the ceiling and the walls and the water.

It was secure: he had hardly dared hope for a slip there, even by Sidhe magic. He caught suddenly at the bars as giddiness betrayed him and whirled his senses reeling about the vault. Firinne's hand fell on his, a touch so light he could scarcely feel it.

"I do take it," he went on doggedly, in his ragged voice, "that your quarrel with this place and its lady is no casual matter. I mind Ceannann mentioned some lady of Dun Glas . . ."

"Moragacht is her name," Firinne said in a small voice. "This keep is all her making. The evil in this valley is her evil. Oh, stranger, if you could possibly swim from here . . . if you could go quickly—you might escape. A man could slip between the bars . . ."

"Escape to where?" he asked.

"He could never make it," said Ceannann from behind him.

Caith turned his back to the bars and leaned his head there, dizzied with the pain, letting his eyes rove the circuit of the vaulted ceiling. He recalled dimly the view of the keep from without, a tortoise-like mass of stone set on the very rim of the water, so unnaturally made on unstable ground, with no stone below it to quarry for its building, no hill to raise its cellars above flooding nor rock to buttress it against its own great weight. He smelled magic, and corruption, as if it seeped up from the wet stones and trickled down the walls. He recalled the storm that had driven him to the cottage, and his ride that ended on the loch shore, and with a sudden chill and a dazed contemplation of the water beyond the grating, he could think of one reason why he had been left free between these two stone-backed cells, in the witness of the lady's two fair captives.

"The beast," he said. "It can reach the loch. Can it not?"

"Yes," said Firinne. Ceannann said:

"I think it must already be there."

The water was the vault's only source of light; and its illusory glow was like the sheen of a hostile weapon, or an enchantment. For a moment Caith slipped away, and found a dark place behind his eyelids as he leaned his back against the iron bars and tried to catch his breath. He reached for faery, a refuge against that gathering shadow, but each time he failed he believed a little less, and the darkness in faery only thickened. Something stalked him there, something well at home in that darkness.

He opened his eyes wide—his head rolling, his heart laboring as he recovered the pewter light on the water, and the black iron grating that closed off the vault from the loch—but he had stood too long: his knees had gone to water, and that darkness hovered behind his eyelids, waiting to claim him, as he felt the bars slide through his fingers.

Dubhain, Dubhain, Dubhain, what is amiss, where are you? Badbh and Macha, why can you not hear me?

Ceannann said, low-voiced, "She's won his friend's Name of him. What might she do now?"

"The sun is sinking," said Firinne. "We might call her, we might bargain with her, do you think? She might hear us . . ."

And Ceannann: "Hush, hush, —has he fainted?"

The waters were grey, chill, and full of shadows, no place for a man born to air and sunlight, but Caith wandered there, within the edge of the loch that had surged up like a flood toward the meadows of faery. He was outside the silver gates . . . he was at that place again, he had gotten at least that far, but found those gates shut more tightly than the grating in the vault, and he could not find their sides or their top, their silver metal burning to the touch as the chill water swept about him in violent tides.

But he did not drown. He looked about him in bewilderment, at grey brightness. The sun slanted rays down into the upper levels of the loch, and bubbles sparkled, rising through the water, past the incorruptible silver.

But he could not stay near that light. Currents swept him inexorably farther from the gates and swept him to some greyness within the loch he did not know. At the heart of the loch there were caves, there were cold springs and fountains where dark things laired—he knew this in the way one knows such things in dreams, and he knew that although he could not drown, he could die in this dream . . . because it was a wandering of the soul, and because the creatures here had existence in this place, and could kill, and seize the souls that came to their hands.

There was a creature that ruled this loch. It was Sidhe, a sort of Sidhe, old and wicked, and he had about his neck the pierced stone that would show him its nature in the world of five senses, if he dared look: reason might say it was better to search it out and look and know the enemy for what it truly was, but fear said such small, unpracticed magic might only draw its attention . . . and by that, ensnare him: like all faery gifts, the elfshot stone was full of conditions and bargains; and a greater Power could turn such a weapon in a man's hands, oh, so easily, and aim it at his very sanity.

"It is ourselves she wants," Firinne said. "Why does she aim at him? It's nothing but wickedness . . ."

"She is sporting with us, do you not see? There was never time for him to get away." Ceannann's voice was hoarse and small. Then Firinne's:

"She will kill whatever we touch. Even this man, only because he was beneath our roof. Like the poor goats. He weighs the same in her intentions. She will do anything to force us."

"No! She mustn't. She mustn't. Whatever cruel thing she does, keep thinking of that. We'll have to see him die if he stays here; but he might get as far as the shore, and he might call the Sidhe through, mightn't he?"

"The Sidhe are helpless. Did we not see the pooka fall?"

The arrow hit and he flew helplessly from Dubhain's back. But now, instead of participant, he saw himself strike the ground with a violence that he remembered in his bones.

He saw blood—his own. He saw the pooka turn to smoke and plunge into the loch, there by the unwholesome weeds, where Dubhain had gone down. Dubhain had not deserted him. Dubhain had been overwhelmed by the *draiocht* in this place—perhaps had met defeat altogether . . . in which case he was doomed, himself.

Which he would not admit to the power of this place. He began to struggle in the currents, to search with what strength he could, as long as he could, there seeming no other hope of escape.

Then he saw the dark shape which haunted Loch Fiain, a vast shadow which brushed seal-like through his mind, and, with the passing of one huge flipper, ghosted away, leaving a stench of horror in the water, for it was a thing without a skin, and the bones of dead men were its bones, and the corruption of the deep loch covered that membranous, veined surface. It went with a sound of waters and with the grinding of ill-joined bone against bone; its entire body shifted and shaped itself to the currents, sometimes seal-like, at other times like a great fragile sac of pollution.

This was the evil. This was the power here, one of the dark Sidhe, bound to the witch's service.

Dubhain was such a creature, at heart, though not such a great one, before the bright Sidhe had turned Dubhain to their use.

But the dark Sidhe, if they slid to the evil here, would want Dubhain back, this great dark one would hunt him relentlessly, and claim him for its own: that was another thing Caith knew without reason—the whole loch spoke now to Dubhain, calling on him, calling to him, calling for him to merge himself with the loch. For the likes of Dubhain these waters held such wicked power, such gentle seduction. Be free, it said, once one knew how to listen to it. And, Free, Free, Free, the echoes said out of the deep, with nothing of ease or grace in that cold voice. It was the killing-rage, it was the blood-lust, it was the raw power of the earth and the waters it offered, and a man could hear it, and shudder in the least small temptation of his soul to believe it offered to him.

But Dubhain must not give way to it—by the geas on both of them, he had no power to give Dubhain up, and,

by the Badbh, he swore to disown the damned mischief-
bound wight at least three times in a day—

But not to this. There was a sort of a man, at least a
feckless, reckless youth, lodged in Dubhain's dark soul;
and by what in him was a man, he would never give
that part away, of Dubhain or of himself, not to the cold
deep.

Yet if Dubhain once fell under the spell of the loch,
and called to him in turn—the only creature, by the
geas on him, that he might have for company, then the
geas would work against them both, and for the power
of this place. He suffered a shiver of fear at that
thought, for that place in Teile, that woman and that
man and that boy he protected: if *he* should slip to the
dark side, oh, he knew what wickedness he would do,
earliest and worst of all the harm that was in him to do,
precisely because there was something he loved, and he
must not. He had met his father. He had seen what was
his heritage. And he had never been so afraid as now, of
what this place and the *draiocht* might offer him.

He searched madly in his dream, poked into dark, unsavory holes and crannies, desperate to find Dubhain or,
at worst, the remnant of Dubhain and draw him out, before he slid deeper into the loch and its darker haunts.

But the darkness rose out of the depth on its own
search, stirring the currents, shaping itself to its own will,
fierce, and desirous of harm.

"The sun is almost gone," said Ceannann.

"Hush, let him sleep," said Firinne. "What has he to
hope for?"

"If he had a weapon," said Ceannann.

"What could that avail him against the beast?"

"Hope of revenge," said Ceannann. "It would deceive him of that, at least."

It hunted, and the thing that it hunted, poking its long
neck among the reeds about the loch-edge, was small

and dark, with fierce red eyes. That thing scuttled and
dodged with great cleverness, but the hunter was quick.
Caith shuddered at the shadow's close passage and
found his own hole to hide in among the reeds, battered
by the current it stirred; he rested there, watching the
beast swim and turn like a great seal in a patch of sunlight. It called to its prey with great squeals that echoed
through the depths. It breached and dived and searched
the places a dark one would choose ... and missed a
flitting shadow among the reeds, as it carried its search
around the loch. Its squeals and echoes diminished in
the distance and Caith plunged through the slithery,
loathsome reeds, before his quarry could take flight.

"Dubhain," he said, "I need you! Carry me out of
this place!"

" 'T is yourself," came a voice like a flurry of bubbles, as a pair of red eyes glowed in the soft grey am-
bience, among the spiky shadow of reeds and
water-grass. "'T is yourself maun carry me, my Caith,
hae ye not heard me at all? No more can I do for ye."

"Dubhain, *come* to where I am. A place on the shore.
A dark place. I need your help!"

He tried to go closer. But Dubhain retreated, quick
and wary, and the baleful eyes resumed their red, frightened stare.

"Dinnae tempt me, man. Dinnae come near. . . ."

"Then how can I carry you, fool? How can I bring
you out of the loch? You make no damned sense!"

"Hsst," said that voice, and the shape seemed to
glance aside distractedly. "It rises, it rises, —flee, man,
while there's time!"

Came a sudden upwelling of cold water, a marked
change in the currents, as if a stream had broken upward on the slope beneath him. The beast came like a
geyser from the deep and Caith turned with nightmare
slowness, seeking the grey shallows and the upper
banks, in its direct path.

He broke the surface, came up in dry air with a gasp

for breath and a pain in the shoulder that sent his senses reeling. His reaching hand caught the cold bars of Firinne's prison and, muddy and bloody as he had been before, he stared stupidly at the changed water, for the grey daylight was gone and the water was stained with bloody sunset. The bars were lifting, slowly, as hidden chains hauled the gates apart with a clatter of ratchets and clank of iron.

A touch came on his fingers where they rested on the bars—Firinne's hand, reaching to his for comfort. "Your friend has failed you," Firinne said. "Swim for the outside, try to reach the shore; there may yet be time. If you were outside the lady's wards, perhaps there you could call him. . . ."

"Call him," he echoed hoarsely. 'Him' had no meaning. 'Call' was what the beast was doing now, incessantly. Words rattled hollowly in his skull. In his mind he still saw the grey water and the shadows, felt the chill currents—felt another presence, too.

Caith! it cried in panic. *Thou fool!*

He slipped his hand from Firinne's and struggled to his feet.

"Fool, is it, —ye damnable traitor! By dread, and by pain, is it? Damned wretch, you knew, you knew and you Saw this before we ever came to this valley! Dump me off your back—is it not enough? Is it not enough pain now? What in very Hell d' ye ask?"

He heard no answer. He staggered free of the bars and with a great breath, grasped his wounded arm by the wrist and hurled that shoulder against the stone wall.

The pain burst and blinded him; he heard Ceannann and Firinne cry out in dismay at his madness; but he stumbled a step away and flung himself at the wall with all the strength left in his legs.

"*Dubhain!*" he shouted, as the shock reeled through the marrow of his bones. He could not see, could not tell up from down, and an ankle turned. He fell, with another jolt of pain, onto his right hip, and sat there helpless as a child while the fog cleared from his eyes and the pain ebbed down to a measurable pain, and the vault in its deepest shadow gave up a dusky naked figure, all crouched and bowed.

"Dubhain," Caith said in the voice left him.

Dubhain lifted his face and shook back his hair. The hell-light glowed bright in his eyes and dimmed again. For a moment it seemed not a boy who sat there, but a lump of darkness; a power of faery, as lethal and as quick as the beast.

Then: "Och, man," said Dubhain, rising to his feet and looking about him, "what a merry place ye choose to lodge in."

"Get us out of this place, damn you!" Caith doubled in pain, fighting for mind and breath and control of his chattering teeth. He was on his knees, and the vault around him was fading into red haze. "The witch, the queen here . . . herself knows your name and one Name more than yours, and she has waked things here you will not like to . . ."

A shadow rose up in his vision. For a dire moment, a single beat of his heart, he believed it the beast itself; but it was Dubhain who gathered him up in his arms.

Then the cold and the pain seemed less, and what was human seemed less, in the ebbing away of the world. "Ye hae done well," said Dubhain against his ear, a breath, and another, that let him get his own. "Ye great fool."

"Call me fool, ye thrice-damned wight, call me fool—who got you past the wards? Ye know how oft I called? You know at what cost?"

"Och, aye, man, but did ye need to fall off like a child?"

Caith struggled out of his embrace, hurled himself up, wide-legged, reeling this way and that, indignation lending heat to his limbs and sending the red mist from his eyes. "It was your doing that brought me here! And

if ye'd not run straight at them, ye bloody-minded
fool,—"

Dubhain tilted his head back. "I, *I*, bloody-minded?"

"Get us from this place! Or what are ye worth to
anyone?"

Dubhain's nostrils flared. " 'T is *iron*, man; 't is iron
those wards are, and the pains of hell it takes to breach
it, not for the summoner only!"

"Then why did you come here? There are bars, there
are chains, there are locks. They do go with castles.
What did you ever think to do here?"

Dubhain paced toward the water's edge, then turned
his naked back to that water and to the light. "Why,
man," he said cheerfully, hands spread, "I ease your
pain, is that nae help?"

Caith shook his head and sank slowly to his knees.
"A plague on your humors and your jokes, Dubhain.
Tell me what to do to get us free. These two have no
guilt here."

"Nae guilt at all? Why, what a wonder we have
here—a guiltless man and a guiltless woman! And
where is it writ that I should have the knowing and the
doing, when ye call me into castles of iron and locks?"

"Then be damned, I should have left you in the
loch."

"Nay, nay, now," said Dubhain, scratching his head
and walking bare as any lunatic along the shore, apparently deep in thought. One way he walked, and the
other way he walked, and a light like the moon began
to reflect on the water within the vault, and on the puddles that formed in footprints, as if they were filled with
pale, soft light.

Wretch, Caith thought. It was never Dubhain's tracks
that light attended. Hellfire, yes, marsh-light and will o'
the wisps, but never that pure light, reflecting everywhere now, glistening on the damp stones, with no
source visible. Brighter and brighter it grew, until there

became a source for it, until a ghostly shape stood above the muddy ground.

Soil his feet? No, not the Sidhe. That was for mortals. That was for Caith mac Sliabhin, all blood from head to foot, filthy with mud and sweat, shaking like a leaf in the wind and holding to the bars to keep his feet. Ceannann had ducked his face away, as if the presence blinded him. From Firinne, Caith heard a soft, fearful sob. But he watched steadfastly, as from the footprints on the shore, bars of light went up to the roof of the vault, and silver vines sprouted from them and wove themselves into a shining barrier between them and the loch, up and around and into the stones of the vault.

And the brightness that was the Sidhe took on expression and lifted a hand, never yet touching the ground.

"Man," said Nuallan, holding up a shining bit of silver between his fingers. "This is the key to every lock. Use it, take these two, and be gone from here as quickly as you can."

Caith walked unsteadily from the bars, reached with a grimy hand for the silver key in Nuallan's immaculate fingers. The metal burned like ice, it sweated in his fingers as if it were melting as ice would melt, and the pain of it stung him half to tears, when he had suffered so much else for no reason.

But complain against the Sidhe? Nuallan might abandon him here for another lesson, more bitter than the last . . . and leave him the guilt for two innocents besides. He dared not look the Sidhe in the eye, lest Nuallan suspect his rebel thoughts. He only brought the key to the lock that held Firinne prisoner—it seared his fingers when he put the faery silver into the iron, and his hands shook with the pain, but the hasp gave, and the lock opened.

"Come out," he said to Firinne, opening the bars. His hand was hurting so he could hardly hold the key, but he took it to Ceannann's cell, and opened that lock, too, biting his lip and shaking so he could scarcely, with one hand steadying the other, find the keyhole in the lock.

But when that lock was open the key melted and vanished, and he was left looking at the burns on his trembling fingers, red and deep amid the bloodstains and the mud. It hurt. Oh, gods, it did hurt, and Ceannann seized his hand and cast an accusing glance at Nuallan.

But Caith closed his fingers hard on his before the youth could say a foolhardy word. "He will leave us," he warned the boy on what breath he could muster. "Don't accuse him. He could not have touched the iron."

"Go," Nuallan said, as if he were dismissing the household servants. "And with your lives be away from this place. The sun is setting."

"Lord," Dubhain began, in objection; and flung up his arm against the light of the Sidhe's sudden, angry regard. For a moment it was the dark shape Dubhain had, with the wild mane and the red eyes; then a hunched and naked boy, head bowed to the ground, that much Caith saw, himself blinded and shielding his eyes from that light.

But as quickly as a dream, it was the red sunset about them, and they were on the open, reedy shore of the loch—Firinne and Ceannann in close embrace, a naked, kneeling boy ... and a hurt and bloodied man, for whom, after all else, the burned fingers were only an afterthought, a trivial cruelty to make the eyes water and the heart ache with the desire to do murder on the Sidhe *and* the lady together.

But that was the unredeemed Caith, his father's son, the hasty, foolish man. The wiser one blinked his streaming eyes at the ebbing daylight outside the gates of the lady's castle, and asked himself was their freedom now yet another dream within a dream, and himself lying fevered on a roadside, or in the lady's bed, or in the vault, waiting for the beast. Every part of him hurt, that much he knew for certain, and he dreaded at any moment to see the gates opening and the lady's men-at-arms rushing to take them back.

"Let's be away," he said, and turned to gather up Dubhain. But Dubhain was standing now and staring at the castle in horror plain to see—*Dubhain* was afraid, and when he caught at Dubhain's arm to make him move, Dubhain flinched out of his reach and gave a furious shake of his head.

"He is trapped," Dubhain said frantically. "He is trapped, man! And by your grace she knows his name!"

Nuallan? No. He had seen the clear Sidhe light, he had seen the silver bars and the vines, he had just seen Nuallan standing in clear possession of the field.

"How, 'trapped'? He has the castle, he has the key to their locks—"

"And is prisoner in what he holds." Dubhain's arms were locked about his naked ribs as if he were freezing. "A shell inside the lady's magic, he is, a nuisance, a burr, a gall, but nae more than that—" Dubhain's teeth were chattering, his breath hissing with cold, when Dubhain had skipped barefoot on ground that would numb mortal feet, and gone in a thin shirt whatever the season. "That is a wicked, wicked creature, man."

Nuallan, trapped to the lady's prison? He could not imagine . . . the creature of light, with the silver vines twined all through the stone keep: that was not defeat. Was it?

And what could the lady *do* to a Sidhe in her prison—who, Lugh save him, was the only one of the great Sidhe who might, if only for his own occasional convenience, care about Caith mac Sliabhin?

"What shall we do?" Ceannann asked faintly. "She must not have him. Worse, far worse, than her having us."

"We must go to our father," Firinne said.

"Go to your father," Caith echoed Firinne. Every word he was hearing on this shore seemed full of portent, and echoed off the sunset sky, saying: This is why.

This is the Sidhe's reason. But none of it fitted together, absent the truth from Firinne and Ceannann. "And where and who might this father be, woman who is no wife? The father of you both, is he?"

"Come with us," Ceannann said, already a step and two on his way with Firinne.

There was no other direction that offered itself. Caith caught at Dubhain's elbow to wake him and draw him away from this fatal place—shook at him again as Dubhain cast a look back at the castle and faltered in his going.

"We can do nothing as we are," he told Dubhain, "but get ourselves off the witch's doorstep." Breath came hard for him, even yet. It was surely only the witch's preoccupation with Nuallan that let them slip her notice thus far: he could not walk far or fast, and Dubhain's strength was all the hope they had. "Don't think of him," he warned Dubhain, with a tight hand on his arm. "Don't look back, ye fool, don't be dragging your feet."

"Nay," Dubhain said, teeth chattering, and seemed to come to his senses at last, walking more lively, keeping up with them, if limping somewhat. "Och, what hae ye done with my clothes and my belongings? Where did ye lose them, ye clumsy man?"

They were going toward that place, along the track beside the loch. He had seen it in his dream and seen it that night, and he had no doubt at all that they had to go to where Dubhain and he had parted company—that, he thought, must surely be the farthest boundary of the lady's power.

But it was a long, a terrible walk distant down the loch shore, under the grim witness of the keep.

"Yonder," he said, already out of breath. "Where you fell. We'll get them back." Firinne had never blanched at Dubhain's nakedness, desperate as they all were—certainly there was no way Dubhain could help his condition, but in a saner mind, and for Firinne's modesty,

Caith stripped off his own bloody shirt while they walked and passed it to Dubhain. "Wrap that about you."

" 'T is filthy!" Dubhain objected, a flaring of his usual contrariness, as the keep fell farther and farther behind them. But with no more ado than that, Dubhain wrapped the shirt about himself for a kilt, tied the sleeves together, and strode along at their desperate pace, as short of breath as they all were.

The lady's power, Caith saw in Dubhain's weakness, the power of the stone gods: Dubhain was fighting for his freedom now, as Dubhain had not been able to cross the boundary to enter the castle until someone inside had invited him in. No: more than invited—until someone wicked enough to lure a dark one had Called Dubhain across the lady's powerful wards with all the force of *geas* and Need their damned bond to each other could muster. They, he and Dubhain, stuck together like felons bound by a common chain, and, like the simple, rustic wards of the cottage, the great wards of the lady's keep had suffered in Dubhain's entry—

Suffered so that Nuallan had gotten himself in, and suffered so that somehow Nuallan had flung them outside . . .

But not suffered so that the lady could not draw the nets of her magic tight—a large fish, was a Sidhe lord; and very small the likes of themselves, to slip away while the lady was startled, for so long as the lady was startled, or busy with the silvery vines that, if they kept on as they had been going, were working and prying at the stones of her keep.

Necessity, Dubhain had said, back in the woods where the beast had hunted through the night and the storm; and he had stumbled into it, no mere whim of Dubhain's that had brought him to that cottage, to that keep, to this shore: he could damn Nuallan for what he suffered, but while his mind churned that resentment over—he had to hear Dubhain's protestations, that

Nuallan was not where Nuallan wished to be, either, and that was a frightening thought.

Nuallan had freed *them* and then not been able to free himself? Self-sacrifice was not the great Sidhe's habit.

Draiocht and *geas*. Black sorcery and dire Necessity.

Find their father, Firinne said? Well, so fell the last shred of Ceannann's story. Sibs, they were. And ask why this had aught whatsoever to do with them. They were all of them, and perhaps separately, arrows shot from some power's bow, but ask whose.

And ask why, when they walked by necessity at the very brink of the loch, where they had greatly to fear the beast, there was no more than a troubling of the waters near the shore, only a roiling of mud up from the bottom, as if some great fish had come into the shallows and dived deep and suddenly. Perhaps Nuallan was not so helpless as Dubhain feared.

Then—the same way they had *been* at one moment in the vault beneath the castle, and *been* on the loch shore outside the gates, the particular patch of shore they were walking . . . was not the same patch of shore, and when in astonishment Caith turned to look behind him, they were miles farther down the curve of the loch.

The others were looking back, too.

And the castle was a scant dot in the distance.

"He hae flung us *out*, man," Dubhain whispered. "Or someone hae flung us out of her domain t' be quit of us the while. —Och, the fool, the fool, she hae *got* him!"

chapter

five

A PATCH OF reedy bank at a scant walk back in the direction of the castle, a place where the road ran perilously close against the loch: in the mortal sense there were a dozen like it, and in the fading twilight every place along this cursed shore looked as unsavory as the rest of it, but Caith himself had no doubt it was the place where they had fallen; and Dubhain at a certain step paused—flared his nostrils with a deep breath as if he were about to dive deep, tossed his head, then waded moderately into the reed-choked water, searching for something.

"Have a care," Ceannann said, and Caith thought of the ripples they had seen farther down the shore. As for why Dubhain had caught his breath before touching that water, he felt, even with his mortal senses, the heaviness of the air.

"A care, ye say?" Dubhain had just found something in the calf-deep water, and bent and snatched it up in a dusky, strong fist, triumphant. The stone, Caith guessed, that stone which a creature of Dubhain's shape-shifting kind had always about him, and, recovering which, the wicked sparkle came back to Dubhain's eyes and the confidence to his movements as he went poking about with his toes and feeling about him in the peat-strawed water of the loch edge, a very soup of floating peat and

unhealthy reeds that clung about Dubhain's bare legs
and arm.

"Ah!" said Dubhain, and bent again and retrieved the
sword—of course, the sword, the cursed thing. Caith
caught it crosswise as Dubhain cheerfully tossed it to
him. It weighed what he remembered, it filled his hand
with a known and familiar shape, it settled into his possession like a bad habit, a source of confidence he had
far rather not rely on in the world.

" 'T is no cleaner for its bath," he muttered, wishing
he did have the fortitude to leave it in the mud, but faery would not abide that challenge. The Sidhe would
surely devise some way for him to regret losing it before the sun slipped below the horizon—as the sun was
fast doing now, and the waters of the loch were less and
less to trust, where Dubhain was splashing about to
wash the peat off his legs. "Come out," Caith said, "before you make a supper for what lives there. If your
clothes went in, they're gone altogether."

"No, here," said Ceannann, who was making his own
search on dry land. "This would be it, perhaps."

It was indeed Dubhain's small bundle that Ceannann
had found among the reeds, dry and clean, as Caith
himself was not. Caith frowned as Dubhain held up his
hands for it and Ceannann tossed it at him.

Caith shot out a hand and caught it instead, put-upon
and angry with the Sidhe and their luck. "You've the
stone back, now, wicked lad. So now ye *can* carry us
three, can ye not?"

Dubhain gave an indignant toss of his head and
shook it, the mop falling into his eyes and needing a
second toss, the hell-light glimmering behind that
fringe, translucently sullen.

"You can do it."

"Nay, cannae!"

"Will not, will not, is the word, Dubhain! Carry us
three, or go naked as a jay, for what I care, and give me
back my shirt!"

Dubhain sulked, untied it and dropped it insolently in the water. His next trick would be vanishing, if Dubhain did not get all his way, and that was to no one's good.

"Give me my shirt and be damned, then, stubborn wight." Defeated, Caith flung the bundle of Dubhain's clothes at him. Dubhain caught it with one hand and, with the grand flourish of a bow, swept up the bloody, the cut, the muddy and now sodden shirt from the peat-water with a single finger of the hand that held the stone. This, while two strangers with better sense watched them quarrel like a pair of dogs in a scullery yard.

"Please," said Firinne.

"Oh, aye, *please*," Dubhain scoffed, offering the shirt to him, one-fingered.

Caith jerked it from his hand. "That's *enough*, Dubhain!"

"It's the wickedness of this place," Ceannann said while Dubhain glared. "Friend Sidhe, please, please and politely, by the cup we gave you, come out of the loch."

Dubhain gave a great shiver. It was sense the lad was urging on them both and rare sense the lad had in calling the wight by the obligation he had on him—the boy who had bolted into the trap in the woods had now to advise his seniors to use their heads; and, furious as he was, grudging as he was in Dubhain's case, Caith swallowed his rage and put on a cold courtesy before his temper killed them all on this shore.

"Come," he said, and turned along the shore, putting his back to the lady's keep, and burning with the anger in him.

The pair would have pleaded further with Dubhain. Firinne added her voice to the entreaties, and Caith spun around and walked backward a pace and two. "Come along!" he bade them, "Now!" And he turned about again, acutely anxious, past the rage that had the blood buzzing in his skull: this place, this cursed place where they had fallen, must be the boundary of the lady's lands. Dubhain wished to act the fool here, but he refused to, and if Ceannann and Firinne would not follow him out of here, then damn them both! He longed to be away, into air he could breathe.

But Ceannann and Firinne, at least, followed him, not without misgiving looks back at Dubhain, and seeing Dubhain bent on his own, fey, fickle course, Caith slung his sword angrily to his shoulder and wrung out his shirt as they walked—from white, it had gone a loathsome brown shade of dirt and blood; it was all over with bits of peat from the loch; and Dubhain with his fine, clean clothes could follow or not, for all he was able to care at the moment. He was shamed by Dubhain's flouting him in the sight of Firinne and Ceannann, his burned hand hurt as he wrung the shirt out, but getting the water out was the only saving of himself from chill tonight, and he gave it three furious twists with all his strength, after which effort the wound in his shoulder ached, too, —so much for Dubhain's magic. The pain might even be Dubhain's spite at him, the same as the lady's ... Dubhain might hope he would grovel, as the lady had wished it of him, and by the Badbh he would not, not if he bled his life out. He shook the shirt out, put one arm in it and handed his sword to Ceannann to hold while he pulled it over his head, stumbling as he walked.

Then—while he had his head stuck inside the clammy shirt, he suffered a sudden light-headedness, a thorough confusion which direction he was walking. He fought his head through the collar and caught-step at the same time, finding himself, as he staggered, facing backward, toward the distant castle, toward Dubhain.

That had been the boundary they had passed just now, the limit of the lady's land, and they all had crossed save Dubhain—which gave him now an unbearable sense of unease. He knew that feeling, and damned it, and spun about again, tugging the clammy shirt down about his ribs and his waist. Every breath felt lighter,

but the geas with Dubhain pulled at him, wrenched at
his very soul—

So let it worry Dubhain, was his thought, beneath the
anxiety, and he kept walking, with the feeling rising up
and choking him with nameless fear.

Firinne cast a glance back. "He's following us."

"Oh, how not? There's mischief to do." Dealing with
Dubhain, one learned churlish answers, and he regretted
his at once; but the pain in his hand and his shoulder
was consuming his good sense and the loch was a sheet
of gathering dark all too close to the edge of the road.
The beast might be watching them while Dubhain
lagged and argued and made himself a cursed obstacle.
"Forgive me," he muttered to Firinne, "but I know his
ways."

"You have the calling of him," Ceannann said.

"Oh, aye, you see how far that goes."

"But he follows. He obeys you."

"For his hide's sake." He knew how narrowly it was
true, and what danger Dubhain was in, near this dark
place. The feeling of danger was running up and down
his spine of a sudden. He paused, turned to see
Dubhain's shadowy shape, a mere gleam of white, clean
shirt in the dusky distance, and furiously beckoned him
to catch up with them—

Dubhain, the wretch, looked about him and behind
him, as if he might have meant some other Sidhe.

A second time he beckoned him, and Dubhain laid a
hand on his breast in mock astonishment.

A third time. Then Dubhain flung wide his arms and
began to run along the trail, quickly as a Sidhe could
move, jumping the weeds, his kilts flying, cavorting
like a very fool.

Caith let go a weary curse and stayed to suffer his
antics. Dubhain had to flirt with the brink of hell, *had*
to walk the edge to the last moment.

"Oh, master!" the fool cried at the meeting, flinging
himself to his knees.

"Wicked creature," Caith said. And because he had his own share of hell-bent temper. "Will you carry us?"

There was an instant, foreboding frown, and Dubhain leapt to his feet and looked away.

So—so, he surmised in better sense, it might be the truth Dubhain had spoken, not a whim—*could* not, Dubhain had insisted, and by Dubhain's manner he almost did believe it: either that, despite the stone, Dubhain had not the strength here, or, more likely, Caith surmised at a second thought, Dubhain feared his own nature in this wicked place.

But Dubhain admit to it? Never.

"Behave," he told Dubhain soberly. "Walk with us, where these folk tell us."

"Och," Dubhain said with a flourish, "aye, with them. A father we're seeking, now. Their father. And husband and wife, are they? Hoosht, what merry wickedness!"

"Hush, damn you! —Forgive him. He wants a bridle on his tongue."

"Och, such a wit, the man!" Dubhain swept a bow, the doffing of a cap he did not own, as he skipped backward a pace and walked sideways in court of Firinne. "But this deceiving of your guests, madam, surely I do forgive, counting our mutual friend here, and him an unmannered fellow. —But a prince . . . did I tell ye that? A *noble* man, my master is. . . ."

"Sidhe, be quiet!"

A second bow, and a skip. "And yourselves, fair brother, fair sister, by no means common shepherd folk, are ye? Sae delicate and mannered ye are, and wi' such a dreadful enemy as Herself—or is it your pretty faces and pretty selves she covets?"

"Peace, damn you!" For a moment Caith wished him back the other side of the boundary, but that was dangerous. He caught Dubhain by the shirt instead and marched him a step and two off and aside. "What in very hell d' ye think to do, you wretched creature?

What harm have these folk done you? Or will you not be content until the man takes his foot to you? I'll not blame him!"

Dubhain rolled his eyes and turned his long jaw to the coming night and the hills, sullenly refusing any answer. Then, with a twist, trying to escape him: "Mayhap they lie. What d' ye think of that, my dearest lord, my fair master, my darlin' Caith? D' ye think all truth flows from that pair? Or that Himself is safe abed in his own land tonight?"

Dubhain Saw things; and Dubhain was distraught—it was the truth and a warning Dubhain was giving him in his impudent way, and only a fool would ignore it. He made his grip on Dubhain's shirt a flick of his hand, a careful straightening of the wight's white, spotless collar, with a hand that trembled and an arm that ached with a gnawing, persistent pain.

"Sweet Dubhain, fair Dubhain. How could I mistake ye? Tell me: give me your advice. What should we do?"

"Oh, do as the pretty pair pleases. Do what they please, when they please, but list' to me, my prince, this is a very dangerous place."

"I did mark that."

"Ye maun jest, prince of murderers, but listen, this is a deep and fearsome loch; this is a castle built of blood and blackest spells, and whatever the lord Nuallan intended is most direly gone awry."

The pain distracted him. He could not bring his wits to bear on anything but the betrayal the bright Sidhe had worked on him and on Dubhain, even if he reasoned that it was a fruitless resentment. The Sidhe would do as the Sidhe would do, and sometimes mend what fell aside.

"The fingers," he said, holding up the seared and swollen joints. "I cannot hold my sword as is, —and ye say it, an unwholesome venue, this."

"If ye will entreat me well, aye, I might deal wi' it."

"Please," he framed with his lips, and as quietly as he could, said: "Prithee, *sweet* Dubhain."

"Can ye, wi' more passion, and louder, sweet Caith?"

"I *beg* thee, villain!"

Dubhain took his hand and kissed the fingers, and the thumb. The pain was cooled, like the touch of ice. Licked the wound, and Caith snatched his hand away in furious offense.

Dubhain grinned at him. "Ye dear, sweet, and bluidy man."

"Foul creature."

"Sweet Caith." Dubhain whirled and skipped away along the trail, a white-shirted wraith in the night. And was gone for an instant, and there again, where the meadow began. Caith trudged after him, the slower, mortal way, working the hand lately burned, sullenly glad and grateful that Dubhain was in a helpful mood, even suspecting Dubhain, in his own way, felt a human fondness for him.

But that was a man's thinking; and a man's way into trouble with the Sidhe was ever to think their reasons were a man's reasons or that gifts from such as Dubhain had no barbs in them at all.

The meadow, so fair and smooth under the starlight, was a treacherous ground, full of bogs, and full of pits and watery holes in the dark. If the beast stayed near the water, it had enough water here to enjoy, Caith thought, and wondered if the road at the loch's very edge might at least give them better ground to run—for the little distance that they might have the strength to run at all. He was exhausted. Firinne and Ceannann slogged along with a strength born, he was sure, of desperation; while Dubhain skipped and dodged the watery patches as if they were on an evening's walk.

"You could work a spell on us," he said to Dubhain when Dubhain was in reach. "You could make the walking easier."

"Cannae," Dubhain said surlily, maddeningly, with a shake of his head and a glimmering of red in his eyes.

He had had experience enough of Dubhain's moods, and one hesitated to ask in the first place, Dubhain's cures being all rough-edged and full of regrets at leisure. But this fey elusiveness—this Cannot, and this glimmering in his eyes and this skipping about—this had a worrisome quality.

He dared not ask again. Dubhain was with them. Dubhain had helped him, and: A wicked place, Dubhain had said, trying to warn him. He most of all feared that Dubhain might be feeling other than horror at this place, and that Dubhain might be suffering the lady's spells in a different way than he might. Dubhain walked with him a time, but there was no comfort in his presence: Dubhain seemed anxious, perhaps sunk in thought. But when Caith next misstepped and soaked an already soaked foot, Dubhain hauled him up by the arm and laughed at him.

"Wretch," Caith muttered between his teeth. "Find me dry shoes and a cloak, can you not? When I freeze, what will amuse you?"

"Lazy fellow."

"Oh, aye, lazy." He bantered with Dubhain to lift Dubhain's spirits, and was relieved when Dubhain answered him in good humor, enjoying his gibes. But there was a darkness ahead, and it seemed to him a sheen of loch water, bending that way. "The loch comes inward, ahead. We're walking toward it again."

"But a higher bank is there," Ceannann said.

"Are you sure?"

"Aye," Ceannann said, and he had no better advice—no word at all from Dubhain, who strayed off into the dark again.

But the ground did grow drier, and rose, so that they were climbing slightly, then took a sharp upward slope, onto stony soil and among whin and heather, woody clumps that caught the feet and got in the way of a straight climb.

The loch curved around the shoulder of the hill, and there was its dark water thankfully far below them, a pitch black pit drinking up what light there was—but they had out-walked the beast, Caith told himself, sitting down a moment on the stony ground. His shirt had never dried, but it was sweat, now, that made the cold spots when the wind blew, and blow it did on this mountain-side. He was winded with the climbing, but he had finally warmed himself through, and if they could keep that warmth by gentle, steady climbing until the morning he thought he might have the strength to make it.

Something thumped and banged above them, so that his ears did not at first know what it was. But, looking up, he saw the rags of cloud that had stolen in over the black height of the mountain above them, and that sight struck him with anger and bitter despair.

A second thump came from the sky above and a drop of icy rain hit his leg.

"Get up," he said, hauling himself to his feet. "Keep moving."

Firinne and Ceannann offered no argument. They were looking at the sky upslope, too, and had doubtless felt the drops on them. They had come far enough to feel some safety from the beast and now the very mountain turned on them, and ambushed them with bitter wind that blasted suddenly down the height, carrying a spatter and then a deluge of cold rain so gale-churned it filled the air and came in with the breath.

Sweaty warmth went instantly to rain-cold, sodden clothing, hanging with twice its dry weight before they had gone a dozen feet up the mountain. The lightning showed a stony, heather-clumped slope, heart-breakingly steep, the same that they had sat down to rest on before attempting, but they had no choice now.

"Dubhain!" Caith shouted out, but wherever Dubhain

had gotten to, it was not with them. He saved his breath after that, needing it all, driving himself uphill in the surety that if he lost the warmth in his body, he would freeze—it happened to the unwary in the hills, and there was not, in the heather and the small stones, even a way to make a shelter. Only if they came to some natural split in the mountain flank, a stream-course, a corrie, even a pile of rocks, the three of them might huddle close together and weather the cold until the morning sun.

In the lightning flashes he searched desperately with his eyes for any such place ahead or to the sides of them; and he hoped for Dubhain—but Dubhain, curse him, was nowhere in sight, off about mischief, it might be—while Ceannann and Firinne were occupied with themselves, forging steadily ahead of him with their young and unbattered legs, their small, desperate party so straggled out on the mountain that he could not at all times see them. Rocks turned underfoot, leather soles grew slick, the brambles and heather caught at clothing and at skin, in the gusts of a water-choked wind that threatened balance on the precarious steep. Caith found himself falling behind, and beginning to shiver so that he risked his knees in every uncertain step.

"Ceannann!" he shouted against the gale. "Firinne!" And angrily: "Dubhain, damn you!"

But he knew beyond a doubt now that he could not hope to close the gap with the pair ahead of him. They might realize he was gone, perhaps. Perhaps Dubhain would deign to find him—or Dubhain was off in the way Dubhain would, on such nights, witless lad, off through the storm and the rain like a very fool, dancing along the mountain in the lightnings. That was the reward of trusting the dark Sidhe.

But at this slower, saner pace he was managing better. He felt the cold less, and he made up his mind to go on up the mountain at a slant, and shelter wherever he could find a nook out of the wind. A stream-cut or a falls was the most likely; and that he had crossed none, upward bound, meant there was none such on the slopes directly above.

Taking that slantwise course around the mountain shoulder, he must eventually cross one: rainwater poured off a mountain in any fold it could find, and it was folly to climb straight up to the summit—they had been going wrong. He could not think what had possessed the lot of them except exhaustion and blind panic, or a Power's ill will; and he shouted, trying to make Firinne and Ceannann hear him—inexperienced of the mountain heights, they might be, and in far direr trouble than he was, in the cold and the wind up above, but he could only call their names and hope a fluke of the wind carried his voice up above. He was doing all he could for himself, to keep on his feet and to keep searching, in the lightnings, for some place out of the wind and the icy rain. He was not half so cold, now that he had left the exposed eastern face, and he was spending far less strength now that he was not driving himself like a fool straight up the mountain—

But in a sudden, cruel gust around the mountain shoulder the rain blasted at him, and stole the warmth he had won. He began to shiver, and the shivers made his knees unsteady, made his steps wander and his ankle turn dangerously on a misstep as the damned sword banged about his left side, hampering him in his reach for a hand-hold.

He did not know now how far he had climbed. His legs were beyond burning with the climbing, and his feet and fingers were so numb with the cold that he could not tell now what his hands were closing on for a grip or where his feet were, among the stones and the gnarled heather-stems.

His foot slid. He took a painful fall onto his hip and his elbow, skidded a distance and crawled up the flat rocks again, on a steep, stony stretch where he discovered at least a knee-high ridge and a growth of heather between him and the direct sweep of the wind. It might be the best he would find. At least he had found a breathing space, the brush broke the force of the rain above him, and the stone of the mountain felt warmer than the rain on his other side.

It must be goat-herding that had instilled such endurance into the pair of fools that had gone up the mountain—that, and no sleepless nights and no wounding with arrows and no beating by the lady's servants and chasing after faithless Sidhe: so he thought, lying under the driving rain; and if the beast should slither up the slope and seek him for its supper this very moment, he swore he could muster no great fear of it, not in the bitter wind.

"Hoosht, now," Dubhain exclaimed, arriving with a skip and a hop down from the rock above him. "There ye are!"

"A small rest," he said, tilting his head back. "A short sit." He could not even muster delight to see the rascal, or to think that Dubhain would help him up. He was no longer sure he even wished to get up. It meant a farther walk through the cold, against the battering wind, and that was a great deal to ask of a man who had already achieved a comforting numbness on one side. The bruises there had ceased hurting. All that side had ceased hurting at all, and Dubhain asked him to get up and go on?

He did not think so. What was more, he did not care. He was through with the Sidhe, with their games and their jokes and their ill-treatment of him. Even Dubhain's. "Go find Firinne," he said. "The Sidhe have such a care for them, go find the fools. I'll bide here a while."

A woman stark naked could not have lured him onto his feet now—that Firinne was alive he did hope, in what little he cared; he hoped with a little less concern that Ceannann was: the boy was not that much the fool, and what could he plead for his own good sense, leading the pair straight up a mountain as if they were going somewhere?

Or had Ceannann been leading? He could not remember, for the life left in him, and he did not greatly care about that, either. There was only Dubhain's dark shape squatting by him, a shadow in which the eyes shimmered the faintest of red, and there was Dubhain's hand, shaking his shoulder.

ChAPTER
SIX

THUNDER CLAPPED AND lit the mountainside, a stark play of rocks and midnight shadows. "Man," Dubhain said somberly, arms on knees, "things are grievously amiss with the world: here and now I can say to ye what I dared not wi' the twain to hear."

"Say on," Caith said, obligingly. His head was against the stone, a heather twig was sticking his neck, and a heather stem was gouging his back, for what he could tell, either one of them of much more consequence in his thoughts, while the rain pounded him in cold gusts and sheets.

"We must rescue Himself out of that Place."

"Oh, aye."

"For our ain sakes, man."

"Aye. Bid the rain stop. Find my cloak. I think I left it in the castle."

"The man said: worse than her having *us*. *Us*, it is, and: Go to our father, the woman says, and off we go, wi' these shepherd folk, like good fools. Hae ye no a sma' curiosity why Himself flung us out?"

"Or she did."

"Perhaps. Perhaps neither."

"Neither?"

"There is the Sidhe about our pretty pair."

Tricked, had they been? Led this way and that and

131

left in the cold? Another damnable Sidhe trick on them?
"Of what sort?"

"I cannae tell. The watery folk, I do think."

Caith made shift to get an arm under him and lift his
head.

"What, that *you* cannot tell? Did we not sleep under
their roof? Did you see nothing then?"

Dubhain stood up and set his hands on his hips, towering dark against the lightnings. "Oh, aye, my fault, it
is."

"I mean no fault in you, ye fractious wight, I but ask:
are they the same?"

Dubhain glanced at him sidelong, the corner of an
eye. "I cannae say."

"Art held from saying?"

"I am nae oracle, man, I only came back in the dark
t' find a fool and warn him."

Dubhain did *not* know, or some magic constrained
him from saying—and Dubhain so hated to be in error,
or constrained in any particular.

"Warn me about them?"

"We hae lost what help we had, man, we hae lost
Nuallan, and d' ye see the Daoine Sidhe coming wi' the
horns of faery and the bright banners flying?" A pass of
Dubhain's hand about the windy dark. "I see nae such
help about this loch or these hills. That is nae simple
witch, man, that is a thing sae powerful a'ready a Sidhe
lord hae mista'en her, and set himself and all his magic
in her keep. D' ye nae understand the Daoine Sidhe
themselves could nae breach her defense? Ye had t' ask
me in; and after me, why, the lord Nuallan had nae trouble at all—maybe far too little a trouble: the lady was
sudden and subtle. The wards went shut, while we
sailed through like minnows in a sieve, did ye nae feel
it? The fair folk cannae breach her walls, no more than
before, and Himself is in nae comfortable circumstance
tonight."

"Why did he fling us outside?"

"Ye were nae listening, man."

"I understand about the wards, damn you. Why send us outside? Was 't Nuallan or the lady cast us out?"

"Why, ye were nae great help, my Caith, stumbling and witless as ye were." Dubhain squatted down again and gazed at him, with the fire in his eyes gone dim again. "And she hae let fly all the pretty sparrows—being occupied wi' the greater gift in her nets. Or perhaps not. Wi' such a power ye cannae trust. And wi' the watery sort . . . 't is me own ilk, pretty Caith, and ever so wise and wonderful as we are, we are a wee sma' bit an impulsive kind."

"A damnable weathercock." The wind whipped behind him and under him as he shoved himself up and tried to get a leg under him. Just that he managed. "Are they waiting or have they gone on?"

"Och, nay, they're sitting in better comfort than you, sweet Caith. There are walls up above, a ruin o' sorts, which I think ye may find more pleasant than here."

He was half frozen, so stiff he could scarcely climb, and Dubhain told him there was shelter? He swallowed a curse, shoved his other leg under him, and stumbled a step and two uphill, using his hands on the rocks to steady him.

Dubhain shoved him from behind, hand on his rump, and such was his weakness he would have fallen and failed the climb, without that. He climbed and he panted and he climbed and he panted, and gasped, halfway to the wind-scoured clouds:

"Did they know this was a place to go? Is this a place they knew?"

"Och, aye, they did seem to." Another shove heaved him a step as his legs tried and failed, and he caught himself and struggled further. "Their father's castle, they said. And a deal else, by now, but I could nae rescue a fool and hear their private talk all at once, now, could I, darlin' Caith? And I did think ye might want a bit of help."

The crest of the hill loomed up against the lightnings, jagged and strangely shaped, a work of masonry and not nature, clearly so. He had to pause for breath, Dubhain shoving at him as he was—he slipped to one knee to rest, but Dubhain seized him by the arm and dragged him up the next distance, with him trying all the while to use his legs or get his breath, at the least. He mistrusted Dubhain now, he mistrusted where he was going: it was a sudden helpful mood Dubhain was in, and his reason went scattered a moment as Dubhain carried him along—Dubhain's reason was balanced on a knife's edge of *geas* and the allure of wickedness, from moment to moment on a night like this, and with wicked and ancient influences on the wind.

"Ye would not like the lady of the loch half so well," he panted next Dubhain's ear. "Mind, I do bear with your pranks and your jests. Would she? I do fear the lady is humorless."

"A great failing," Dubhain agreed, and with a blithe strength no mortal could match, hauled him roughly up a last crumbling slope toward a shadowed wall and through a doorless gate, into darkness.

"A man could break his neck," he protested. His eyes strained to see and found nothing at all to tell him he had not gone blind. His feet were on a level stone floor, and the icy wind was dead here, not warmer, just dead, except a faint, dank breeze that smelled of age and rot. He feared going farther, he feared Dubhain might have gone out of his kinder mood, but he dared not loose his grip on Dubhain's sleeve—Dubhain was having his small joke with him, Dubhain with a chance to discomfit him could not forego that, no more than down on the hillside. Surely that was all Dubhain was up to, and it was no worse purpose he had.

And of a sudden they were facing an outside door, the lightnings glistening on stone, up a few steps to a letting-forth into some hidden, now roofless hall, where the rain and the storm had free rein, and the wind skirled madly about in attempts to escape the jagged walls.

Huddled together in the shelter of the half-ruined arch, he saw Firinne and Ceannann, who leapt up to meet them.

"I hae found him," Dubhain said, "half-frozen that he is."

Wherewith Dubhain let him go. Caith's legs went and his knee and then his elbow met the unforgiving paving-stones.

He could not even muster a curse for the creature, or hate him for dumping him like a sack of meal before his fellow creatures—Dubhain had done someone a kindness, so of course Dubhain had to make up for it, in Dubhain's own perverse set of balances.

"The poor man," Firinne said, and knelt down on the rain-slick stones, this fair-haired, Sidhe-touched creature, to try to persuade him of her good intentions. Ceannann hovered by, too, offering to help him up, but he flinched away from their ministrations, would not have either of them touch him, them with their deceptions and their lies and their misleading him about their nature—not even that he blamed them, Sidhe having a necessity to do that sort of thing, deceiving and misleading and tricking the mortal world, but he was willing to bear no more of it, and wished most of all not to be some Sidhe's plaything tonight, or to deal with them—he had no wit to match with their cleverness, not now.

So he eluded their doubtless good intentions, said not a word of complaint, and edged over into a shallow, rubbled nook next the threshold and the remnant of the vault. There he hugged his arms about himself, tucked himself up small and shivering in this refuge where few drops reached, and hoped that the wind would not shift. The stone floor was cold under him and the stonework cold against his shoulder, but die? Dubhain would not have that, no matter the cold that had his teeth chattering and his bones knocking together. No, Dubhain would get him through until the dawn . . . never ask in what comfort.

But Dubhain settled down next to him, snuggled close against him. "Here, here," said Dubhain, and caught him in his arms, constrained his shivers in a hard, fever-warm embrace, and breathed against his ear: "Pretty Caith."

"Be damned to you."

"Our hosts were sae worrit about ye. They would hae gone themselves."

"They lost me in the storm."

"Ye lost yourself, ye fool. Ye turned off the trail."

"What trail? What cursed trail?"

"Hush. Hush, while they settle to sleep, our pretty ones." Dubhain's embrace half smothered him. "Wi' nae mistrust of us, 't would seem, or they are sae desperate for rest as yourself, my bluidy prince—"

"Not the habit of the Sidhe."

"Nay, but sometimes we sleep."

"Should they trust us?" he asked, foggy-witted, and asking before he thought. Dubhain laughed, a touch of blithe wickedness, and hugged him close, while the shivers diminished.

"Nay, never. But they are nae creatures of the changing moon, I judge, nae e'en as much as the bright Sidhe. Watery folk though they be, 't is the sun they favor. And that is a peculiar kind."

The warmth had reached his other side, it seemed, and he could at last draw a small, sane breath, thinking that he should move, now that he was not in imminent danger of freezing. Dubhain would play some malicious joke on him; but he could not bring himself to relinquish the rest or the warmth while it lasted.

"I've no experience of them," he said, only half awake.

"The sun folk? Strong they are, some sae silly a man can trick them. Some mad as goats in spring. Most hae the Sight in great measure—but it comes and it goes for them. Dark ones of that ilk—"

"Of the sun folk?" It seemed to him he was losing pieces of what Dubhain was saying, and he was sorry: when Dubhain would talk on such matters, one could learn things.

"Oh, aye. There are. And watery ones and dark ones, every sort that ye could imagine."

"I never saw them."

"Of their will ye ne'er do. Ye're a man, ye silly. And the sun is full of lies, dazzle and dance—did I say they were honest? Or fair-tempered? The moon for changes and the sun for hard-handed trickery . . ."

Dubhain's voice was fading to him. A new spate of rain had started, and the wind carried a few cold drops into their shelter, but not enough to matter. He said, "I'd have taken the sun for bright—" And he was slipping away, he knew it, uttering foolishness.

Dubhain said, against his ear: "Man, ye're going. Mind where ye wander when ye dream, tonight. Her nets are spread wide."

He tried to take account of that, and to draw back from the edge of a sleep so precipitate and so needed he felt his wits scattering in all directions. But Dubhain whispered, "I shall carry ye tonight, my Caith. Ye stay wi' me." . . . and he was carried in a rocking silence that took on the easy nature of a horse's motion, with never yet a sound except the thunder.

Then the air was under them, and the loch water a black pit below the mountain. Beware the beast, he tried to say, even knowing he was dreaming, but he could make not a sound. Lightning flashed around them, and Dubhain's pooka-shape ran at easy stretch in the flickering light. The hellfire was banked and lazy in the eye he could see from time to time, a glassy rim of red. The lightnings reflected there, more pure and more placid than the fire. They flickered over Dubhain's sleek hide and lit the windswept walls of the glen, high, high above the troubles and the fear in the glen.

Then Dubhain struck some slope in the sky, and it was down and down, a long leap headlong toward the loch. Caith clung to Dubhain's neck and he might have cried out—at the very moment Dubhain hit some level in the air that pleased him. Dubhain's stride was smooth, but the pace was a gallop now, effortless, as seemed—Dubhain was satisfied, Caith thought, having scared him with that descent.

But it was a perilous place they had come to. From moment to moment in the lightnings and ahead and below, he could see the lady's castle crouched like a living creature at the end of the loch. Lower they swept— "Be careful!" he said, and bit his lip, for the pooka-shape was contrary, and took its inspirations from his warnings.

Lower still, at the level of the tower roofs; and Caith gripped the smoke of the pooka's mane, recalling how Dubhain had gone out from under him at the lady's borders, had turned to smoke and vanished . . . or had that been another dream? They flew above the keep of Dun Glas and he saw the faint cold gleam of moon-silver pouring through the bars of the vault and onto the black waters of the loch, faint gleam, but a sign of the Sidhe held and holding there, still alive.

"M' lord," he said in his dream, although he knew Nuallan was too far to hear him. Or Nuallan could hear him very well. And that made it a foolish thing to do.

Then a dream opened like a door within his dream— a black plunge toward the castle, in the heart of which the lady waited, bespelling him, weaving magics, he did not know how he knew, but he heard the thunder of the cauldron, the blackness and the fire was all about him . . . and Dubhain shied up and skyward with him, snorting and shaking his mane, up and up, with great leaps of his black, lean body.

Only when he was high above the loch did Dubhain settle to a long, free-running stride, up where the wind blew, no longer cold, only an element in which they moved, faster than thought or wishes; and Caith no longer knew where they were, or where they were going, but the flight was high and it was wild and it shot through the crooked course of the lightnings and the deafening buffets of thunder. The whole sky ripped in front of them in a white, jagged rent, and Dubhain leapt above that stroke of destruction, through a thunderclap so great it shocked his heart and mind at once. For an instant he was numb. Then he caught the rhythm of the running and the malice and the freedom a man could not, dared not, learn to love.

Perhaps it was Dubhain's own dream he was slipping into. He tried to remember he was a man, and that he could not fall down to the beast like Dubhain and come back again, but he felt laughter racing under him like a shaking of the earth, headed for a plunge like a suicide off the edge of the sky.

"Dubhain!" he cried, but they were already gone, a dive like a bat, sheer delirious plummet through the wind, a clap of thunder and the earth abruptly under him: he jolted aware in Dubhain's embrace, under a sudden spatter of cold rain, with the memory of lightning still branded in his eyes.

They had never left the ruin. The lightning flickered and flashed and the thunder rolled above their heads as the rain poured down in a fitfully-lit veil outside their shelter.

He was not cold. The wind and the rain soaked him and soaked Dubhain, vast grey curtains of it blowing across the ruin in the lightning flashes, a violence churning about their mountain that made trivial the violence of the mortal world, a violence great and as wild and heartless as the magics of the Sidhe. Men perished. Their houses and the works of their lifetimes were swept away in an instant. What cared such forces?

It needed a while to recover his own self, while he lay half-awake and warm and letting the flashes blind his eyes and the heartless power run through his mind. He had to find the measure of his own thoughts, the feeling of the mountain, of the Sidhe, different than himself, had to feel the simple, mundane fact of soaked clothing and the limits of mortal wit and mortal senses—that was where Caith mac Sliabhin touched the world, that was all the wisdom he had, that he wished the cold and the discomfort back, to be sure he was a man and no other than that.

The storm blew past in a last spatter of wind-blown drops. Came a silence as dreadful as the storm, when a man could lie against unnatural warmth and remember the night at a distance; but by the first touch of the daylight the recollection of it began to fade like any dream, leaving him only pale, water-puddled stone, the huddled shapes of Firinne and Ceannann in deeper shadow, their fair heads bowed together in slumber, themselves all damp with rain. Thunder muttered in the far distance, as the storm walked away over the loch and the end of the valley.

Last, Dubhain stirred and stretched, dislodging him from his warm rest.

"A fair dewy dawn," said Dubhain, arching his back. "And the pretty pair all asleep yet. What shall we do and where shall we go now, me darlin' Caith?"

"Give over," Caith said. His stomach was empty, he was soaked to the skin, and long enough from his last meal to think of that first. "Find us something to eat, kind Dubhain, fair Dubhain, can you manage?"

"Och, we *begin* with polite asking. How rare."

"I do ask, Dubhain, most politely."

"Why, then, let us see." Dubhain scrambled up with a lightness which he could in no wise muster, swept a grand bow and skipped off through the doorway.

Then, while Firinne and Ceannann slept, Caith gathered himself up in the grey morning light and went as far as the tumbled ruin of an upper level, and up a rickety short stairs to what had been a walk along the wall.

The world was wide from there, the mountains, the broad valley, the hills in velvet folds, and a score of waterfalls begun by the rain last night, white threads on dark rock, bright streams running down to the loch and whatever lay beyond. There it would find escape or come up against the mountains—but by the placement of this fortress here, and by the fold of the mountains he saw, he would wager his only shirt there was a pass through the mountain ridge in that fold. This keep had been built on this difficult height for some reason, most likely to guard that narrow water below, either keeping something in or keeping something out—and either circumstance indicated a passage existed there.

Yet, unassailable as this fortress might have seemed to attackers, and dizzyingly far above the water, it had fallen to some violence, and the owners had not rebuilt it. By the unrotted condition of the wood—he gave the railing a shake—it had fallen within mortal memory. That told a tale of sorts: not all that long ago a fall, in mortal lifespans, but either forgotten or the land left so desolate around about it that not even the remnant of its country folk came here to plunder it of iron for their smithing and stone and wood for their cottages and fences.

With the lady of Dun Glas for a neighbor, there might be a reason—and in that consideration, there might be a curse on the place, although he often could feel the harm clinging about a place, and he felt nothing in these stones, felt—if anything, a sense of sadness and confusion.

But the wind whistled about this exposed height, cold and damp with recent rain, and he set carefully in his memory that prospect of Loch Fiain and that fold of mountains as a way they might walk out of this cursed glen, bearing generally west. That was all he had climbed up here to know, and it was with a sense of

where he was going that he took the shaky stairs down
out of the bitter wind.

Firinne and Ceannann were awake now and watching
him, sitting together in their shelter. "As well we make
a fire," he said to them as he came down. "There's
wood enough, and Dubhain is off catching breakfast of
some sort."

"Aye," Ceannann agreed, and rose stiffly, limped
over and helped him break free some of the wood from
the caved-in tower, splintered and, under the rock, a little drier than the stairs.

"Would we'd had it last night," Caith said. "Will the
room down there vent enough through the doors, do
you think?"

"There is a hearth," Ceannann said, "if the chimney
still draws."

And Ceannann disappeared into the interior of the
only intact room, into which, Caith could see from
where he stood, either door cast dim daylight this morning, revealing its dusty and ordinary nature.

So, well, Caith thought cheerfully, a fire might dry
their clothes and give them a good start on the day, if
they could sit awhile in a closed space with a good
blaze in a fireplace, the Badbh take the witch and her
men: her hunters might smell the smoke and they might
see it against the sky, but warm clothes were worth the
risk—

So he thought, until he took his first step down into
that shadowy place, and then all cheerfulness drowned
in an oppression so thick it seemed to come in with the
breath.

Last night, coming through here with Dubhain, he
had felt that same smothering feeling, and wished them
immediately out of this room. But he saw Ceannann
paying it no heed at all, and pride held him still—if it
was a haunt, it was also daylight out, now; and if it was
left from the violent death here, why, one could look for
that in such places, but a comfortable fire usually kept

such ghosts quiet, at least until nightfall—a bit of bread or a sup of beer could do better than that to appease it, but, he thought, the ghost in this room would have to go unmollified until Dubhain's search turned up breakfast.

And there was indeed a fireplace, in which Ceannann was, fearless of haunts, peering up the chimney looking for bird's nests and fallen tiles.

So, Caith thought uneasily: it had been dark when Ceannann and Firinne had gotten here, too, which meant Ceannann had either spied the fireplace in the pitch-dark in this room last night or Ceannann did indeed know this place, as a ruin or before its fall—their father's castle, had Dubhain not said they claimed, last night?

Anything was a possibility, considering that there was Sidhe magic involved with them. He did not trust it. He did not wholly trust Ceannann, who had lied to him, and he had never forgotten that one lifting of the sword against his back. That—was a thing about a man never to forget, whatever his justifications.

No, he did not intend to fall into their deceptions, not twice, not considering what he had met at the other end of Gleann Fiain, not considering the powers at work at the other end of the loch, and not considering the feeling lingering in this room, which Ceannann blithely or conveniently ignored.

A little mad, Dubhain called their kind, and talked about the sun and lies. Dazzle and dance, Dubhain had said last night, and something about trickery.

A shadow dimmed the light from the inward door—he looked that direction in alarm; but it was only Firinne, venturing into the doorway and down the steps as Ceannann pronounced the chimney clear. Caith stood with arms folded and watched Ceannann set to work with the wood they had brought in, trying to break tinder and kindling from it, with a heavy stone from the damaged mason-work.

It did not break willingly, Sidhe magic or no. Heavy pounding produced a few splinters.

"It must have been green oak they used," he observed, remembering the weight of it when they had pulled it out of the rubble. "And a wee bit damp, even so." He was about to say his sword might split it, if he could get it on end.

"It's what we have," Ceannann said shortly—and, As ye will, man, Caith thought, resolving to hold his peace and his offers, hereafter, while the lad went at it in increasing temper. He was not for any quarrel with the Sidhe—but, Macha! the boy was a hot-headed fool.

Green oak for certain, he decided: it had cured hard as iron, it was not all that dry after the storm last night, and if the sun-born Sidhe had not a trick or two better than that with the fire-making, Ceannann was the only one going to get warmth out of that wood until Dubhain turned up. He wished Dubhain had not left him with them in the first place. He wished Dubhain would hurry back—the Sidhe loved best of all for a man to offer them a chance for mischief-making and the causing of pain, if not *his* Sidhe, then very easily this pair, if they *were* of the fair folk . . .

Fair *dark* ones, had Dubhain said, or had his wits been addled last night? It made no sense to him, except it wound round and round the thunderous memories of the lady of Dun Glas, and the old gods, the staring-eyed gods, that the young gods had sent down to hell . . .

But the young gods had not banished the Sidhe— whether all the Sidhe had existed then, or the tall fair folk, the Daoine Sidhe, Nuallan's sort, had come only with Lugh . . .

What were the sun-born kind? If there was the dark about these two, they were not Lugh's offspring. The Daoine Sidhe might be. But Dubhain's kind would not be Lugh's either, now that he thought about it.

Older, might the dark Sidhe be? Old as the old ones? Old as the god in the vines?

Fond of blood, they were.

He gave a twitch of his shoulders and looked toward the light of the door. He had felt much more sanguine about the morning and about them, until he came down here into this shadow, and he thought now he might be wiser to go back outside, with the wind and all, and wait for Dubhain. He could tell the pretty pair he was standing guard out there . . .

Stones rumbled and clattered. Firinne had pulled a piece of wood from the tumbled ruin in the corner of the room, and, having scared him *and* her brother, brought them firewood as dry as the dust she had raised, and brittle-looking to boot.

A helpful young woman, Caith thought, more forgivingly, and sent his darker thoughts sailing away, in favor of letting Firinne deal with her brother and his temper—persuading Ceannann to abandon his efforts on the oak for wood that split far more easily into kindling.

And should he offer his sword to the work now, after Ceannann had bashed himself red-faced and panting with the rock? Not he. He stood and watched, arms folded, while the larger kindling made a heap, the splinters went inside it, and Ceannann and Firinne, bending close to the fireplace to shelter their work, signed at him to move just so to block the wind. He did that, and watched, from his respectful and safe vantage, waiting, perhaps, for sun-born magic, better than bashing wood with rocks.

But for his magic, Ceannann pulled out a fire-kit from his pouch, flint and steel and an ordinary little packet of oiled willow-shreds, the lady's guards having evidently neglected to rob the lad of his personal possessions, while they were carrying him off. Caith was mildly disappointed, and mildly put off, wondering if helplessness was only the pretense they were maintaining for the mortal fool—an inconvenient pretense, if it was, and a slow and a chilly one, involving a great deal of whacking flint against steel, and a great deal more of

Ceannann's short temper. Mad, Dubhain had said of the sun-born folk, and he had seen nothing yet to say they were not both quite mad, and both quite ordinary.

Then he remembered the stone he wore, which might show him the truth of them. But he was not certain he ought to do that, either, before Dubhain came back . . . much as he doubted there was any Sidhe that would prefer to go cold and wet, when fire-making would be the natural gift of a sun-born kind, at least a man would think that was the case.

Sun-born *and* the watery kind? And dark, as well?

Dubhain had not made thorough sense on that point. But the pair seemed more feckless, still, than threatening, and meanwhile Ceannann, having gotten a wavering little flame out of the wood, seemed in far better humor, even pleased with himself. The fire was lit, Ceannann began feeding it, and Firinne got up, she said, to go after more of the dry wood.

"The other will burn, now," Caith said, forestalling her, though his real thought was that her tugging carelessly at timbers among the rocks in the corner, stones that had held their place for no few years, now, might loose a slide from above or below. He took up instead a piece of the damp oak from outside and handed it to Ceannann. Ceannann accepted it in fair good grace, even cheerfulness.

So he squatted down and passed Ceannann pieces from their small woodpile, if that kept the peace and kept Firinne from starting a rockslide in the ruins. Sidhe were all a touchy lot, by his experience, and he saw no usefulness at all in breaching whatever pretense at mortality they chose to keep. If they wished to do things in the manner of ordinary folk, that was well, let them, and be polite and pass the wood. They made their fire with ordinary flint and steel, as they had touched the iron bars, but that they could touch iron proved nothing, except that the dark in them must be stronger than the light, the same way that Dubhain could pick up his sword from the loch—albeit, granted, with no great desire to carry it in his stead.

So Ceannann could carry steel and work with it. And, now that he recalled the pots in the cottage, only one of which had been copper, Firinne could deal with an iron kettle, and an iron pot-hook, and had an ordinary knife for her bread, while m' lord Nuallan would not eat the bread an iron knife had cut.

Wards, the two of them had set up, against faery, was it? Yet had not recognized Dubhain's nature, when Dubhain had skipped, invited, through their doorway and those wards had fallen? Blind, the luck could make one . . . but against whom were the wards, and why had their breaking made it sure the house would fall to the lady's men, who certainly had nothing of the Sidhe about them that he could see?

Breaking the luck, he supposed, breaking the luck of the house might do it—but the luck against which the lady, she of Dun Glas, had been working all this time—and was the witch that weak, until, that night in the cellars of her keep, she put out her nets and, quite by chance, snared a lord of the Daoine Sidhe? He found difficulty believing that.

But certainly the luck about the pair was not all bad. And perhaps they were steadily working a magic that took all their effort, and they could not let it go out of them to make simple fires. He sat with arms crossed on his knees, thinking and wondering, and having no certain answers for his wonderings at all.

The little fire had been gold, bright gold . . . but with the adding of more splinters, it had gotten to be a very bright little fire, uncommonly hot, he was thinking, just as the fire went from gold to blue.

That was odd. Ceannann sat back and stopped feeding it, and Caith supposed he was finally about to see something remarkable . . . as the blue centered gold ran down the splinters like a rime of light. It met the dusty stone of the hearth, spread from there, and ran up the wood it touched and covered it . . .

Gold-rimmed blue became black-hearted then, and the black grew until the blue was only the outer shell of it. That, Caith thought, that was certainly unlike anything he had ever seen.

Then, at the heart of the black, a wisp like smoke appeared: where that white was, the wood turned quickly to red embers, and the water in the wood snapped and spat red sparks across the hearth. Caith jumped at the sting of an ember and scrambled up and back. So did Ceannann and Firinne.

The white wisp showed darknesses like eyes. Moragacht was Caith's immediate fear—he hovered in doubt whether they dared douse the fire, and what they could find to bring water enough, but the fire roared up until it consumed all the wood at once, wet and dry, alike. The death's-head in the smoke formed jaws and filled its empty sockets with the shadow of sullen eyes.

"Murderer," the apparition said—it seemed to look straight at him, and his own guilty soul said, fearfully, It knows. In the next instant the fire seemed to suck away all the warmth it had given him. The stifling closeness of the room seemed overwhelming, threatening. "Murderer," the ghost said louder, to the world at large, no longer speaking to him, he thought, and dared draw a breath again, chilled and shaken. Only the eyes of the apparition remained, a trail of fire that whirled suddenly about the walls and toward the rubble where Firinne had gotten the timbers. It wished to go up there, Caith thought, up the wreckage of stairs to a floor which no longer existed—he knew that without knowing why. But, frustrated and angry, finding no way up, it shot around the walls faster and faster, up and down and around and around, while they ducked and dodged—it was not them it was seeking, he trusted that, in the very instant it rushed at his face.

He stepped back, and spun around . . .

And was in the same room before the fireplace, on a rainy night like last night; but the fireplace showed no ruin, and there was a chair before the fire, two great hunting hounds, and a man sitting there he both loved and called lord. . . .

Ceannann mac Ceannann was this lord's name, of Gleann Fiain; while the name he called himself was Padraic, and the body he had a fiftyish, stout-limbed man's—chief of the household, he was, in this grim fortress which was not their proper home, nor a home they willingly occupied.

And this night Padraic, he, with a shapeless terror in his heart, devoutly wished them elsewhere and wished past choices unchosen.

He had a cup of the barley water in his hand, as he crossed the room. He offered it to his lord, and stood there leaning on the mantel while the mac Ceannann drank, musing darkly into the fire.

But as well as Padraic knew Ceannann mac Ceannann, as long as they had been close as brothers, he could not tell tonight what his lord was thinking, whether mourning over Fianna, gone and in her grave, or over choices already made, or brooding on the midnight and the choice to come, it being both the twins' birthday, and the same day a year ago that Fianna had died—laid to rest in a cairn of stones, in the lower hills, was the lady of Gleann Fiain, not the first or the last of the misfortunes of the house. On this day for fourteen years some new and terrible grief had come to them; and a new one was coming, neither of them had any doubt.

"Are they abed?" the mac Ceannann asked, touching Padriac's very thoughts.

"Aye," he said, quietly. "Siobhan is with them. She will not leave—or sleep, tonight."

"Good enough," the mac Ceannann said, and looked him in the eyes, resting his hand the while on the head of one of the two hounds. The mac Ceannann had aged sadly in the last bitter year, gone entirely grey, while the

lines that laughter had once made about his eyes had
become a map of sorrows by tonight's firelight. " 'T is
almost the hour," the mac Ceannann added softly.
"And a bitter thing, Padraic: she has saved us for the
last. —Was I wise?"

It was a terrible question. What could he say to his
lord? No? They had done the best they knew. Or should
he say, now, You should have quit this fight years ago?
It was too late for that, and the dead would not come
back again. He squatted down in front of the fire and
looked up at his lord, his hand on the worn wood of the
chair.

"You could not have surrendered. It would have done
no good. 'T was never only the child the woman
asked."

"And which child?" the mac Ceannann asked, to the
heart of the matter. "Can you say which is which,
Padraic, even yet?"

They talked awhile, in the dying of the fire, of small
things that would not stay in the mind of a living man,
while harm hovered all about the keep, harm from out
of the earth and out of the loch, and from all the dark
forces of the air . . . and both of them knew it was coming. There were few of them left now to defend the fortress, the scant remnant of the men and women of
Gleann Fiain, in the ruins of what had been a rich land.
The cattle and the sheep had died years ago. The farmers had fled, or were dead with their flocks, the year
that a great beast had come up from the loch, which
they had hunted to no avail. The airy hall of Dun Glas
had passed into the hands of their tormentor, and this
high, rough keep was the only refuge they could find
. . . built against the pirates, who had used to come up
the river from the sea, in their grandfathers' time.

Now it was the last refuge of the lord and the people
of Gleann Fiain, the twenty and nine of them remaining
who had not died by the beast, or the famines, or the
plagues.

"Bid the household all go," the mac Ceannann said. "I have a foreboding, Padraic, that tonight is the last. Bid them take whatever they need of the stores and go, tonight, before the hour."

"My lord," Padraic began. It was an argument ten years old at least. He would not go, the mac Ceannann knew that very well.

"At least the youngest should go," mac Ceannann pleaded with him. "At least the young lads, and their wives."

"And leave us old men defenseless?" he said, weary of the yearly argument. "And them dishonored?"

"To flee plague? To flee the things ye cannot see or feel? What defense, Padraic? What defense can there be?"

"What pride do you leave us, then? No, lord. They will not."

"Put it to them. Give them all the chance, I say. Before midnight, Padraic, swear it."

"I will," he said in a low voice, to give the lord mac Ceannann peace of mind in something, at least, for the hour that remained, but none of the lads would go, and none of the wives, either. They had sworn it in blood, the men, young and old, who had stayed around the mac Ceannann when the others fled; and if he gave the mac Ceannann's word to the lads that guarded the wall tonight, they would give him back glum stares and ask who else was going. They had done the same last year, before four of them had died.

And the women had sworn their own oath, or whatever women did when they banded together, and worked their women's magic against the witch, with singing that set a man's skin to itching. Them there was no persuading. They had no retreat: they were mortally engaged, in ways, he suspected, that no man could be.

The mac Ceannann drank until his head nodded, until the hand with the empty cup dropped from the chair arm. Padraic was satisfied, and, tenderly easing the cup from mac Ceannann's numb fingers before it clanged against the pavings, set it aside on the hearth and began his rounds that he made every night, checking all the doors and all the shutters, in the remote chance (for all the lads and lasses of the house were careful, and it could only be done, on this night, by magic) that someone had been forgetful.

When he had assured himself of the downstairs, he climbed the stairs, inspecting the tower shutters as he went, and, on the upper level, stopped by the twins' room—he put his head in, saw that shutter latched, that latch bound with rowan sprigs and barley knots. Their nurse was sitting there, the twins soundly sleeping, and he was about to go on his way, but old Siobhan got up from her bench, came quietly to him and whispered to him that she was cold, that she needed to get another blanket from the chest in her room ... what could a man say? It was a fearsome station the old woman kept, braiding her barley strands and muttering to forces a man did not deal with. What wonder she might wish a comfort tonight of all nights? "Watch them," she asked him, and, feeling the chill in the room himself, he agreed.

"But hurry about it," he warned her. "I'm on my rounds."

"Aye," Siobhan said: his own mother's cousin, the old lady was, withered and stern and utterly devoted— the one who truly grieved for Fianna tonight, he thought, more than the mac Ceannann could, the truth be known. Aunt Siobhan had been Fianna's nurse, and now the twin's guardian, and mourning tonight, and working her angry, women's magic, her little knots and mutterings ... that had not saved Fianna from her folly, or her death.

Fianna's troubles were at an end, one could hope that much for the lady, charitably, at least, and try to feel no anger while their own troubles spun down to the end—

and all of it, the whole damned business for the sake of Fianna and of the twins lying in their beds.

Their fourteenth year, Padraic thought with unease, and look at them, alike as mirrors of each other, and them still so close it set a man's teeth on edge. Ask the one and the other might answer. They talked in turn, one finishing the thought the other had begun. Sibs did such things, his nephews, rest them, had done it, and there had never been two less fey lads than those two born in Gleann Fiain—but this pair was such that one would lift his head suddenly and the other, without looking, would answer an unasked question of some third person in the room. They would not by any persuasion be parted ... even newborn, they had screamed themselves sick when Siobhan put them in separate cribs. Siobhan had given in to have peace, and, against his own opinions, and little by little over the years, the whole house had surrendered to them, the whole of Gleann Fiain had surrendered their lives to the damnable bargain Fianna had made to get them—made, and broken, and defended them with charms and spells. As children, neither twin would let the other out of sight, if they were brought out of doors, and if by chance one strayed, the other followed at a run, or if held from following, went mad with fright, and the other raced back to comfort the twin.

Now, at fourteen years, and it long since causing talk among the last loyal servants, they slept each night in each other's arms, two heads together on the pillow, fair hair mingled, their very breath in unison.

That they were fey went without saying: fey, apparently more Sighted than was comfortable for anyone to be, and it was with a dose of whiskey and honey they were sleeping tonight, if he could rely on Siobhan's tricks, for the twins well understood the hour and the day, if they had had no Sight at all to trouble them—they missed their mother, one could pity them in that, and all their birthdays ended full of death and evil.

Would that, Padraic thought, standing there at the foot of the bed, would that lady Fianna had remained barren, and would that the mac Ceannann had never had a son, or a daughter, or whichever, if either, the Daghda help them, was lawfully his: or would the twins were both of them in hell, before they came to this. Fianna had lost two babes, and bargained with a wise-woman to have the twins, that was what Siobhan had maintained, but what Fianna had confessed to her husband, the mac Ceannann had never told even to him. Women's magic—magic with the Sidhe, the women had said, some sort of women's doings in an ancient grove down by the loch, into which no man could inquire.

Fianna had borne the twins, then, in due course, and, contrary to the men's natural expectations, the women of the house had gone about that day close-mouthed and grim, and gone down to the scullery and the kitchens to gossip about the birthing. The women had all known something their lord should have known that day, that had been certain at the time, but their law was something else, and uncatchable. A man could only surmise that in some way Fianna had broken faith with them, or betrayed them, or offended their sensibilities, the Daghda might know, but no man had understood the offense, then. No *man* understood now, but Siobhan kept making her barley knots and muttering to herself. . . .

And that night the twins were born, the wise-woman the women talked about had turned up at the gates, all cloaked in costly black and claiming her choice of the twins . . . Fianna had gone white as a fish's belly and sworn she knew nothing at all of any such woman—had sworn by Lugh and by Danu that she had made no such bargain.

While all the women gathered in angry whisperings and mutterings among themselves—fear had run through the scullery and through the upstairs halls, and the women sent dark, fearful looks at Fianna's back that hour, he had seen it, every man in the house had seen it: in the mac Ceannann's silence . . . what could a man do?

If perhaps the gate-guard had been more courteous, if perhaps the mac Ceannann had listened then to the whispering among the women—but, no, the mac Ceannann had taken Fianna at her word and bidden the lad at the gate give a short answer to the woman at the gates—besides a loaf of bread and the pity one might give the mad.

That very night the guard, a young man, had fallen dead at his post with no mark on him.

And the women had answered no husbands' nor fathers' questions, not for threats, not for beatings, not for the magic the men made . . . as soon talk to the stones of the walls.

Came the twins' first birthday, came the witch to ask her due, and this time Fianna was contrite, at least toward the witch, and sent word to the gate, begging to be excused of the bargain she had made. But the witch was off in a fury and Fianna began to confess things and rites to her husband then only some of which Padraic had heard, the Daghda save them from reckless women. The mac Ceannann heard her privily, and to this day would not tell him everything, only that he forgave Fianna whatever she had done, and loved the twins so much he said he could not decide, himself, either: how could he let the witch choose one, when he could not?

The third year the witch came back. The mac Ceannann had met the witch at the gate himself, offered her wide lands and herds and his protection if she would give up her claim to the child—but she would not agree, and stalked away along the loch, until the woods swallowed her up, and a flight of ravens went up from it.

That night the ewes all died, and the bleating of orphaned lambs was pitiful all across Gleann Fiain.

The Daghda save them all, so innocent the twins looked, now, sleeping—

If they never had been born, he thought. *If* he had followed Fianna and the women into the woods that night. If the mac Ceannann had only honored his wife's unholy bargain and not fallen into Fianna's wrongdoing himself, denying what Fianna had sworn, foul as it was. . . .

All of these things, he thought, while Siobhan delayed over-long and longer about fetching the blanket, and he paced the floor and grew increasingly uneasy, thinking of his uncompleted rounds.

The lads on the gates and on the wall were not careless. No one would take chances this night of all nights. Everything was shut. If something wanted guarding, it slept in this room, in this bed. . . .

Something banged, downstairs. Fear leapt up in him. That would be her. He had to go down to the mac Ceannann. He had to be before his lord in dealing with the witch—it was Feargus and mac Guigan on the lower door, but the mac Ceannann might well awake at that thump and take matters in his own hands; and by the gods, he meant this time to part the witch from her head.

Something splintered. He was across the room in two strides and jerked the door open as the twins started awake, calling out, "Uncle Padraic!"

He looked back, his shoulders against the open door, as the twins scrambled from their bed. "Stay inside!" he bade them, and shouted down the hall for Siobhan, but the old woman was already running as fast as she could, the blanket left lying in the hall. The twins ran and clung to him in fright, but he shoved them into Siobhan's care and ran down the hall, and down the wooden stairs as fast as his legs could carry him—

The lower door splintered—a darkness flooded into the hall, overpowering the fire. It surged across the floor and toward the stairs, all shadow and teeth . . .

"Lord!" he shouted, drawing his sword—but the stairs broke, swept from under him, and the beast struck out in every direction at once, splintering wood, scattering fire, crazed with the killing, as men rushed in and died.

This much he saw, in the dark and the ruin, before his life went—

"Padraic?" Firinne was asking urgently. "Is it Padraic?"

He did not know where he was. He was murdered here, in this room, he was a murderer, himself, from Gleann Teile: he was old and young, angry and crazed, and the next breath would not come into him, the beast had torn out his throat . . .

"The fire, the fire," Firinne cried, and dived toward it, caught up a burning piece of wood in her bare hand and whipped it into her lap, smothering the ember with her skirts, bent in pain, and the smell of burned cloth was in the air—while of the fire there was left only a heap of glowing embers, giving off an ordinary red glow and an ordinary heat.

Suddenly there was breath to be had in the room, and Caith drew in what he could—but he had *been* Padraic, he had died in this place, he had seen, with his dying sight, his lord die, and from a heart more loyal and more giving than his own . . .

Of that came the anger, the consuming anger, that entangled with his own rage at all masters, and the one he served . . . he did not know what to think, or understand what raged through him. It hurt to know that great a goodness did exist, and had died here, all for nothing, all for a senseless woman's madness . . .

"Oh, Firinne!" Ceannann whispered, and Firinne bit her lip as Ceannann unfolded her seared palm, but she shook off his help, seeming grimly triumphant with the prize she had for her pain—a charred splinter, a piece of the inside stairs, saved from the burning.

A chill went down Caith's back. In that instant he remembered women's magic, he remembered the stairs buckling under him; and the mac Ceannann's death, ripped limb from limb, the mac Ceannann had been, and last of all, the beast came to Padraic . . .

"Oh, ho!" Dubhain said cheerfully, a sudden shadow in the doorway. He skipped barefoot down the stone steps, a brace of hares dangling broken-necked from his hand. "Breakfast! And a fire all down to coals. Here's quick work!"

Chapter
Seven

Dubhain proposed to cook breakfast over those same coals—not a breakfast that at all appealed, considering the nature of the fire, and what had happened in this room, Caith thought, but, on a second consideration of his weak knees and hollow stomach, the witch's cauldron would not disgust him this morning, if porridge came out of it. The sun had followed Dubhain through the doorway, and when one thought of food, . . . there followed close upon that thought an intimate knowledge of the ruin, and the cellars.

"One wonders if it was plundered, at all," Caith murmured, putting practical banditry to the fore: if there was horror left in this place, he was surely on fair speaking terms with Padraic, at least; and Dubhain was back, to deal with the other ghosts that might lurk about.

While, below, if the lower stairs were intact, he had a curiously vivid recollection of the scullery, the larder, all the lower portion of the fortress, where, considering the hall had had no survivors to scavenge it, nor invaders to loot it . . . there might well be jars and well-kept stores such as three and four and even seven years would not have spoiled—flour for cakes, and salt, and honey . . . those might not have lasted, granted, unless

159

the stoppers were tight, but blankets were possible, and bowls and pots and pans ...

Dubhain had squatted down and, with a small flint blade from his pouch, set to work on his catch, Ceannann was consoling Firinne for her burns in the light of the far doorway, and no one paid attention to him as he rose, dusted off his hands, and walked back where the stairs had stood.

The downward course did look intact. The inside was dark, but not a disturbing dark, so long as Dubhain was within hail. He surveyed the possibilities and the hazards of the pile, as the stones were resting, and heaved a timber aside.

Stones shifted and rolled. A shattered skull rolled out from the heap of rubble. That gave him a queasy feeling, when he realized it must be Padraic's; but he squatted down and shoved it back decently under the pile of timbers and rubble that partially filled the corner, if a felon's touch counted for a burial, and the touch of a caring hand. Immediately the place did feel better, but with Padraic's dying fresh in mind and memory, he became a little less eager to go below and search the dark down there, stirring up ... the gods knew what.

"What are you after?" Ceannann asked, at his back, and his heart skipped a beat.

"Oh, a barrel of this or that." He did not like Ceannann at his back, where he was perched. He could not say why, he only looked across the room, to the fire. "Dubhain, leave me the skinning, here's work your eyes are apt for, you dark-loving creature. The storerooms are below. Would there be whiskey, d' ye think?"

"Och, now," Dubhain said, and immediately came over, bloody-handed as he was, and peered down into the lower stairway, before he started down.

"It was the cellars," Ceannann said doubtfully, as Dubhain nimbly picked his way through the ruin of tumbled stone and splintered wood. "There were two rooms beyond."

"Are yet," Dubhain's voice floated up to them, echoey and chancey. Stone crashed. "Well, well."

"The roof might cave in," Ceannann fretted. "Tell him be careful."

"Be about the skinning, lad, d' you know how?" A lord's son Ceannann might be, but they had a superfluity of lords' sons and daughters in present company, and, starved and weak-kneed as he was, the hares Dubhain had already brought were a surety, and he was more interested in what Dubhain might turn up below, considering the night he had just spent, and the wet clothes he was sitting in on this windy mountain-top. "One would be the store-room," he called down to Dubhain, "and the other the scullery, with a door leading out to a stairs down to the spring. Ye might get some light on the matter."

"Och, ye were fixing our breakfast, pretty Caith, not giving advice, were ye, and whence d' ye know such things?"

"A passing breeze told me." His legs were shivering under him. He shifted to squat on the verge of the stairway, arms on knees. "It also says there might be a blanket or the like down there, if there was no plundering, and who would do that, with the folk of Gleann Fiain all in the beast's belly?"

"Who indeed? I may hae found a door here." Dubhain's voice was faint and far. "Oh-ho!"

Came a dreadful crash and rattle of stones. Caith flinched for fear of the entire floor going. A cloud of dust rose out of the cellar. But there was dusty sunlight in the depths then, and Dubhain popped into view, a shadow in the grey light, his eyes glowing faintest red.

"The bones of dead men," said Dubhain, "and the strewing of grain about, but the mice hae had a' that. Was there aught else ye said ye'd be wanting?"

Mice and moths. Against those marauders no shelves were high enough, and barrels and burlap were no defense. He had not thought of them, and he was disappointed in his hopes. But Dubhain vanished again and in a moment skipped up on the littered steps to hand him up a white rock the size of two fists. Salt, by the sticky feel of it. That was welcome. "The mice and the foxes hae had a share," Dubhain said, "but we hae the last lump. Hold a bit."

"Something to carry the thing in, Dubhain, sweet Dubhain. What else?"

"A mort of empty barrels. The wee pirates hae had a taste for barley."

"Cloth, then. A blanket. A bit of rope."

"Nay, rope there is, but ye would nae trust it, man. Ah!" Dubhain came back into view and handed him up a nest of shallow copper pans. That was a prize. They cooked their suppers on makeshift spits, and never had had a plate or a pan for boiling.

"Porridge we can have, when we find some farmer's field. But blankets, pretty Dubhain. Sacks. Rags. Something against the cold."

"Against the cold, is 't?"

"Aye," he said sharply, teeth chattering, and *felt* cold of a sudden, a chill down his backbone which had nothing to do with the wind between the two doors. He turned his head and saw Ceannann at the coals, cooking their breakfast as if he felt nothing, and Firinne in the inner doorway. But his hair prickled, and he shivered, hearing a small crash below. "Dubhain, do ye feel anything? I'm not liking the feel here, Dubhain."

A few more rattles came from below.

"More dead men's bones," said Dubhain. "Nae few souls hae perished here."

"Leave them!" There was a very bad feeling to the room of a sudden, not Padraic, he thought, but something slower to wake and far, far more dangerous. "Dubhain, get up here!"

Dubhain's shadow appeared in the milky light below, and Dubhain's eyes glowed like coals, disquieting as the feeling of something in the room with them. And never yet had the twins seemed to notice it.

"Dubhain, my friend, come upstairs, will ye, quietly, the while?" The sight of Ceannann and Firinne oblivious to the cold spot in the room lent him no comfort at all—like two children they were, absorbed in their own doings, while this thing prowled the margins of the room, more aware by the instant. Whatever it was, it was nothing of the light, either moon or sun, and he was not altogether certain Dubhain was safe from it, as Dubhain quietly came up from below and laid something on the dusty floor.

"Och," said Dubhain, "the blood, the blood hae waked it. It was stirring about last night, I felt it, and the pretty ones did, and we preferred the rain in the courtyard. But by day, . . . well, 't is quieter. Dinnae provoke it, and keep an eye on our pretty birds the while."

At which the feckless wight dived below.

"Dubhain!" Caith whispered furiously. But Dubhain had left a pile of moth-eaten cloth beside the bowls, a blanket, it looked to be, and he glanced back to the room at large, torn between his misgivings toward the ghost and the prospect of warmth from the draft Dubhain had started with his opening of the lower door.

With half an eye to the room and the twins, he shook out the grey blanket . . . full of holes it was, but it held together when he flung the dusty thing about him. In a while more he was shivering violently, the way a man would, who had passed beyond chill and begun to warm up again. Meanwhile Dubhain clattered and thumped about in the cellar like a good haunt, and whatever had stirred to wakefulness in the ruin seemed to have no possessiveness at least about the blanket—which in good chivalry ought to go to Firinne, he grudgingly supposed; or to the boy, Firinne having her abundance of skirts and petticoats to keep her warmer than either of them.

But in the miles and the weather a man turned selfish with the necessities, and chivalry got very much to the rear of him. He thought: Turn about with the boy at best, once they left the fire; and he was, even so, grudging that charity with their only blanket, when a thundering slide of stones happened below and whatever lurked hereabouts sent a chill through the air.

"What was that?" Firinne asked, looking anxiously in his direction.

"It's all right," he said. There was a sudden stillness in the room it was hard to break, a presence that had almost settled to sleep again, and now stirred to wakefulness.

Dubhain came thumping up the steps on bare feet, his arms loaded with blankets, a jug hooked by his fingers, and a coil of rotten, moldering rope over his shoulder. "Breakfast," Dubhain said cheerfully. "And I hae stolen all the best fra' the moths and dispossessed a mouse or two fra' the pantry. They could nae gnaw through the pots, me darlin's. Thank me properly."

"I'll kiss you myself, ye rascal, if that jug's what I think."

"Two more such below, the falling shelf did for the rest." Dubhain carried his prizes over to the coals, well pleased with himself, and squatted down and pried the crockery stopper, that mice had been at, but they had had no luck. Dubhain had a swig of the contents and a grin was on his face as he offered it with a bow to Firinne.

So it went around, Firinne to Ceannann, and last to him. It was passable good whiskey the lord had had in store, thank the Badhb for stout crockery. He poured a little in the dust, for Padraic, and for ... whatever it was, for its good will if it owned any toward the living.

The spot dried to dust as it hit. He poured a bit more and it vanished in the same way.

And a third time. Three was a lucky number.

At least one felt one could breathe in the room, now,

and Firinne heaved a sigh. So did Ceannann. So did Dubhain.

"A polite ghost," Dubhain said, because he could *not* hold his peace.

"Hush! forbear." He took his portion of their breakfast, brushed ash from it—with no spit and no pan when they had started their cooking, it was make do and be thankful for it. And a far better breakfast than Nuallan was having this morning, he congratulated himself, picking well-done meat from the bone. What with the whiskey, and the blanket about him, and the heat from the coals drying his clothes and his shoes, he was feeling far more sanguine about their escape.

But what they should do, now, whether to escape the glen or whether, as he had far rather do, considering the aches he had waked with, they should tuck down in this ruin a few days and catch their breaths, he had had no word from Dubhain—and he preferred Dubhain's advice, with the Sidhe in question.

"So where now, Dubhain?" he asked, leaning on his elbow. "What now?"

"Why, we go on as we were," Dubhain said, flipping a bone into the coals. It hissed, and burned briefly, and went to ash. A man could not but stare at that, and not feel so comfortable reclining there.

"Our one father," said Firinne, "died here."

"But our other," said Ceannann, "is still to find."

"Two fathers," Caith said, as the Padraic-memories stirred up in him uncomfortably vivid, of *draiocht*, and bastardy.

"Ye'd tell us, perhaps," Dubhain said, "how this wonder came to be." He wrenched off another joint. Crack. "And what help it might be to the Sidhe lord we hae left in less pleasant lodgings last night—if Herself hae not made breakfast of him. Is 't her doing that this place is in ruins?"

"Aye," Ceannann said.

"And born of the Sidhe," Caith said, straight to the

point, since Dubhain was here to deal with the consequences. "—Are you not?" But Padraic had believed only one of them was Sidhe. "Twins, you are."

"Twins." Firinne broke her silence. "With different fathers."

He regarded her doubtfully, although Padraic had known that: it fit that memory like a key in a lock . . . but there was so much no one had known.

"It is truth," said Firinne.

"What else is truth?" Caith asked. "Twins, well. But what more? What ought friends of yours to know, if we made common cause against this lady of Dun Glas? You slept—upstairs in this keep the night it came down. And why? What was the quarrel with her?"

A midnight rite in the hills, Padraic's recollection was; women's rites, women's powers. Most uneasily, Caith remembered a sad, frightened woman he had never met.

"Our mother," Ceannann said, "our mother was the lady of Gleann Fiain, when we lived in Dun Glas. She wished to have a child, and she went to the spring in the mountains . . ."

"Are we to another ballad?" Caith said, his skin prickling. "The last was the harper. Were you ever a harper?"

"No," Ceannann admitted, and looked into the fire.

"Now, see," said Dubhain. "Ye do offend the man. Ye hae such a mortal lack of grace. —Pray go on, young gentleman, and what did the lady do?"

"The lady who lived by the spring—" They never called the name of Moragacht when they could avoid it; and with a witch or a power, in Caith's experience, there was every good reason to be careful. "A wisewoman was all she seemed to be, at least as I heard the tale; and she did live by the spring." This with a scowl—but it fit no memory of Padraic's, and Caith raised a brow. "Our mother bargained with her to have a child. She let the lady weave an enchantment over her, and she did everything that the lady said."

"Wi' what bargain?" Dubhain asked. "There maun always be a bargain in such affairs."

"There was," Ceannann said. "The witch said our mother would bear twins, and that the witch would choose one for herself on the night we were born."

"Foolish woman," said Dubhain with a shake of his head, and Ceannann frowned.

"She wished to have a child," said Ceannann. "She thought that she could lose one for the sake of the other she would keep. She never planned for our father to know."

"But when we grew in her," Firinne said, breaking her silence, "she regretted what she had done." A poke at the coals with a rabbit bone. Sparks went up like stars, and the end of the bone went to ash. She dropped it all into the coals and drew back her hand in haste. "It was a night magic; and she had to have a lover."

"Of the witch's choosing."

Firinne nodded, her eyes downcast, and she lifted a shoulder in a shrug. "And once it was done, you know, then—it was too late to change the bargain."

"Our mother," Ceannann broke in, "was not a stupid woman. She must have been under a spell from the time she went up to the spring. And the way it was, she had sworn to the witch that she could make her *choice* of us; if the witch took the mortal one of us, it would put her husband's true child in the witch's hands and a selkie-child on the throne of Fiain."

"A selkie," Caith said, with a feeling of cold down his back, and a stir of longing. A power of the sea, that was—the beloved sea. But Dubhain moved uneasily.

"That was the bargain she made," said Firinne, never looking at him, never acknowledging the dire and wonderful nature of the creature. "That was the lover she had, only one night. Only once."

"That does often suffice," said Dubhain.

"Behave," said Caith. "Go on, lass."

"When we were born, and the witch came to make her choice, our mother confessed to our father what she'd bargained with the witch, and that the witch was promised one of us. But she didn't tell him about the selkie-lover. She never told anybody that but the women who knew it already."

"And you," Caith said.

"And us, when we were twelve."

"The witch came back every year to ask," said Ceannann. "But our father wouldn't give us up. And the sheep all died. Our father hired a priest to set wards about us and all about the loch. But every year something worse would happen, until finally the beast came, and we had to move out of Dun Glas."

"The priest?" Dubhain asked.

"He died."

"She should ne'er hae broken an oath to that lady," Dubhain said with a shake of his head. "It gave her all manner of power against ye. —That is nae common witch, ye maun know."

"We do know," said Ceannann. "We do, that."

"So you lost Dun Glas and you came here," Caith said. "You refurbished this old place, and you held out—how long?"

"Till our fourteenth winter. The priest died in our eleventh. And the most of the people in the twelfth. And our mother in the thirteenth. In the fourteenth, she killed our father and all the rest, and ruined the hall here."

"Twice seven years, seven for each of ye," said Dubhain. "That was a great spell the witch was working, and a great protection ye must have had."'

"How did you escape?" Caith asked, and sat up. Padraic's memories did not extend beyond the beast's foray in this room, and they were too vivid yet, a fast-moving shadow full of claws and teeth.

"One of us," said Firinne, "took the other to safety."

"By magic," Caith said, recalling the twins in their bed, inseparable; and by experience in the affairs of the Sidhe, he had a niggling suspicion there was much more than something unnatural in it.

"Aye," said Ceannann.

"Escaped where? To that cottage?"

"Aye."

Padraic's memories were a momentary blackness. And pain, oh, yes, pain. "And that cottage was defense enough—for how many years? You've more than fourteen winters."

"Twenty and one."

"Anaither seven," Dubhain said under his breath.

"She never came," said Firinne. "We found the sheep and the goats gone wild. The beast found us, but by that time we had our wards set, and she could not get so much as our flock."

"Very strong, those wards were," said Dubhain. "I could nae pass them, meself—excepting your hospitality."

"And why?" Ceannann asked angrily, in the way of a resentment put away but never forgotten. "What had we done that you had to break our defenses? We had done no wrong to the witch, and she had nothing in us to take hold of but a promise we had not made for ourselves. And what was that to you?"

Caith shrugged. "With your beast on my heels, young sir, I ran. And that was not my choosing. What the Sidhe chose to do, and why, you've only to look at Dun Glas. That is a powerful witch, who can hold *him* against his will."

"But none of it would have happened if you hadn't come there," Firinne said. "None of it. And it went wrong, everything went wrong. . . ."

"Ye did nae ask, lass," said Dubhain, "*which* power drew us to your door."

For some blind reason he had not even thought of

that possibility, and the thought was like a blow to the stomach.

Besides . . . a small something went bump at the back of his memory and tumbled into place when Dubhain said what he had said.

"*I've* a question," Caith said. "The witch's men had no time to ride out from Dun Glas and attack you *after* we came down into the glen. It's much too far. Either they came from closer, or they started earlier. And how did the witch know the wards would be down?"

"She would," said Ceannann, "if you were hers."

Caith fixed him with a cold stare. "If that were her treatment of her own, man, I've seen better. And thanks to your driving us off your land, where we might have saved us all a deal of trouble, one of the bright Sidhe is in her hands, our particular lord of the Sidhe, in which we have a pressing interest—"

"Please," said Firinne.

He could not say why he took fire so readily with Ceannann. His temper had led him astray so many times, and he smothered it.

"I meant," Ceannann said hotly, "if she'd sent you and you not known. That could happen, man. I didn't call you a liar."

"Hoosht, now," said Dubhain. "Ye two, like two cocks in a henyard . . ."

"Ceannann, please," said Firinne, laying a hand on his arm, and Caith looked down at his hands, found the meeting of thumb and first finger smoother than they ought to be, and wondered about that rather than killing Ceannann. There was the red, healed brand of a rose on either finger, itching like mortal sin at the moment, and he shut his fist to take away the sight, thinking suddenly of the central question, the thing Padraic had not known and regarding which they had deceived even Dubhain:

"The truth," he asked of Firinne. "Which of you is the selkie?"

"I am," said Firinne; "I am," said Ceannann.

Temper rose up, quick and continually frustrated. "Has either of you ever once told the truth?"

Their brows furrowed, and Ceannann looked down rather than meet his eyes. "Truth . . . we aren't sure."

"Not sure, man!"

"So perhaps the witch herself can't tell," Firinne said.

"And can't separate you. Is that a fact?"

A wincing. A glance down at her hands. "Perhaps."

"Someone hae laid it on them, perhaps." Dubhain sat, chin on fist, listening, with small movements of his almost-brown eyes. "Perhaps before they were born. I feel the strength in the bond o' these two, but I get nae sense at all about the source."

A geas so strong the twins themselves might not overcome its command to keep the secret, or even know their own natures? He was far from convinced, and slid a glance toward Dubhain, wondering how far a Sidhe gave it credence. "Could *you* not know what you are?"

"Och, man, magic is such a troubled pot. Ye stir a mother's desire into it, ye stir in a witch's schemes, and a priest of some power's counter-workings, and ye cannae say what kind of stew may come fra' out of it . . . nae thing convenient for the mother or the witch, by the look of this hall—" Dubhain's eyes made a circuit of the ceiling, and flicked back to him, faintly red in his shadowed face; last, then, to the twins, with a cynic look. "And shall we go and ask the selkie, now? This is the father ye wish to find?"

"We cannot defeat her ourselves," Ceannann said, "the two of us, or even yourself, m' lord Sidhe."

"M' lord, I?" Came a little lifting of Dubhain's brows, the tweak of a wicked grin. "Och, now, such a polite young man."

"He doesn't know you," Caith said darkly, disturbed at this sudden merriment. He wanted a word with Dubhain, aside from them. He saw an amusement he did not like.

"We need your help," Firinne said in a small voice.

"It's power she's after, power to take and to have and to have more. If she takes power from him . . ." A little tremor came into Firinne's voice, and she lifted her hands and let them fall. "I don't know what in the world might prevent her, then, except our father, or yourself. M' lord Sidhe, can *you* not find him? Can you not tell the Sidhe what happened in this glen, can you not—?"

"Oh, they surely know," Dubhain said. "The halls of hell do *know* what happened, lass. The question is what the Sidhe may do about it. —D' ye know your father? Hae ye ever met him?"

Said Ceannann, in Firinne's silence, "Our mother never saw him after."

"Well," Caith said, settling back upon his elbow with a sigh. "Well, but we have no help else, if you can find him, if you can call him, whatever it is you can do."

"Perhaps we have the calling of him," Ceannann said. "But our mother thought not. We—"

A step scuffed, outside, in the daylight. Caith stayed a move of his own and held his breath, saw Ceannann and Firinne and Dubhain in the same blink glance toward the door, before he rolled onto his knee, for deeper shadows . . .

The white skulls of two hares shone almost under his hand. They were the hides and whole heads Dubhain had cut off and tossed aside. And in the few moments as they talked something had gnawed them almost clean, bits of flesh still clinging to bone bright as milky glass.

Revulsion hit his stomach. He drew his hand back and scrambled to his feet as he heard a step just outside the door, and while he was drawing his sword, a man's shadow was on the edge of the threshold, a man who must have smelled the smoke, and whose shadow grew an arm and a sword the instant before the man himself rushed the entrance.

"No!" Firinne cried, embracing Ceannann, and,

sword in hand, Caith could not draw a breath to move, the presence in the room grew so intense and so violent.

The intruder screamed and fell backward in his tracks—limp before he hit the stone, arms and legs twitching loosely as if an unseen pack of wolves were tearing at the corpse. Caith caught himself and breathed the breath he could finally find. Cold, god, he was cold, and Dubhain was grabbing at his arm and shoving the twins toward the cellar stairs on the other side of the room.

Caith let himself be drawn along past the doorway, where no other fool showed at all; and, he could not help it, he glanced down at the twitching corpse. A curious white spot gleamed and widened at its forehead, bone, the flesh being eaten away as if teeth were gnawing it with frenzied speed.

The mastiff dogs flashed into his mind, lying by mac Ceannann's chair, tame to his hand; but it was not only the dogs, it was . . .

A yank at his wrist hauled him in Dubhain's wake, down the cellar stairs into the grey, dusty daylight, and through the rubbled ruin of the scullery, toward that clear view of sky.

But Dubhain dived back inside again, and, fearing Dubhain was going back to fight the creature, Caith grabbed at him.

In vain. "Fool!" he began to say, but Dubhain snatched up a jug from the floor inside and came back in a great hurry.

They fled out the door onto the narrow ledge and a sudden halt, over a view straight off the side of the mountain and into the sky.

It was Dubhain's snatch at his shirt that prevented him going right off the step, with Ceannann and Firinne already on the downward slant, sharply to the left, and his heart suddenly laboring to catch up to the rest of him.

"Fool, *I*?" said Dubhain, and flung an arm about his,

the jug handle caught in a finger, the two of them walking like lovers downhill, his legs shaking so now he might have fallen down in a heap. "Stand and gawk, will ye? Linger to bid the haunt good mornin'?"

"The dogs," was all he could say, between breaths and trying to keep his feet under him. Sweat was running in his eyes and he was chilled through. Dubhain laughed wickedly and shook at him as they walked.

"Hoosht, now, afraid of the dark, are ye?"

"It was the dogs, it was something else . . . in it . . . too . . ."

"The father. The father, the lord, an angry, angry spirit . . ."

Padraic had tried to tell him something that was still rattling around in his skull, something Padraic was ashamed to think, but that was it, he thought, all that anger and all that madness was the mac Ceannann . . . that, the witch had left of him.

"Only he would not . . . kill the twins . . . but any creature else . . ." Breath failed. Vision almost did. His ankles turned on the rocky track and he would have gone down in a faint, if Dubhain had not had an arm around him. As it was, Dubhain hoisted him up with a roll of his head and the sky and the mountain steep swinging giddily in his vision. He had his feet under him at least, and a death-grip on Dubhain's shirt, Dubhain giving a little dance step and laughing.

" 'T is light on your feet ye are, me darlin' Caith."

"Aye." He was too exhausted to quarrel with the wretch, he was only thinking of getting down the mountainside without falling down it. He saw Firinne and Ceannann ahead of them, two heads and one grey blanket . . . which he had not. "Oh, damn it to hell, I left the blankets . . ."

"Ah, well," said Dubhain, "I provide for ye and look how ye care for things . . ."

"There had to be . . . another man . . ."

"Chary of that door, he'd be."

"Going around . . ." He tried to look over his shoulder to see, and Dubhain swung them around, balancing on one foot above a sheer drop, that was Dubhain: but he was not even thinking of falling, he was looking up at their last view of the face of the keep for a while, the steep, rubbled shoulder of the hill about to come between them and that doorway. Whether anyone was coming around the keep, it was already too late to see, and Dubhain spun them around again as his leaning almost pulled him over.

Almost. The wretch. "There could be somebody," Caith said, and caught a whole breath, but his legs were no better: the cold was leaving his limbs, but only enough to let him know where his feet were. "I couldn't see."

"Nae riders on this slope, at least," said Dubhain briskly. "A horse could nae do 't."

"Fools would *wish* to do it." He was looking down into the shadowed deep of the glen, the sun not yet over the mountains, but it came past the mountain shoulder and made Loch Fiain a lying sheet of silver far, far below; and the forward thrusts of the mountain on the other side a velvet heathery orange and purple. A man could think it was a safe place. The air was rain-washed and clean. With a breakfast in him and warmed by a fire, however unwholesome, and with the smell of the clean air, a man could think not all the world had gone to dark and mud . . . if he did not remember that the horror up above their backs existed here because of Moragacht and the powers that she called.

A man could think, if the twins had gotten themselves away as they claimed, the twins had a luck about them, and it had struck twice, counting that they were free this morning, and a man was dead, and the lord Nuallan stood in their place in m' lady's prison, with the cauldron and all.

"Let be, let me walk," he said: he had caught breath enough, and warmed his limbs at least enough not to fall down the mountain, and he was off his balance and at the mercy of Dubhain's inconstant humor as he was, with Dubhain's arm between him and a fall to the loch.

"Ye'll break your neck, my prince."

"Rather the witch's. I'll live so long." He wished then he had not said it. Some sayings hit the air and hung there, fraught with meaning a wicked power could take and use, but it was true, now, that he had to go back to Dun Glas, it became true that moment that he admitted the Necessity.

Geas. A little one now, but on his life, he had made that pact with the Sidhe, and had second thoughts about trusting his own legs, since his wit showed itself none so keen.

Of course that was the moment Dubhain let him go, and he staggered a downward step on uneven rock, on the narrow boundary of earth and empty air.

That would wake a man and start his heart to beating.

chapter
eight

HEATHER GREW MORE frequent, in small tough clumps, clinging among the stones. The rain-fed spring Caith had searched for so desperately in the night was here, cutting its way into barren rock, a white thread that plunged a long, dizzy distance down the steep, toward its soiling in the loch.

Here the twins turned aside from their course across the mountain shoulder, and took the steep, slow descent, climbing from one rock down to the next.

"What are they doing?" Caith asked. The twins must be following some childhood path, some foolhardy short-cut which grown men were hard put to follow. "What are you doing?" he called out to the pair some little distance ahead of them and down a tumble of boulders. "Is there something we're looking for?"

Ceannann steadied Firinne as she jumped down to him, from a cascade of rocks, and Ceannann did not answer him.

"Surly, now," Caith muttered, but Dubhain, squatting by him, hopped down on the same course, jug and all, and landed and spun about with a skirl of his kilts.

"I'll catch ye, man, 't is no great bother. Jump!"

Boys and a hoyden lass had the spring in their knees to bounce goatlike down the slide. His had carried him too many miles and taken too many falls already, and that rock was rounded on its top.

"The hell with ye," he said, got down on his knees, turned around and slid off the drop, losing skin on the rock. The sword banged at his side, and having it fall down into the rocks or off the mountain would be, he thought, a splendid piece of luck.

By the time he turned again, Dubhain was already skipping down the next two rocks. Dubhain turned to wait for him there on that flat place, beckoning him impatiently with one hand, the whiskey jug unbroken in his left.

He did it as he could, at his own pace, and with the loss of more skin on his knees and his hand. One of the young pair was Sidhe, and lending the other strength, he told himself, while Dubhain, damn him, was naught but a force of nature, the night's own wind skirling and sporting down the mountainside. A man could not hope to keep up with the likes of him, or to land so lightly as Dubhain did on bare feet.

No, a man was apt to break an ankle, or his neck, and a man could not make all the descent at once. He had to sit down at a flat place by a thread of a waterfall, with a third of the descent to go, his heart thumping as if it would burst, and the sweat running on him. The water spray that the wind dashed on him from the falls was as cold as a Sidhe's heart, and it numbed his hands when he dipped up a drink from the pool to ease his throat.

Then the memory of Dun Glas came back to him vividly, the vault and the silver vines trying to grow through the stone—but not a memory. In his mind, Nuallan stood as he had, still with the light of faery about him, but other branches had grown up among the silver, and a black rose budded and in the light of Nuallan's presence, unfolded petals to him. Nuallan put out a hand to it as a breeze shook the branches, and instead of the rose, Nuallan touched his thumb against a thorn. Blood started bright on his moonlit hand, blood-red in mortal day. Nuallan put the wound to his lips, thoughtfully abandoning the rose.

"My lord," Caith whispered, affrighted—'my lord' was not a claim he had ever owned to with Nuallan, or to any creature in faery or on earth, in his heart of hearts, so it must be Padraic's pernicious influence that lent him that sudden terror, which he did not like. . . .

But he recognized danger in the black branches, and knew that Nuallan should not reach toward that rose—but who had ever cheated Nuallan before, and when had Nuallan ever understood the meaning of duress? And if Nuallan fell, if Nuallan failed in that place, then where was he?

Nuallan recognized his presence, then, and looked at him as if to say he had not seen him until now and did not wish to see him here. Play not the fool, that glance said. Quick, run away from here . . .

He took it for warning. He tried to remember where he was, but remember he could not. Nuallan's pale face became Moragacht's dark smile and Moragacht's basilisk stare—her with the empty bed and the hunger to take and use: the carnal and the charnel were one thing in that bed, and a Sidhe lord would not satisfy her long, nor could he, nor Dubhain nor any creature on earth or in faery or in hell. She was appetite incarnate. She had begun with cleverness and now wielded power that a Sidhe lord could not resist.

Nuallan's will? It moved at her command. Nuallan's strength? She directed it. She directed everything they did.

Why let you escape? he imagined her saying. And imagined her smiling, answering her own question, What matter? You'll come back.

He did not wish to hear that. He tried to look away, and started when a heavy hand landed on his shoulder and shook him hard.

It was Dubhain, and the bright empty sky, and Dubhain's fingers biting into his shoulder.

"Ye witling!" Dubhain cried. Like the wind, Dubhain might have come up the rocks, in the blink of an eye and the drink he had taken, everything might have happened: his soul was still wide open to the knowing and the Seeing of faery, he was still half here and half there, and only the pain of Dubhain's grip held him to the mountainside and his sight to Dubhain and the sky.

"He's in trouble," Caith said, catching a breath.

"We are *all* in trouble, man, and more than trouble, when ye go wit-wandering like that! She reads the waters, that's where her magic lies! We could nae cross the stream, we did nae count it wise, man, and here ye do all but bathe in it!"

"Ye said nothing to me about reasons, ye cursed wight! Get your hand from my knee!"

It was more than the torn skin Dubhain mended, it was a giddy wave of power that came from his knee up and through all his limbs. The breath came in at his nostrils and went out to the ends of his fingers and his toes, and charged the air he breathed. His hair might have crackled. It prickled on his body, the way amber would make it, rubbed across the skin.

"She says," he said, "we haven't escaped, that we're doing what she wishes . . ."

"Oh, aye, and the naughty wench is sae honest, is she not? Gie me your hand, man, up you go—"

He needed no help. He heaved himself to his feet and made the jump, free of Dubhain's hand, in a darkness that had nothing to do with the sky. It was the dark force of Dubhain's strength that steadied his legs and gave him the agility the sun-born Sidhe shared down below, crazed, themselves, but not crazed with the wicked delight that was Dubhain, a strength that had the lady's power running like a growth of weeds through it. Dubhain grew chancy and fey, and himself no less, Caith the killer, Caith who was already damned with kin-murder . . . he could almost weep to know the strength Dubhain would give him if he grew any more foolish, and the least small corner of his sanity could feel the terror of things sliding amiss with them all, the small indulgence growing to self-satisfaction, and that, to the desire to overthrow all sense, all restraint of action . . .

The shocks of the landings came one after the other, now, he had gained so much downward speed. If Moragacht had done all of this, everything, Fianna and the selkie and the ruining of Gleann Fiain and all of it, from the beginning, for the very purpose of laying her hands on one of Nuallan's kind—if that were true, and he did not admit it, still he was not caught, *he* was not her servant and would not be. For one giddy moment he flew, and in the next absorbed the shock of landing with his knees, one great boulder to the next, until, at the very bottom, he came to a running, downhill halt, no saner than he had to be when he looked at Firinne, and at Ceannann, the both of them seeming shocked at him.

"Go on," he said, waving them ahead. "Go on." It was pleasant to be feared, even by such a feckless lad. It was pleasant to feel no pain at all.

But it was very dangerous. Of such feelings a man ought to be very afraid, if his wits were not utterly sunk into the spell that fed his arrogance. He knew that, and he warned himself, as Dubhain landed near him. He drew a deep breath and walked like a sane man, afraid now that Dubhain was on that same slippery edge of the dark.

"You should not," he said to Dubhain finally, "you should not do that to me. Do you hear me, wight? I *detest* your constant hands on me!"

"Ye like it too well," Dubhain gibed at him, and then was gone.

"Dubhain!"

Badbh and Macha, he thought, turning to look full circle about him, in the hopes Dubhain had only skipped away too quickly for his eye to see: Dubhain could do such things, and he hoped with his heart and soul he had, this time.

But there was no Dubhain. There was no Dubhain, and the last time Dubhain had vanished . . .

Macha, we aren't done. We aren't through what Dubhain Saw.

"Ha! Scared ye, did I?"

His heart thumped, not alone for the tweak at his hair and Dubhain's sudden presence by him. For a moment . . .

"You damned fool! It's no place for your jokes . . ." No, he did not mean that. He caught at Dubhain's sleeve, entreating him from his threatened desertion. "Stay. Stay, Dubhain."

"Please?"

"Wretch. Walk with me. Stay with me. I have *need* of ye, Dubhain. It's the lord Nuallan in difficulty, remember, and ourselves will follow him . . ."

"Oh, aye, d' ye lesson *me*, man?"

He did not let his temper answer that. He smoothed Dubhain's sleeve of the wrinkles he had made in it. "Stay, Dubhain, fair Dubhain, let us give her no victory."

Dubhain blew a breath out his nostrils, and swung away from him, walking downhill at an easy pace. Caith went beside him, or behind, where the going was hard, and saw Dubhain finally distracted by the flit of an insect, the sweep of a bird skimming the slope.

"Do we trust them?" Caith asked finally, with the twins far down the slope ahead of them. "Or was that ado by the fire this morning all another skein of moonbeams? 'Not know which is which.' They make me uneasy, Dubhain."

Dubhain was silent a moment more, walking slowly, for Dubhain, with now and again a skip in his step, hands clasped behind him as if they were on an afternoon's stroll, not on a steep mountain descent. "And

which is the selkie? I think one and I think the other.
That is a spell, my Caith. Lying in the same womb, who
knows what spells they might hae worked, or had
worked on them? They see what they see and no more."

"Could *you* forget what you are?"

A skip on a projecting flat stone and a shrug, head
bowed. "Could I do such a thing? Nay. But sun-born
folk? It might be a glamor the selkie child can cast everywhere about. Och, who knows what such creatures
may think or do?"

"A dangerous sort."

"Och, aye, nae question."

"But a selkie can take mortal shape." So he had always heard. Often one could trust the old women to be
right.

A dark chuckle Dubhain gave, and a wicked wink.
"The lady wife could hae said. I wonder which were
the greater pleasure, and in what shape? A cold and
clammy fellow, but of endless variety and dimen-
sion . . ."

"A wicked mind you have."

"Why, nae curiosity? And the lady at the end of the
loch for Fianna's matchmaker, and the great selkie
obeys? I hae question o' that. I hae great question o'
that, sweet Caith, but these sparrows hae nae answer."

It was a question: why the selkie had agreed, or
whether the selkie had anything to gain. And why . . . ?

"If Herself could command the great selkie himself,"
Caith asked, "then what use, a selkie's child?"

"An excuse for a quarrel, and all it let in?"

"But what use a bright Sidhe *or* these young folk for
her magic, if she could command the selkie?"

"One maun ask."

"You missed the ghost, this morning. *I* made close
acquaintance of it. A fellow called Padraic. He served
the mac Ceannann, in that hall."

A swift glance of Dubhain's dark eyes, in which the
red was kindling. "Say you so?"

"From out of the fire. The beast killed him." He tried not to remember that. "The fire conjured him; the lass singed her fingers saving a bit of wood before it died. This is no maiden's keepsake she has. . . ."

"Mayhap she is nae maiden. Hae ye asked? Shall I?"

"Damn your humors." The ghost was all too vividly in memory, and the collapse of the stairs and the dark; the fall at his left hand was straight to the loch, down a hundred feet and more. "Did you find aught but the hares when you were out and about, this morning? How did that man get past you?"

It implied fault, perhaps. And Dubhain was never at fault. He gave no answer but a lifting of his shoulders and a frown.

"Nuallan bled," Caith pursued him. "I saw it in my dream. There by the falls. A prick of the thumb."

"By the falls?"

"In Dun Glas, damn you, I saw the vault in Dun Glas, and Nuallan isn't altogether ignoring her. There were roses, black ones, and he pricked his hand."

"Roses, ye say."

"What does it mean?"

"Nae good thing." Dubhain gave him as straight and sober a look as ever he had given. "My prince, I See no roses, 't is no' any roses she offers him, but mortal Sight does queer things. This is true: if he were nae holding against her in some degree, we would nae be free where we walk, and her borders would be somewhat wider than a day ago."

"We need the Daoine Sidhe. We need their help, Dubhain, —beg if we must. They can't realize what is happening here . . ."

"M' lord called ye to Gleann Fiain. *Thou 'rt* the help, man, ye did nae realize it?"

"I? Badbh and Macha, Dubhain, —no."

"Things hae gone vastly awry, man. Yet we hae these pretty sparrows for guides. And ye *will* swear by the battle-crow. Fickle she is, fickle as the old ones, my darling Caith, ne'er trust her."

"What are the fay *doing*? Where are they? Whence comes this silver gate?"

"What silver gate?"

That Dubhain had seen nothing of the sort, that Dubhain knew nothing he was talking about, set all his estimations in disorder.

"Between myself and faery."

"Oh, that gate."

" 'That gate'! You drive me mad, damn you! It's no joke!"

"Why, everything's a joke, man. The lord Nuallan and the lady, 't is a great joke, that."

"How? How is it a joke, Dubhain?"

"To her, man. She hae a wicked disposition. Roses, ye say?"

"Black ones."

"I should nae expect white."

"What if she's doing all of this, what if it's all her working, us coming here, us taking out with the twins? I was in hell, Dubhain, I looked into hell, and the old gods . . ."

"Man, I told ye, 't is her view of things. 'T is the draiocht she works, and wi' a lord of the Sidhe in her black nest, och, nae doubt she'll be reaching out again, as far as she likes, the next valley and the next and the next. She'll reach for us when it pleases her."

"And what can we do, with the gods of *hell* at her calling . . ."

"Och, but 't is all her view, man. Calm yoursel'."

"I was *there*, don't tell me so! You couldn't breach the wards—"

"Sweet Caith, I maun tell ye a thing about the *draiocht*: 't is a simple bargaining—ye maun gie as much as ye get."

"What do you mean?"

"Ye maun allow your victim t' gain something, the

same as you; only ye gie him the gift nae sae easy to use, whilst ye gain the thing ye wish. I hae thought about it one way and the other, but now I would almost wager 't was she that blinked at us slipping out—she let that pass her and, because she let us pass, in the balance o' magic, she gained the greater prize in him. 'T is all a fencing match—'t is press and retreat, and rapid as thought, a duel of magic is. And m' lord of the Daoine Sidhe was a wee bit greedy and far too sudden wi' her. He tried to take—and she let him, whiles she . . . took him."

"Nuallan made a mistake."

"Oh, aye. Such as any swordsman may make on any day. Nae great one, but such as can kill ye. And mind ye, Nuallan went suddenly into this match wi' her, but she hae prepared three long sevens of years for this— *knowing* what she wants most, what's more, and he hae all to guess. 'T is a great advantage in magic, when what ye want, what ye'll take, and what ye'll allow, is all a puzzle to the enemy."

"This woman and her beast and her gods couldn't take an unwalled shepherd's cottage without four years and two score men to do her work, she could not compel the lad and lass alone without—"

"Ask what that lad and that lass *are*, my prince."

Caith looked down at the pair, ahead of them on the descent, which must lead them to the loch shore again, or to running water.

She reads the rivers, Dubhain had said. And if there was a danger in crossing running water, how should they get beyond that valley without doing that? Or would they turn aside again, and climb laboriously above the water which inevitably must run in any cleft between two rain-swept mountains?

Give and get, Dubhain said.

"And how far and how long can she reach, Dubhain? Beyond the glen? To the great sea? Can you at all guess?"

Dubhain shrugged and gave a troubled shake of his head. "I can nae think on 't," was all he said for the moment, but a little further on, did answer: "She could, aye, I do fear she could, and if she grows much more powerful, reach as far as she likes, but ask me nae more such questions, man, on what she can and cannae do."

Dubhain was on a precarious edge, he saw evidence of it in that brief silence: a question had sent Dubhain's thoughts and Dubhain's wishes back to that place against his will, and in the way faery ran threads through all the world, the lady had been perilously close to them for a moment, a mere thought, a simple wish away from reaching them.

And for a moment after answering him, Dubhain skipped away on a series of scattered flat rocks, boylike amusing himself, or, more desperate, taking deliberate risks on the steep, to distract his thoughts.

Dubhain was worried. That did come through, plain as plain to him.

If mortal legs could have stood the pace, Caith would have argued for going on: but it was as safe and comfortable a nook as they would find on this mountainside, this small corrie where, autumn though it was, not all the trees had cast their leaves: the mountain and the leaved trees broke the wind somewhat, and there was no dearth of water, with the spring gushing bright and cold out of the mountainside ... they had to drink, no matter the risk they ran of the lady's magic.

The water was cold enough to numb the day's hurts and bruises, but they took no longer about drinking or washing than they must. Stay away from the water, Dubhain bade them before he went out in search of their supper.

So they made their fire and they settled to wait. Caith found the driest ground he could on the smoky side of the fire, because the smoky side was the warmest, and

Firinne and Ceannann had a blanket to keep the chill off their backs.

They could watch themselves, Caith decided. They both could make a supper for the clattering beast, for what he cared at the moment. He did not take it greatly amiss that they did not offer the loan of their blanket, even until he should get warm, since Firinne had been the one to rescue it. Probably it never occurred to the girl he was cold. But the blowing smoke was warm all about, and he only wished to lie down and shut his eyes. A risk, that fire was. If it were mortal folk they had most to fear, it would be foolishness even to think of it; but if the lady's hunters were out and on their track, it was no smell of smoke or gleam of fire they needed.

But to hell with it, was his estimation, once the heat had eased the ache in his limbs and let him lie easy. With two Sidhe about, if he was not safe to lie and rest, he was not safe to wake, either.

Except he dared not truly give himself to profound sleep without Dubhain near. And he was perilously tired, and close to that black brink. A little nightmare or two tonight—he was too weary to care, if before that he had a little rest; but there was more to fear in his dreams than his memories. There was far more of substance and more of betrayal.

Yet he remembered a leaf—a particular red and yellow leaf, a larch, it was, with flecks of black on it, and it had fallen down to the spring—he had noticed it for its color against the dark: that was safe to think of, so he set his mind very narrowly on that, for rest from his cares and the dangers about them, and he mindfully shut his eyes.

But a current caught that leaf, sucked it from the spring down into the brook in a trice, and he knew where it was going, a fast, helpless course toward the loch below, where something waited, for the leaf . . . and for the dreamer.

He wished to break away. He wished to take his eyes away from the leaf, but it met an unexpected falls, and plunged into white water, and into the pool below.

Then the world went dark indeed, dark as the waters of the loch, that were night turned liquid, heavy with peat. He was blind in these waters, and he knew by the wash of a current that a great body had brushed past him, and that the current had met the loch.

He could not tell where the shallows were. He tasted blood and salt, and a second time that cold current rolled over him. It called, strange lonely squeals into the dark, that went away and then came back. It knew that he was there, and it searched, a wave in the pitch darkness that brushed him with a chilling cold.

"Dubhain!" he shouted.

Immediately he waked, threw his head up and was halfway to his feet when he saw, in the dusk and the firelight . . .

Firinne and Ceannann were kneeling on either side of the little brook, with their hands joined above the water, and dark threads of something flowed and dripped about their fingers.

"Macha! What are you doing?" He came at them—grabbed Ceannann by the shoulder and tore them apart from each other, all but pulling Firinne into the water. Their two hands showed red stain in the firelight, blood dripping freely into the innocent brook.

Ceannann was on his feet; Firinne was, and Caith reached his hand across the tiny brook to steady her, getting her blood on him when she shoved his hand away.

"We are no children!" Firinne cried. "Don't treat us like children! Don't touch me!"

He took back his hand, sticky as it was, and hesitated how to deal with it. He wiped the blood on his bare knee, having no desire to break Dubhain's enjoinder himself and put his hand in the brook. "He said keep out of the water—"

"We were not *in* the water."

"Oh, aye, well, blood was, and that's worse."

"You don't know!"

"Deal with your sister," Caith said to Ceannann, and turned his back on the affair, because he honestly did not know whether he had done good or ill. He only saw Firinne's anger with him starting a quarrel between himself and Ceannann, which could lead to worse than that, given the boy's own temper. He wanted nothing so much as the sleep he dared not take, but he could only go back to the fireside and sit, angry, leaving the twins to mutter and whisper in their own secrecy, and to bind up their self-dealt wounds.

He had not gotten all the blood off. He sat down in his place in the smoke and rubbed at his hand and his knee, which left a grit of leaf mold. He was thoroughly disgusted, and tired, and hungry, and abandoned to deal with a pair of obstinate young fools, who worked magic without consulting anyone and cast a spell in the witch's teeth, what was more, with blood, which the stone gods liked well with their sacrifices. Blood, and drownings, and things that went down to the bottom of the loch and lay there.

Not children, Firinne had said, indignantly; but what they had just done argued otherwise—wait until he had his eyes shut, indeed, when they knew what Dubhain had said. Never argue against advice sanely, oh, no, they sneaked their business, and the Badbh knew what else they might be doing when no one was watching. He recalled the strike Ceannann had made at his back. He recalled them both through Padraic's eyes, sleeping in each other's arms—the same way they had slept last night, in the storm; and the memory gave him the same queasy feeling Padraic had had about it, a thing not right, far beyond the mortal, petty wickedness a man could imagine in that bed-sharing. The feeling that walked up and down his backbone was of some vaster wrong, in the way of nature itself, the way rain did not fall up and the river would not flow uphill.

Draiocht? he asked himself. It was in their mother's milk. It was in that hall, it was under its stones, it was deep in the bogs and the loch of Gleann Fiain.

Dubhain came in on a gust of wind—late, to his summons, and blithe as a May lamb. He had four large hares this time, fat ones; quick and easy hunting in this wooded nook between the mountains. "Hey," said Dubhain, "sae glum ye are. Here's supper. How are the coals? Ready?"

"Beyond," Caith said with a shiver, and got up to help skin and dress the take—and to have a muttered word with Dubhain: "Did you *hear* me, you? Did you hear my warning?"

Dubhain seemed nonplussed. "Warning, d' ye say?"

"I dreamed, I slept, I was in the loch, and these—these *children* we plucked from the witch's den were spilling blood into the brook, didn't you feel it?"

"Nay." A frown was on Dubhain's face. He was skinning one of the hares, and the flint blade made fair short work of it. "I did nae such thing. In the loch, ye say."

"I slept." He knew he was at fault, and knew Dubhain would remember it at his expense. "And while I slept they were working some kind of magic, themselves, with blood and water."

"Were they, now?" Dubhain was maddeningly unconcerned. He parted a hare's neck, with a crack of bone and gristle. "Nae ghostie here to feed, I suppose. Well, 't will feed the foxes—"

"Macha and the Badbh! Take it seriously, ye smug wight." He rubbed the heat that was stinging his shins, and lowered his voice. "And make no jokes about ghosts or magic. What did you find out there?"

"Oh, I went along the ridge a ways, and looked for the fay ye'd expect, but the lass is fled a'ready." Now Dubhain was not smiling: a brow was cocked beneath his forelock. "I cannae find the fair folk. I cannae find so much as a path that would lead me there. The springs yonder—nae sign of the fair ones, and naught of the darker sort—but I would nae flirt wi' my own kindred near this loch."

Then Ceannann came over to the fire with something on his mind, and sat down by them without their leave. "We are not such fools," he said angrily, "as to betray us to the witch. The water runs down to the sea from here, not to Dun Glas; it was a magic our mother showed us if ever we could make it work. That was what we were about."

One could take it for a young fool bent on his folly. One could take it for one trying to bridge the angry silence. Caith deliberately chose to take it for the latter.

"Ask beforehand. Warn a man."

"You are not my master, man! And what do you know about it?"

"More than you think," Caith said in labored patience, "but if you doubt my advice, ask Dubhain, and trust that *he* knows something."

"Hoosht," said Dubhain, "ye maun ask, but I hae nae the calling of any selkie, nor he of me." A second crack of bone. Another head and skin joined the first. "Bluidy work, it is." Dubhain licked his thumb, and Caith frowned and flinched, seeing that red glimmering in Dubhain's eyes.

"I'll spit them," Ceannann said, anxious to move away for the same reason, it might be; but Firinne moved in before he could leave, and sat down quietly. Like two children, indeed, anxious to be forgiven, fearful of their rough company; while Firinne's profile, against the fire, her fine-boned, pensive face, and its halo of light, reminded him why he had almost succumbed to temptation under her roof.

Almost. He watched her instead of Dubhain, as she poked at the coals with a stick of wood. It took fire and she threw it in, and added another.

"A wicked night," said Dubhain. Crack. "Easy as

kiss me hand, these creatures are to catch. They trust a calling."

"Let be," Caith said. He had seen Dubhain at work too often, thinking about it soured a man's appetite, and Dubhain knew it. "Think of the daylight, Dubhain, think of a summer day."

"Bright as our pretties' hair. D' ye think, my Caith? Willing ye were once . . . to think on 't."

"Wicked creature. Mend your manners. 'T is the witch talking to you."

"Och, and not a wicked thought in his head. What a wonder!"

"Forgive him. His mother foaled him headlong."

"I forgive him," said Firinne, and looked at him, instead, all shadow, with an outline of golden light. "And you."

He saw Dubhain lift his jaw, saw the spark of malice in Dubhain's eye and the quirk of Dubhain's lip. But he countered meekly with a sketch of a bow. "For the laying on of hands, aye, I take your forgiveness. For the other . . ." It was a question he supposed he should have asked, although he foreknew the answer. "Did the selkie *answer* you at all?"

"No," she said, downcast. "Not a bit. Nor ever has, for all our calling, in trouble and out of it."

"But there was a great working in the way of him, wi' the witch against ye," Dubhain said. Crack, the fourth neck. "That for the foxes. The fay hae fled this valley, having better sense than we. And does not the selkie as the selkie will? I hae heard they are a flighty sort, nor here, nor there—"

"Dubhain."

". . . and mad, most times."

"Dubhain!"

"Go, go," Firinne said. "You'll burn them, likely. Leave them to me. Away!"

With a wave of her hand she assumed possession of

the coals and the hares: men, even a dark Sidhe, were advised to give up their efforts.

"A determined lass," said Dubhain. "An armful."

"By the Badbh, you're . . ." But least of all did he wish a quarrel with Dubhain tonight, and he saw himself on the brink of it, with the hellfire glimmering in Dubhain's eyes and the wicked smile at the corners of Dubhain's mouth. "I beg ye, softly, softly, Dubhain, come away and speak with me."

"Nay!" The frown was instant. Dubhain flung his hand off his arm, got up and spun away.

"Dubhain." He began to be afraid. It had all too much the tone of the madness he had seen before in this cursed glen. "Softly." He picked up the whiskey jug as he rose, and that brought a spark of interest to Dubhain's eye. "Come, fair Dubhain, sweet Dubhain. By the bond the bright Sidhe set on us, ye fractious creature, —have a wee drink."

It was precarious. The madness was there. But Dubhain came back to the fire and took the jug.

"Sit down, sit down." The thought of Dubhain off in the woods alone the last hour, searching for some way to faery, frightened him, now. Dubhain was their surest, quickest hunter, but his poking about the brush might have started more on the boundaries of faery than four unlucky rabbits: the loch was very near, down the slope and at the end of their little corrie.

"The witch is aye humorless," he said to the wight. "An ye go to her, ye'll lose *me*, ye silly creature, and what would ye do, then? Ye'd fair pine away."

"Never!"

"And I'd *win*."

Dubhain's nostrils widened. "Win what?"

"Why, what is there ever to win? Which of us is the more clever? Even if you drag me down—it won't be *my* fault. *You'll* have failed, Dubhain. You'll have failed, and that makes me the better of us, and the cleverest."

"Out on you!"

"Brave Dubhain. Did I say ye v
strong? Clever, now . . . perhaps."

"No perhaps, man." Another swig fr
a glimmering of the eyes, but the fires
now and a wicked smile danced across D
Dubhain had thought of something, Cait
look, something most likely at his expense;
was *with* him now, wholly.

"You'll not get the chance at me," he said,
down completely. "If that's what you're thinki

"Ha," quoth Dubhain.

Now, best that bid, he thought at the lady o
Glas. Pay for it, he might: and Dubhain knew wh
was about, too, but never dare to rub *that* in . .
would undo all the good he had done and se
Dubhain's mind scurrying after mischief he could do i
stead. Dubhain would not be bound to a good deed, no
Dubhain, no.

But when the rabbits were mere piles of bones, and
the twins had made their nest under Firinne's blanket,
on the other side of the fire, Caith lay down to sleep at
Dubhain's side in full confidence that Dubhain's
thoughts now were bent on pranks to play on him, and
not dream-traveling to Dun Glas.

Dubhain ran a finger over his arm, which Dubhain
knew he hated, leaned close and whispered: "Pretty
baggage, the lass is. And never a wicked thought in
your mind. That's not like you."

"I've troubles enough." He tossed onto his side, disquieted. "And if I don't sleep, wight, we'll be the
slower tomorrow and you'll be carrying me."

"Oh, should I?"

He lifted his head and cast an angry glance over his
shoulder. "I make you a bargain. A truce. A truce for
seven days."

"Nay, ye're a clever man. Ye'd fling yourself to the
beastie and win that way."

verge of tears, he was so weary,
so exasperated with the creature.
with his eyes shut. "I'm no chal-
ye feckless spook. Far too easy a
your worst. For a prank, damn
that satisfaction."

his arm, not gently. "Dinnae jest on
is nearer than not tonight."

pegrace. 'T was the Sidhe damned
and master Pure and Noble first of
et me sleep dreamless tonight. Either
me."

jest, man. There's powers abroad.
fled this place."

sleep. And let me sleep, or I shall
ey and more strange . . ."

to his arm, which he felt more dimly.
ake it back!"

ubhain. Dear, sweet Dubhain. Bless the good
en, root and branch, bless that fool Dubhain, and
r us from Dun Glas." His senses were fading. He
the dark, the true dark, which held no images. One
could wonder how Nuallan fared, but he would not leave
this dark and this peace to know. "A few hours. Tomorrow's all to find. Mind the fire. Don't dull my sword.
Break the branches, and toss them in the fire, there's a
good lad. . . ."

Dubhain's hand slipped over his, Dubhain's fingers
closed on his. Dubhain spelled him to sleep then, as
Dubhain could, when Dubhain would . . . Dubhain
whispered, last, in his ear, "Caith, my bonny, damned
prince, he hae heard them. Wi' blood they called, and in
the great ocean he hae turned his face about. He is
caught, too, and cannae help himself. Roses, ye say,
black roses . . ."

196

Caith sighed,
so scant of sle
He lay flat
lenge to
mark.
Nual

CHAPTER
NINE

THERE WAS DARK about; dark and the clasp of Dubhain's hand on his; Dubhain himself seemed fast asleep, and the fire was down to a sullen heap of embers. But something was amiss. Caith could not tell what had waked him at first—he had dreamed, he thought, of something threatening standing near him, and felt a lingering impression of something cold and wet having touched his cheek just before he waked, but that could well be the dream. . . .

Then he heard a soft snuffling, like a dog smelling after a scent, pass above his head and close to his hair as he lay still on the ground, while his heart thumped and the sweat started on his skin. He squeezed Dubhain's hand—Dubhain should not be asleep, certainly not this deeply asleep, and it was no stray dog that searched their camp. He feared to make the slightest move. It went off into the dark, then circled back near him a second time. He could hear it breathing, but its feet made no sound on the leaves. Right against his ear, the panting came, and again that cold, wet touch, this time at the side of his jaw.

He remembered the intruder in the keep, the face going to white bone before his eyes. He scarcely dared breathe. He feared what he might see if he stared and he feared what it might provoke if he made even the slight movement of shutting them. He stared into the night sky above the branches and listened to the sound move away again.

Then he squeezed Dubhain's hand, hard, the second time, and whatever was in their camp slunk away, he could feel the lifting of the terror like a weight from his chest. He sat up and put a stick of wood into the coals, and another. In a moment they took fire, and light spread out, throwing the trees into stark relief against the night and blinding the eyes to the hostile things that might prowl beyond that circle: he was not sure whether he liked having the fire or not.

But now Dubhain lifted his head and sat up, blinking. Caith looked at him, then saw, off at the limit of the light, four small rabbit skulls, gnawed clean.

"Macha!" he swore, on the drawing of a breath, and tucked his knees up and hugged his arms about himself, the sight afflicted him so.

"What?" asked Dubhain.

"The skulls. The thing from the keep, Dubhain, the mastiff dogs . . ."

Dubhain cast a glance where he waved his hand, then shook his head. " 'T is gone back there, then. It forgot where it was. Nae matter."

" 'Nae matter,' ye feckless wight! We've camped above some grave or other. Murder happened here!"

"Pish. And *you* affrighted, my bluidy prince?" Dubhain gave him a second, sidelong glance, and grinned, while Caith rubbed his arms against the chill. "A mastiff dog, ye say. And murder in this place."

"I don't know. Something drew it. Or death to come. I don't know why I think so. It hasn't the feeling of the Sight. Maybe it spoke to me."

"Who, the dog?"

"Out on your jokes! More than the dogs, Dubhain, I told you it was more than the dogs. And you were fast asleep. I couldn't wake you. Or were you pretending?"

Dubhain had no answer for that question, and some-

how avoided looking at him or answering—Dubhain
would never admit to fault or failure, and Dubhain had
slept through the visitation by no choice of his own.
Few the powers that could do that to a Sidhe, and that
was as troubling as the haunt itself.

Meanwhile the twins were stirring awake. Ceannann
sat up and looked around, and Firinne was leaning on
her elbow, looking at them.

"A ghost," Caith said surlily, still unnerved, and in
no mind to drop off to sleep again in this place.

"Wi' a taste for rabbit," Dubhain added, with a nod
at the pile of skulls.

The twins scrambled up in dismay, and Ceannann
went and looked at the skulls, and gave a visible shudder. Firinne joined him, wrapping the blanket about
both their shoulders.

"Let's be going," Caith said, rising to his feet; he had
no disposition even to shut his eyes again this close to
the keep, and he had rather make progress out of
Gleann Fiain, walking toward the sea as they were. He
longed to find this selkie father the twins were seeking,
anything but sit and wait for the lady's beast or the
ghosts to overtake them in this haunted place. A wind
was rising, whispering in the trees, and he might not
even have noticed it without the ghost brushing close to
him, but the whole of nature in this place felt disturbed,
now . . . maybe from the blood, maybe from what it had
attracted.

Not even Dubhain argued against going, and, none
gainsaying, Caith kicked apart the coals of their fire—
kicked them into the brook, to be sure of them on a
windy night.

It hissed, the embers drowned, and steam went up in
the dying light. The dark after that was all but complete
under the trees. Digest that, he thought to the witch who
read the rivers, who had tried to draw him into her
power, the witch, *and* her bloody, eldritch gods . . .

Foolish gesture, he thought, then. To spoil a stream

was not lucky. But what else was he to do with the fire, in a rising wind, with heaps of autumn leaves about, to send fire sweeping across the mountain? He stood there blind, with the light all drowned, and the deed done, and wondered if they were wise at all to go haring off into the dark, or if his gesture just now, at which the rightful Sidhe of the place would have taken high offense, had been an offense to the lady. He hoped it had. He hoped it had been satisfaction to the little Sidhe who had been frightened away from its spring. That was Caith the fool, justifying his temper after he had done a thing, and after he was facing a night and a walk darker than he had thought.

But Dubhain's eyes saw in the dark with no trouble at all. "Come," said Dubhain, and Caith picked up the whiskey jug and followed without question, a perilous step across the little brook he had defiled.

Perhaps the lady of Dun Glas was sleeping at this hour. Perhaps she had not noticed his deliberate challenge.

Or perhaps she had.

The wind was at their backs around the low shoulder of the mountain, a broad, broad mountainside, tangled with whin and rough with rock, and slow going in the dark, for a man. Caith stumbled and felt his way, Dubhain and Firinne and Ceannann getting to the fore of him, and the gap between them growing wider and wider.

Lose me, he thought angrily, leave me to be eaten by ghostly dogs, will ye? You'll be sorry, Dubhain, you'll have no butt for your jokes but Ceannann, and the lad's a sullen, ungrateful sort.

Deserve each other, you do.

As he scraped the skin off the side of his knee, and burned his hand on the heather he seized to hold him.

But Dubhain turned up in front of him, a shadow against the shadow of the mountain, his eyes glowing a faint red at their bottom edges, and Dubhain had nothing to say to him, only waited his coming in chilling silence.

"Run a race across the mountain, will ye?" Caith muttered, but still Dubhain said nothing, his humor seeming as dark as his shadow, and as chancy as the night around him—it even occurred to him to wonder if what stayed for him and reached out a hand to haul him up *was* Dubhain at all.

But it felt like Dubhain's hand, and it let him go again, and the shadowy figure took the cumbersome jug and went ahead of him. He could not see Firinne and Ceannann—ahead of them, again, whether waiting or walking on, heedless and careless of their whereabouts.

He was relieved to see the pale banner of Firinne's hair when they had gone a little distance farther, Firinne and her brother well ahead and still going, oh, aye, while he and Dubhain—he prayed it was Dubhain— kept their own pace behind. It was not what he would have advised, spreading out like this, but Dubhain's silence encouraged no objection, and Dubhain's eyes glimmered with ghostly red fire when Dubhain chanced to look at him, or when once Dubhain caught his arm to haul him over a difficult and blind step, and drew him close on a narrow, flat stone. Then the red was more than a little, and Dubhain said in a low voice,

"Steady, my prince."

"D' ye know where we're going?"

"To hell, my prince. A bluidy piece o' work."

He thought Dubhain was laughing at him. He saw that narrowing of the glimmering fire. But it was not a pleasant warmth, and not a pleasant joke. Dubhain might be Seeing ahead of them. Dubhain was thinking of mischief, perhaps, drinking occasionally from the jug, and enjoying scaring him ... but Dubhain in his darker moods was more honest, and the whiskey made him fey.

He was thinking of that when he put his foot wrong,

and slid off the mountain. He made a wild reach with one hand at brush and rocks, breathless with fright. But he had no time to plead. Dubhain's strong hand closed on his wrist, Dubhain's dark voice said, somberly, "Nae sae fast, my prince," and drew him smoothly upward, as if his were a child's weight, until he set his feet on safer ground.

No jest or jape Dubhain had for him after that, and that was unlike the wight. Dubhain only walked ahead of him, sometimes a shadow in his sight, sometimes out of sight altogether, leaving him alone on the mountain—he could seldom see the twins ahead of them, and that far in the lead. He grew desperate, fearing he was losing all hold over Dubhain, or over them, and struggled to go as fast as he could, reckless of the steep slope.

"Dubhain!" he whispered into the dark and vacant air. "Dubhain! Come back here!" But call out aloud he dared not. He only kept going as best he could, and trusted the mountain not at all.

The skinned knee and lately strained shoulder had time to stiffen before the sun began to light the sky at their backs—before the mountains above and about them took on shape against the sky, and the greys turned slowly to heathery purples and oranges on the hills and to faint gold in the heavens.

Then he could see Dubhain, between him and the twins. Even when his desperate effort overtook the wretch, Dubhain said not a word, and the twins stayed far ahead of them.

But once the air had warmed a bit, and when there was light in the sky, Firinne sat down to rest in a place with a far view over the loch, and Ceannann sat down.

Thank the gods, Caith thought, more than glad to overtake them and to sink down beside them. He was utterly winded, and once he had sat, hardly had the strength to stir.

But Dubhain, having set down the jug at Ceannann's side, stood looking thoughtfully out over the valley, the far mountain and the loch far below them. He had a pebble in his hand, idly tossing it, and then—

—hurled it down the stony slope, where it dislodged another, and skipped and tumbled down toward the loch.

"Dubhain," Caith protested.

A second pebble followed.

"Dubhain, forbear. Come sit."

A third, magic threes. He did not like that, and got up and went over to Dubhain. "Come, sit down," he said, resting a hand on Dubhain's shoulder. "Talk to me. Fair Dubhain. I'd have your advice. . . ."

Dubhain gave that aversion of the head and hunching of the shoulders that meant refusal and evasion. Then he lifted his face and the whites of his eyes showed in his mop of mane. Another voice than Dubhain's said:

"Silver in the waxing moon, iron then becomes. Ask then the ransom of the Sidhe."

"Moragacht!" Firinne breathed, at his back, as he caught Dubhain by the elbow and shook him, poised precariously above the loch as they were, the way the pebbles had gone.

"Dubhain, come back to me, by the geas we neither choose, Dubhain, ye damned, contrary wight . . ."

Dubhain went vague and grim, and seemed to have spent whatever it was, but there was disquiet on the twins' faces, as if they might bolt on the instant. " 'T is a fit," Caith lied. "He has these. —Come, come, Dubhain, wise Dubhain, talk to me." Waxing moons, he thought in desperation. The moon was in its waning course. Last night, it had been behind the mountain—the night before, hidden in storm, and what was this about silver and iron? The power of the Sidhe and the power of the banished gods? It was the waning of the year, autumn days spinning down and down toward that hinge-point of nights, that letting down of bars between the

realms. In the next course of days the moon must come
full again, and the new year begin . . .

Macha, he did not like the thoughts that stirred. The
days ahead were too fraught with unstable powers, the
Samhain was the next full moon, and came the witch
reaching out now to touch them in the sunrise, when
they ought to have been safe, outside her lands—and
touching the one of them they needed most to trust?

Dubhain blinked at the dawn sky, then shook himself,
dark hair obscuring his face, and staggered so that Caith
put out a hand to prevent him falling, foolish thought.
Dubhain walked barefoot a little distance from them on
the precarious slanting stone, and set his back to them
all, a grim figure against the sky and the mountains,
shoulders hunched and arms folded.

Then damn the witch, Caith thought angrily, and
went out on that perilous slant himself, for the witch
had touched Dubhain—even embarrassed him, who had
no shame. It was a kind of perverse innocence in
Dubhain, and the witch had no such right.

But he approached Dubhain carefully, warily, and
was not at all surprised when Dubhain turned his head
and he saw the balefire glimmering in those brown
eyes, even by beginning daylight.

"The witch waked in a bad humor," Caith said. "So
will she do as she pleases with us? I think not."

The fires burned no dimmer. Dubhain held his arms
folded tight, and madness boded in that frown.

"She has made a mistake," Caith said, "when she
spites us. A little more, and she may make us angry."

Dubhain's laugh was quick and merry as a wicked
thought: his arms came free and he spun half about and
scooped up another, larger stone from beside the rock.

Out it sailed, far, far off the mountain, until the eye
could not find it in the gulf.

It was excessive, perhaps. But Dubhain was that.

Excess was his own besetting fault. Excess had led
him to trouble before this, and his saying what he had

said and Dubhain's hurling the stone hung in the air with a finality he could not shake. He saw it in the twins' faces, distraught with what they had heard, or Seen with the eyes of the Sighted. They seemed appalled, as if they knew not what to make of the allies they had gained against the witch.

"Come," said Dubhain, skipping barefoot from the side of that rock down a series of flat stones that a mortal eye might not pick out as safe. Dubhain found a rapid, reckless course along the edge of earth and sky, a quick, white-shirted wraith that he could not keep up with.

But free. Free of the witch, free of spells, he had won that.

And, coming down a different course of like stones, Firinne and Ceannann were quicker on Dubhain's track than he was, and left him picking a slower, more careful way along the slope, the jug in one hand, the other hand for the mountain, where the way grew unreasonably steep.

Dubhain had something to prove, or Dubhain was still feeling the lady's hand on him, and was showing out.

"Break all our necks," Caith muttered.

But soon afterward, in the deep chasm of the loch, he saw the wheeling course of a gull, and then another one, a white, swift bandit streaking high above the slant. That gave him hope for where they were going. Gulls came inland—but they were free creatures, and there had been none at all, he recalled, in the darkness of Gleann Fiain. Yet they were here, and the mountains still showed promise of opening before them.

He clambered over rocks and along perilous slants, slower always, until at last he saw the twins and Dubhain all standing against a bright slice of sky, as if there was something there to see. He made what haste he dared, and arrived out of breath and sweating.

It was all open sky ahead. They had crossed the

mountain shoulder, and a low and rolling land spread below their feet. At their left, the dreadsome loch poured out its waters into a river that went on and on into that land of autumn hills, a winding above which gulls flew willingly and on which the sun shone with a fair, bright light. He blinked at the vision, in that way a man did when faery played its tricks, and the haze was still on the horizon.

"The sea," he said, between breaths. "The sea," Firinne whispered, too, and he had no doubt at all: he felt it . . . he had grown up hearing the gulls and smelling the salt water, and that memory pulled at him like a mother's unheard voice, oh, Macha, it was good to be near it again.

And Dubhain, standing in the wind, with a flat rock for his vantage: "He will be there, the sun-born will. In the salt sea he smells the blood. The gulls hear him coming. The land feels the thunder of his waves. The sun turns to brass and the gates of faery shiver—"

Dubhain turned about, with the red fire sun-dimmed in his eyes, with a frown on his face, with a word more on his lips he did not speak: Caith saw him smother it, and saw the uneasy glance at the twins.

Then it came to him what uncertainty Dubhain had about them, and that they had never known what the selkie's part in this was, or even whether the selkie was a bright or a dark force, for or against the Daoine Sidhe . . . while, fool that he was, he might have the answer himself, banging about his chest and his neck for months—so accustomed he forgot most times that he carried it at all, the elfshot, the discerning of seeming from being.

The sight would blast you, Nuallan had said, picking it up and calling it to his attention.

And when they turned and resumed their downhill course, following Dubhain toward that distant flat, he began to think of it constantly, and at last furtively laid his hand on it, wondering if he should ask Dubhain . . .

but Dubhain was fey and strange at the moment, flitting down the rocks out of reach and impossible to ask—while there was no better chance than he had, with both of them below him, and unawares.

Still, he hesitated, little enough confident that he would like the truth he might see, little enough certain he knew enough to judge. If what he saw was strange, how was he to know whether it was fair or foul? He had never yet dared look at a Sidhe, only at the things the Sidhe had touched, and he had never made sense of those at all, except that through the stone, blessed things looked brighter and cursed things had a kind of grime on them . . . and the sword he carried was a black thing, with the print of his hand on its hilt.

But Nuallan had directly called it to his attention, when they met, Nuallan had set the thought of it into the matter at hand, when Nuallan had seen it before and done nothing. Nuallan had only warned him against looking at Dubhain—had he not? Perhaps it had been an honest warning—for once in his dealings with the bright Sidhe—in calling his attention to what he should remember he carried.

Things of faery slipped the mind and changed on a man. He could not remember now whether Nuallan's prohibition had extended to anything else. Macha, it was enough to drive a man mad—like swimming through dark water, it was, trying to remember the most necessary things of faery. But Nuallan had intended he remember, and do something with it, Nuallan had not bespelled him to remember . . . perhaps with his own fate on him, Nuallan had feared the witch would see it and take it from him, and it was somehow important she not do that.

So perhaps Nuallan had bespelled it, only to be forgotten when one saw it—

Foolish, if they needed it, was it not? Or why else had the witch not taken it from about his neck, when they had gotten everything else he carried?

He had no ties to the twins, at least, and if they were foul beyond belief, he did not believe the sight would blast him, as Nuallan had said—he had seen horrors aplenty and gone unblasted yet: it was only his peace of mind it might work on, if he were fool enough to try it on Dubhain, that had been Nuallan's meaning—had it not been?

He thought about it, and thought about it, and finally, at a breathing-space in his descent, and while Firinne and Ceannann were occupied climbing down a steep slope below him, he lifted the stone on its cord and stole a single glance.

Sun-glare flared through at him, so blinding that he dropped the stone and rubbed his eye, leaning against the mountain with his other hand, that held the cursed jug. A dark spot was branded on his vision, in which drifted a red shape with different layers, one on the other, changing red to black, none of it making mortal sense.

That was a Sidhe? That was what they were? Dazzle and dance, Dubhain had said of the sun-born kind.

And, in the same way the twins professed they could not tell which of them was which, the stone both blinded him, and showed him one single creature between them, that kept changing even the shape branded on his eyes.

So much for carrying the stone all this way, with it banging nuisancefully about his chin, and making him look the fool, perhaps even to Dubhain, certainly to Nuallan. It offered only further mysteries, solved not a damned thing, and for a moment, light-blinded and leaning helpless against the mountain, he longed to rip the cord from off his neck and pitch it off the mountainside, he was so wroth with it, and in such blind, stinging misery from the use of it, and so angry at the Sidhe's deceptions. He all but despaired, for a moment, of finding any help below, not from the twins, not even from the selkie. Ghosts haunted their sleep and kept them walking all night, the witch's men were on the hunt—the corpse on the floor of the keep attested to that, if they had had any doubts—and they had, sooner or late, to deal with the hunters out of Gleann Fiain: no mortal horses might cross the slopes they had crossed, well and true, Dubhain knew that better than any, but the riders of Gleann Fiain surely knew their own land— might come afoot or might know some pass farther back along the loch, once they knew where they were tending.

And knowing the nature of the twins, how much guesswork did it take to know where they were going, even better than they did? Macha, it had all the smell of the ambush on Guagach's banks, the one he had walked into, feckless as Ceannann, and how many times did it need for them to learn these men were no fools?

And who ever had promised them that the witch's resources were all bound to the loch itself? While their own were running low, now, and they had no sure promise of help where they were going, sleepless and with so much effort . . .

But in the pain of the stone, at least, he had seen a truth to give him sober thought; and with his eyes still half-blinded and running with tears, he drew a breath that smelled of heather on the mountains, not of loch water—and that promised better than where he had been. He heard a gull cry and remembered the sea, and by then he could see enough to take a careful course downward, not so quick as the others, not so sure-footed, but steady and stubborn.

That was how he always kept up with Dubhain, knowing he would get there, himself, the cursed man, and the sword he carried. Even the stone gods had their mortal followers, and if they needed something done they called on them, and it happened at their pace.

He was the wager the Sidhe had made. He could do no better than he was doing, nor guess more than he did, if they left him with no better counsel than they had given him. But *geassi* bound the Powers, too, to silence, precisely on the things mortals had to work out for themselves: that was how the magic worked, when it worked, if it worked. Even the Sidhe could make mistakes.

Think of m' lord silver-hands in his cage.

And, oh, now, the twins slanted their downward course toward the river itself, unasking, unadvised—

Anxious to be out of the hard climbing, they might be. Or drawn by the fey blood one of them had. But *he* could not overtake them to argue the point, while Dubhain—

Dubhain, seeming to consent to this course, skipped effortlessly down the stones, and among the heather-clumps, apart from them on the mountain, hands folded behind him, head bowed in thought.

Brooding on something, or scheming, or thinking of mischief, Dubhain seemed to be. At least the witch and the powers under-earth had not gotten him—Dubhain might be touchy and sullen, no unusual thing, but this skipping about, this brooding on devilment, that was Dubhain's very self, and Caith took heart in that much, dark as it seemed.

For all he could know, too, the twins' course toward the river was advised and ordained.

Except—except this morning, he had talked of going back to Gleann Fiain. Macha, he did wish he had never said that—he wished he had never put that boastful thought into words and flung them into the haunted air.

Still, what more could the Sidhe ask, once they found the selkie? And Dubhain, a creature of the dark and the waters, what did he care for the wars of the great ones, at all? He had nearly lost Dubhain this morning ... it had been that near a thing, that moment on the mountain ridge. The Sidhe surely knew the weakness of Dubhain's kind. They would send someone else. They were through with this, they had done all they could.

No such, no such, said the pebble that rolled downhill, dislodged from beneath his foot. It bounced on the flat stone that Dubhain trod, and skipped and sailed far, far out into the sky before his eye lost it. Dubhain stopped and looked up at him, as if asking was it his doing, that stone.

By afternoon, the land was scattered hills, the skirts of the mountain, that spread down onto the whin and rock and grass of the rolling downs. The hazy difference between the sky and the land ahead grew stranger as the sun sank low, edged with pale uncertainty.

And from blackest despair in the morning, Caith found himself arguing with a rising, giddy hope, that there might indeed be a Power nearing them that was everything they needed. Gleann Fiain and all that darkness and mountain steep seemed another world from what they saw, and rest and help and sleep seemed all possible tonight. The setting sun danced merrily on a lazy westward bend of the river as they descended to its very shore. Peat-straw had washed up as a golden margin along the river edge, where reeds were few and the banks were autumn grass—a brightness was on the water so different from the dark glen it might have been a passage into faery itself.

They might yet be free of Gleann Fiain and quit of their obligations to fey fools, Caith told himself. They might find the selkie, send him off to quarrel with the witch and themselves linger near the sea, walk the shore and smell the salt air and be free of hurt and need for a while. There would be fishermen, there would be crofters about these hills—rich as the land was, one expected flocks and fields, fat cattle and sheep and, like a stone net spread across the land, the drystane walls that farmers made.

But such as he saw were tumbled down in places, uncared for, and gorse and broom were the crops.

Perhaps the farms lay more toward the sea. Perhaps it was cattle rich lords pastured here, although one would expect to see some sign of the herds, even on resting pastures. It was the fading season. They might have driven the herds down to winter byres already . . . it was toward that time, that unstable season of the year. But it made the land feel vacant, and chancy. And there were no signs of recent presence. And they had seen no falls, no barrier between the loch and the river.

In that mind, he grew uneasy as they walked along the shore, the more so as the rolling hills before them obscured the sea from his view, and the shadows grew longer. The twins kept on at their walking, while Dubhain walked the crest of a nearby hill that he had no strength or will to climb. How long did they purpose to walk tonight, and to what end? One place was like another. And where were Dubhain's thoughts, in his wandering off like that? He was almost willing, now, to beg ease of his aching legs and his scrapes and bruises, whatever the unpleasantness of Dubhain's magic when it touched him. . . .

He was all but willing, but not yet, and increasingly out of sorts with Dubhain's solitary bent. He thought of shouting at him, and bidding him come walk with him, since walking was what the twins seemed inclined to do forever, but he wished no dealings with Dubhain when he was in this fey and dark a mood—no good could come of it.

Then, past another small knowe, and where the shore widened out to a gravelly strand, he saw nets drying on the shore, and what must be a fisherman's bothy, a hut of fieldstone built up against the hill and almost into it.

He drew larger breaths and doubled his pace to overtake the twins, limping as he was, hoping for welcome and a driftwood fire and, if the fisherman was charitable to strangers, a supper that was not rabbit.

Except that the nets, when he overtook the twins among the frames, proved frayed and rotten. The thatch of the hut had looked sound as the stonework, but when they came near, it turned out as weathered grey as the fieldstone. Worse, when they reached the door of the bothy, it hung aslant on two leather hinges, the third rotted away, along with the lower corner of the door itself.

"Abandoned," Caith sighed, and, with a second glance about, wondered how long it took of hanging in the sun and the wind before well-made nets rotted on their drying-frames. A year or so, he reckoned. Less than ten, he was sure.

"There might be food," said Firinne, "or fishing hooks."

There might be. It needed poking about inside a ruin as dead as the keep on the hill, and, as their luck had been running, he had far rather have Dubhain do all the opening of doors—if no wards prevented him, or if Dubhain at all liked the smell of it.

But when he looked around, Dubhain was not with him or anywhere in sight—probably he had found something else to distract him while they were walking through the veils of the hanging nets, in the quirky, un-announced way the rascal could flit off. He might be around the other corner of the shanty, he imagined, having come around the hill, and he walked to that other side to find him, but there was not a sign of him.

Then he began to grow anxious, and looked around.

"Where has the Sidhe gone?" Ceannann asked, from behind him.

Off among the nets, Caith thought disgustedly, but he had no patience to answer the boy—or to look the fool in Dubhain's pranks. Dubhain was either playing games, now that they had reached some sort of destination for the night, if one could call a dusty, abandoned shanty a destination at all—or Dubhain was squatting down by the river, poking at something he had found, or tossing stones in, a dangerous thing to do, with the water flowing out of the loch not a few miles away, but never expect Dubhain to stay the narrow course, and never try to explain him to anyone.

So he left Ceannann perplexed, set down the jug by

the side of the house, and went along the river-edge, among the frames with their rotting nets, expecting Dubhain at any moment to leap out at him or tweak his hair or some other such foolishness. They were not in imminent danger. To Dubhain it was an invitation to mischief.

But the wight was not there either, or was hiding half in faery, as he could do, perhaps listening to the search for him and smirking to himself. There had been that business last night, when he had challenged Dubhain's cleverness, and Dubhain had been so fey and difficult, since—like this morning, on the mountainside. Or all afternoon, that Dubhain had refused to come near him . . . if he could only trust it was one of Dubhain's pranks, if he were absolutely confident that were all it was, he could damn the wight with a clear conscience and go his way until, an hour from now, Dubhain sprang up with some wicked trick to scare him.

But if it was a prank, it was cursed ill-timed, and dangerous with all they had at risk, and tired as he was and angry as he was, he cared not now what Dubhain did to him, so long as Dubhain showed up safe and in good humor. By all the rules he knew, at least of Sidhe magic, a spell always found its way into the weaknesses of a thing—and Dubhain was both the greatest strength in their company and their chiefest weakness, in ways not even he was apt to be. Whether the witch's workings were the same as Sidhe magic, and bound by the same strictures of give and take as Dubhain had claimed, he did not know how to guess—but magic was magic in its grossest points, he supposed, and this disappearing of a sudden truly began to frighten him, along with the vacancy of this place, and the vacancy of the land, and the twins' insistence on walking near the river.

"Dubhain, you rascal. You're not helping us. I did take ye for cleverer than that." That last, he said to sting Dubhain's pride, and give the rascal the excuse to appear, scare him, and claim some plausible excuse for his vanishing—oh, not weakness. Not that he might have been tempted to a wickedness greater than his ordinary wicked self. Not that something was whispering to him out of the water and out of the earth and bidding him play the ultimate, wicked, unexpected prank.

"Here I am, Dubhain. Ye can't touch me and get away before I catch you."

But it drew not a flicker of a misbehaving Sidhe. Not a stone. Not a breath of whisper at his ear.

Shaking his head, he walked from among the nets and around to the back, half up on the knoll, and down and around again, giving Dubhain every chance at scaring the sense out of him, but there was never a hint or a sign he had been there. The twins stood and watched this foolish, helpless search, perplexed, and shrugged and looked troubled when he gave it up.

"You cannot find him?" Ceannann asked.

"No, damn him," Caith muttered, twice foolish answer to foolish question, which he wished instantly he had not said; and, the hut being the only resource before them, and the only place else to search, he went to that, took hold of the door by its edge and dragged at it.

The leather of the middle hinge gave way, and the door sagged down of a sudden and scraped his ankle as it swung open on its last. He swore and recovered himself on the uninjured foot, holding his ankle, with a view of the dark inside—no ghosts, no bogles evident. And no Dubhain.

Ominously enough, too, the place was still stocked. No fisherman would have left his nets, and, by his experience, neighbors who knew an old man had died would by no means have left his belongings for the badgers and the foxes. Yet the light from the open doorway fell on clothing left hanging and cooking pots left unthieved. A cot, a table, a chair, floats and weights and other oddments of the fisher's trade . . . all abandoned. If there had ever been a boat, he had seen none near the shore, so one could choose to believe the fisherman had taken it and abandoned what might even have been a seasonal abode—years ago, perhaps simply because the fishing failed.

But in such haste? Or in expectation of return the next season?

Maybe his boat had sunk—but why had no one missed the fisherman, and come looking, and eventually carried away the goods, if the man had drowned and they were going to waste and ruin anyway?

Its condition had all the look of a place under some curse, if he had to hazard a guess, a place where the neighbors would not willingly venture; but he could most often feel a Sidhe touch in a house that was quiet enough, or feel a haunt if one was about and ready to wake, and this small hut and its gravelly shore was void of all feeling of harm or help, except his niggling unease that it existed so conveniently and so conspicuously in an otherwise vacant land. He even held up the elf-shot stone, with a trepidation of seeing something otherwise invisible. . . .

Blurred, unnatural shadow fell on the cot and the wall, and for a moment his heart jumped, but the twins had moved behind him in the doorway, blocking the reflected sunlight.

"D' ye feel anything?" he asked them. One of them being Sidhe, he thought he might expect some advice or some opinion, or even some explanation why they had come straight for this place. But they shook their heads to that question, seeming more interested in the shelves.

"There are blankets," said Ceannann, and, "Shelter," said Firinne.

Shelter, the woman said. Macha, he was exhausted, and without Dubhain to keep the dreams away, he did not wish to sleep, least of all in a place this strange. The sea was where they were going . . . the shore was where he had far rather sleep tonight, if he could only muster the strength to keep going. It was the only thing that

beckoned to him with safety, and he had not the
strength to reach it.

But plead with the selkie-child? Who was listening to
him, at all, when Dubhain deserted him and the fey
twins were at the shelves and the sun, the traitor, was
slipping to the horizon?

Maybe, after all, the twins knew where they had to
be, and where were they going, before the sun set, if not
here, where luck had led them ... and for all they
knew, the right luck? The twins came out of hazards un-
scathed, the twins kept their lives, and got to safety ...
stay as near to them as he could, that was the wisdom
that offered itself in Dubhain's absence; and if the
selkie had swum the river to the getting of the twin with
Fianna, it could certainly reach them here, in the way of
the Sidhe, just as fast as the selkie willed to reach
them—which would be with all the speed its scaly kind
felt necessary.

Meanwhile the twins were into the shelves and pots,
interested in plunder. Firinne had already gotten off
with the only blanket from the mountain keep, and
shared it with her brother, but never once, not once, had
they considered him on the way here: Firinne had had
the blanket to herself all during the climb, the warmest-
clad of all of them, with her abundance of skirts and her
plaid, and with the strength of the Sidhe to sustain her.

Now, like a good thief, she was losing no time in
searching through the shelves and looking into the jars
for whatever spoils she could lay claim to.

Well, fisher-ghosts and Sidhe be damned, he said to
himself, he was weary of going cold. He spied a man's
shirt hanging on a peg, nothing fine, but good muslin,
and clean, given the dust from its hanging on its peg for
years. In a small tarred box below a counter, he found
good stockings, more than one pair, and in the same
box, a leather bag the thong of which broke to powder
when he opened it. In it he discovered a razor, a whet-
stone, and a good knife, not too far gone in rust, along

with a few fishhooks and some weights wrapped in cord that might still be sound enough to land a fish.

Worse and worse news for what had happened here, then. What with the knife and the cord and the hooks, the little bag was the sort of kit a fisherman might habitually take with him, if he liked his comforts, and used his razor for more than shaving. But the fisherman was gone and it was here, and his need was.

"We could stay here," Firinne was declaring to Ceannann. "We could mend the nets and be fisherfolk."

Macha save him, it had all the echo of the cottage in the glen, above Guagach's haunted waters, a high, hollow echo of folly. He heard in that utterance the very words Firinne must have used six years ago, when they fled the beast. Padraic's memories were as dim to him now as yesterday's dream, but they rose up in bitter rage at Firinne, for all the death and the pain and the destruction her mother's folly had brought down on Gleann Fiain. Nothing would happen, no, no one would die, they would live on forever in an idyll of innocence. Why, Ceannann, Firinne would have said, just as blithely, looking about the cottage, we can live here and be shepherds. . . .

Did you never care what was going on around you? he longed to shout at Firinne, himself: did ye never ask who lived in that cottage before you, or what happened to them? He hated such fecklessness. He had lived in his own illusions, on the shores of the salt sea, and he had cherished his own misled dreams, and he knew the harm it had brought on him and everyone he touched—in his bitter home-coming, and his youthful delusions who his father really was—Macha, it was the oldest of stories. He did nothing new. There was no new wrong-doing under the sun. There was nothing new of folly either, or fond delusion.

Or perhaps it was the truth he hated most of all—and he was no one to lesson them. He could not, in his own heart, and apart from Padraic's bitter feelings, fault the twins too much, who had never known any life but the one their foolish mother and mortal father had given them, their little shadow-play of happiness between murders and calamity—

How could they have known better than he could have known his own truth? When the Sidhe damned a man—they owed him no truth. They gave him no leeway, and no excuses. That was for men to have, the better to deserve their fates.

And were they thieves? They were a lord's children. Who had denied them anything? Who had ever told them the cost of their illusions and the glamor of the pretendings that a fond father cast about their nursery, while the gate-guard died, and the flocks died, and the people died bloodier and bloodier deaths? They were safe. They slept soundly. No one had told them the cost. And were messengers ever guiltless of bitter messages?

Have peace with them, he decided. If they proved contrary tomorrow, he would seize the best of everything himself and leave them to their fate: thus, twice or so in every hour of his life, he deluded himself that he had a choice—or that they had. He did not know their fate, he did not wish to know it—he could grow angrier and more desperate for himself if he let himself think long in that vein, and he refused to listen any longer to their childish play and their bubbling delight over a dead man's leavings. He only appropriated a cooking pan and a cup, that was all else, with apology to the dead. He put the small things into his own pouch, wrapped the pan and the cup into a piece of muslin Firinne had not yet found, tied it up in tarred cord that had not rotted too badly over the years, and took his pilfered goods outside. That was all he needed, besides the shirt and the stockings, all the wealth, at least, that m' lord Nuallan was likely to let him keep, once they had rescued him . . . as was only Nuallan's due to be

rescued, and Caith mac Sliabhin's just fate to go penni-
less, oh, aye, it was.

He had to get his breath of clean air, after the inside
of the hut; and, walking out and around under the sinking sun, only to see what there was to see, and perhaps
to climb the knoll for a view of the sea—he lifted the
half-rotten lid of the cistern beside the house and found
the recent storm had filled it almost to the brim.

Here was water that had flowed from the sky, not the
loch, and it was better to him at the moment than the
things inside the house. He took the immediate chance
to strip off his tattered shirt and wash the grime off,
then sat down to shave and attend his sore feet, while
the twins were at their business inside. Gone all desire
of further traveling tonight, gone his restlessness to
reach the sea by walking another night. His knees
ached, and his stomach was empty, and once he had
washed, he felt far saner and calmer—still concerned
for Dubhain, aye, but ready to settle for the evening and
let tomorrow's troubles come tomorrow.

Besides, he reasoned with himself, the wight did go
off at times for simple reasons that made perfect sense
to Dubhain, however ill-timed. Responsibility was not
often foremost in Dubhain's thoughts. It was not often
in Dubhain's thoughts.

But in that consideration, if Dubhain had felt hungry
and decided they were staying, Dubhain might even be
off chasing their supper, in perfect innocence. He had
done that before.

That, and looking for the local Sidhe. That was far
more likely. Where there were mountain springs one
could expect a few of the elusive little folk; where there
were broad grassy meadows like these beyond the hill,
there well might be one of the domestic fay; and
Dubhain might easily have hared off in court of one, if
the fay in question was at all comely—

Or he might, third choice, be off exploring in faery,

if the way into that land was at all easier from this valley—as well it might be.

On that thought, Caith leaned against the rim of the cistern and made a cautious venture himself in search of such a passage, always so easy for him—always far easier than he had liked, before Gleann Fiain.

Easy this time: he fell, in that sudden vision— tumbled headlong, not into the fisherman's cistern, but into a frightening grey vacancy, where up confounded down and everything spun topsy-turvy.

Then, turning slowly until down was up, and watching the insubstantial bubbles rise through the insubstantial water, he knew where he was—back on the very edge of Moragacht's domain.

Of the silver gates of Nuallan's land, he saw nothing, only drifted in a terrifying greyness, not mist, not fog, not water—no feeling at all. Dubhain's vanishing was not at all one of Dubhain's pranks, nor even Dubhain's choice, he knew that now, and he felt a foreboding fear that if he looked about again, something would be at his back—a fear so acute he tore frantically away from the greyness, desperately imagined himself leaning on the cistern rim, then, and after a breath or two, was there again, alone, panting after breath, and with no sense of rightness in faery or out of it, at all. The sunlight seemed dimmer, the rim of the sun below the hill now . . . that much time had just passed, in a single curious slip.

"By the geas," he muttered, shivering with the earthly wind on his damp skin. "By the geas, wight. Ye must answer me—come to me. Now! I give ye no choice!"

No answer came to him. He waited. And in the midst of numb fear, the wind persuaded him to think of other, more practical things, at least long enough to pull on his stolen shirt and change his ragged stockings for a dead man's.

But he could no longer bear the stillness outside or

the prattle of careless suppositions from inside the shanty—and if there was a danger in faery, he could not deal with it while that chattering was going on and that foolishness was distracting him. It wanted caution, more than he was going to have from the twins tonight, he was sure.

He ached even getting up again, but he slung his sword to his shoulder, and went walking along the river shore, out of earshot of the twins, where the setting sun stained the grass and cast long shadows. He watched the ground as he walked, kept an eye to the river, arms hugged about him against the chill that rode the wind out of the mountains. One might hope, he thought distractedly, that the sea wind would come in soon, and bring its milder air. One hoped it might bring more than that.

But it seemed no good to beg the unhearing Sidhe, or to threaten to walk away and leave the twins to whatever guilt they had inherited by being born. The Sidhe would have no mercy for the twins for what they were and had no such mercy for him if he failed them . . . directionless now as his kindly Sidhe lord seemed to have left him, or helpless as his foolish Sidhe patron was now, there was no knowing.

He could suppose, in the absence of other evidence, that the twins were indeed the important matter, that they were set in his charge, for him to do for them what he could . . .

Or perhaps he was to destroy them. That was the Sidhe's principal use of him. That was his particular talent in the world. Perhaps they had no wish to have the selkie involved and he was to do general murder. They left him to guess which.

"Dubhain," he pleaded with the indifferent breezes. "Dubhain, if this is all a joke, I do own ye far the cleverer. Ye've affrighted me, I admit it, to all the height and depth of the world I do admit it, and ye can come back, now, Dubhain, at any time ye will."

Only the wind whispered to him down the knowe and the peat-water sighed among the reeds, while the sun died at sea.

Once in dread, once in pain . . .

The thought struck him then that the sum of his Callings might not add up to three: once in the yard of the cottage, with the beast at his heels, once into Dun Glas . . . and never since, if one counted only the times Dubhain admitted to coming at his calling . . .

Not at your calling, Dubhain most carefully had said, when he had arrived on Guagach's bank, to take his pooka shape and bear him to Moragacht's border. Dubhain had made a curiously careful point of it that he had come at Nuallan's summons, and that it was Nuallan's bidding he was doing—which he had thought mildly strange of Dubhain, then, but he had written it down to Dubhain's reluctance to carry him at all. . . .

A third calling yet to make? Macha, what worse was there to face, than the cellars of Dun Glas? What worse, oh, gods, had he deserved, in the balances of magic— and what worse harm could a man find, in this fair, sunlit land?

The fisherman might have known that answer. A prudent man might have taken his boat and fled as far from Gleann Fiain as he could, once the keep above the loch had fallen.

But leaving everything? His razor? A good shirt? A knife well-honed and old in the man's possession?

Everything they had found here spoke of sudden calamity, the nets rotting on their frames and the door and the shutters shut, until the weather broke the door hinge and the rot ate away the bottom corner, letting in the breezes and the foxes to their mischief.

And was this fair land all vacant, and was all there had ever been here this one solitary fisherman? This river might be, for all that he could tell, some rustic borderland of faery itself, where the Sidhe, bound by the *geassi* of their own magic, could leave only clues

and signs of the mortal world. Things of faery matched
their counterparts in the mortal world at very odd
points; and every choice regarding those counterparts
was fraught with consequence.

In sudden fear that he might have strayed over some
such boundary unawares, he looked back toward the
hut—but there was Ceannann sitting on the cistern
edge, working over some bit of plunder, as sure a proof
as he would have that, wherever this land was,
Ceannann, at least, and the hut, were all part of it.
Firinne was not in sight—but she was inside, plundering
the last, he had all confidence of it.

Then it came to him that, having fled the hut as far
as the bend of the river . . . here he was helplessly looking back to it again, sure that if he *did* wish to find
Dubhain again, doubtful blessing, then he dared not
leave this place.

Doubtful blessing, but without Dubhain, who would
keep the dreams away, and who would be with him on
the road he was damned to travel, and what creature
in the world would he ever know was absolutely safe
from the curse he bore . . . save only Dubhain?

So, furiously angry, and rubbing his arms to warm
them, he found himself walking aimlessly, helplessly
back to the abandoned shanty, still hoping that Dubhain
would appear, but not believing that his appearance was
imminent—still hoping his surmise was wrong, and that
he might be spared worse than he had suffered, but all
but out of hope for himself.

Ask why it was on him to suffer the pains of hell for
this vain, this feckless pair of fools.

Ask why a lord of the Sidhe stood where he did now,
or whether it was to Nuallan's good or his own or the
witch's, all that he had done so far. Belief was tottering.
Courage was. He gave a pleasant face to Ceannann because the anger in him was so extreme and so murder-
ous, and he gave a shrug to Firinne when she put her

head out the door of the bothy, asking where he had
been.

"Oh, talking to the river," he said, "and the air and
all." Like Dubhain, he had to tread the brink of killing
anger, but he lacked Dubhain's innocence. He had to remember the greater danger, that not only did his anger
get the better of his sense, the worse thing was . . . he
so enjoyed it while it had him.

Either his fey saying or the expression on his face put
restraint on them, though, because they were quiet, and
seemed afraid of him.

A driftwood fire threw a pleasant warmth over the
evening, while the beast, if ever it ventured out of the
walls of the glen, proved not to have eaten every fish in
the river. Ceannann had, with an unwonted industry,
and probably at Firinne's urging, put together a lure and
a hook, and showed skill with it, what was more. Three
fat trout had ended their lives flopping on the stony
bank in the very last of the daylight.

A whole trout apiece, cooked over coals on a proper
grill in the outdoor cookpit, rubbed inside with a few
herbs that Firinne had discovered growing wild against
the side of the hut, along with a little salt and a few
crystals of honey from jars in the cottage, was not at all
a supper to disparage; neither was the whiskey of
Gleann Fiain an inferior drink. With both to warm his
stomach, and sitting in the lee of the bothy wall, a small
fire in front of him and one of the fisherman's blankets
about him, he recovered a more charitable opinion of
Firinne and her brother—well, at least so far as their resourcefulness about the fish extended.

And, uneasy as the place was, at least nothing had
shown up to gnaw the fishes' bones, either—so thinking, Caith glanced off where he had flung his—not into
the fire, but into the dark beyond it, deliberately to pac-
ify a hungry ghost, if it was there, and to see whether

it had stayed where it belonged, behind the walls of Gleann Fiain.

If the ghost from Gleann Fiain had not followed them, and if no fisherman-ghost was haunting the shanty, they might, he almost began to hope, pass a peaceful night, and surely make the sea by tomorrow night. He was far more sanguine, with supper in him and a blanket around him.

And if a cruel-humored, prankish Sidhe could only hear a man and turn up, after all, safe and free and with some plausible, feckless excuse for his absence, he could sleep the sleep of his life tonight.

"Missing a good supper, Dubhain, d' ye hear me, ye wicked wight? I feel sorry for ye."

"Where would he be?" Firinne asked, when he said that aloud. "Where can he have gone?"

He gave a shrug. "Where he pleases. Chasing the fay of some spring, the lascivious fellow." The firelight warmed the stone and thatch of the abandoned hut to a lived-in look. Worn-out nets held the weathered thatch down, probably the reason it had lasted so well. The ropes that depended about the head-high eaves had for their weights fishing floats of green glass that shone like bubbles behind Firinne's pale hair. In that firelight glow, he recalled why he had been so drawn to her, which had nothing to do with her cooking or (he had to admit it for the truth, now that he had had his supper and mended his mood) her greater presence of mind in getting out of the mountain keep with her blanket and a cooking pot, certainly better than he and Ceannann had done; and, as for her sharing with her twin and not with him—how could she reasonably deny Ceannann? And what did she owe a chance stranger?

Her life, he thought nastily. Her freedom. And Ceannann's.

With whom she shared a bed at night. Padraic's recollection of standing at the foot of their bed—was of all Padraic's memories the most persistent, fraught with omen and the imminence of Padraic's own dying. It struck the same note as sounded in his own sensibilities when the twins, as they did now, would look at him at the same moment; or speak one on top of the other, as they had begun, ever since the ruin, to do more frequently—either more frequently, or he had, with Padraic's sensibilities, begun to notice it. Wrong, his instinct clamored when he saw it. Unnatural.

Someone should do something, it said, on his conviction of geas-bound wickedness between them, whom no one had succeeded in separating, not their nurse, not their mother, not their mortal father, and, so far, not Moragacht nor the Sidhe. A child, the lady of Gleann Fiain had longed for; twins, Moragacht had promised her; and, before or after their birth, someone ... *some* power had bound the twins as they were bound— damning all Gleann Fiain into that bloody bargain.

A man might come between them, the thought arrived unbidden, considering Firinne among the glass bubbles. His blood moved faster in him, and he conceived a righteous, temper-ridden notion of setting nature right and breaking the unnatural bond that some fool priest or some dark and magical force had set on two children. Let the powers at work here test damnation for damnation—curse for curse, let the witch of Dun Glas try his for bloodiness and persistence, and let the balance of magic at work here weigh their suffering against his for lord Nuallan, and decide whose was the greater force.

Ceannann remained the center of the problem, Ceannann was persistently the spoiled, angry child that Firinne had to placate, just like at the cottage. He vividly recalled his second encounter with Ceannann, Ceannann armed and distraught, oh, aye, distraught as a man would be for the safety of his sister, but the more he considered the devastation that bond had already wreaked, the more watching them together set his teeth on edge—watching the way they set about, now that

supper was done, Firinne bidding Ceannann do this and
Ceannann do that . . . as if *he* were not sitting at their
fire, too. He waited, irked at being ignored, for either of
them so much as to look his direction. He watched sullenly as Ceannann gathered driftwood to keep the fire
going through the night, a task in which he might have
helped. Ceannann might have turned about and said,
Lazy man, bestir yourself. He would not, he decided,
have taken offense at that, no matter Ceannann's usual
tone in such remarks.

But he might not have existed at all in their small
world, the two of them talking together, making their
plans together: what wanted doing, they evidently considered themselves quite enough for, as they had in the
fishing and in the making of supper, and so long as they
were enough, and so long as he did not speak to them,
evidently they needed not notice he was with them.

The longer he sat ignored, the more he felt that as a
slight, even considering the perilous nature of the night,
and the fey character of the twins. It was not, he was
sure, even an intended slight. It was the unnatural way
of them. That was the very heart and core of the vexa-
tion he had in being left responsible for them.

Share the shanty with them tonight? His thoughts
were all too dark for that . . . too dark and too dangerous, and he did not like the fact that his temper was
bounding leagues ahead of his reason, tonight, in a
coming and going of anger and ease that had been going on in him ever since the keep. He knew in all good
reason that his imagination of having Firinne was mad,
and that the notion that he could, by the oldest and most
primitive magic a mortal could work, shatter the geas
that bound the twins, was a foolish, reckless thought.

Granted, it might even work—if the breaking of the
geas did not blast the man that did the deed.

It *might* even be Nuallan's magic urging him to such
a reckless step, as a means the witch might not be able
to prevent—but a geas strong enough to destroy Gleann

Fiain entire was nothing to attempt on a whim and at such—a man could not but think—intimate risk.

The more he considered matters sanely, the shanty, too small and too dark for three people to take their supper there, seemed far too close for him and the two of them lying down to sleep inside. It was a fey, difficult night, the river shore was quiet, they were well out of the dreadful glen, and, what was more, the inside of the hut was blind to the outside, without its rotten door and flimsy shutters affording any barrier against whatever might prowl the shore tonight.

"On his way, your father is," he remarked, as the twins were going inside, still without seeming to notice his presence. "And if he does show his face, how shall I know him? Fins, has he? A seal's coat?"

"We have no least idea," Firinne said solemnly; and Ceannann, behind her:

"Our mother would never tell us that part."

"I wager she did not." He could *not* govern his tongue—and it was not all dealing with Dubhain that made him as he was. There was his father's cruelty in him, and Ceannann was frowning when he went inside.

The door scraped to, the bar dropped with a definitive thump, shutting him out, without them ever once asking did he wish to sleep inside, or did he feel any unease in the open tonight.

Well, damn them and good night, he thought, refusing that final provocation. Give him his sword and a wall at his back and a clear field around him, if he had to use it. Give him no Firinne to draw his mind down forbidden paths all night. He had a good fire going, he had his blanket; he had the clean wind about him instead of a musty thatch shedding spiders and mouse droppings on his head, they had the shanty to themselves, cot and all, and if the beast should come clattering out of the river, by the Badbh, the twins' luck hitherto had been potent enough to save them, and fatal to those standing near them. So he intended to look en-

tirely to his own safety, and damn Firinne, too. It was
foolishness he had been thinking tonight.

He thrust another stick into the coals and watched it
take fire, with nothing more on his mind than that,
thinking that after a drink and a meal and his walking
half of last night he should sleep like the dead. But
sleep perversely eluded him now. His blood kept racing,
and he sat half-mad with angers and suppositions and
fears for things to come ... he did not even know
where he had gotten them or why he entertained them,
but they bred like vermin and left his blood racing with
anger and his hands trembling with exhaustion as he
took up a small stick of driftwood and broke it in
pieces, casting them one after the other into the firepit
and watching them burn.

The mutter of the river and the snap and flutter of the
fire were the only sounds. For a time he could occupy
his anxious mind with listening about him, like a proper
sentry for two fools' sleep. But the silence grew lone-
lier, his own prospects more frightening, once his
thoughts drifted to wondering what Dubhain was about,
and what the Sidhe might ask of him on the morrow.

A pebble shifted, across the faint glare of the fire. His
eyes lifted as instantly as his heart thumped. Two red
shimmerings a little brighter than the dark showed
above the fire-glow, then a dusky, familiar face.

"Dubhain, damn you!" All his calculations and his
defenses went tumbling down, and left only temper ...
which with Dubhain was never the best course. He expected laughter, then, and the inevitable foul trick at his
expense, but if Dubhain was here, anything was welcome.

Dubhain whispered, "He answereth, man, he maun
answer the blood, the twain hae had that much for true:
bluid is the binding of him and heart's bluid is the binding of me. Call the third time, my prince. I hae nae ither
means to return t' ye."

"A third time. A third time, is it?" Fear settled sickly

cold in the pit of his stomach, and anger welled up out of it. "And who laid this on me? Was 't you, is this your damned *joke*, after all, Dubhain? If it is, then set to, draw blood and be done, don't leave me here with this pair! I own ye the cleverer, I flatter ye, ye damned wight, anything ye wish, I will grant, but don't leave me alone to deal with this!"

"My doing? Nay, my damned prince. I would 't were."

"Damn you to hell, then, Dubhain! —No! Wait! Don't go!"

"Invoke me wi' more passion than that, man, and use your wits, this time, such as they may serve ye . . ."

The red glimmering faded on the other side of the smoke and Caith leapt to his feet in indignation, but there was nothing to see, not the least shadow of Dubhain's presence. Disconsolate, he sank back again and wrapped the blanket about himself.

Oh, far too much now he wished to believe that Dubhain's jokes and Dubhain's treacheries had their limits in Dubhain's conscience, he longed desperately to believe that, in their years together, Dubhain had learned some love for him, some remorse for his wickedness and his changing humors—oh, dream that Dubhain did any kindness that had not its obligatory barb in it . . .

Dream then that the river ran backward, and first explain to Dubhain what compassion was, and try to make that word at home in his heart, before one ever tried to explain to him what loyalty was, or why one friend would stand by another at no profit or amusement whatsoever to him.

Macha, was that too much to ask of the gods, once, someone who was sorry for what happened to him, now and again in a lifetime of paying for someone else's sins?

He raked his fingers through his hair and flung back his head. It hit hard against the stone wall of the shanty—which hurt, and reminded him of a stone flung by Guagach's banks, and a pain over his heart and a spot of blood on a white shirt.

That told the tale, if ever he could muster the courage to face it: it was the fair warning Dubhain gave him of his own character, the honesty Dubhain was compelled to show him, like any good Sidhe ... or wicked one.

Oh, aye, whoever lived by magic was bound to such little honesties: it kept the Sidhe pure, it kept them out of harm's way when the difficulties came, it let them work their spells on a mortal, fallible man and it gave them all the power of their wicked innocence.

Damn the wight!

The door scraped, softly, opening. A pale shape whispered out of the doorway, pushed the door shut again, and loomed over him the other side of the smoke, him with the tears seeping in his eyes from the crack on his skull.

"Was someone here?" Firinne asked. "Has your friend come back? I thought I heard you talking to someone. Or did I dream it?"

He was in no pleasant mood, nor willing to wipe his eyes with Firinne to witness it. "Come and gone," he said sullenly, in as faint a voice as might not disturb the night and wake Ceannann inside. "Go back to sleep. 'T was nothing. I only thought I heard something."

With a rustle of her petticoats she came around the fire, looking at him, but he would not look at her.

"Quarrels among us now can only be the witch's doing," she said, sinking down, elbows on knees, beside him. Every word she spoke seemed to hang in the air, weighted with Necessity and omen. Her coming out here gave him no easier feeling at all about Dubhain's skiting off the way he had—if he had not dreamed it all. He set his jaw and looked away, as plain a hint as he could give that he wished she would go back inside.

"Perhaps," she said softly, "if we laid out food for

the Sidhe, he would come back. I saved a little fish for breakfast."

He had to laugh, albeit bitterly. "Not he. Not that one. He's none of the small folk. What your cup of milk could not bind in him, cannot be bound at all. Go back to sleep."

"I can't sleep." With a second rustle of her skirts she sat down on the ground beside him, only for the companionship, it might be, but he was in no mood to suffer anyone in patience. He hurled himself to his feet instead, clutching his blanket about him, and stalked off along the river shore into the night—churlish behavior, it was, but the wind dried the tears in his eyes and chilled the heat in his heart to a cold bearable resignation, and at least he had not shouted at an undeserving innocent, or cursed her, or, thank the gods, done any worse thing. He only wished to lose himself in the wind and the river sound for a while, until Firinne had the sense to go inside and leave him alone. He could only hope that when the twins' unearthly father did show his face, the sun-born Sidhe would be far more reasonable to deal with than his two offspring *or* Dubhain.

He had behaved badly with Firinne just now. He did not think that he had deceived her about his fit of fear and temper, and now he supposed he looked twice the fool in her eyes—thrice more so, to be standing out here in the cold, while she held the warm fireside, waiting for him to gather his composure, he supposed. Doubtless she had seen the tears.

But it was more than his privacy he had sought: it was escape from all of it. He felt as if, in the moment of her nearly touching him, the world had tilted and he had slid to the edge of it, with a very last handhold on safety, and if he once let that go, and let her grow close to him, no sane man or woman could reach him, or them, and nothing could save them from disaster. . . .

"Ahem."

He spun about in blind fright, his hands to his sword as his pilfered blanket tumbled about his legs.

It was no apparition of shadow and clattering stone, it was only a man sitting on a flat rock, in the dark, an old man whose face was stubbled and weathered like a man who had lived his life in the sun and wind, whose cloak was far from rich, and whose white hair, such as remained of it, blew in an untidy ridge in the stiff wind. It was not quite the dreadfulness and dignity one expected of the Sidhe.

But a man who dealt with faery learned to take nothing at its outward seeming, and most of all learned not to be rude with any creature who might be Sidhe: it gave them license. He was not sure whether he was safe to let go his sword hilt, but he refrained from drawing the weapon, or making it obvious, and he bent cautiously and gathered up his blanket, not failing, as he did so, to see the stout stick showing from under the old man's cloak: a walking-stick, it might be, but such a stick in expert hands was not at all to discount as a weapon.

"Who are you?" he asked.

"I might do the asking," the stranger said cheerfully, in an old man's rough voice, and with the lilt of the remote, ancient places of the land, "seeing ye've made yourselves free o' me hoose yonder."

It might indeed be the fisherman who owned the place, except Caith thought, the items left, and the nets left rotting on their frames.

"If the place is yours, we do earnestly beg your pardon. But the dust lay so thick about, and the nets in disrepair and all . . ." It was a perilous thing to challenge a ghost. Some took it very ill to have their death proven to them.

"Ach," the old man sighed, slowly standing up, leaning on the stick. He had only one leg, Caith saw then, and that could explain a great deal else, about the abandoning of the nets and the house, for one, without at all

invoking the Sidhe. "Well," said the gaffer, " 't is free
ye are of the place, for aught I care. Me daughter persuaded me to leave the auld hoose, gie up me nets and
sell th' boat doon th' river."

"So you still live near here?" They had seen no
plume of smoke such as a chimney might make at sup-
pertime, but then, they had been busy with fishing and
other matters about sunset—and he ever so much hoped
to find an ordinary explanation for the vacancy of this
shore.

"Oh, a wee o'er the hill. Me daughter wad no ap-
prove th' auld man abroad a' sich an hour, but I smellt
the smoke and a', and I asks mesel', who'd be settlin'
in here i' these wicked days? —Is 't the fishing at a'
ye're after? 'T is gone, man, gone, th' day ye'd make a
good living fra' the river Fiain, but e'en yet ye can find
a fat 'un or two, on a good day, if ye do ask. —Hae ye
had any luck at all?"

"Oh, a couple or so," he said, taking the trailing blanket over his arm, folding it to hide the sword, and de-
bating urgently in his mind whether the old man was
only what he seemed, a trusting old grandfather who
truly ought to ask himself whether the occupiers of his
old shanty might not be bandits keenly interested in
finding better plunder.

"Ye wad na' hae a dram o' the barley for an auld
man, would ye?"

The whiskey was undeniably about him, and with the
chill undeniably riding the wind out of Gleann Fiain it
seemed very ill-mannered to send the old man off into
the night, especially seeing they were occupying his
house and making free of his pots and pans—although
his daughter must be rich, to let good pots go to ruin.

But if the old man was, as might well be, simply the
Sidhe who ruled the place, then it would be exceedingly
well done to have given him his due at his asking.

And if he should turn out to be the selkie they had
come to find, it might well be a testing, and best entreat

him well, if there was some test or some geas about him they had to break to gain his help, and not have him diving off into the river and leaving them.

Or if it was, after all other chances, only a lame old man come out on a long walk to his outworn house, well, then, ply the old fisherman with whiskey and send him home sleepy and safely clear of trouble that no one else needed know about. Dubhain's deserting him to-night, along with his own impulse to walk out here in the cold wind and the dark had, to him, a sudden, most definite sense of Sidhe magic about it.

Perhaps, he thought, the selkie was indeed testing him, or the local Sidhe was offering him a chance the magic wagered his faults would not let him take: the Sidhe were very keen on such tricks and traps, exactly the sort of thing that would give a Sidhe just cause for anger at him: what Dubhain had said of Sidhe magic had offered him a glimmering of the truth he had long suspected, that Sidhe magic was far and away more potent if it could set a man in the wrong, and if it had offered him escapes the magical three and seven times.

"Oh, aye, we might have a drink," Caith said. "Whiskey out of Gleann Fiain, last of the stock, it is, and served in your own cup, besides."

"Heh," the old fellow said, and, spry for a grey-beard and well-practiced on his crutch, he hopped down off the little rise and swung along with him toward the bothy and the firelight.

"My name is Caith, by the way. Caith mac Gaelan." It was dangerous to give a true name to the Sidhe: and one could reckon that a Sidhe would never lightly give his own. "And who might you be, besides the owner of this land?"

"Liamh mac Kiernan, auld Liamh, they call't me, when there was more folk about. Och, was they big ones?"

"The trout? Oh, aye, grandfather, three fat ones, long as my forearm."

Old Liamh laughed merrily. "A half a score such wad ye take, upon a time, and salmon, too, i' the spring, the pretty fishes running up to the loch and beyond. Ye'd see them leaping at the sun, a' up the river Fiain, when the old laird was alive."

"Him of Gleann Fiain, d' ye mean?"

"Och, aye, as long as Himself was on his high hill, the fishes came, but when the keep burned down, then the glen came grimmer and darker, and the fishes came fewer, and, och, the clatterin' beast was out an' about, a horrid beastie, all clatterin' an' rattlin' wi' dead men's bones."

"Was it?" Nothing now seemed chance at all. "Did you meet the mac Ceannann? Did you deal with him?"

"A fine, fine man, the mac Ceannann. He gie'd me leave to draw fishes fra' his ain loch, and paid me besides, in cheeses, meself being the only fisherman who'd dare the loch f' him." He chuckled as he hopped along on his crutch, and a hale old fellow he was, for a mortal, not seeming so much as short of breath. "Himself wad ca' me up to the hall on the hill and ask me the doin's on the loch and doon th' river ... hoo, 't is a lass, yonder, is 't?"

Firinne was standing by the door in the firelight, watching them as they came; while not a word he had heard from the gaffer yet had told him a truth he was sure of, or made him any surer of his nature.

"Was it fishing that you lost the leg?"

"Me leg?"

"Was it fishing ye lost it?"

"Aye, t' the beast, it was."

"In the loch?"

"In the deep of Gleann Fiain, man, I was drawin' in me nets like always, and snagged something beneath the water. Up it comes—" He gave one hop as he swung his stick at the night sky, then had it to lean on again. "I stuck my foot at the beast and it bit it right off and dived doon wi' me nets and a'. —Why, 't is the laird's ain daughter. 'T is Firinne! Firinne, lass!"

Firinne stood staring as the old man hopped briskly toward her; and at the very edge of the yard, in the maze of frames with their rotting nets, every sense of the Sidhe flared up, a prickling of Caith's skin and a shortness of breath.

Then of a sudden it was no man beside him, but a three-legged dog, or a wolf, that, before his heart could take another startled beat, snarled and streaked straight for Firinne.

"Shut the door!" Caith cried. *"Shut the door, woman!"*

Firinne seemed to come from trance, then, and spun inside the shanty and dragged at the broken-hinged door, trying to pull shut what might not be able to shut, for all he knew. Where Ceannann was, or whatever help Firinne had from him with that door, it was not closing well; and Caith ran with his sword in his hand . . . he did not even remember drawing it, except the weight was swinging with his arm at every stride. The black dog was growling and snapping at the ragged door, trying to force himself through the broken bottom corner.

But seeing Firinne was safe inside and he was alone out here with the creature, he skidded to a halt short of what no longer was a dog, but a one-legged man hammering at the door with his stick, then a woman in ragged skirts . . . or a goat hung about with seaweed, or a sheep, or a pig, or a clattering collection of bones, changing shape with every thump of his laboring heart.

"Dubhain," he gasped, "Dubhain, if ye'd kindly take notice." He slid his finger along the edge of his sword, drawing blood, Dubhain liking it so well. "Dubhain, sweet lad, I've caught the creature. I have it trapped. Will ye come now and dispose of it?"

The beast had abandoned its attack on the door. It turned and eyed him. In that shapeless, skinless body it had settled in, veins stood out, knotting and twisting;

then sinews bunched along its grating, disjointed bones and it lunged toward him.

He cut at it and swung the blanket at it to confuse its rush, but some part of it hit him like a sack of stones and sent him flying. He landed on his side with his sword arm beneath him and his legs all this way and that. His eyes were still full of red flashes as he scrambled back to his feet to face the beast—he made out its retreating shape through the flashes in his sight, and he charged after it as it lurched through the nets and frames, tearing down half a dozen poles, swathing itself in rotten nets and adding a wooden clamor to its bony clatter as it ran for the river.

"Damn you!" he howled after it, as it churned into the black water, leaving a pale froth in its wake. He almost had a second cut at it—close enough to have his feet wet to the ankles in the slosh it made as it dived.

Lock-water, it was, and it had tried to draw him in deeper. He realized his danger and leapt back to dry land in haste, but it was already faery about him, or hell ... he stood in the vault at Dun Glas, and Saw a tracery of black rose-branches about the cage of light. So near Nuallan he was standing that he could see the fine dew of sweat on Nuallan's cheek. He heard the thundering of the cauldron, saw the Sidhe lord's eyes half shut, and he flinched from the sight, so unmasked and desperate the Sidhe magic was, the light shining out through Nuallan's flesh as if it were his strength melting away—

Silver in the waxing moon, iron then becomes ...

The shadows of stone images were about that place, deep in the dark, the gods with staring eyes. A rose-branch twined through the cage, past waxen flesh, and the black thorns of it drew blood ... curse Nuallan, oh, aye, he did, three and four times a day and oftener if he thought of it; but this—this torment was wickedness, this was Moragacht as he had known her, working against reason that resisted her hungers; and as Nuallan turned his head and looked off toward the dark, it was such an expression of intimate desire, such a longing as anyone could have toward a forbidden, destructive thing, that a man with his own soul to guard was forced to flinch away from it. The blood moved hotter in his veins, and he was smothering in the lady's presence. He longed to flee back to the mortal realm, to distance himself from what was happening here . . . it was consent the lady wanted, consent was the geas on her.

He understood it. He knew that kind of domination, he had fought it and lord Nuallan had never faced it, not m' lord innocence, m' lord of the lily hands—that now were beaded with blood. The lady whispered to him knowingly through the hammering and the fire, and he turned his face to her, when he would not—no!

With a thump of his heart he caught his balance— stood on the river shore again with his sword in hand. Firinne was running toward him from the house, terrified. He caught her in his arms in his own fright, his heart beating hard, Firinne asking him, he thought, through the roaring in his ears, whether he was hurt. He did not know. He had let fall the sword—dangerous, foolish abandonment on this shore, but then he was not thinking at all, he only remembered the fever and the death he had fled, he had his lips on hers, and that was not closeness enough. He began to slide her skirts up, found bare, warm skin beneath his fingers, while she covered his neck with kisses.

"You dog!" Ceannann's voice cried out of nowhere. A hand landed on his shoulder and hauled him half about, a fist cracked across his jaw, and in that blinding pain, he let go Firinne to seize Ceannann's shirt, with the only thought in his head that of beating Ceannann senseless before Ceannann got in another blow. He heard Firinne shouting at him through the roaring in his ears and the shadow in his eyes, he felt her pulling at his arm, not the least hindrance to his reach for Ceannann's throat. Ceannann was trying for his at the same time, and the two of them shoved back and forth among the tumbling poles and the falling nets.

"Ceannann!" Firinne cried. "Caith! No, *no*, you fools, you fools, it was her, all of this was Moragacht, do you hear me, Ceannann? No! It wasn't his fault! Caith!"

He had his hand on Ceannann's throat, letting the boy batter at him as he would while he strangled him.

But of a sudden a powerful blow landed on his back . . . from what third quarter he could not imagine. It caught Ceannann, too, once, twice, then him, across the head, and they had to break their holds on each other to fend off Firinne, with a net-pole in her hands and wrath on her face.

"You very fools!" she cried. "Both of you!"

"You let him touch you!" Ceannann shouted at her. His voice cracked. "You take up with this . . . this . . . this thief, this bandit!"

"Bandit, am I?" A man liked to know how he seemed to others. It was enlightening. Worse, it had been true, once. "And yourself, ye spoiled, selfish, unnatural boy . . . maybe your sister is weary of you in her bed, d' ye think?"

Ceannann went for him at that, but Firinne hit him over the head and shoulders with the pole and he staggered in his tracks. "No!" she shouted, the tears running on her face. "Ceannann, no!"

"I should let you rut with this goat? Is that what you wish?"

The pole sank to the ground. "No, Ceannann. Ceannann, come back to the house, come. Please."

Ceannann was listening, at least, gasping for breath. Ceannann was as bruised as he was, Caith had no doubt, with the desire for combat running out of him: Firinne had not spared with the pole, and sense was coming back to him. A man of more years than Ceannann ought not to have said what he had just said to the boy. It was not a thing Ceannann could forget, it

certainly gained nothing with Firinne—and anything he
said or did now, Ceannann would find offense with, that
was clear to him. It was dangerous even to bend and
pick up his sword from the stones where he had
dropped it, but he was not leaving this quarrelsome
ground without it, and now it was only retreat he intended. He kept a wary eye on Ceannann when he retrieved it, perversely not willing to give him any sign of
truce, with the anger still buzzing in his blood, but he
mustered the sense at least to walk away from the
twins, then, along the shore, back toward the mountains,
letting Ceannann think what he would of his retreat
from the field: it was not an opinion he valued.

"Caith!" Firinne called after him, a high, anxious
voice. Perhaps she thought he was deserting them both
in their danger. She had reason to fear, seeing he left
her with a fool for her protection.

Ceannann had been bullying her lifelong, for what he
could see of matters between them. Take up with anyone and Ceannann undoubtedly threw a tantrum. Need
anything for herself and Ceannann needed her attention,
immediately. It was a twisted, unnatural obsession the
boy had, and, by the Badbh, he wanted setting straight
. . . but not here and not by him. Desert them, oh,
gladly, he would do that at the moment—but he had no
such choice.

And the moment he even thought of leaving, he
found himself halted on the river shore, looking at the
night sky above the mountains, with his heart pounding
in mingled fear and foreboding.

The mountains might make a wall, he thought, higher
than any king could build; but the evil and the corruption flowed out of Gleann Fiain with the peat-water, just
the same. Whatever folk had lived here, including their
fisherman, were surely bones in that misshapen body,
and souls in its dark belly. Particularly horrid, he found
it, that magic could make them speak, and walk, and do
the beast's bidding, the way the old fisherman had come

out and spoken with him, so convincingly that he had all but invited it across the threshold.

He felt a chill when he realized how very close a call it had been—and it had even had the flaw, damn his foolishness, a very host of flaws: its story had not made sense, but the longer he had listened, and the more he tested it, the more committed he had become to testing it further, until he had walked beside it and taken it to the house.

But he had never given it the peace of the evening and never trusted it completely: therefore it had had no power to come at him without disadvantage, which a creature like that did not like. It might also have smelled the magic about him: the *geassi* that bound him to Dubhain and to the bright Sidhe might have lent him enough magic at odds with its own purpose that, in its low cunning, it had declined to take him on ... saving itself for its try at Firinne and, one supposed, an unwarded doorway.

But that charge, too, had been a futile effort ... too far from the seat of its power, he supposed, this hunting-hound kenneled at Dun Glas.

More, he found his sword blade sticky to the touch, and he wiped it with damp grass and dried it on his kilt—the cursed blade, the unlucky thing that he could not lose—

Macha, he wished Dubhain had never found the sword in the loch. It was a stubborn thing, with an affinity for wicked blood. He had blooded it on himself, tonight, and then on the clattering beast, and the cursed thing was too often in his hand the last few days—let a stone rattle and he was reaching for it, like a child for his mother's hand.

And with that sword, like many a thing bespelled and wicked, a little use became more use, and a feckless, unthinking reliance. He was not doing at all wisely today since Dubhain had left him, and he realized it with a sense of shame and a wondering—he could not help it—whether Dubhain had honestly won their contest, or whether his declaring the contest at all was the chink through which the witch's magic had gotten at them. It was his own cleverness she had tried, and so far—what had he managed and how far had he outwitted anyone?

He squatted there in the dark, having slid the sword back in its sheath, holding it on his knees and asking himself why he had treated Firinne like a whore in hail and full sight of her brother. He had known Ceannann was awake, what with the creature scrabbling at the door. Even if he were a thorough-going villain, he had no need to be a fool—but, no, he had clean forgotten how the twins answered for each other, how they would not be separated, even when it was that very geas he was trying to break.

And Firinne was fey, and young, and if ever the witch was going to insinuate a spell onto the twins it would be Ceannann's temper and Firinne's hunger for any small scrap of life—he Saw that with the True Sight, now that it was far too late to mend. He could not so easily help them now as he might if nothing of the sort had ever happened between them. With his temper and the damned sword so ready to hand, he was dangerous to them, and he had the most dire, sudden fear borning in him . . .

For who could say it was ever the witch's power just now that had blinded him to consequences? He had desired Firinne as long ago as the cottage. A moment ago he had desired her with a deafness to common sense that had all the feeling of geas about it—himself, himself, the Sidhe's own criminal, that they sent to do the things in the world that the immortal Sidhe did not desire the guilt for . . .

Macha, what do they expect of me? Is it rape and murder they call me to, next? Is that the game now, to loose or to end the twins' magic in the world? And which?

He knotted his hands together against his forehead,

elbows on his knees, and he sat out in the dark a long time, trying to calm himself, trying to achieve peace and patience with Ceannann and Firinne, at least within his own heart—trying not to think of his own fate at all, or thinking, when he must think, Please, Dubhain, this is not what I have to do, this is my own wicked imagination at work—is it not?

There cannot be another Calling yet to face, —can there, Dubhain?

But at last he took account of where he was, and in what danger, sitting alone on the shore. Much as he dreaded to go back to the house, it was folly to sit here until the beast slipped up on him in the dark.

Besides, the wind had chilled him through, and the fire was still burning by the shanty, and he had left his blanket in the yard.

"Dubhain," he whispered as he got up. "Dubhain, will ye come back now?"

For sometimes, in the after-moments of the worst and most perilous magic, when it ran utterly amiss, as perhaps the lady's attempt on him had, other things could go so far astray, and a clever Sidhe might slip through the slats, if only for a moment.

But in the way of magic when one needed it most, there was no favorable answer, no answer at all.

He reached the shanty and found his blanket lying where the beast had struck him down. He bent and picked it up. The door was shut—barred against him, he was well sure, as he settled at the fire. Silence prevailed inside, and the disturbing image came to him of the twins entwined in each other's arms, snared again in their mutual obsession.

Was it the nature of them? He had shaken Padraic's indignation from him enough to ask himself that: and, aye, he decided, aye, it *was* wrong, the way it was wrong for a babe to stay in the womb forever. Never truly born to the world, they were—and his wicked act might even have been the only hope for them, the only hope of breaking them free . . . if only he knew from what magic it had come, and he most strongly suspected Moragacht, suspected it with a dark memory of fever in the blood, that still had him disturbed.

There was a smear of blood on his hand. He discovered it, dark in the firelight, but it was nothing of omen, only where he had cut his finger. He sat down by the dying fire and sucked at the wound. It tasted of salt, and iron, of chanciness and such things as the dark gods desired, a man could not forget that, who walked with the likes of Dubhain, and Dubhain himself was under some compulsion—

Heart's bluid is the binding of me. . . .

Call the third time, my prince . . .

Nuallan was listening to the lady. Nuallan heard the thunder and the spells; and once man or Sidhe began to listen to a forbidden thing, he said to himself, then he began to tell himself there was no harm, or no use holding off, or no escape—might he not? And who, since the foundations of the world, had ever taught m' lord Nuallan about self-denial, when fruit from the very trees of faery had fallen into his hand at his bidding, and everyone about him bowed and did as he wished, without demur. Yes, my lord, at once, my lord. Nuallan was more helpless and more innocent in his way than the twins could ever be.

While Dubhain . . .

He hugged his arms about himself. He doubted all his choices, and repented most of his decisions, and asked himself why, why, and why sleep eluded him tonight, weary as he was, and shivering with cold. Doubts and forces seemed to run through his veins as if there were war going on in him, his hands trembled with it, and images of stone gods and silver vines chased each other through his vision, as if he were half ready to fall into that place, as if, if he would consent, he could be there, and all doubts would end, and he could sleep . . .

Dubhain could come there. Dubhain was very welcome there.

Dubhain simply could not come *here*.

He heard the baying of some hound, far away on the mountain. That made him think of the mastiffs, and the mac Ceannann, and of the ruins only a mountain away from them—howling at the moon, he thought, wondering what time it was, but when he looked at the stars, he recalled it had chased the sun to its setting, its thinnest paring.

Witch's moon. The dark of the moon had to be tomorrow night, then, troubling thought. He had lost track, in the storms and the climbing. Spells went better or worse on such nights. And in the fading of the year, with one realm rubbing up against another—

Silver as it waxes, iron then becomes . . . Which did mean the moon, of course—one year's dying, at the Samhain eve? Samhain was at the full, a fortnight away, yet.

But the old gods had had different rules, dealt with the dark, and blood . . . the earth was where their power rested. If it was not the new year the witch was looking to, if the Samhain moon was not the power the witch was seeking, but rather the fortnight before, when the leaves were falling and life was uncertain—

Ask then the ransom of the Sidhe.

And ransom, was it, once Moragacht's power was established? He was her gift to the powers she courted. She needed Nuallan's consent, but a misguided, even a forced consent would do. She drew her power from out of the earth, woman's magic, from the bloody and banished gods, and of a lord of the Sidhe, as of a man, she had to have his consent before she killed him.

Gods . . . *tomorrow night.*

He leapt up and knocked on the door of the shanty. Knocked, and banged on it a third time, with his fist.

"Go away!" Ceannann shouted at him from the other

side of the door. "The door's barred, and we've nothing further to do with you tonight!"

"Something's wrong."

"Oh, aye, something's wrong. Something's wrong. We're asleep, man. We've no interest in your fancies. If the beast comes back, deal with it!"

"Lad." He gathered up his patience. "The moon. We were not hearing what Dubhain was telling us this morning. When you work magic, something is owed the other side, is it not? The greater the magic, the greater the gift must be, and the witch was obliged to warn us directly today, about the silver, and the iron—it was the witch's moon this evening. Tomorrow is the dark of the moon, d' ye understand me, it's not our year's-end she reckons, it's some older reckoning, nothing to do with the younger gods—"

"Go to sleep!"

"Ceannann, I was a fool. I apologize to you, and most of all to you, Firinne, but we have not the night to wait for your father. We have to go to the sea—"

"Now?" Ceannann cried. "In the middle of the night? You're drunk or daft, mac Gaelan. Have the rest of the jug and go back to sleep."

"Lad," he said patiently, reasonably. "Twice now, I beg forgiveness of you and your sister. I swear—I did not mean to affront her, or you, and will not, again. I was wrong. 'T is the third time I say it. Come out and gather what we need. We've a walk before us."

"No!" said Ceannann. "Not with you and not in the dark!"

"Lad." Restraint and reason came harder with every breath. "If I need that door down, I can take it down. The Sidhe is not faring well in Dun Glas, and will fare worse tomorrow night, d' ye hear me?"

"All the more reason to stay inside tonight!"

"Open the door."

"No!"

"You—" No. Temper would not improve matters. He

did not batter the door: he rested his clenched fist carefully on the stone beside it. "Firinne, —Firinne, will you reason with the man? It's a long walk to the coast. If your selkie father is late, or constrained somehow, let's halve the distance. Shall we lose everything, for sleep ye've had some of, at least?"

"We've had no sleep!" Ceannann cried. "We've walked half of last night and had you to deal with in this one, and if our father can't reach us here, then what earthly help is he? Go where you like and ask your friend to go with you, if you can find him, if he's not been one of the witch's creatures all along! And for what we know, *you* are!"

He could not prove that even to himself. He lied, knowing as much as he did of magic: "If we were hers, would a bright Sidhe have ransomed us out of Dun Glas? 'T is the gods of hell she bids to let loose, man, and this river is no safe place tonight or tomorrow. Open the door, and let's be on our way while we have time left to do anything at all."

"Do *what*?" Ceannann cried. "Why should we care? 'T was your notion to tag after us, 't was your notion our father could help you, none of ours. We're safe here. We can fish the river, the two of us, and be very comfortable . . ."

Macha, it was catching. "With the beast at your door at nights? When the whore of Dun Glas has a Sidhe lord to open the gates below? You—" He swallowed 'fool' and continued mildly, letting his fist rest tamely against the wooden frame. "She owns all the land hereabouts, lad, from the mountains to the sea. Where are the people here? Can you answer that? D' ye remember Gleann Fiain at all before the beast came? This land is despoiled of people, flocks, everything that ought to be here. This is not safety. Listen to someone who knows the world, lad, listen to someone who's been farther than Gleann Fiain in his life, and dealt with wickedness besides this wicked woman. Ye cannot temporize with it. I know."

"By what do you know?" Ceannann challenged him, and the intemperate man shouted back:

"Because you cannot with me!" He drew back and kicked the rotten wood without a further thought: it crashed in, the bar fell, the twins cried out, and he stood facing them with his hand on his sword, because he had no idea what Ceannann would do.

But Ceannann stood embracing Firinne, her arms about him, and their eyes wide in the faint firelight from outside.

And if that did not curdle a man's blood, he could not think what would.

"I will swear to you," he said in a harsh voice, "I will take you toward the sea, as far as I can, by morning, I will find your father if there's a father to be had on this forsaken shore, I will put my request to him, myself, and thereafter I've no care what ye do or where ye settle. My care is a fool of a Sidhe lord who's about to become a witch's key to bloody hell, and once I free him there's none so ready as I to see the back of two greater fools." He found himself shouting, and the two of them staring at him like two mice caught in the granary, which was not the help he needed. He lowered his voice and mastered his temper. "I beg ye, lad, I do beg ye, I've a black and a wicked temper, and I beg ye to use softer words with me ... if Herself has a way to us tonight, I tell ye contritely, 't will be your tongue and my temper, or the other way about. And I would not willingly do you harm, lad, not you nor your sister, but you will provoke me, if ye do not what I say, now, and very quickly."

Ceannann's anger was ready to boil up, he saw the scowl gathering, and the pride, and the foolhardiness, but some sense held the lad, and Firinne silently pulled him back.

"Everything's packed," Firinne said. "Only let us

take our blankets, Ceannann, let's go, we shan't have any sleep, anyway, if we don't. Please, Ceannann, don't fight with him. . . ."

"He's a common bandit."

"Nor common nor a bandit," Caith muttered, and looked the place over for weapons. "The boat-hook, girl, the pole with the spike—four foot of that 'twixt you and the beast, if it gets past your brother and me. Take it, and leave all the rest. You can come back here for it, if there's a coming back at all." He snatched a piece of cord from a peg, took the fisherman's knife and cut the cord, pierced the blanket and tied it and had a cloak. Last of all he gathered up a plain pole from the corner, thinking that his advice to Firinne was good for any of them.

"Come on," he said then, and kicked the wreckage of the door aside, waving them out into the night. He stopped to pick up his own small bundle of cooking-pan and cup, that was all, before he started them off, all of them with their poles in hand, and Ceannann's thoughts doubtless of bashing him with his or putting the spike of the boat-hook in his back.

He waved Ceannann on ahead of him, and Firinne, too, in that reckoning, and the twins struck out seaward along the shore at that tireless pace of theirs that was the cruelest weapon they owned.

Complain, and bid them go at a pace a mortal man could bear? It was a comfortable load he was carrying and a comfortable pace, for a man fresh from his bed in the morning, a man who had not been knocked head over heels by the beast, tonight, and if he had no sore jaw and sorer disposition, and if he had slept more than a moment or two in recent nights.

A bit more, he told himself, with the breath already hurting his side, where a rib caught a stitch, a bit more and he could gladly pitch Ceannann into the river. But he did not damn them, either one. Things were far too chancy for that.

Came the sound from the hills again, the howling of dogs, out in the mountains of Gleann Fiain, and he doubly cursed his folly, that he had ever delayed going to the sea.

CHAPTER

TEN

CEANNANN AND FIRINNE strolled along the shore in the starlight with their boat-poles in hand, letting them trail, at times, in an indolent, snaky line through the weeds that grew along the riverbank—no more trail than they made with their walking, Caith decided glumly, and held his peace about it.

The falling dew had made the grass and the rocks alike slick and treacherous going, and, now that the wind from the mountains had sunk away, and the air had grown still as one might expect at a certain point of the night—but the sea wind still failed them, the air stayed bitter cold, and now a mist began to rise from the river surface, making for the first hour a pale sheet over the water and slowly curling outward through the low places.

"Keep from the edge," Caith said, when he saw them chancing it too far and walking ankle-deep in mist. "Macha, the beast could take your leg."

"Mind your own," Ceannann retorted, and muttered to his sister, as they walked: "Where's his friend? That's what I'd like to know."

"I don't know where he is," Caith retorted, at their backs, and Ceannann swung around.

"Don't know." Ceannann was walking backward, a

perilous act on the foggy edge. "I'll wager you don't know."

"Ceannann," Firinne said, and, catching at his arm, made him turn about again.

"You take his part. I don't know why you should take up for him. . . ."

"There's a great deal you don't know," Caith retorted, utterly out of patience. "And walk or wade, as you please, boy, I've no stake in the matter."

"Oh, aye, you don't."

"I wish your sister's safety, and her life and her welfare, which is in continual hazard with you."

"Oh, with *me*, is it? The beast likes your company. It likes it well enough it came up out of the glen with you to eat our flock and break the wards that protected us for years, it liked you well enough it came walking up on us at your side tonight, mild as milk, until it took after Firinne! You kick our door down, you hale us off into the dark on your advice, and, nay, no, we shouldn't ask where the Sidhe has gone, we're not to know that, and you've no idea—"

"Watch where you're going, boy!"

Ceannann scarcely escaped walking into the reeds.

"Ceannann," Firinne reproved him.

"I don't know why we should trust him," Ceannann cried. "I don't know why you always take his word over mine of a sudden!"

"Trust me or not," Caith said. "Fall in the river if you choose. 'T would please *me* no end." He was short of breath and shorter of temper, and he let his steps lag, wishing the twins to go ahead of him and mind their own business, as they had before. Ceannann fell angrily silent again, while Firinne—

Who could know about Firinne? Firinne had her eyes on where she was walking and her wits clear on present circumstance, so far as he could tell, while Ceannann was being the fool for both of them.

Ceannann might well go at his back. He had once. A

man who would, would do it twice. Child-like, the boy was—angrily jealous of his sister's looking away from him, the more so as Firinne found a choice in the world besides him and he still had no companion but her— that was his considered reckoning: a boy with more anger at the world than sense about his dealings with it, and more reliance on his sister than she had on him.

And because Ceannann was as he was, the witch had a fool's temper to use, so evident a weakness that a man could all but see the black tendrils of Moragacht's spells working through it, far, far more evidently now that Dubhain had left them: Ceannann had respected Dubhain, the gods knew why—feared him enough, perhaps, to keep a civil tongue in his head, or, more likely, was bewildered by him, and never knew which of them was master.

More, Caith thought, *he* had been outside the hut most of the time the twins had been searching through it—which left him now with no idea whether Ceannann might have not found another knife among the oddments of fisherman's gear, and hidden it from all of them—a close-quarters weapon far harder to see in the dark than that spiked boat-pole the boy carried.

That consideration, far more than the stitch in his side, kept him lagging considerably at their backs as they followed the river, to avoid having Ceannann behind him. He had no idea what specific cause a hostile magic might stir up between them, but he little liked the way his own temper had let fly past his better judgment just then, words he had not needed say, and *he* had been guarding his tongue.

Warn the boy? Nothing he could possibly say to him was going to fall on sensible ears. He heard the faint mutters of argument ahead of him, as it was, Firinne doing her best to reason with the lad, by the sound of it, and to whatever she said, Ceannann shook his head fiercely—so even she could not prevail with his young highness, who clearly knew better than any of them.

Meanwhile both of them kept walking on the flatter, easier ground near the river, against his advice—not so near the water as before, true, to that degree Ceannann had taken his warning, but, if only because he had said it, Ceannann must appear to do the contrary, acting the boy as well as the fool.

All this Caith observed and held his peace, thinking in his heart, Very well, if the beast swallows them whole, if the Sidhe can do no better than send me fools, what affair is that of mine? Did m' lord Nuallan make me their keeper? It's only Dubhain's guess we were to take them anywhere at all, and what care I if the beast makes breakfast of them both?

Then he amended that judgment: It can have Ceannann, for what I care. Firinne has had him to deal with. How can she know better?

While, past the next few hills, the river-course grew wider and lower and more reedy along the edges. "We should go up," he said, seeing how the cold fog was spreading now from the water to the shore, and about their legs. It lay in the low places in the meadow as the land descended, pale, diffuse pools of starlit mist.

But when he made that sane suggestion, Ceannann muttered something surlily to his sister that sounded very much like a challenge to her to go ahead, go off with him, since that was what she clearly wished.

For a very little more, Caith thought, he would call the boy aside and batter sense and restraint into him.

But, no, that was his own temper. Any lessoning of Ceannann might go further than he wished, and he was determined to hold himself sane and not to challenge the lad's jealousy tonight or tomorrow.

Better, he thought, if he could cry halt and all of them sit and catch both breath and sanity for an hour, in the hope of that sea wind to clear the fog that, in all reasonable expectation, they were only going to have more of as the land dropped toward the sea. But the twins showed no tiring at all, and Ceannann kept walking, no longer indolent strolling, but a pace Ceannann surely knew was painful for him—while the fog grew deeper over the land and the gap between them widened.

The cold air remained still and hushed, except for his own hard breathing and the persistent quiet rush of the river, that drowned all slighter noises. It was that hour when the night-creatures had fallen to silence and sleep and the birds had not yet foreseen the sun—the dark before the dawn, Caith thought to himself. In air so still it was full of tricks, and underlain by the river sound, he believed at times he still heard the howling from the hills, but in the dark it was easy to imagine a remembered sound. At other times he thought he heard the beat of hooves, the same way, but it might have been the rhythmic whisper of the water.

Twice and three times that happened to him as he walked, and he stopped and listened, wary and mistrustful man that he was, not liking to dismiss so much uneasiness, and so much that rode, like faery, at the edge of his five senses, and under the sounds of his own struggle to stay with the twins. He never heard it when he was stopped, or in the troughs of hills. It was as if the air had a life and a heartbeat too faint to hear, as if his senses might, as sometimes they did, unwilled, reach into faery to warn him of what mortal ears could not hear.

Another hill and over, and he walked faster down the slope this time to overtake the twins with their Sidhe-born strength. The effort was almost beyond him, and at the last, seeing them start up again, he had to call their names louder than he liked at all.

It was Firinne who made Ceannann wait. Ceannann gave him a surly look while he held his side and caught enough breath to speak sanely.

"There's something in the hills," he began.

"Something in the hills," Ceannann mocked him.

"Boy,—" Macha, it was always the wrong word with the lad. Hostile working tangled all about them, and he made a dismissing, deprecatory gesture. "Forgive me. Something's out there."

In the cellars of Dun Glas, the boy had shown some compassion. On the road outward, he had shown some resourcefulness. Since they had set out tonight, not a whit of sense . . . but now Ceannann as well as Firinne did look toward the hills, frowning, as if some least unease had gotten past the clamor of Ceannann's jealousy.

"I've seen nothing," Caith said quietly. "It's distant. Riders, I'd judge. Maybe something else, not their friend." Unlucky to name a ghost, unluckier to attract one by imprudence. "The same that's followed us from your father's keep."

The twins looked not at all comfortable in that.

"Naught to do but keep going," Caith said, "but they've naught to guess, either. They know we'll be following the river."

"Then well we *didn't* go off into the hills," Ceannann muttered.

Ye did not hear, Caith thought, appalled by the boy's notions. Ye fool, lad, ye've no craft at all where it counts . . .

But going off with them into the rolling land, laying traps and ambushes with two innocents for his help . . . he thought of that and judged that Ceannann, from his own understanding, might be right about their chances.

Besides . . . they had to reach the sea.

"The fog will hide us," Firinne said, "if it stays."

"The witch's damned weather," Caith said, "and not what I'd trust, over all."

"We daren't stand here," Ceannann said, and he found no argument to that. He was willing finally for them to work whatever magic they could on him, much as he loathed the feeling of the Sidhe touch, but Ceannann's impatience put him off. "Ye daren't lose *me*," was how it came out, and Firinne brushed his arm as if to say they would not, by her will, but Ceannann,

with a cold look half-backwards, and already two steps
up the hill, said,

"Then keep up, man."

Damn the boy, he thought, too quickly to stop himself, and instantly wished to avert what he had hurled
into the winds of magic, but he could not somehow find
forgiveness in him. Safest, then, to wish safety for all of
them, Ceannann with them, because he was Firinne's.

Perhaps he should go off from them after all, and
fight the fight he understood, from ambush and with
stealth—and let the twins deal with their father. If it
was the witch's men behind them, and they had brought
horses up over the hills of the little glen, by Guagach
and over the mountain there, as they might well have
done, then the witch might have been casting her spells
for days to prevent them, as well as sending her riders
to cut them off from the sea, long since knowing the
track they would take. The woman who had schemed so
long for this would have foreseen every move they
made, and the *draiocht* she wove worked through the
long time as well as the immediate. She might well
have sent an ambush out to their rear, and thrown her
nets about them in haste only when they made their
sudden bid tonight to reach the sea.

But trust that, since they were free, Nuallan's magic
was still working, too, to what degree a mortal could
only guess, but if the moon could not be hastened in its
course, and Moragacht's purpose attended that immuta-
ble hour—then wisest for m' lord white-hands to give
his mortal instruments a wee, small help tonight, never
minding his own discomfort for a trice . . . like the impulse that had brought him at the shanty door, and, subtle as a kick, had his good hound on his feet and
frightened of the hour.

Except the Sidhe's hound was not wise enough to
know which kicks came from the lady and which from
the lord. Good sense said now that he might thwart
Moragacht by cutting off the mortal reach of her power,

but he felt queasy at the thought of going out there alone.

D' ye hear me, Dubhain, thou lazy wight? Another Calling? And heart's blood, this time? Is it mine, is it mine will satisfy ye this time, ye black, intemperate creature?

Maybe that thought was where his courage had left him. He slogged along the meadow, up to his knees in fog, and wondered in a fey and angry mind whether he ought not to go out there, make himself a target for them and be done with it. Dubhain might save him. It might get Dubhain free of the witch, poor wight, the bright gods save his wicked innocence. Maybe that was what he had to do.

It might be cowardice that he followed the twins, then—knowing that the force that had parted him and Dubhain was no whimsy of the bright Sidhe, but a magic that had all the smell of lord Nuallan himself about it. Give to get, kept ringing in his ears with every step he took in the wake of the geas-bound, fey and fated offspring of a selkie and a fool.

Give up the strongest half of their pair, to have the geas drawing them back together with, point: dreadful force; and, point: a geas unrelated to the matter at hand, which the witch might not unravel without distraction *from* the matter at hand.

And, point: be there within Moragacht's walls, to pluck black roses, smile at the witchly lady, and court disaster. . . .

Was that m' lord's plan, against the powers of hell? Was that the wisdom and the foresight?

Macha, he did not like to think at the moment how angry he was, or how much at times he longed for Nuallan to suffer something beyond the pangs of inconvenience. From moment to moment he hated Nuallan more than he hated the witch, and, oh, that was considerable tonight.

Meanwhile his side ached, the breathless air grew

thicker with fog, and if the morning stars were still visible above the hilltops, no stars shone on the river. The
shores were all wrapped in mist that grew thicker by
subtle degrees, and the gap between himself and the
twins was steadily widening. He made an earnest effort
to narrow it, called out, faintly, "Wait, plague take it,"
while Ceannann and Firinne pursued their way on a
rapid downhill into the mist. His voice lost itself in the
fog and the whisper of the river.

They paid him no need, and they might have helped
him—doubtless Ceannann would not; Firinne might not
be able to oppose him. It might even be that they did
not know how to extend their magic to someone outside
their geas.

But in only as long as it took to crest the next small
knowe, then, he had no sight of them at all.

That was not Nuallan's working, he was well sure.
No sight of them, no sound but the river, then a feeling
of presence in the night and some sound just out of
hearing, that might have issued from out of the earth. It
might be some ominous echo resounding through
faery—or it simply be the sound of pursuit coming
closer to him.

"Dubhain," he muttered as he walked, leaning heavily on the pole, and using it to probe ahead of him.
"Dubhain, lad, I truly, truly understand this now. I
freely own ye the winner in our quarrel, I'll carry ye on
my back a mile, I swear 't to ye, sweet Dubhain. . . ."

He lost all hope that Dubhain could slip around the
edges of faery to cheat on their side—worse, if *he*
slipped into the lady's magic from time to time, what of
Dubhain's temptation to it, and what might the witch
offer Dubhain to win him?

"Two miles, Dubhain."

Twice was never enough.

"Three, ye hard-hearted wight."

Macha, would the calling would be that easy, or that
cheap?

"Three's the bargain, is 't not, in faery? Thou 'rt bound, d' ye hear me, Dubhain? She cannot have ye. I will not let ye go to her, d' ye hear, we left that gloomy place once, I'll drag ye out of faery with my bare hands if I have to . . ."

Mistake, that was, even to think of going after him: the fog hid the mortal world from him and in the next step the grey desolation of faery and the mist of the riverside fluttered back and forth in his senses. For the next few steps, he did not know whether he was walking or floating, could not tell solid earth from the insubstantial—something was near him as the river's noise faded from him.

That was what he held to, in the treachery of that slippage. He could not remember if he had found Dubhain. He recalled the feeling of something near him in faery, but he could not recover it and he dared not reach back to it. The cold mist of the mortal world was flowing about him again and he heard the river lapping at the unseen shore. He cast about him in fright for a moment, trying to assure himself that he remembered aright and that the river belonged on his left—surely he could rely on that memory.

But he had lost other points of bearing, impossible to recover—for the mist-laden dark gave him no indication how long he might have spent in that fey, foolish slip. His straying into faery seemed to him to have been only the space of a breath or two—but one could never rely on time in faery, and now he did not know how far Firinne and Ceannann might have walked ahead of him, or whether he had stepped out of that realm at the same place on the river, or where the horsemen might have gone in the meantime. He could hear no clues but the river, and he cursed his judgments in general: unnecessary, to have quarrelled with Ceannann; unnecessary, his dealings with both of them that had set them at odds with him . . .

Or maybe wholly Necessary. Maybe Necessity was in

full course now, unstoppable—it was surely not all his
fault that Ceannann was ahead of him, refusing help.
The one of them was Sidhe, well and good, one of them
had gotten the other away safely from the mountain
keep while their defenders died for them . . .

But their defenders died, all the same.

They might be losing this battle, he thought. They
might come too late, and they were held to a mortal's
pace—so who was the weak link, that the magic would
come at, now? His breath as he walked came like the
wind of a bellows. The hammering in his ears might be
his heart or the thunder of hell. He kept at the pace he
set and stumbled through the mist until, despite the pole
to feel ahead of him, he misstepped into boggy ground,
and slid suddenly knee-deep into cold water.

At that touch of running water the *draiocht* flooded
through him, quick and bitter chill, full of shadow-
shapes. The brazen thunder threatened him, and a
mournful squealing reached through all the borders of
faery—the shelly-coated beast, finning along on the currents, smelling the blood and searching the waters for
him and for the small, elusive, red-eyed shape it hunted
there.

He struggled across the boggy spot, hauled himself
up by a handful of reeds, and recovered solid ground to
walk on, with an acute stab of pain in his ankle he dis-
missed at first as a scrape on some sunken rock or
branch, while his foot was numbed by the cold, but he
recalled then it was the same foot the beast had bitten
when he had outrun it above the glen, that wound which
Dubhain had healed in the cottage that night, and that
set the fear in him. He limped among the reeds, swearing in crazed cadence to keep himself moving, remembering his own advice to the twins to take to the higher
ground—but he trusted Ceannann to do exactly the
thing he had told Ceannann not to do, and hew close to
the river—

No hard work for Ceannann, no rough ground, oh,

never: Sidhe magic knew better, Sidhe magic never failed the twins nor led them into danger . . .

" 'T is why m' lord lily-white is languishing in the lady's hall," he muttered to the empty, fog-chilled air. "Sidhe being so clever and all. Dubhain, Dubhain, Dubhain, ye vain, silly—"

His pole told him there was bog in front of him and he shifted course, came on another arm of it and shifted again, and at last in desperation climbed the bank onto sound earth and knee-deep grass, abandoning at last what he was sure was the twins' path. He only hoped now to reach the sea when they did, if the beast had not swallowed them whole, and if the selkie was any friend to the bright Sidhe at all . . .

It did seem to him, as he reached the higher bank, that the fog was lighter about him, if not thinner, and the light grew as he walked, until he could at least dimly see the ground beneath his feet, and eventually the ruddiness of a morning sun came through, a wan disc all but lost in the haze. He limped along as fast as he dared on the slick grass, until his breaths came with a coppery edge and the ache that had begun in his foot ran up to his knee—Macha, if the witch had an advantage over him, she had not failed to use it, and every step cost him.

"D' ye hear me?" he panted, climbing the crest of a dew-wet slope. He reached the top, leaning heavily on the boat-pole, and caught a startling sharp pain in the shoulder as he started down the other side. "D' ye hear me, Dubhain, sweet Dubhain, ye lovely, vain, and fractious wight? Listen to me and forget that silly baggage, her with the tower and the silver cage—if she can cheat, then so can—"

His foot flew out from under him. He slid on the grass and hit his knee on a rock, and that hurt, and the ankle hurt—he had gone down with it sidelong—but the pain in his shoulder was suddenly acute. He swore to himself and rocked and held the injured arm against

him, telling himself he must have wrenched it holding
to the pole as he fell, but his imagination painted the
first and now the second of Dubhain's healings inexorably unweaving themselves, the way the witch in Dun
Glas had unwoven her magic, and soaked her sheets
with his blood, and cast him in agony onto the mud of
her cellar.

He dragged himself back to his feet, caught his balance, and, finding the pole now painful to lean on,
abandoned it—all the while with the copper taste of
pain in his mouth and the recollection what pitch it
could get to. He did not know if he could bear it—he
told himself it all must be Moragacht's work, not
Nuallan's, his talking to Dubhain had only rattled the
bars of faery and annoyed the baggage, who was taking
it out on him, and maybe neglected other Necessities,
all to cause him misery . . .

But was that not what the Sidhe desired, was that not
their great and wise plan, with the witch's men riding
the riverside in hunt of all of them, and himself the
hindmost?

Macha grant they were men at all that hunted them.
He did so yearn for a cut or two at them if they overtook him—and he still could make no speed, not with
the mist that made the slopes and the grass treacherous,
not with the pain that blurred his eyes. The mist was
milk and brass, now. His heart was like to burst from
exhaustion and fear, and his steps reeled like a drunken
man's, but the effort of keeping his balance took his
mind off the pain, and made his head light—he had
struck a rhythm of sorts to his going, between the moments of giddiness or the unevenness of the ground.

Every time he blinked, now, he saw black branches
twined about silver bars—began to see, worse, two lovers twined in each others' arms, one shadow, one bright
as the moon, and that one passing into eclipse. He saw
bright blood on pale flesh, and a Sidhe lord's eyes half-
shut, half-dreaming, half lost in ecstasy.

Thorns tore his hands and caught at his clothing in that world. He lurched free into this one, slid on the wet, fog-hazed grass, and lay there two breaths before he could summon the will to get up again. The sword swung across the reach of his good arm, and hampered him in his rising—he thought of flinging the hated thing away at last: that would spite the Sidhe. Like the elfshot stone that banged about his chest and neck, it had never been any good to him; it could not cut through to the truth, or protect him against his enemy, and it had brought so much of grief to the wrong people. But he was too busy keeping his balance to deal with it.

"Dubhain!" It was all the breath that would come out of him, and the thumping filled his ears . . . that dull hammering in the earth that now seemed imminent and all about him. He found himself facedown in the grass, and terror brought him crawling to his feet. He ran through faery, on the earth, he had no clear sense in what realm, or what choice he had now but keep going, doubled and lurching with the pain of wounds that, for what he could tell, were all bleeding afresh.

Brightness grew as he climbed, as if the mist and the sky had become the same thing. He staggered, panting, up a hill into a white fog of a brilliance he could not understand. The hammering had the rhythm now of waves on some unseen shore.

It was beyond him to run, now. He did not know what realm he was in—but he smelled the salt in the air, he felt the clammy damp about him, and he saw sand between the hazy clumps of grass at his feet.

Perhaps he walked, after all, near the earthly sea. Perhaps his own legs had carried him, or Nuallan's wish had, but the intimacy of the lovers threaded through his pain like a fevered and present dream, and the sun rising in his sky, if it was the mortal sun, came up on a man struggling and reeling with every step, a curious kind of dance, he thought, against the sky.

'T is the great sea the baggage desires now, he

thought, and she shall not have it. He wove a step or two, asking himself where he was going, or to what, or wondering whether a step now through faery could land him in her hall, and bring his sword with him . . .

The earth dropped out from under his next step. He yelled in startlement and flung out his arms, not knowing how far the fall was, or in what realm . . . hit sand as he landed on the slant, and that, too, slid out from under him, sprawling him flat on his back.

The wind was all but out of him. It was a moment before he could even move. And the pain, oh, the pain had his eyes watering, so that it was only slowly he could roll to his elbow and get his knees under him, and that, feeling wholly the fool.

For he had fallen nowhere remarkable—only off the edge of the land and onto the edge of the sea, a narrow sandy strand dotted with black humps of rock. The waves had eaten the shore away where he had walked and he had walked blindly right off the edge of it—the glory he had seen around him was the sun through the fog, the very sky all but under his feet as he walked that crumbling edge.

A very fool, indeed, he was, lying at the bottom of an undercut cliff and wondering how he was to get up and where he was to find the breath to go on from here. He looked dazedly at rocks rising out of nowhere like misty black ghosts, at the bright curl of the incoming waves in the fog, that rolled up on the beach.

But one black rock was moving straight toward him, a shadowy low bulk among the rollers washing in on the sand, that came aground, then heaved itself up onto the foggy beach itself, a painful, rippling progress of vast weight. It was a whale, he thought, that had resolved to swim ashore, and he watched it in mingled fascination and distress—an ominous creature, almost certainly—and it dawned on his dazed wits it was the creature he had come to find.

But, he asked himself, despairingly,—was it helpless as it seemed, and had the witch overwhelmed its magic?

He reached out an awkward elbow against the stone and sand that made the cliff above his head, and levered himself to his feet, managing to stand, at least. The creature had stopped, exhausted, rocking with the incoming waves. It made another great effort as a wave came in, and then the water retreated, leaving it mostly aground. Sand crusted its hide, from its rolling and lurching inland. The scars of years and battles with great monsters scarred its flanks, and, as it blew its bubbling breath out its blowhole, it stank of death and salt.

Another wave rolled in, and it heaved itself farther up on the beach. The creature's determination was pitiable, not threatening, and he watched helplessly, not knowing what to do, whether to drive it back into the sea for its own good, or whether to be a fool in the privacy of this shore and wish a dying whale good morning.

It made a low moan, gusted another breath through its blowhole, and blinked at him, its great eye, startlingly like a man's, running tears through the crusted sand on its blunt head. It lay in the wave-washed track it had begun to make on the sand, the plowing of its flippers and its great body, three and five times the size of a man. Its hide, he saw more clearly now, was full of sores and scabs, and crossed with scars. Above it gulls gathered, crying banditry and plunder in the dawn.

It gusted another sigh. And as he chanced to look it full in the eye he was bewildered at his own perception, for it was no whale, as it had seemed, but a sea lion of prodigious size. Tears ran down the deep channels beside its whiskered muzzle and spotted the sand before its chest. It waved one flipper like a breathless man about to speak, and all its manner spoke of grief and sorrow.

"Man," it said in a voice as gentle as its gaze, "man, what do you seek of me?"

Could a man be astonished that it would speak, so

prodigious and so strange a creature? And could a man, however desperate, ask violence of such eyes? Ask amiss of the fay, and expect a curse, and not blessing.

"We came for your help," he said with all humility. "And your blessing, lord Sidhe." He felt compelled to add that last, with no idea what moved him, except that calm voice and those eyes that seemed to have the sorrow of ages in them. "You'd be the selkie of Gleann Fiain, would ye not, m' lord?"

"The selkie of Corrigh," it corrected him gently. And time raveled faster or more strange, as a warm wind began to rise from the sea, flattening the grasses on the crest of the denes, and while it rose, this poor, bemused creature lowered its head and scratched at the scabs on its chin with the claw of its flipper. "But I do know Gleann Fiain, to my lasting sorrow and my earthly regret."

So this was the hope they had raised after so much effort—a mournful giant helpless under its own vast weight. Sand clung in pale patches to the fur of the sea lion as it had to the whale. The place it scratched with its claw bled afresh. It seemed very old, its scabs crusted with sea growth, and its grey fur was crisscrossed with the black of old wounds.

Yet he tried, with all respect to it. "Lord of Corrigh," he said, "the lady of Gleann Fiain bore twins, and every man and woman and child of that land is lost for their sake, because of the witch in Dun Glas. They've come to you for help, if you can give it, lord, and they can't be far from here!"

"The blood," the selkie said, "the salt in the blood."

The wind kicked up in a sudden terrible gust, blowing at cloak and hair and kilts, and Caith raised his arm to shield his face from the salt spray and the sand it kicked up off the strand—

Then he realized he was using the wounded one, that the pain in his shoulder and his ankle had diminished to a faint ache—a powerful magic, a kindly, gentle magic bestowed unasked, and he did not know what to say to it . . . or what it might ask of him.

But as he looked at it to thank it, he saw the gentleness gone from its eyes, and those dark and suffused with a wildness different than the malice of Dubhain's kind. Mad, it seemed, eyes rolling, body rocking as the wind blew. He was half afraid of it, with no understanding what he feared, except the mystery and the power it raised. It was calling the wind, he was sure, scouring the fog to a thin mist over the shore. It rocked and darted its head this way and that, groaning—no, *singing*, in harmony with the wind that roared and rushed about the land, scouring up the beach, stinging bare skin, blinding the eyes.

Had he thought the creature harmless or helpless? The creature heaved itself closer, and loomed up and up, seeming utterly drunken with its power, and he was a prisoner in the nets of the storm, in skeins of stinging sand. He wished to distance himself from its wildness, and he could not so much as step backward when it heaved toward him, a shadow like a man's worst nightmare, that moved with the thunder of the great sea waves, that thumped and pounded the shore.

But he did not go down on his knees, quaking though they might be, and he did not draw his sword against it: years of dealing with faery had made him wiser than that. He felt that advance as a testing of him, a geas on the creature, or its simple, natural madness trying to turn away fools and selfish men—for no man with his own life foremost of his wishes could stand to face the shadow it became, its breath cold with ocean depths, its moaning the sound of the ocean storms.

"Sidhe!" he shouted at it, when it seemed about to crush him. "I'm still here! And of frights, I've seen grislier, and had far worse! Give over! Ye hold no terror for me!"

"Death," it moaned, "death and *draiocht*, and the end of peace, thou frail and bloody creature! Sae easily ye break—ye cannot compel me, nay, your kind will never force me again!"

"The witch of Gleann Fiain is your enemy, lord Sidhe, d' ye not remember the woman? And the rightful lady of the glen, the witch's beast has killed her, and her lord, and all the people of the land, except your own children that call to ye, d' ye hear me, lord of Corrigh? Nuallan of the Daoine Sidhe has sent me, a prisoner of the witch himself . . . so mind your manners, ye hulking creature, I take no blame for your troubles, and I'd help *you* if I could, if a mortal could repay the likes of you for the grace you've shown me!"

Sun dazzled him as the creature above him shrank and fell—until it was a white unicorn whale lying beached before him under a brassy sky, a creature struggling to breathe, its blowhole working. It swung its head, scarring the sand with its horn, and stringing sandy tears from its eyes.

"Selkie!" Caith cried, as it battered the sand, fearing for it as much as fearing it, now: it could be any manner of creature, at any moment, but the one it was now stood to destroy itself, threshing about like that. "Selkie! Listen to me! Moragacht is the name of her, Firinne and Ceannann are your two children . . . ye know their Names, now, ye cannot lie down and die of any geas, ye silly fool! Behave yourself, and take some other shape, more useful against the *draiocht*, d' ye hear me, m' lord of Corrigh!"

If it heard, it could not answer. It uttered squeals as plaintive and strange as the voice of the creature in the loch. It battered its horn against the sand, destroying its own self, bloodying its hide and threatening its eyes.

But the sky, a blaze of milk and brass, abruptly darkened as iron-hued cloud came scudding in off the sea, turning the waves to lead. Thunder rumbled aloft. This wind was cold, and smelled of storm. It whistled about the rocks and flattened the grass of the dene above his head. "Selkie!" he shouted, scarcely able to look at the creature, now, because of the sand in the wind. A gust hit his eyes, and he rubbed at them with his arm, fearing what dire shape the thing might take next. "Dubhain! Dubhain, come reason with this fool!"

Lightning flashed and thunder cracked, so close to him he staggered from the blast. Rain followed, spattering him with cold, heavy drops, and through the lightning flash branded across his eyes he saw in the unicorn's place a mass of old nets and weights and floats—

Was that it, he wondered with a sinking heart, fearing that he was made entirely the fool. Was *that* what he had been pleading with?

Then that mass of rope and net moved and hove upward in the flickering of the lightnings, as if the flotsam of the sea had taken unnatural life. Old nets were its head. Fishing floats were its eyes. Its teeth were splintered wood.

It was indeed a test, then, a bond on the selkie that would not let it go to their help without a trial and would not let him ask it or entreat it as he chose, either. Moragacht's doing, he was sure. Moragacht's magic was working even at this very border of the sea and the land, trying to seize the creature or to confuse it; but by Macha and the Badbh, neither would he let the witch have her way—this lady who smelled of roses and rue, roses he could all but smell in the air, now, and the sweet, pitying voice he could all but hear whispering beneath the selkie's wind. He seized a trailing end of rope as the mass swung its ungainly face toward him. It shook itself then—it roared like the groaning of timbers, and it crashed down in the lightning flashes, all in wreck and ruin.

"Selkie!" Caith shouted. "Selkie, you of Corrigh, the third time, hear me! Your children are in mortal danger, your children of Gleann Fiain—the witch's men are on the hunt, d' ye not hear them?"

For that sound of horses was back, the strangeness

that had haunted them from the walls of the glen and chased them along the river shore. All about him he felt the imminence of sorcery and calamity.

It was the white whale, then, that blew steam and blood and sank again in exhaustion. "Death, death, and death," it mourned, with its head on the sand, into which its tears still ran. "So many the brethren, so sharp the iron, oh, man, man, man, the slaughter is bitter and death hae ye brought us, death was always the ending of the matter—"

"Sidhe, listen to me!" Caith cried, remembering the arrow, and the lady's chamber, and the pain—a blind, dark rage, it brought on him, that was no small part of fear. That rage of his had damned him once, and he could not trust his own heart for reason when the temper rose in him, no more than he could trust the Sidhe when it shifted continually. He fell on it and tried to still its threshing and its battering of itself. "Ye will not destroy yourself, lord selkie, nor will I kill thee—'t is thy own foolishness, to trust nothing, with the witch of Dun Glas trying to kill thee. —Give me your true name, ye stubborn creature, and gie me your help, and bring my foolish friend back, if ye can hear him, in any wise. . . ."

Suddenly it was a man he held pinned, a young and handsome man with wild, fair hair, with eyes as mad as the unicorn's. All out of breath this stranger was, and with an eel's slipperiness, still fighting to reach the sea—but damned if he should escape now, Caith thought, and the same as the docks of his boyhood, he threw his arm across the selkie's throat and flung him head-backward on the sand so hard he went all hazy-eyed and dazed.

"Now," he said, panting for breath himself, and, leaning on the selkie's throat with his arm, he carefully lightened his weight. "Now, ye fool. I have got ye, and ye owe me the wish of my heart for it. Defeat this witch."

The madness at least dimmed. It was the sad, wild eyes that regarded him, now, so gentle, so wise that nothing could wish to harm the creature, but that was only another of its shapes. The cold rain pelted them both, and the lightnings flashed overhead, making the pocked sand white, and the puddles sheen with fire around them.

"Man," it panted, "by the salt and by the blood, and by the tides that flow in mortal veins, ye maun answer: who hae held me? And is it the bright Sidhe ye serve?"

"Caith is my name," he said, without even thinking: its power struck like a serpent, so subtle it was, and so absolute its magic, compelling the truth—but having said that truth, he was not bound to let it go. "Caith mac Sliabhin. And yours, lord Sidhe?"

"Corrigh is the name I gie ye. And is the lady dead, now, her of the fair glen, and is the green land gone waste?"

"Gone all to grass, but no flock to graze there. More graves it has than people. And only the two bairns left, of all the house of Gleann Fiain."

"The last worse than the first. Pity the servants of Moragacht."

He did not understand that saying at first, and then did understand what the selkie meant, remembering with the vividness of Padraic's recollections the men who had kept the watch on the wall that night. Send the young men away, the mac Ceannann had begged Padraic, but they had not gotten the warning, they had never gone—and were they now the very servants of the witch that he yearned with all his heart to kill?

The notion shook him to the heart, and the tears ran from the selkie's eyes, as its breath labored beneath his arm.

"A small evil to bring a greater one," the selkie said. "The getting of children to the death of me . . . the waters hae flowed down to the sea, and, ah, the sea . . . the sea maun swallow a' the wickedness. 'T is the nature of me, man, for wickedness I hae drunk to the dregs, and I am filled with destruction. So ye maun do murder on my kind. 'T is the calling they hae set on ye fra' the making of the world."

The thunder crashed, shaking him, but he did not let go, nor could he let go of what it said to him, nor shake it from his sense.

"No. Not I, selkie. Not I." He found breath hard, in the clenching of his limbs to hold the creature—harming it was all too easy, now, and its suppositions were far too dire: he feared it might change again for fear of him, and the both of them would be damned, then, all for nothing. "I will not harm thee. Not I. Never fear me."

The lightnings sheened across its eyes, and on the puddles about its head, one and the same blind illusion. "Ye hae nae choice, man, 't is the nature of you and me. The sun will nae shine nor the moon rise wi' the world as it is."

He shook his head, fearing truth, fearing traps. "No. No such thing, m' lord Sidhe, not I, no. I *will* not. . . ."

"They hae sent ye, man. What other choice hae ye but this?"

"Sent me. The Daoine Sidhe hae *sent* me? The bloody hell they *sent* me for any such thing, lord—not me, the hell with them all, that they should *send* me for this! Plague take them!" He trembled, holding the creature as he was. It had Ceannann's face, it had Firinne's, it became the face of something wiser and more beautiful and more ancient, and it gazed at him the while with all its compassion and all its fey madness.

"Ye maun do it, man. For that right ye battled, and ye hae won. Ye maun use what ye hae gained."

He listened. He had no choice but listen, holding it as it was, but by the Badbh, he was not required by any geas to have its blood on him, he was not required to do what the Sidhe sent him to do, *damn* lord Nuallan, damn the twins and the folk of Gleann Fiain and the Sidhe and all, he would not kill the creature.

He drew back his elbow from the selkie's throat, and his hands from off his arms, and scrambled for his feet, quickly, if it was in the selkie's mind to change again.

"Not I," he said. "Not I, lord Sidhe. The hanging of a witch, now, that, I will with rare gladness; and the killing of her hunting-hound i' the loch, that, will I, m' lord of Corrigh, with no remorse. But not—" He backed away, with a hand held in the air, and the thunder rolling and the rain pouring down on them both as the Sidhe arose in his young man's shape—he dared not offer it a friendly hand for help, or for peace. He did not even know the right and auspicious words that would make it believe the things he said. He only knew he had let it go, and it *was* free, and that, by that freedom, the fate of them all could change.

Then he heard a sharp small hiss pass his shoulder, and saw in shock the creature's whole body shaken, and the dark feathered shaft standing unreasonably in the selkie's heart.

The shock of that sight was still going through him as he spun about—it was still painful as he flung himself toward the eroded shelter of the hill, searching through the grey, blowing mist for the bowman who had struck the selkie with an arrow from behind his back.

But there was no sound but the wind and the crashing of the waves—while he held his sword in his hand, and kept his back against the sandy curve. Thunder cracked. The whole sky was dark and stormy above him as he saw the selkie lying bleeding its life into the sand.

Angry, oh, yes, he was angry ... he was trembling with the anger, and asking himself did he have the courage to leave what might be his only cover, to drag a wounded creature to safety, when it was dying for what might be his fault, at least as fault weighed in the scales of the immortal Sidhe. The selkie lay there looking at him, still alive, for the while, still in human shape, and its lips moving in words he could not hear or it could not say in this realm.

He saw its eyes move up, then, in startlement, and fix on the bank above his head, and he swung the sword up at the dark body that hurtled down on him, a mass of cloth and solid limbs and kilts. Its fall tore the blade through it and all but out of his hand, brought it down on him as he staggered for balance and tore the sword free.

Macha, it was Ceannann sinking against him, Ceannann's bleeding body he was holding upright in his arms, with the hot blood flooding over his hands. His heart went cold as ice. No, he protested to the Sidhe and to the gods, he could not have done it, he could not have killed without looking, or knowing who it was—

"Damn you," Ceannann said, and caught after a breath, trying to staunch the blood with his hand . . . he had that much presence of mind. Caith let him down to the sand and pressed a wadded fold of the boy's cloak across the wound, holding it tight; blood kept coming, flooding through the cloth onto his shaking fingers. "They're chasing us," Ceannann said, and fear was in his eyes, as his hands clung desperately to Caith's sleeve. "Firinne can help me. Find her. Firinne can make me well."

The final lie—but the blood was coming too fast, and Ceannann's eyes were already dimming. Caith held him, shaking, powerless to do anything while that frightened, mortal grip was on him—Damn you, he kept thinking, angry at the boy, for no sane reason except he should not be dying; and the death of the selkie yonder, lying like a heap of weed on the shore—could any of it be chance at all, and not the work of the Sidhe that sent him here?

Draiocht and geas. Ceannann might well be Sighted . . . and had Ceannann Seen his own death in him? Had Ceannann then not had every right to hate him, and was it not generously and bravely the boy had dealt with him, always? He had raised the sword at his back. He had not struck that way—who could know whether he would have?

The life went from the boy. The sea-green eyes kept staring, fixed on nowhere at all, and the cold rain fell on them, while blood mingled with water and flowed into the puddles, as if it were nothing precious to anyone.

"What do ye ask of me?" he cried at the storm and the wind. "What have you brought me to, ye damned, righteous bastards, but everything you cursed me for when I did it for myself? —Dubhain, is it not enough? Is there ever enough blood for them? Find me enemies to kill, ye damned wight, no more children! Is this their white-handed *justice*?"

He longed for the witch's men, he longed for them with all his heart.

But he heard instead, through the rolling of the sea and the rush of wind and rain, a sound to chill the blood—an animal's cry, it was, and a keening like an orphaned child.

The twins, he recalled in sudden dread, . . . the twins that could not be parted. And that was Firinne.

chapter
eleven

THE KEENING DIED away down the wind, and the noise of the waves and the roar of a spate of rain drowned the sounds of movement—no telling even from how near or far down the shore that cry had come, or whether—counting the father—a woman's throat had uttered it. Firinne was out in the storm grieving and lost, and, the Badbh knew, perhaps not even sane, or in mortal shape any longer.

And oh, he wished to go no further in dealing with the twins in this sad and bloody business—he ached to kill the men who had made him kill Ceannann, a last murder, and after that he longed to fling his sword into the sea and be quit of all obligation to faery.

But most of all he did not wish to discover what was wandering lost down that shore, and he did not wish to face Firinne with the truth of Ceannann's death; but, be it geas or the wakenings of his own conscience ... he saw the slim chance of finding her as the chance to do something right, once, to unravel disaster about Firinne before the nets could close: Go free, he would tell her, go away, the spell is done, the geas unwoven, the witch has no more claim on you.

He wished to hope that that was true, at least, and to believe, at least, that it was Moragacht and a long-ago curse that had ordained the selkie's death.

279

But, failing that, faery had ordained Ceannann's at his hand—was that not so?—in the selkie's place, or because Ceannann was what he was, in all things an innocent, and caught in the witch's magic.

Perhaps the weight of guilt was still Moragacht's. Perhaps it had come to be his, now. The scales were all out of balance, and a mortal man did not know how to read them any longer. He only knew that the arrow that struck the selkie had passed his unguarded back. Granted the archer would target the more dangerous enemy first, why had that archer, seeing two of them, not had a second arrow ready for the string and killed him, too, before he could so much as turn around—if not for the boy coming blindly up behind him?

Looking for the selkie, Ceannann had been—perhaps knowing the witch's men were close, but without the least notion that he was there. Ceannann's arrival might well have saved his life, and cost Ceannann's own— fool to the bitter last, coming over the ridge like that, as it ill-chanced, at a man an arrow had just missed, never mind he himself had just fallen helplessly over the same edge in the fog, never mind he had struck out at a descending shadow without even thinking it might be an ally—

Macha, he might find a thousand reasons for what his hand had done, too skilled and too quick, but none, none that made it better than it was—none that called the blood back from the sand, or mended anything in the tottering, wind-scoured world.

The selkie had seen the Necessity of his own death, and maybe more than that. The selkie had sought that death of him, *insisted* on it, at his hand . . . knowing what?

That it might spare his children? Sidhe of his acquaintance were not so selfless. That it might tip some balance to faery? He did not even know what he had already cost, or done, or what power he had just helped . . .

And, thus ignorant, he went to find Firinne, not even sure what he might find, and, finding her, persuade her to deny what the Sidhe might demand of her?

Badbh, he said to himself, ask the cost of that, and what possesses me to think I know?

"Dubhain, Dubhain, ye have your blood, is 't not what ye asked? Heart's blood, brimming over, innocent blood, none of the guilty—does that not free ye, Dubhain? . . ."

A dark lump lay in the rain-haze ahead of him, on the sandy stretch between two great black rocks, a body beneath a dark grey cloak, it might be—all but certainly not Dubhain, and most like Firinne.

He stopped, fearing the archers had found her, too, but he feared, too, to go straight to it, with the steep rocks on either hand, and with the cliff above. He went around the one rock on the seaward side, instead, until he had another view of the body.

"Firinne?" he asked it, and, it lying so still, he walked up to it, sword in hand, and with an eye to the cliff and all about, then nudged it warily with his foot.

It was lighter than he thought. It was a man, with no face, and no entrails.

He drew his foot back in haste, and asked himself whether the beast might be loose on this shore, and taking the witch's men by mistake. He thought not. He asked himself what he was to do now, or what was sane to do, and he made up his mind to go down the skein of sand to the south again, out of this blind jumble of mist-scoured rock and blowing rain, in which a man could not tell what he was walking into. Dubhain had not come back to him. There was blood enough for any Power, and a Sidhe lying murdered, and Dubhain had not come back. The powers were still out of joint, and something boded happening that had not happened, or something had changed the rules, and held Dubhain from him, in which case—

Something blocked the wind from his back, and he spun full about.

"Firinne," he said, but the woman had a fold of her cloak up for a hood and he could see a hand, and half a face, and one dazed and staring eye, that held everything a man might imagine there—horror, madness, welcome, anger. It was all that.

"Firinne," he called her name more gently, respectfully as one had to speak to faery when it was all in the right, and he did not even yet know which was the selkie-child. "Your father is dead, lass. Ceannann is dead. D' ye know that, Firinne?"

"Ceannann's gone to the sea," she said, and added, distractedly, faintly: "My father's coat is mine."

Mad, it sounded. It was shadow, it was woman, the hand that held the cloak beside that single eye let it go and the cloak fell. Shadow existed across her face, where shadow had no reason to be, making pieces of a woman, and threads extended into shifting darkness, widening, and growing, until the part that was Firinne was the small center of something vast and constantly changing. He tried to back away, but terror or blind foolishness held him fast, watching the shadow-pieces blow and billow about her in the wind, like grey veils, like blowing nets, or seawrack, or thrust up like the ribs of things dead and stripped of flesh.

But that hand, that sliver of face, stayed constant, and that eye which was fixed on him was terrified, asking him to say things he did not know how to say, or asking him to do things he could not do; and he could only stand there with his back unguarded and himself helpless to leave or move or say anything. He did not wish to face the creature she had become. He feared what she might become next. She flowed toward him, and her father's terror was about her, her father's power, as the girl-child reached for him . . . him with Ceannann's blood still on him, and the guilt of Ceannann's death to make it impossible for him to win over her. Wrestle her father, aye, when he was in the right. But he was guilty now, and his skin was clammy with it. Geas seemed on him. His wits would not hold what was happening, as if it, too, had shapes and shadows extending into faery, and into hell.

The sword fell. He did not feel himself dropping it. His fingers were numb. He only heard it hit a stone, like the ringing of a hammer, like the thunder in Dun Glas.

"Caith," she said, faintly, this half-Firinne, half-shadow—even the single eye changed color constantly now, pale to dark to grey and green again by the instant. Her hand was on his left arm, what touched his right was cold and strange—but the one eye was still Firinne, lost and frightened by the world. No match for the witch, he thought, not Firinne, no match for the fate she was born to . . . not willingly a killer.

"Go to the sea," he said to her, with what courage he found against the magic, "go to the sea, Firinne. Do you hear me at all?"

A change happened, sudden and terrifying. Tendrils whipped out of a form that was not Firinne, nor any creature he knew. Then Firinne was back, at least as much of her as had been. He could not but think of the dead man, a hollow thing—the mac Ceannann's man, once, he might have been, but the creature she was had no knowledge of that, and perhaps no knowledge what it had done. He knew the mindless release of hurt, the anger . . . he felt it now, wanting his hands on Moragacht. But they were near Firinne, near a creature who did not understand what was happening to her, and he brushed the cheek he could see, ever so carefully, trying not to have his hand shake, either with fear or with his anger.

"Firinne, lass. Your father was a gentle Sidhe. And Ceannann's father was a gentle man. Not all the world is Dun Glas, girl, not all the world is wicked. Some did love you. D' ye recall your mortal father? D' ye recall old Siobhan? Or Padraic? The witch killed them, and you cannot belong to her. The things she wishes cannot come true, or 't will come a bloody, a wicked age, where good folk cannot fare well at all. Help me, lass. I need your help. Or go to the sea."

Firinne held his one hand—the other brushed his arm, strange, and not pleasant, and yet careful of its strength.

"Moragacht." It was multiple voices, like shadows of sound, and something looped suddenly about his back, and held like rope, or net, with vast strength. But the eye that looked at him was wide and terrified, shimmering with tears. "I cannot hold a shape. Caith. Caith, hold me, someone love me ... once ... and I'll do what you ask. Only once."

Macha, he thought, and nerved himself to put his other arm around her, or such as he could feel—none so bad, it was, but not a woman's shape. He kissed the half a mouth that he could see: his stomach was queasy and his mouth met cold flesh, like the dead; it was not courage that kept him from flinching, it was fey anger at what delivered her to this; it was not passion that returned a second kiss, it was a damnation to the witch that made Firinne and the Sidhe that damned him to the things he did—save me from *this* folly, he wished the Sidhe, sunk deeper and deeper into what was chaos, and shadow, and killing cold. He kissed her full on the lips, once, twice, and the third time deeply, for faery luck—it was wickedness, tainted as he was with Ceannann's blood and her father's all at once.

But the kisses she gave back were spells, each one, each one a slippage of the soul toward some unguessed brink ... he forgot himself until the third, and then no longer knew where it was leading, except the wind was roaring now with voices, and the arms that held him turned cold and far too strong.

Firinne, he called to its new-born innocence, Firinne ...

But there was no reaching the selkie-get now. It explored its new delight in violence, it flowed in through his skin and rummaged through his vitals with cold abandon, taking love, doing as it pleased. There was nothing he could protect from it, not the love he still had or the longings he held secret . . .

And faery . . . that place, too, it found, and he tried to protect it—it went up in fire, and thunder, and sank down into dark, where the stone-eyed gods waited, motionless.

But it veered away, then, like the beast in the grey waters . . . it streaked for the sunlit waves . . . and home—his home, not a kindly one, granted, not a home that he should ever long back to, but he was a boy again, sitting on the rocks of the harbor, pitching stolen bread to the gulls, thinking then how the water blamed no one and accused no one—how it was stronger than the men who beat him, stronger than the storms above it and the rocks of the shore . . . all of that was around him, the smell of the salt wind, the groan of ships against dock, the crash and sigh of the great salt water—

Sweeter even than faery, it was to him, and more forgiving, because it only killed, it never damned.

In that thought, he found a kind of peace with it, and let it do what it liked with him, with the blood in his veins ebbing and rising with the waves and the tides . . .

Dubhain! he thought to call, because mortal sanity said he could drown here, and geas would not let him die, not here, not this way.

The creature ebbed away then with casual disinterest, and after a time he opened his eyes on cold, rainy daylight, lying half in the water, watching a smooth, grey back breach the surface of the green waves and dive into the sea . . .

A second time it breached, south, and shoreward.

There was no third time. He heard the gulls crying and saw the setting sun. He had cold water lapping against his side, moving his hand and his foot, and that water was red stained, with small curls of blood going away into the current. He held something in his hand, that looked like a black stone, but his fingers were numb and he could not feel it, he only held it as something he had and would not let go, but what it was he could not decide.

The rain had gone down to a cold mist, now, the sun a wan red disc above the waves. The rocks and the rolling dunes stood like ghosts themselves, black shadow-shapes in the haze.

But the sea did not have Moragacht's magic in it. It had its own. It was still clean. And it had loved him, as much as its cold heart could. It left him not empty, but somehow bereft, and if he lay here it would take him, and all he had to do would go undone.

His limbs were half-frozen. Ice rimed the plaid of his kilt, and he could not feel his left side. And that was the westering sun, at which he felt a sense of urgency and disaster, but he could not remember why, he only knew he would freeze to death if he did not move. He bit his lip until he tasted blood, and got one knee under him, and managed finally to rise, taking three steps this way and three steps that before he could steady himself.

He had dropped what he had carried in his hand. He saw the water washing it at his feet, amid the froth and the bubbles and the sand, a lump of burned wood, urging it at him, with every roll of the sea against the sand. Firinne's piece of wood. He bent and picked it up, almost falling in the act, and looked out at the sun, that reddened the white sky about it, and reddened the sea.

There was somewhere he had to be going, immediately. His wits were not altogether sound, and blood was running down his hand and dripping on the sand, but he recalled Moragacht, then, and the moon, and the sea—he kept remembering, and growing warmer and angrier with every staggering step he took. He found his sword. He tucked the cindered wood into his belt and gathered the sword into his hand—straightened a second time with his head spinning and the roar of the waves making direction uncertain. It was the witch's men he had to dread, he had that recollection back, along with the selkie's death, and the god in the dead forest, and the castle hulking under the waning moon, fatal and fell.

Something disturbed the sand behind him. He spun about, ice making his kilts heavy, and cracking on his sleeve. He saw a shadow across his own, from behind, again, and he spun again, and held his hand from striking at the empty air.

That was too much. The temper rose in him. He turned around a third time, and this time, as he watched, a dog's footprints marked the wet sand near him.

His heart went cold in him. He turned very calmly, and began to walk away, not quickly, not steadily either, worse luck. Run from it—acknowledge such things— and open the path for them, that was what he had done. "Dubhain," he said softly, trying not to fall, but his steps were all unsteady, and he could hear the snuffling of the hounds on his track, heard a growl, and the sound of pads striking the sand . . . that was enough. He began to run, his side already hurting, ran among the black rocks, and weaved and dodged as if the stone could barrier what had no form. . . .

Straight into someone's arms he ran, arms that slid around him, and held fast.

"Och," Dubhain said against his ear, "when ye go a-courtin', ye dinnae go by halves, do ye, me darlin' Caith?"

"Damn you!" he cried, and struck out to be free, but he was nothing against Dubhain's strength, nothing against any Sidhe. He could only lean against the wretch and catch his breath, and take the warmth Dubhain lent him, warmth that burned and hurt, it was so extreme.

"Let me go!" he cried, trying to move his arm against

Dubhain's strength. "Let me go, damn you!" He had the sword still in his hand and he tried to fling it into the sea for once and all, resolved to be quit of the Sidhe, but Dubhain caught his arm, and held it fast, his warder and his keeper, and the only friend that would not die.

"Nay," Dubhain said, holding him fast, "nay, dinnae believe so, my prince, 't is hell waking wi' the dark of the moon, and we maun do what the bright Sidhe hae bidden us."

He stopped fighting Dubhain's hold. He let his sword arm fall, and Dubhain let it, and Dubhain's hands rested on his shoulders, lending warmth against the chill, ease of pain, so much so that the numbness left, and the lesser aches hurt. His face was wet. It might be the rain, and he stood there staring out at the sea, at the rain-washed calm of it.

"Not for the likes of thee, my Caith, ye're no the sun-born kind, and ye dinnae breathe the water, ye great fool. Whate'er were ye thinking of, t' lie down wi' such as her?"

He did not know, now. He could only shiver in the cold, and shiver harder, until Dubhain took his hands away, and left him warm enough to live.

He put the sword away in its sheath, heard a flurry of hoofbeats by him and felt a spatter of sand. A black horse sped an impatient course along the water's edge, in the sinking sun. Dubhain's clothes and belt were where he had shed them, and Caith picked them up without thinking, watching the wicked creature skite along the water's edge, flirting with the sea and making a game of it.

"Dubhain!" he shouted at him.

A moment more the pooka-shape had to defy his calling. But it came about again, back toward him, a phantasm, a thing half smoke, half horse, and full of violence. It shook its mane and bowed its head to him. The sun had gone now, behind a thick bank of cloud, and the sky and water had gone to iron grey. The fire

was in the dark eye that regarded him, the faintest glimmering.

"To Dun Glas, is it?" he asked. He wondered even
. . . whose the summons. But he had no choice. He
seized the cloudy mane and hurled himself up to the
pooka's back.

At once Dubhain was off, scattering sand from his
hooves, splashing through the leaden water, and then
over it, and faster, faster, with every stride, racing the
dark moonrise.

The sun could still cast shadow. And some smaller
darkness loped beside them, doglike, as Dubhain's
course turned and his long body gathered itself and
stretched. His hooves touched the grass atop the dunes
and two rough strides thundered on the earth—only
that. With a death-grip on the mane, Caith risked a look
back, fearing what might be behind them, but his hair
was in his eyes and his cloak flew about him, and he
could not see.

Dubhain was the greater danger, himself, the abandonment, the delight in the dark and the glow of hellfire
in his eyes . . . not the fair, bright banners of faery to
carry against Dun Glas, not the pure or the kindly or the
innocent. The iron the bright Sidhe could not touch, that
was the weapon, that, and the anger and the unrepen-
tance that would not own a master, not in faery, not on
earth, and not in hell . . .

The witch of Dun Glass wished to have them. And,
Macha, she should have them, as they were, as far toward her as they could reach . . . when they reached the
sea, there was nowhere else to go but back to her.

Geas and *draiocht*. Someone's drew them. And he no
longer cared which power that was.

chapter
twelve

THE SUN WAS all but faded now, the dark moon going with it. It was the witch's night coming fast, and the cloud above the mountain walls was veined with lightnings and murmurous with thunder. That very storm that had passed over their heads they now overtook at the edge of night, as it broke against the mountains and wreathed the summits in cloud and the sea-born mist.

They climbed through the pass with the selkie's wind at their backs, until its warmth met the cold on the mountain height in a thunderous shock of lightning. Rain sluiced down the Gleann Fiain mountainsides in freshets, every one the witch's grammarie to read, but Dubhain leapt them, spurned their edges with a thump of his heels and an insolent and wicked delight.

Then Dubhain took a sudden plunge and the mountain dropped away under them. Rock and brush came up, stark in the lightnings, and if Caith had not flinched at obstacles before this, now fear sent him utterly off his balance—he thought Dubhain had meant to leap that space between the rocks ... and then thought not, as Dubhain recovered his footing and took his second such leap downward, bringing the night and depth under them. Dubhain's hooves jolted onto rocks he could not see below them, and Dubhain leaped again, one crazed turning after the other—Macha, Caith thought, it was the breakneck course the man-shape would choose, and this one with two feet too many for the mist-slick stones.

Scare him? "Damned *fool*!" Caith screamed into the wind, when pooka feet skidded over an edge. But Dubhain found a landing and bucked for sheer pleasure, then soared out and down, crack! onto rock, and thump! onto muddy earth. Uprooted gorse and heather showered down with them at that landing, Dubhain sliding hindquarters foremost down the hill, providing a pooka *could* mistake his footing, then, finding a place to turn about, launched onto a forward skidding course down to the very shore of the loch, a very witch's cauldron, frothing in the lightnings and shivering with storm. Dubhain sported through the stony shallows, sending up lightning-lit drops, before he landed on the dry ground with a shock that went through Caith's bones and began to stretch out and race, sometimes through the water, sometimes beside it. "Dubhain!" Caith cried, trying by his grip on his mane to pull him away from that edge, but he locked the rest behind his teeth. Encourage the mischief and there was all too much of it—suddenly a giddy flood of strength was flowing into him now from the pooka-shape, numbing his wounds, keeping the cold away . . . such strength was all at once pouring through him as he could not hold and keep his reason—it came from Dubhain, it came from the storm, he did not know which. Dubhain was drunk with it.

Then he suspected it was neither—not preventing them, no, the lady in Dun Glas sent her spells through the storm and the wind, poured her magic into them on this her night until it ran through bone and nerve and there was no distinction between themselves and the storm . . . they were everywhere across the wide sky, they were in the lightnings and across the waves, too much to be aware of at once. They could *be* anywhere, in the loch, on the shore—

He kicked Dubhain, hard, in the flank, Dubhain

squealed and jumped in indignation, and they were *on* the ground—kicked him again, he did, and the hellfire blazed in the pooka-shape's eye, and glowed in the nostril he could see as it bent its head around toward his leg, teeth glowing blue in the lightnings.

"Mind where you're going!" He kicked Dubhain with all the force he had, and jerked his fistful of mane—the angry head swung back, Dubhain reared and leapt forward—another kick, and Dubhain ran, hooves striking stone only occasionally. The hellfire burned bright in his eye, and the cold wind around them burned like a winter gale. There were bucks and kicks, sideways and backward, there were shocks against the earth and shakings of the head and a sound Dubhain had never made, neither horse nor human, something of pain, as the shore and the storm flew past them.

Ask if Dubhain remembered the boundary, ask if there was a thought at last in a pooka's head but its freedom, and its own will, and the drowning of its rider . . . but every kick from Dubhain won a kick in his flanks, and every shaking of his head a jerk on his mane. There was a howling on the wind, and, beside them in the loch, a great smooth back broke the surface and washed the shore with the wave it left behind, a wave that ruffled up Guagach's black water as Dubhain crossed that stream in two strides, and tore along the bank. Power tingled in the freezing air, the pooka-shape threw a flurry of kicks for pure extravagance, and the next stream they crossed, Dubhain did not disdain, but splashed through it with a vengeance, before he struck out along the road that began there, smooth and deceptively civilized.

Now the keep of Dun Glas was in view, and Dubhain gave a snort of fierce pleasure and took to a course above the earth as another breaching and sounding in the loch sent a wave that washed through the marshy channels and over the road.

They were all but at the boundary, Caith recognized

the shore and the patches of reeds, tucked Dubhain's parcel of belongings tight against him and seized a double handful of Dubhain's mane as it came up at them. The ground was full of darknesses with the allure of hell itself, between the puddles that flickered and flashed with the lightnings, but the power was singing in them, tingling in the air—he could never stop Dubhain now. He only watched the place, and felt the uncanny force of it in the air raising the hair on his arms as uncertainty entered Dubhain's breakneck gait and Dubhain shied toward the loch.

Caith drove both heels in his flanks, and Dubhain squealed and jumped with all that was in him, across the boundary of Moragacht's land—was panting as he ran, now, onto the farther turn along the loch shore, and hellbent toward the bag end of the glen, where the fortress of Dun Glas squatted with its stout and lightless towers.

Rain spattered down, and Dubhain's breath whuffed in steady rhythm with the pounding of his hooves on mortal earth. Dun Glas jolted nearer, the iron bindings of its gates flickering with marsh fire and the water lapping at its stone.

"Slow, slow," Caith breathed, hauling at Dubhain's mane, for he did not seem inclined to stop, even with the stone of the keep rushing at them as if they were falling at it.

Dubhain did slow, then, his breaths coming in great gasps, like nothing Caith had ever seen him do. The glow from his nostrils lit the stream of his breaths as they came up to the gates, and he shied aside and struck out like a crazed thing, at what to Caith's eyes was black and empty air. It was no little ado to slide down from his back, and Caith found his legs wobbling under him as they took his own weight. He still had Dubhain's mane, and leaned against his steaming shoulder, while Dubhain shook his neck and threw his head and snorted, not leaving the pooka-shape.

"Dubhain," he said, shoving at him. "Dubhain, ye troublesome wight, come, take your right shape. I need ye. . . ." The lightnings flared above the stone, the thunder deafened, and Dubhain shook himself the second time, and backed and spun as he grabbed at the mane. "Hold!" This as Dubhain reared up and came down, wild-eyed. He dropped the bundle of Dubhain's clothing, made a grab at Dubhain's nose, trying to force him, but Dubhain snapped at him and he held to the mane instead, carried off his feet as Dubhain reared and in a circle full about.

Macha, it was a perilous and ridiculous plight—he could all but hear the witch laughing within her walls, as Dubhain came to a shivering stop and he kept a desperate hold on him, leaning on his burning shoulder, in front of shut gates and grim, dark walls.

"A fair good race to come here," he breathed, with the rain coming down on them, and Dubhain's heat all that was between him and freezing. "And what do we do with a witch's gates, Dubhain, d' ye know?"

Knock politely, was the thought that occurred to him, then, foolish as it seemed under other circumstances: but that iron-bound oak was not going to fall down for their wishing it, and polite requests sometimes worked, with the Sidhe, at least. "Stay there," he bade Dubhain, not at all convinced Dubhain understood, as he edged away from Dubhain's side. He struck the towering doors with his fist, once, twice, and three times. "Moragacht!" he shouted. "Ye've visitors at your gate, and by the hospitality you afforded me, you are bound! Let me in!"

That last was inspiration—for the baggage *had* sheltered him under her roof, even if he had refused the cup that might seal the obligation—at least he might sting her pride.

For answer, lightning struck the wall above him, marsh-fire flared on the iron of the gate. He stumbled

back to Dubhain's side, shaken, and seized his mane for
fear of losing him.

"Dubhain, lad, we have a wee difficulty here. Will ye
spit out the damned stone? Can ye, pretty Dubhain, fair
Dubhain?"

The lightning rent the night around them, and
Dubhain flinched. Dubhain *tried* to take his human
shape, he thought, the witch's doors were still shut, and
the baggage was laughing at him. That was enough. She
struck at them with magic, that was one thing; but
she struck at Dubhain's dignity with her damnable
joke—and that, that made his blood boil.

"Well enough," he said, taking a good grip on
Dubhain's mane, "well enough. —Lord Nuallan, wake
up, you've company outside."

Lightning struck the ground beside them. Dubhain
shied and would have run over him, but for the hold he
had on him, that let him drag him to a halt.

"Easy," he said, shaking in the knees, and patting
Dubhain's trembling shoulder. The hell-light was
brighter in the eye that he could see, it flared from the
nostril—Dubhain's temper was rising, too, and he suspected in the witch's methods a direr threat to Dubhain
and to him than a shut door and an insult. Dubhain in
this form had the Powers in the earth whispering to
him, Dubhain was all too corruptible in this shape, and
he was fighting it with the temper that could turn on
him at any moment.

Work his sword through the gap in the doors to raise
the bar? The doors were set too close, the lightnings
came down like defending armament, Dubhain was
helpless—he would go after the cursed stone in
Dubhain's mouth if he could hold his head down, and if
he had a chance of getting his hand back—but that
failed: Dubhain shied and would not let him at his head,
at which he knew the witch was laughing, inside her
walls. He swore at her, down to necessities and faery
for his sole resources, not knowing what he was dealing

with, or even what he had left to do, with the dark
moon set as soon as it had risen, and Moragacht's
power beginning to shake the hinges of the reasonable
world. He was blind even to what she was doing in
there . . .

Fool! he said to himself on the instant, and lifted the
elfshot stone.

He saw the gateway open, all choked in thorn-
branches, with here and there a thread of silver ivy—
and in the blink of a startled eye, the branches put out
new shoots on either side of them, those shoots instantly growing leaves and thorns. Before he could drop
the stone and find his retreat, a thorn raked his arm and
snagged the sleeve between himself and Dubhain, another and another grew between them and leafed and
bloomed with a black rose as he tried to keep his hold
on Dubhain's mane—Dubhain reared back, pulling at
him, and almost tore him free.

But he could not keep his hold—threads of Dubhain's
mane tore away in his hand, and his last sight of
Dubhain was the pooka-shape with eyes all fire and
fury, breath steaming red, snapping and striking at the
branches and tearing himself bloody on the thorns.

The vines carried him inward, then, and he was nowhere, standing, floating, he could feel nothing but bitter cold, could see nothing until the dark gave way to
faint shadows, and the shadows to faintest hints of
stonework—cobbles winding up a hill and into utter
dark, a view of the castle's inner courts appearing and
disappearing with the lightnings.

The witch invited him to go ahead—but if he turned
back without advancing another step, he could get
through the thorns, back to Dubhain . . . he felt that un-
spoken assurance, too—understood it the way faery's
understandings came with his foolhardy trespasses, the
way it had in other places, and in his Sighted dreams. It
was the same as Dubhain had outright confessed to
him—faery had to warn a man, there had to be an es-

cape; and hell, evidently, conducted itself under the same strictures.

So here he stood, himself, alone, the one necessary thorn in the witch's workings against the Sidhe, a small thorn, at that, an all but invisible splinter of a thorn, the not quite fair chance Nuallan was due, perhaps, or that he himself was due, if he weighed at all in the balances of the Sidhe—he was here, and if things were going better for the Sidhe, *he* would not be here while a stronger Sidhe could not pass the gates or recover his saner form.

Not good, he thought, not at all good, if he was all Nuallan had gained, with the duel of magic down to its last moves. The witch had the castle, had the loch, had Nuallan locked in and Dubhain locked out. Not what m' lord would have chosen: Nuallan had far rather have had Dubhain, he was sure. Or Firinne. Or one of the flitting Little Folk, if it came to that. Of weapons Nuallan had, Caith mac Sliabhin had to be the very bottom of the bin . . .

Yet m' lord lily-hands had come asking him that day in the forest, and *bidding* him and Dubhain come pry the twins out of Moragacht's hospitality?

If there were subtle victories on their side, he could not imagine what they were, and if there was something he could do alone, he had no idea what it was.

But retreat? About to Moragacht's boundary, that was how far they might get, before everything from Gleann Fiain to the sea was at the witch's beck and call.

So . . .

He took the step into that flickering courtyard, saw the cobbles glistening with rain and lightnings, the marsh-fire standing on iron chains as it was outside.

But retreat was still possible. He felt that of a certainty. The witch invited it. And when he did—

He drew the sword. Marsh-fire spreading over it and onto his flesh. He heard the quiet thunder in the stones, and recalled the cauldron rocking where Moragacht had dropped the cup, the red wine seeking channels between the stones.

He took the third step—and found himself halfway up the cobbled road, on the very track they had ridden that night, himself sick with his wound.

And the way back . . . still existed.

Damned cheat, he thought. She kept changing the rules, giving him chance after chance after he rejected retreat. So retreat was defeat. And, on his own, he would never accept the course his enemy chose. This skipping up the hill on her magic left him no choice where he would be. No knowing how far a fifth step would carry him. Or into what hazard.

"Dubhain," he said quietly, hoping he might invite him by that means. "Dubhain, do you hear, Dubhain, lad? You'll be missing a good argument."

No answer came. The echoes of his voice died beneath the thunder.

"M' lord Nuallan?" he called then, expecting his voice to be louder and stronger than it sounded. Nuallan, Nuallan, Nuallan, the echoes gave back, and died, too.

So, well, Dubhain had inured him to frights. Realizing his fingers on his sword hilt were clenched in a death-grip, he let up his hold and let the blood return. Foolish man, he said to himself. Fear was not his friend now, and the witch so desired it.

A rose-shoot extended down across his shoulder, and leafed as he struck it away. It pricked his hand, and the wound ran a thread of blood, that he sucked at without thinking.

He took the fourth step.

He caught his balance on the brink of a pit that breathed with icy cold. There was stone overhead and on either hand, a narrow hall, inside the keep, he thought, and there was no more way forward. But he tested the darkness with his foot, felt stone, and took the fifth step.

Firelit pillars towered about him, a hall of statues, living forms: their nature changed with the flickering of the fire and changed back again—the stone-eyed gods, the god in the woods, changing position in the uncertain light, or in the coming and going of his own fey Sight—he could not tell. They seemed to move and threaten him. And constantly he heard the thunder of the cauldron, bronze crying out with a hoarse voice, through the very stones under his feet.

Quickly, the sixth step.

He was near a small and lavish table, in an intimate, fire-warmed room—a red-haired woman was seated at one end, gowned in dusk and rose; and m' lord Nuallan . . . waxen-skinned, his hands bearing the marks of thorns . . . rested his hand on hers, pale fingers twined with hers. The room smelled of roses, of wine, of rich food—and treachery. Lord Nuallan smiled at the lady, with the servitors standing about, in armor, some, in dusk and gold, the others. A gold wine cup was in Nuallan's other hand, and Nuallan lifted it to him.

"I thought you might win through," Nuallan said. "My dear and stubborn servant. *Where* did you leave Dubhain?"

"Outside," he said, finding breath difficult in the warmth and the perfume, and the opulence all about him, . . . a banquet, it was, a feast, Nuallan with his lily fingers locked in the lady's, servants to wait on him, of course, servants, all this time, that *he* had been in the pains of hell. Damn you, he longed to shout at Nuallan, for Ceannann, for Firinne, most of all for Dubhain, bleeding on the thorns—

Nuallan held out the cup to him. "Come," he said. " 'T was all a testing, Caith, my dear, gentle Caith. The dark of the moon is here and our game is won." The other hand wove fingers with the red-haired woman's, and the scratches on it were suddenly healed, as Nuallan gently laughed. "Come, man, thou 'rt *free*, was it not

ever thy fondest wish? Drink the cup. It never held
harm for thee."

"What of Dubhain?"

"What would you, with Dubhain?"

"That you had dealt better with him." He seized up
the elfshot in haste. The witch frowned at him, a
frowzy, sullen woman, and the creature holding her
hand was one of her men-at-arms.

"I counted," he could not resist saying, with a certain
smugness. And took the seventh step, magical seven, as
the witch's voice rang after him, screaming at him, "Be
damned with him, then! I need thee not, and hell will
have him!"

He was in the dark before that voice had died, smelling age and wet stone, hearing the ominous lap of water
against the shore.

"M' lord?" Caith said. His eyes were still full of the
light above. It was a moment before he saw the faint
glow at all—like glass, the silver vines that made the
cage in the midst of the vault—like glass and gossamer
the Sidhe lying prone in the midst of them. Too late, his
heart said, at first, despairing, until he saw Nuallan lift
his head, and strive to stand—far too arrogant to stay
sitting like a sensible creature, no, m' lord had to be on
his feet, his hands struggling for purchase on the vines.
Nuallan gained his feet, and said, in a faded whisper of
a voice,

"It took you long enough."

Macha save him from his temper. "Oh, aye, we dal-
lied among the wee folk and had a feast . . . damn you,
come out of there and lend a hand to your own rescue!
Call Dubhain through!"

"Thou 'rt late, Caith. Thou 'rt well late, the moon is
at its dark, and I cannot reach him. —Do not!" Nuallan
said sharply, as he lifted the elfshot stone to be sure of
what he saw. "Fool, did I not warn you?"

"Then how do I believe you, damn you? And where
can I walk? If I take the eighth step, where will I be?"

The Sidhe stretched his hand through the bars. "Here. Take my hand."

Not to look, this one asked of him. It was what Nuallan had asked. It was the same. In faery, that often *was* the true answer. Again—often it was not. He heard the thunder again now, beneath the stones, worse, he heard the lifting of the water-gate, as the ratchets and the chain clanked, opening the vault to the loch.

He reached out his hand, he took the eighth step.

"The right hand, Caith."

The right hand. The sword hand. The creature was full of conditions and fancies, and the gate went on rising, to what purpose he could well guess. Lightnings flickered outside and danced on the water, and the thunder in the stones confounded all sanity.

"Caith!"

He traded his sword to the left hand and held out the right through the dim bars. Nuallan's fingers touched his, and at once a pain shot through his thumb and forefinger as if he had taken up a burning coal. He could not break away, as the pain shot through all his hand, like ice now, as he gazed in shock at the Sidhe's ice-pale eyes.

Then the Sidhe let his hand go—a key had appeared in Nuallan's fingers, silver and shining with a fierce, pale light.

"This," said Nuallan, "this prize is not hers."

Wherewith the bars were instantly gone, and Nuallan was gone, leaving him the lightnings, and the sheen off the unbarriered water. He did not even cry out in his indignation, he simply shifted his sword to his aching hand and cursed in silence the Sidhe, the beast, the witch, and his own foolish, simple trust of Sidhe promises.

Nuallan was free, he supposed. The key that opens all locks, m' lord had called it, and never told *him* that he still had it, and that the witch had been searching for it. *Dubhain* had not told him, and Dubhain should have

known . . . if geas would let him speak, if Dubhain was
still free at all, and not dragged down to hell. Nuallan
had gotten the twins away, for whatever cause he had
served; he had gotten the key back into his own world,
but he had brought it into the mortal realm in the first
place . . . and what had Nuallan truly gained in all of it,
if not the rescue of himself from discomfort?

He wished he had never come back at all. Let the
bright Sidhe languish in the witch's bed, *let* him spend
a hundred years in thrall. What was that to him, after
all, or to the dead, or to the world outside Gleann Fiain?
Could they not spare a bright lord a century or so, and
teach the damned fool what it was to suffer?

Most likely the world could not endure that. Most
likely the world would miss mac Sliabhin far less, and
the Sidhe cared only to have Nuallan back—what matter a mortal, more or less? Nuallan would not come
back for him, not here. He waited, in the dark, looking
out toward the water, with fading hope of any rescue.

But, by the Badbh, he thought, if the beast could
swim that water, so could a pooka, and so could a man,
and given his choice, he had rather not deal with the
beast in this narrow space—get him outside the walls
again, get him to Dubhain if Dubhain could not come to
him . . .

He moved. The ninth step. He was in firelight, face-
to-face with Moragacht, and among her men. She
screamed, her face contorted with rage, and her men
closed in on him on every side, seized him in their arms
as he used the sword for the bludgeon it could be at
close quarters, fought with elbows and feet and knees,
until the sheer weight and number of them overbalanced
him and bore him crashing down sidelong, with the heat
of the fire perilously close. He kept fighting and they
tried to force the sword from his hand, tried to force his
arm into the fire, failing that, while he tried to tear free.
The thunder was in his skull, now, and the witch was

shouting orders to have him alive, for hell and her gods ...

"Mine!" she kept screaming, "him and the Sidhe!"

Fire seared his hand. He let go the sword, helpless for the moment, with a man's weight across his throat—as the recollection came to him, of fire, and coals—*coals*, by the Badbh. He remembered what Firinne had left him, while they were twisting his one hand behind his back and fighting to turn him onto his face—he got his free hand under him, pulled the bit of wood from inside his belt, and flung it among the coals. They shoved him down, hard against the stones, and his hand came down in the coals, scattering them as he rolled onto his back to escape the heat, looking up at Moragacht and the sharp-edged knife she had.

Well, he thought, with the witch's men dragging him to his feet—that effort was for naught. But Moragacht turned suddenly to the fire—the very air screamed as the light of it went all but out.

So suddenly the men let him go that he fell on the hearth on his side, his ears full of that shrieking as he saw blue light running over the wood and the coals, and them turning to ash on the instant. Black was inside the blue fire. A tall shape rose up in fire and white smoke, roaring and wailing ...

"Padraic!" he shouted to it. "Padraic, man, set *to*—" The pain of his hands was enough to take his sense away, enough to summon souls out of hell, if that was what the Sidhe favored ... and not Padraic only, in the shrieking chaos of voices and rushing of trails of fire out of the fireplace and about the room. The ghost-fire consumed wood to ash as it touched, and had stones falling and the draperies going up in flashes of red flame.

Fire caught the hindmost of the men, that ran into the hall, living torches carrying the fire where they fled. The booming of the cauldron resounded through the

keep, a clamoring and shrieking attended it . . . the fire
was everywhere about him.

"Dubhain!" he yelled, trying to get to his feet. Burning wisps were floating in the air, comets of fire
shrieked past him, and his legs wobbled and went out
from under him. A timber crashed down, close beside
him, and went to ash in the blink of an eye. Stones fell.
A dog's footprints showed in the ash beside him, a
panting breath and something wet brushed his ear, and
then a howling burst into the halls of Dun Glas, as the
fire blazed up, and mac Ceannann's hounds went hunting in flame and falling ash.

He struggled for the door, and fell, made it into the
hall and reeled back and forth between the walls and
down the corridor as best his legs would bear him. Fire
was everywhere, and the stones quaked with the thunder below them. He reached downward stairs, and lost
his balance on the second step.

Strong arms caught him from behind. "I hae ye,"
Dubhain's voice said against his ear. "I hae ye, my
prince, and hell gaeth wanting tonight. Where would
ye?"

"Out," he said, on the breath he could catch.
Dubhain's hands and arms were scratched, Dubhain was
dripping wet, and cold, and not a stitch had he on—he
had come that quickly. "Out of this cursed place!
Nuallan is free . . ."

"Up wi' ye, then," Dubhain said, and heaved him up
onto his feet, hastened him down and down the stairs he
suddenly feared he recognized.

"I cannot swim the loch!" he said, but Dubhain
stayed not an instant for his doubts, Dubhain swept him
along and down. Fire lit the stairs from above. The floor
jolted, and a massive jagged gap opened between two
steps below.

There was no more going back, none. He stripped
burned skin from his hands, trying to keep his balance
against the wall as Dubhain drew him along faster than

his legs could manage. He caught his breath only when Dubhain stopped to push the door open onto the vault—firelight showed on the water below them, and showed another shape as well, a huge hulk in the water, half on land.

Caith balked, then and there. But Dubhain seized him and hauled him along down the steps, down and down while the black, glistening thing lurched toward them with a clattering of its ill-assorted bones. It was a race for the open ground, as they reached the very last steps with Dubhain's speed and it lunged to cut them off, hissing as it came.

Dubhain jerked him off the steps and in the next stride had his other shape, the pooka blacker than the night around them, and the hellfire gleaming alike from its eyes and the beast's.

Caith seized Dubhain's mane—had not even the footing or the strength to get astride: Dubhain surged across the muddy vault and hit the fire-stained water with a jolt that all but lost him, the illusory mane slipping through his fingers, the water around them aglow with fire and awash with the power of the beast as it came about after them.

A long, low squeal sounded through the water in front of them, and Dubhain veered, drove through the water toward the shallows and up, and up to the blessed air—there was no keeping his grip beyond that, with the water dragging at him, and the heaviness of his own body pulling Dubhain's mane through his grip. He fell, breathed water and choked and fought his way to the silty, reedy edge, among the rocks, looking back for fear of the beast behind them.

A great violence churned up the loch, a huge crooked fin lobbed the water, a sleek grey back broke the surface in clear pursuit, and after that was a roiling of the reflections out in the deeper water, as burning wisps of ash came drifting down like snowflakes out of hell.

Dubhain squatted down by him, in the icy water.

"Och, such a lovely stew. And the selkie is the stronger, now, d' ye think, my Caith? A wicked, wicked lass, our lovely Firinne, wi' such a bluidy grudge—"

Caith stared at the troubled surface, coughed water and wiped his nose, numb, except the burns that hurt with the chill water, but he had no complaint for that. The rest hurt less with the cold, and he was not willing to move for the while.

But Dubhain set a hand on his shoulder, and at that the cold grew less, as the wicked strength came into him. He tilted his head back, to see the smoke billowing out of the keep, and moved to protect himself as a wave from deep in the loch rolled ashore and splashed them both.

"Come," Dubhain said to him. "Come, hae ye not invited me to this merry hunt? We'll dance wi' the wind and the rain tonight—"

A howl rang down the shore, and the waves splashed out of time with the wind.

"Out on ye," Caith said, and took solid hold of Dubhain's arm, with an eye to that troubled water.

The creature that had haunted the loch was Moragacht's hound, indeed, fat, and greedy as the mouth of hell—but Firinne was Sidhe, not a creature of the *draiocht*, the child of father sea, cold and cruel as she could be. He did not fault Firinne. She was what she was. So was he, and he did not belong in this place.

"Och, hey," said Dubhain, hauling him up to his feet—and the lightning struck the mountainside above the keep with a crack like doom. "Ill-tempered, the witch."

"Come along!" he said, thinking of the likes of that bolt landing closer. "Get your clothes, wicked creature—this is no weather for games. Come away!"

The hell-light glimmered in Dubhain's eyes. Merry wickedness danced there, and in the light from the fires above, a grin flashed.

"Dubhain!"

"Oh, aye," Dubhain said, and went and caught up the bundle of his clothing from before the gate—pulled his shirt on there in the fire and the destruction, and wrapped his kilt about him, clean and mostly dry, oh, aye, of course they were, and Dubhain himself in a rare fine mood.

The key, Caith had time to think, was safely back in faery, the key which all Moragacht's magic had not discovered, the key that Nuallan had said would open every gate—including the silver gates of faery itself; and, presumably, the gates of hell. Hand him *that* to carry, had Nuallan, and for a lark, escort the selkie-get from out of the witch's hands? Then break their restraining geas by bloody murder? Damn him!

The vault came down, with a sound like thunder. The towers followed, falling inward. A great wave rolled out from the shore and sparks flew thick, whirling on the wind.

"Hoosht!" said Dubhain, skipping up to him, catching his arm, drawing him to the road. "A grand, great bonfire ye hae raised, my prince."

"Good riddance," he said, walking with that strength Dubhain lent him, a giddy, unworldly flood that made a dangerous stirring in his own heart, with the headiness of the storm, the lure of the hellish power in the earth and in the sky of this place.

"Black roses," Dubhain said, looking back. "How pretty they do grow ... d' ye no see them, Caith, all along the way?"

Caith caught his arm and dragged him along a resisting step or three before Dubhain shook free.

"I can walk for myself, man!"

"Fractious, we are. Come, Dubhain, fair Dubhain, ye'd hae hated her."

"The moon will come new tomorrow," Dubhain said faintly, and with a shiver unaccustomed in him: "Och, man!"

A grisly thing lay smoking in the road, one of the

witch's men, Caith supposed, escaped from the ruin, but not so far. A second time he seized Dubhain, this time by the sleeve, to draw him past, and the lightnings showed him a sword lying in the rain and the ash, under a blackened arm.

"Damn the thing!" he said. "Damn it to hell!"

He yearned to walk past it, ignoring Sidhe gifts. But it would come back to him, he had no doubt of it. With a shudder and a curse he picked it up, hot as it was from the fire, and carried it, there being no choice at all.

chapter
thirteen

THE RIPPLES WENT out from the great creature that
breached and dived in the loch. They flashed bright
under the sun, and rolled among the reeds, and a little
distance up Guagach's stained stream. But a selkie
would not stay in the loch ... the next surfacing they
saw was farther on, and the next waves came more
faintly, a mere rocking of peat-straw against the shore.

The new moon was in the sunlit sky. Ash was still
sifting along the way. The wind kicked it up, and blew
it, and Dubhain was in a rare fine humor, skipping
along, halfway up this hummock and that, prying into
mischief, startling a frog the beast had missed in its
hunting.

"Leave it be!" Caith said, when Dubhain gave brief
chase. "Macha, is there no end? The creature's lived
here through all of it—give it peace!"

"A canny wee creature," Dubhain said. "D' ye ken,
the frogs hae a king? A great green fellow, he is, all
over wi' spots—ye may hear him piping the kindreds t'
the springs again, it hae said as much."

"Lies," Caith said.

"I? Mistake the truth?"

"Bend and break the truth, and trample on it, daily,
ye wicked—"

A strange figure caught his eye then, a brown, hob-

309

bling thing ahead of them on the shore. He gave a quick and uneasy thought to the sword he wore, and the remote chance there was of meeting any traveler in Gleann Fiain.

"And who would that be?" he asked; and the moment he asked it was gone.

"Who?" Dubhain asked.

"I saw someone. I swear to you, there was someone on the road."

"A touch of the fever, it might be. Or the fay. The gates are opened, the sun is risen wi' the new moon, and the horns of faery hae sounded, did ye nae hear them wi' the dawn?"

He was too weary to argue the matter. They had walked all the night, rested seldom. Neither of them knew what might have escaped, besides themselves. And m' lord Nuallan—who never yet had said kiss my hand for the rescue.

But there were signs of healing already in the glen. The morning sun laid a touch of gold on the water, where only grey had been. The howling in the hills was gone, one could hope, satisfied.

They did not catch the Brown Man. But they saw him again, well up on the heights, and heard the faery pipes. A little frost lingered where the shadow fell, but the sun found it and melted it away.

A graven stone they found, later that day, half of a god, but it lay in the loch, head foremost, and overthrown. Dubhain pitched a flat pebble across the loch, but the waves swallowed it quickly.

"Enough," Caith said. Dubhain grinned at him, and skipped the flat stones along the edge, defiant of disasters.

The wight never missed a step, not one.

ABOUT THE AUTHOR

C. J. Cherryh's first book, *Gate of Ivrel*, was published in 1976. Since then she has become a leading writer of science fiction and fantasy, known for extraordinary originality, versatility, and superb writing. Her *Downbelow Station* and *Cyteen* won Hugo awards. She lives in Oklahoma.